THE KITCHEN SINK SUTRA

PATTI MURPHY

PUBLISHED BY SMALL TOWN BOOKS

For Memère
Music I heard with you...

~

Sutra:
    (noun; from the Sanskrit)

(1) A collection of aphorisms relating to some aspect of the conduct of life;

(2) A Buddhist teaching.

~

CHAPTER 1

High Blood Pressure

Nobody ever waits until Friday afternoon to tell you *good* news. I'm sitting on the ass-numbing bench outside the principal's office reflecting on this truth and passing the time by skimming through a mental list of possible offences that could have landed me here, but frankly I'm having a hard time coming up with anything substantial.

Yes, I've been using a parking spot that strictly speaking wasn't mine, but no one had been using that spot since last term and anyway, that probably merits an email, not a touch on the arm and a soft, "Ms. Sutton, can I see you at the end of the day?"

And yes, I've been wearing jeans on days that have not been officially designated as casual, but I was teaching sculpture to the Grade Eleven class and we were working with drippy clay for Christ's sake, so it wasn't the best day for Vera Wang, not that I own anything by her. Or anyone, actually.

And I've almost convinced myself that it's nothing important, the principal probably just wants to "touch base" (he's big on those kinds of buzz words) but then I notice that two of the secretaries in the office won't make eye contact with me, even though I've been sitting here for half an hour, and the third secretary, the only one who will look at me is giving me sad little smiles, like you might give to someone who's waiting to have their cat put to sleep.

Before I can put any more serious thought into my worries, I'm ushered in to see Mr. Peck, the principal, and I am informed in the most positive tones that although my work last year was exemplary - "...the kids are so productive, so *engaged*..." - he's going to have to let me go.

For a moment, I want to laugh.

"Are you firing me?" I say and I am instantly dismayed by how squeaky my voice sounds.

"Oh, good heavens, no! Not at all!"

"So I still have a job?"

He leans forward, his head tilted very precisely and his eyes fixed on mine, and I can tell that this is something he learned at some management course ("Non-Verbal Methods to Pin Your Listener to their Chair," 10:00 a.m., Conference Room B) and he launches into a little sermon about being an administrator in such tough times - he's a great patron of the arts himself and it breaks his heart to let me go - but unfortunately, I am surplus to the system.

"Surplus," I say. "And that's different from fired, how exactly?"

"Ms. Sutton, I don't think you should choose to see it that way," he says, and I notice that his dress shirt is as crisp as if he's just taken it off the hanger and I wonder what he does all day that he can look so freshly pressed at 3:45 p.m. "Look at it as a chance to pursue other opportunities. Of which I'm sure there'll be many."

Except no, art teacher jobs are not falling from the trees these days, particularly not after the school year has already started, and there is a thrumming in my ears and I need to get up and leave but I can't actually feel my feet.

"...happy to provide you with a reference and wish you the best..."

The click of the door closing behind me is unnaturally loud, like a gunshot.

All of the secretaries are gone.

I SUPPOSE it's noteworthy that the first person I think to call, once I've collected my jacket and bag, isn't Alex, my girlfriend, partner and the presumed love of my life, but instead my best friend Pam, because I know that Pam will be outraged and supportive, whereas Alex will just be pissed, but not for the right reasons – she'll bang on and on about how I should be showing my work more and how that place never deserved me, when all I really want is a longish hug and possibly a tumbler of vodka. Both of which I know I can get from Pam.

I am just about to dial Pam, when my cell phone rings.

"Olivia?" A tiny voice, far away, or maybe frightened.

"Yes?"

"This is Penny Clarke. I'm with your grandmother at the hospital. She's had a stroke."

A WORD ABOUT FAMILIES.

Christ.

They're not always what you expect, are they?

My grandmother is a saint. Now, I know that almost everyone thinks that their grandmother is a saint - a paragon of generosity and wisdom and warm chocolate chip cookies, but most people's grandmothers don't have a handwritten note from the Queen, thanking her for the lovely baby quilt and the packet of jam pennies, do they?

Nana Sutton, (Violet to her friends,) is my mother's mother, and she is the centre of my family - actually, for most of my time on this planet, she's been the only real family I've had. I lived with her whenever my mom was away on a trip, which from about two weeks after I was born, was most of the time. Gradually the time between Mom's trips got shorter and shorter until one time when I was about three, I think she just forgot to come and pick me up. (I suppose it's a complicating fact that I'm not entirely sure who my father is. This is partly due to the fact that the stories my mother has told me over the years about my father's identity have had little discrepancies. From what I've been able to piece together, he's either a potter who lived on an island in the Mediterranean, or he's an Australian river guide somewhere in Egypt.)

This has never mattered much to me though because my Nana has always been more than enough.

Which is why, as I make a headlong dash for home to throw some things in a bag, all I can think is that it's been two weeks since I spoke with her, our regular phone calls having slipped away in the insanity of my life lately - Stresstember and the school year starting up again, Alex's business at such a critical point - and the last time I hauled my ass to Stafford Falls was Mother's Day which was - one-two-three... shit, four months ago. I'd been so busy after that, teaching summer school (remedial English to potheads, never again, but we really needed the money) so there just hadn't been time for a visit, but back in May, Nana had seemed fine, maybe a bit subdued but as she herself said, at 78, she wasn't a spring chicken.

And so I drive. And drive. It is the longest drive of my life, that trip to the Falls, made worse by the fact that I lose all cell reception during a call with Pam and I can't seem to get Penny Clarke back on the phone. I wonder where my mother is (Madagascar? Mali?), I wonder where Alex is (London? Paris?) and mostly I wonder why the hell nobody is ever around when you need them. Somewhere in the middle I become convinced that Nana has died, that I am too late, that Penny Clarke just couldn't tell me over the phone, but six frantic hours and many miserable cups of coffee later, I am jogging across the parking lot of Stafford Falls Hospital and speed walking down the shadowy hallways until I spot Nana's best friends, Penny Clarke and Angie, huddled in a waiting room near the ICU. Penny Clarke fills my ears with medical jargon, while Angie just stands by looking stricken and patting my arm, and then they usher me into a dim room where Nana is propped up in a giant hospital bed, framed by glowing computer displays, wires and tubes snaking in and out of her little blue hospital smock, but alive, thank God, alive! And she smiles when she catches sight of me which makes everything inside me melt and all

I can think, the thing that keeps running in circles inside my head and which I can barely keep from saying out loud is, my God, when did she become so tiny?

"Oh, pet," Nana says, and her words are muffled by the clear plastic of the oxygen mask. "You look so tired. Come and have a little sit down."

IT TURNS out that she started feeling dizzy at Mrs. Tyndall's funeral lunch in the church hall. ("I don't know how poor Mr. Tyndall is going to cope without her, I really don't, the poor man doesn't know how to make so much as a cup of tea," Angie says, shaking her head and tutting.) Nana, who had been running the dessert table, had been too busy to stop for a bite and so at first she thought maybe it was just hunger, but then the headache hit and her cheek felt all tingly and finally it was the look on Angie's face that gave it away — Nana was trying to tell her that they needed to put out more lemon squares but the words must've been coming out funny because Angie just blanched and hollered for Penny Clarke, who called the ambulance.

"What a sight I must have been, being wheeled out of the church hall," Nana says. "But those paramedics, they were the nicest boys. Very polite."

I'm wishing that she would get to the part where people in white coats do brain scans and tell us all how bad it is, but I know that Nana will tell the whole story in her own time with lots of detours, and for the moment, I am so grateful to be sitting here beside her, holding her hand, that I don't care if she launches into the genealogy of the nice, polite paramedics.

Which of course she does.

"The one with the glasses," she says, turning to confer with Angie who is hovering close by, looking like she's just itching to tuck something in. "He's Frank Lamont's son, isn't he?"

"No, he's Frank's nephew," Angie says. "His father is Bob. The plumber."

"I thought all of Bob's boys went into the business with him," Nana says. "Well, good for him though, because he was very professional. Very reassuring."

The praising of the paramedics is interrupted by Penny Clarke who arrives with the doctor hurrying along in her wake. At least I think it's the doctor, because this kid can't have been out of medical school for more than an hour and a half, but he's well over six feet tall and so somehow that's comforting. He tells us that Nana is very lucky - they caught the stroke early, it's all looking good, but they need to keep a close eye on her, probably do some more tests. Penny Clarke is listening with rapt attention and when he's said his piece, she starts to pepper him with questions. I try to follow but she's lost me after the first "ischaemic" and I am so tired and overwhelmed that I feel myself start to sag. Nana's eyes meet mine and there's so much I want to say: how sorry I am that I've been busy, how terrible I feel that I wasn't there for her, how much I love her and how very much I don't want her to ever leave this world. My heart is so full of sadness and relief and worry and guilt that I feel an actual pain in my chest and my hand flutters up to cover it, to keep it all inside. Nana's smile is tiny and knowing and droops ever so slightly on the left side. She reaches over and pulls me to her.

"It's going to be all right," she says, and I am nine years old again and I believe her.

EVENTUALLY THE NURSES insist we leave so that Nana can get some rest and after many kisses and hugs and the promise that I can return early the next morning, I follow Penny Clarke's whale-sized Chrysler through the dark streets of the little town to Nana's house. The headlights of my car wash over the red brick, the tidy shutters, the sprawling porch and it feels like a hundred years since I've been here. I can hear the dogs barking even before I open the car door — a bass, a tenor and a yappy soprano — and I suddenly remember the look on Alex's face the first time we were here. As soon as we opened the car doors that day, we were besieged by jumping, barking animals. Not a dog person by any stretch, Alex was particularly offended by Mortimer's lack of two complete ears. She actually recoiled.

"Oh my God, what happened to him?"

"Maybe frostbite. He's a Jack Russell terrier so possibly a bar fight."

She raised an expensively shaped eyebrow at me.

"He's a stray that Nana rescued," I said. "They don't always come with a full biography."

"And that smell?"

"That would be Lucy. The Boxer," I said as I got out of the car and stooped over to rub the velvety fur on Lucy's head. "She's prone to flatulence when she's stressed. Or when she eats fish. Which evidently she has been doing."

"How many dogs does your grandmother have?" She said this as if she really wanted to ask how many pythons she had or maybe how many heads.

"It varies. Usually a few."

"So, she's some kind of one-woman no-kill shelter?"

Alex still hadn't put a foot out of the car and I was regretting not having advised her to wear less expensive shoes when Nana appeared on the porch, an apron wrapped around her waist and flour on her hands. A black Labrador Retriever was sitting politely by her side. "Olivia!" she called. "Thank goodness you're here! I was getting worried, pet!"

"Oh my God," Alex had said. "You were raised in an actual Norman Rockwell painting."

I had laughed and hurried up the drive to Nana, Lucy trotting along after me, as if we were playing chase.

A door slams nearby and jolts me from my reverie. Penny Clarke has beached her giant car beside mine and is walking smartly up the steps to the porch, rifling through her purse for Nana's keys. The dogs' barking reaches a crescendo as we tread on the worn planks of the porch.

"I'll take these beasts for a bit of a walk," Penny Clarke says over her shoulder, as she wrestles with Nana's deadbolt. "Why don't you put the kettle on for tea?"

It's ten long minutes later before any of the dogs is calm enough to have a leash clipped on and someone pees from excitement right there in the foyer but eventually Penny shepherds them expertly out the door with firm words and then the quiet is absolute and exhausting. I fill the kettle and put it on the stove to boil and I drift to the kitchen table and drop into a chair. The table sits beneath a picture window and although it's dark now, I know that it overlooks the garden and beyond that, the lake. If I looked out I would see the flowers that she spends so many hours coaxing to bloom, I would see the water that she gazes out at while she has her morning coffee. It's the same lake I looked out at the day when I was seven when my mother told me that she was going to Africa for two years without me, the same lake whose surface was covered in creamy waves the day I told Nana I was in love - with a girl named Jennifer — and held my breath after I said it. But tonight I can only see my own reflection.

There's a vase with some hydrangeas on the table, big snowball flowers, and around the base is a collection of amber pill bottles. An alarming number of them it seems to me, but upon closer inspection I see that at least half are for the dogs: Lucy (Canine) Sutton for arthritis and low thyroid, Mortimer (Canine) Sutton for his heart condition, and some sort of indigestion remedy for Ophelia (Canine) Sutton. I examine Nana's pills and they have names that I know should be familiar to me and I think they're for her heart or maybe her blood pressure but I'm not sure, and this makes me feel worse because apparently she's been in ill health for longer than I've known and I *should* have known, I should have been doing something about it.

Beside the pills is the little notebook that she keeps track of everything in: bills, planting dates, phone numbers, appointments, inspirational quotes, clippings she wants to pass on, books she wants to read. She's been filling these up for as long as I can remember and somewhere in this house there is a box full of old ones that she's filled. A record of a life lived, of details remembered. I flip open the cover and there is a business card tucked close to the spine. It's for a real estate agent ("Tyler Cooke with an 'e'") and of course his picture is there in full colour. He's slick and slippery and his name is vaguely familiar to me. He looks utterly untrustworthy.

The kettle whistles, a piercing shriek in the still of the empty house and I jump.

Before the tea has time to steep, Penny Clarke is back and the three dogs rocket through the front door and into the kitchen, nails clattering on the linoleum, a panting, wagging tangle of legs and tails. I refill their water bowls while Penny Clarke hangs her sweater on the back of a kitchen chair.

"Have you eaten? You must be starving," she says. She sets about efficiently preparing us sandwiches and the easy way she moves around Nana's kitchen reminds me of how long she's known my grandmother, how many years of friendship rest between them.

"Thank you so much for being there for her, today," I say, "and for calling me."

She waves off my words as she butters the bread. "I'm just glad you were able to come so quickly."

"I never thought to ask - did you get a hold of Mom? I'm not even sure where she is."

"Mumbai, apparently, or so her office told me." She spreads mustard to the edges of the bread with medical precision. "I tracked down the number of her hotel, but as it was the middle of the night there, and you were on your way... well, I thought I'd leave it to you to contact her."

"I wonder if she'll come," I say and Penny Clarke's silence is so loud that even the dogs stop lapping at their water bowls and look over at her. "I mean, should I tell her to come?" I ask. "Is Nana going to be all right? I didn't understand a lot of what the doctor said."

"It's still early," she says, but I notice that her lips are pursed. She takes great care in selecting a serrated knife from the block and she looks like she's weighing her words. "There are many good signs. She got treatment quickly, she's lucid and she doesn't appear to have any loss of speech."

"But?"

"She has some weakness on her left side so that suggests that there's been some tissue death."

"You mean brain damage?"

"Well, yes, you could call it that." She doesn't take her eyes off the sandwiches she's slicing as she speaks. "And it remains to be seen what other sorts of deficits there might be."

"Deficits?"

"Balance, co-ordination, memory." She brings two plates to the table, sets one down in front of me, then turns back to get the tea pot. "We'll know more in the next few days after she's been assessed by the physical therapist and the occupational therapist, but I'd say it's likely she's going to need some sort of rehabilitation."

I nod and watch her pour the tea into Nana's blue willow china cups. "Is there something I should be doing? Making appointments or calling someone?"

She settles into the other chair and gives me a sympathetic smile. "Olivia, it's midnight. Right now, all you can do is have something to eat and get a good sleep."

I stare down at the sandwich she's made me, cut in perfect triangles, with the crusts removed, but I can't eat it.

"I should've come to visit her this summer," I say. "She wanted to rent a cottage for a week and she asked me to come but I was stuck in summer school and then she said her computer was broken and I said I would help her shop for a new one but I never made the trip. And I should've. I should've been here."

Penny Clarke sips her tea and regards me over the rim of the cup. Her eyes are almost the same shade of cool blue as the cup and I remember how many times my grandmother has said that Miss Penny Clarke is made of equal parts of tweed and cashmere, which is not only a fairly accurate description of her wardrobe, but a keen assessment of her character. Tough and soft, practical and comforting. "You think you've been a bad granddaughter," she says.

I shrug.

"For what it's worth, your grandmother doesn't think so," she says. "You are her perfect, darling girl."

I pick up one of the sandwich triangles and put it down again. "I should have been here."

"My dear, your grandmother would have had a stroke today whether or not you were within the town limits. At our age, these things happen." She puts her tea cup down with a tiny clink. "I will say this though: she's missed you very much."

I can't say anything because of the sudden lump in my throat.

"The most important thing is that you're here now," she says. "She's going to need some care at home for a little while. Can you get some time off from school until we can arrange for nursing care?"

The lump descends to my stomach now, as the events of the day come back to me. "Yeah, I can stay for a while," I say.

CHAPTER 2

Calling Mum(bai)

I t's not so much that I sleep poorly, as it is that I don't sleep much at all, thanks to farting dogs, snoring dogs and one whiney Jack Russell terrier who, no matter how much I plead, simply will not stop pacing and just lie down, and it isn't until I throw back the covers around half past five that it occurs to me that the dogs are stressed, too; they know something's wrong. Nana should be here with them and since she isn't, their entire doggie universe is askew. My universe is feeling pretty askew as well but at least I know a shower and a hot cup of coffee will help. We all pad down the hall to the bathroom, but I gently close the door against my three furry shadows because I just really need a minute to myself.

There's something off about the bathroom and it takes me a minute to realize that it's the absence of the tang of an abrasive cleaner that's making things feel not quite right. And then I notice that the sink needs cleaning and frankly the tub could use a good scrub, too, and this, more than the army of pill bottles on her kitchen table tells me that Nana has not been well. Nana always subscribed to the notion that cleanliness was indeed next to godliness and all of my memories of Saturday mornings involved the comforting lemony scents of freshly cleaned floors and sparkling porcelain. I shower quickly just to get out of the bathroom, and vow that I will clean this house from top to bottom before she comes home from the hospital.

I set the coffee maker in motion and make a mental note to get some coffee, (real coffee, not senior-citizen-on-sale coffee) at the first available opportunity, then I make a move towards the leashes and all doggie hell breaks loose. Each of them is trying to get closest to me so that they can be leashed first, and they're all wagging and snorting with glee, wiggling so much that I can't get a grip on anyone's collar. I ineffectually tell them to sit — Ophelia, the black Lab, sits instantly and regards me with wide, worried eyes - but then Lucy Boxer takes a nip at Mortimer for some perceived slight, and I'm just beginning to fear for what's left of poor old Mort's ears when Ophelia intervenes, nudging Mort out of the way with her big, blocky head and stepping between them. I think I hear Lucy mutter something under her breath and there is a tense standoff but this allows me to snap a leash on each of them and then we're out the door. Before we make it to the end of the driveway though, their leashes are snarled in some kind of elaborate knot and they're all pulling in different directions and I realize that there is no way we're going to make it around the block, so I coax, encourage and finally drag the three of them back up the stairs and into the house.

"Sorry guys, I'm new at this," I say. "We're going to have to go one at a time."

Lucy's flatulence is reaching whole new levels of toxicity so I unleash the other two and hustle her back outside, and we haven't gone fifty feet when she stops abruptly and squats. Big brown puddles spread on the neighbour's manicured grass and this is when I realize that I probably should've brought something to pick it up with.

MANY, many trips later, everyone has peed, pooped and I've cleaned the neighbour's lawn thoroughly. Everyone's enjoying their kibble,

I've washed my hands a half dozen times and I'm sitting at the kitchen table thinking I should make a list, when my cell phone rings. It's Pam.

"I hope I didn't wake you," she says and I can hear her two little girls shrieking in the background, the usual early morning noises. "I wondered how your Nana was doing."

"Pretty good when I saw her last night. I mean, she's had a stroke and the doctors think there's been some damage but she was sitting up and talking and that's good, but apparently they need to do more tests to figure out the extent of it."

"If she's talking and everything - just a second - *Rose! Take that off the cat this instant!* — if she's talking, that sounds encouraging."

"Yeah, it could be much worse. The doctors sound hopeful."

"What about your mom?"

"What about my mom?"

"What did she say? Is she coming?"

"I haven't called her yet."

"Oh, sweetie, you have to call her — hang on... *Martha! Don't put that in your nose!* — Liv, you have to call her, she needs to know."

"I know, I know. I'll call her this morning. Or email her. Or something."

"You can't send the woman an email that says her mother has had a stroke. You need to talk to her in person."

"All right, all right, I will!" I say. "In other shitty news, I got fired yesterday."

"What?"

"Surplus to the system. Although apparently, I was doing a crackerjack job."

"Surplus to the system? What the hell does that mean?"

"It means they have more teachers than they need, do not pass go, do not collect your paycheque."

"Well, shit."

"You said it, sister."

"So what now?"

"Well, today I'm going to go to the hospital and spend the day with

Nana taking care of her every possible need and then... I'm not so sure."

"Sounds like an excellent plan. Did you have time to pack?"

"Some stuff. I was in a bit of a panic, I just wanted to get going."

"Listen, if you can hang on until Thursday, I can bring you more clothes and things."

"Pammy, it's a six hour drive and you've got the girls. You don't have to."

"Oh, I'd leave the girls with Jason, it'd be a holiday. And anyway, you have to have clothes. When is Alex getting back?"

"I'm not sure. I've left her a couple of messages but she hasn't called yet."

"If she's not back before the end of the week, I will make sure you have your stuff, all right?" she says. "Now is there anything else you need?"

"I don't know... a job?"

There is a crash and a wail in the background. "Okay, that was the toaster, gotta go," Pam says. "Just rip off the damn bandaid and call your mother."

We hang up and I hold my cell phone in my hand for a full minute before I can make myself dial and then I bail half-way through and decide to make another cup of bad coffee first.

MY MOTHER and I have a complicated relationship. It's mainly complicated by the fact that since I was old enough to walk, we haven't spent a lot of time on the same continent, and in the time we have spent together, I've ended up feeling like a houseguest who's stayed a little too long, or who used the good towels to wipe dog shit off her shoes.

My mother, Clara, is an economist who works in international development, mostly Asia and Africa, which sounds really wonderful and save-the-worldy when you say it, except that what she really does is consult with big corporations and deliver papers with titles like "Water Privatization in Sub-Saharan Africa: A New Economic Policy of Pillaging." I may be paraphrasing a bit there, but basically, she is the person you hire when you want to figure out how to squeeze the maximum amount of money from the natural resources of a region and apparently, she is very good at what she does. I can't prove it, but I suspect that she was the person who came up with the idea of outsourcing half the jobs in North America to India. And if it wasn't her own idea, then she at least probably did the math for someone. She has taken great pains to explain to me how her work is of tremendous benefit to the resident population of said regions but she generally loses me when she gets into things like "countervailing equity considerations" and so we generally just agree to disagree.

Don't get me wrong: I admire my mother. She's an intelligent, accomplished woman. As the daughter of Stafford Fall's most prominent lawyer (my Poppa) and perhaps the world's most overqualified small town librarian (Nana has one degree in Classics and another in Medieval Literature — she speaks passable Middle English and we read *The Canterbury Tales* when I was five) it was always expected that my mother would make something of herself. And given that her senior yearbook quote was "Anywhere But Here," it's probably not surprising that when she chose to pursue a doctorate, she did so as far away from home as possible. It was, however, a little bit of a shock when she came for Christmas in 1979, several months pregnant with me, but without a suitor in tow.

In her own way, I know she's tried to be a good mother, and on my best days, I'm grateful for that. No matter where she was in the world, she always made sure that I had whatever I needed, including tuition for whatever I wanted to study. (Although she did feel that this entitled her to editorialize about my choices. To wit, "Olivia, you're a gifted artist and you have a Masters of Fine Arts from the best school in the country. I can't help but think that the only reason you've decided to become a *schoolteacher* is because you're too lazy to think of something more *original*.")

But perhaps more than anything, I am grateful to her because she had the good sense and decency to leave me with Nana.

IN A FIT OF COWARDICE, I decide to try her at the Grand Hyatt in Mumbai before I call her cell phone, on the premise that she is not likely to be hanging around her room at this hour and maybe I can just leave a detailed, yet calm message. But two rings after a polite young lady connects me to her room, my mother's on the line.

"Hello?"

Dammit. "Hi, Mom, it's me."

"Olivia? What's the matter?"

"Don't worry, everything's okay. Well, relatively okay. I mean, it could be worse."

"Olivia."

"Nana's had a stroke."

"Oh, dear God. How is she? Is it serious?"

I repeat the details that I know: tissue damage, more tests but lots of good early signs, and my mother is completely silent, absorbing every detail. And then she's off.

"All right, I know someone on the board at St. Luke's. I'll make a call. How soon can she be ready to be transferred?"

"I'm sorry, what?"

"Do you have her attending physician's contact information? I'm sure they'll need it."

"I do, but I think she's fine here, Mom."

"Don't be ridiculous. St. Luke's will have much better facilities, not to mention competent doctors and specialists. She'll be much better off there."

"But St. Luke's is six hours away. And I'm not sure that she—"

A none too patient sigh. "Olivia, your grandmother has had a stroke. I assume you want her to have the best possible care?"

"Of course I do."

"Then let's get the wheels turning. Call my office and tell them -"

"Mom, if her doctors thought she needed to be transferred to another hospital, I'm sure they would have suggested it. And I don't know that Nana is going to want to go to St. Luke's."

"It hardly matters what she *wants*. We have to think about what's best for her."

"I did mention that she's sitting up and talking and is perfectly lucid, right?"

"David Milton's father had a stroke last year and he went to St. Luke's and David couldn't say enough about how they treated him."

"Who is David Milton?"

"The CEO of the mining multinational I worked with in Tanzania. You know him."

"No, I don't know him, Mom."

"It's immaterial," she says and in my mind's eye, I can see her waving a manicured hand, dismissing facts that displease her. "Apparently, the rehabilitation unit is top notch and they had his father back on his feet in no time. I'll call David and see who the head of his health care team was. Maybe we can get the same person for your grandmother."

"Fine, you do that, Mom, but it's still Nana's decision."

"Olivia, this is exactly why medical power of attorney exists. I don't know if you're aware but it's very common for people who've had strokes to suffer personality changes."

"Personality changes?" There's a band tightening around my forehead, the familiar accompaniment to most conversations with my mother. "Mom, Nana asked me to bring her three things when I go back to the hospital this morning. Her copy of *Mrs. Dalloway*, the tin of butterscotch candies she keeps in the cupboard with the tea cups, and a newspaper so she can do the crossword. Does it sound to you like she's suffered a personality change?"

"I don't appreciate your tone of voice."

"And I don't appreciate you trying to take over the situation from the other side of the goddam world!"

"Stop acting as if you're the only family she has, Olivia! I have a right to an opinion!"

"Yes, but since you bring up medical power of attorney, maybe you should remember that Nana was quite clear that she wanted Penny Clarke and me to make those decisions for her, in the event that she was no longer able to. Which in fact she is, so all of this is completely beside the point. So I'll tell Nana that you send your love and wish her a speedy recovery, but I will not march into her room this morning and tell her to pack her stuff because you don't think she's in a prestigious enough hospital."

There is thunderous silence on the line. I take a deep breath and try to infuse my words with a calm that I don't actually feel.

"Look," I say, "I realize it's a shock to hear that Nana is sick, and I'm sorry that I had to spring it on you like this. I will ask her doctor this morning if he thinks she needs to go to another hospital and in the unlikely event that he does, I'll call you, all right?"

"I'll get the names, just in case."

"Okay, you do that."

"I have to go now, I'm late for a meeting," she says and she sounds smaller somehow, like she's even further away than the other side of the world.

"All right. I won't keep you," I say.

"I'll have my office send some flowers. Are yellow roses still her favourite?"

"I think so."

"Yellow, then. Keep me updated."

"I will. Bye, Mom."

I start to hang up but she says, "Olivia? Are you still there?"

"Yes?"

"If you want me to come, I'll catch the next flight."

A flicker of warmth. "I think she'll be okay, Mom. But I'll keep that in mind."

We hang up and I send Pam a text: *I'm never ever ever taking your advice again.*

And then one to Alex: *Where the hell are you?! I've left three messages! Call me!*

IT's an uneventful trip to the hospital, the first few blocks anyway, and then I nearly hit a Buddhist monk. At least, I think he's a Buddhist monk, since he's wearing the same kind of outfit as the Dalai Lama, all wound up in maroon and saffron robes, the tails swept jauntily over his shoulder. One minute I'm driving along, arguing in my head with my mother, thinking of all the things I wish I'd said, and then the next, I'm slamming on my brakes to avoid hitting the little man who seems to have just appeared in the crosswalk. My heart is thumping in my chest because he's literally inches from my front bumper and I'm wondering how the hell it was that I didn't see him, and then I'm wondering what the hell a Buddhist monk is doing crossing the street in Stafford Falls, but he doesn't look startled or perturbed or even remotely put out by his near death experience. He just smiles, this cloud-clearing, beams of sunlight smile, as if nearly being run over is pretty much the best thing that's happened to him all day - and then he bows to me, gathers up his skirts and continues on his way.

I sit there, stunned, watching him make his way purposefully down the street, until the guy in the SUV behind me leans on his horn.

It's still sort of freaking me out (both the near accident and the monk) when I roll into Nana's room. It's not even eight o'clock, but naturally Angie is already there and the two of them are dissecting Nana's breakfast tray with looks of faint disgust.

I kiss Nana's cheek by way of greeting. "Hey, you guys are not gonna believe what I just saw on my way over here." I pause for effect. "A Buddhist monk. Robes, the whole bit."

"Oh, that was probably Tenzin," Nana says. "He's a lovely fellow."

"Tenzin means 'holder of the teachings,' in Tibetan," Angie informs me. Then, to Nana, "He's much friendlier than the other one. I find Rinchen quite standoffish."

"I think Rinchen's just shy, really," Nana says. "And I'm not sure how much English he speaks."

"Rinchen?" I ask.

"He's a monk, also. They usually walk together in the mornings, but he's gone back to the monastery in New Mexico for a while."

"Are you telling me that Stafford Falls has not just one, but two, Buddhist monks?"

"Rinchen means 'precious,'" Angie adds, helpfully.

"When did we get Buddhist monks?" I ask.

"They're helping to open a retreat centre," Nana says. "You know the old Boy Scout camp, across the lake? It's been empty forever but someone bought it a few months ago and they're going to fix it up and have meditation classes and gardens and courses and all sorts of things. Tenzin spoke to our church group. He gave a lovely presentation."

"It had the most wonderful name," Angie says. "Do you remember, Violet?"

"Oh, what was it? Something about perfection…" Nana says.

"Apparently meditation is very good for high blood pressure," Angie says, and then she frowns. "Olivia, have you had breakfast? You don't look like you've had breakfast."

"I had some coffee."

"That's not a decent breakfast, and frankly, neither is that," she says, nodding disdainfully in the direction of Nana's tray. She starts gathering up her things, jamming stuff into her purse. "I'm off to call Alf and get him to pick me up. I've got a nice piece of back bacon in the fridge and I'm going to fix you both a proper bacon sandwich. Won't take more than a few minutes." And then she's gone, moving remarkably nimbly for someone who I happen to know is on her second set of hips.

The quiet in the wake of Angie's departure slowly fills up with hospital white noise, far away beeps and hums and pages for someone to come to admitting. I notice that last night's oxygen mask has been replaced with a little tube that fits in Nana's nose, but her colour isn't great. She looks drawn, not pink and perky like she usually does, and there is still the slightest droop to one side of her mouth.

"How are you feeling?" I ask.

"Tired mostly," she says and she summons a tiny grin. "This is a terrible hotel. The other guests made the most awful racket all night."

"What a coincidence. So did the guests at my hotel," I say and sit on the bed beside her. "I think the dogs miss you."

"I hope they weren't a bother."

"Oh, we got through. But you might like to get Mrs. Cameron next door a nice potted plant when you get home." I root through the bag

I've brought with me and pull out the tube of hand cream that I took from her bedroom at home. "I thought you might like this, it gets so dry in here," I say and I put it on the rolling tray table, beside the congealing oatmeal and cold tea that were supposed to be her breakfast. I take out her slippers and arrange them beside her bed within easy reach, and I'm just placing *Mrs. Dalloway* and the tin of butterscotch candies she requested on her bedside table when I notice that she can't get the cap off the tube of hand cream. She's intently focussed, a deep crease between her brows, but when she grips the tube firmly with her right hand, her left hand doesn't seem to have the strength or dexterity to unscrew the cap. She switches her grip, trying to loosen the cap with her good hand, but the tube slides around. Just as she's worked the cap off, her left hand seems to convulse and a glob of lotion squirts out the top and lands on the pale blue hospital blanket with an audible splat.

For one terrible moment, I think she is going to cry. But instead, she says, "Son of a biscuit!" and then her eyes dart to my face, like a puppy who just peed on the carpet.

We both dissolve into giggles, then straight out hoots of laughter. Nana claps her good hand over her mouth, to stifle the noise, but it can't be held in. We laugh like total loons and when she can finally catch her breath, she says, between gasps, "Oh! Oh, Olivia, your face!"

And we're off again, me bent over double, trying to pull myself together, her tiny shoulders shaking and heaving with the force of her laughter. This is when a wide-eyed nurse runs into the room and I notice that all the computer screens behind Nana's bed are flashing primary colours, and that somewhere in the hospital, her laughter has just set off sirens and bells.

LATER, after all the monitors have been reset and we've both been chastised by the impossibly young nurse, after Angie has come with bacon sandwiches and left with a promise to return with soup, ("Lord only knows what they'll try to pass off as lunch in this place, really, it's no trouble at all, I was making a pot for Alf anyway,"), the physiotherapist shows up. Like everyone else at this hospital, he seems absurdly young, although he assures me that he's fully qualified, which I find hard to believe because he looks like he's just started to shave. His name is Anthony and he turns out to be absolutely wonderful with Nana, explaining everything he's doing, helping her first to sit on the side of the bed, then to carefully stand in order to test out her sea legs. He complements her on her muscle tone and says it's clear she's a frequent exerciser and while they move gingerly around the room, Nana tells him about the calisthenics of gardening and all about the walking tour of the Cotswolds that she and Penny Clarke and Angie took last year. She teeters a little and I want to leap across the room and grab her, but Anthony and his rippling biceps are right there, cradling, steadying. They do a slow shuffle down the hall to the nurse's station and when they come back, he announces that Monday he'll take her down to the rehab room for her first session, but it would be great if she did two more laps to the end of the hall each day until then. He helps her back into bed, takes her hand in his giant paw and says, "Don't you worry, Mrs. Sutton, we'll have you back in your garden before it's time to cover your roses."

The look on my grandmother's face at that moment: flush with the success of her fifty yard trip, looking up at him with such hope and confidence. I want to remember that forever.

THE FLOWERS START ARRIVING after two o'clock: Mom's arrangement, of course, one from Penny Clarke, one from Angie and Alf, one from her church group, one from the library board, one from her next door neighbour Mrs. Cameron (which makes me feel even worse about what Lucy Boxer deposited on her lawn this morning,) and several more from friends and people whose names I only dimly recognize. There's no way they'll all fit in her room and so I am dispatched with two vases of neon Gerber daisies and instructions to "brighten up the waiting room." Halfway down the hall, my phone buzzes. Finally, a text from Alex. I dump the daisies on an end table in a little alcove and whip out my phone.

So sorry about your nana. There might be a guy coming to pick up the car. Will explain later.

I immediately dial her number and get her voice mail.

I call her every hour for the rest of the day but it isn't until ten o'clock that night when I'm out being dragged down a darkened street by Nana's hell hounds that she answers.

And it's not good news.

CHAPTER 3

A Brief History of Heartbreak

I didn't always want to be a painter. For quite a while, pretty much until first grade, I wanted be a cowboy, but when I was six, my Poppa took me with him to Paris. It was a short trip, just a few days, and he only brought me because he intended to have it out with my mother, who was doing some post-doc work at the Sorbonne at the time. It wasn't so much that he wanted to get rid of me - I never felt anything less than cherished in my grandparents' home - it was more that he wanted my mother to live up to her responsibilities and be a proper mother to me. (My Poppa was very big on responsibilities. This may or may not have been related to the series of heart attacks he had in his early fifties.) Nana wanted no part of his plan and I remember they argued about it, which was a noteworthy occurrence to even my six year old self. I didn't realize that the purpose of the trip was to make my mother feel guilty, I was just excited to fly in an airplane and stay in a hotel.

That trip changed my life, not because my mother refused to have me come live with her, but because my Poppa took me to the Musée d'Orsay. He told me about how it used to be a train station and how the building itself was supposed to be a work of art. He tried to explain the difference between the Impressionists and the Postimpressionists and I listened carefully because I could tell it was important to him. But what I remember most is the moment I saw my first Van Gogh.

Now, it is decidedly uncool as an artist to say that your favourite painter is Van Gogh. There is no artistic credibility in that at all, so usually, when asked, I try to come up with someone suitably obscure and tortured, but the truth is, my favourite artist since I was six years old, has always been Vincent.

I stood there that day in the Musée d'Orsay, and stared at one of his self-portraits and he stared back at me, with his flaming orange beard and his swirling blue thoughts, and it was like suddenly, the whole world had come into focus. It was like something shifted in my little brain and I started to cry, not because I was upset, but because I'd never seen anything so beautiful. From that moment, all I've ever wanted to do was to try to make something as moving and incredible at that.

Afterwards, my Poppa bought me a book of Van Gogh prints from the gift shop and I sat in the café while he and my mother had a "grown-up talk," and I drank my hot chocolate and turned the pages of my book and nothing was ever the same for me.

My Poppa died less than a year later. My mother was inconsolable, but then she didn't come to visit for a long time.

IT WAS AT ANOTHER, completely different kind of art exhibition when I first met Alex - a very sad little exhibition actually, the kind with wine from a box and a tray of supermarket cheese cubes. It was supposed to be a good show, a fancy affair at an up and coming gallery, just a group of us who shared studio space and who needed the exposure and encouragement of having some pieces admired or, God willing, purchased, but the gallery owner had pulled out at the last minute, having scored a hot new artist who worked in spray paint of all things and who promised to bring in a much bigger crowd. Feisty little group of rebels that we were, we forged on, managing to secure a dank little space on the fringe of what is considered the gallery district, and we hung and lit and catered the thing ourselves. Hence the bargain basement wine and cheese. Each of us invited everyone we could think of — I'm pretty sure somebody's dental hygienist was there — Pam was there, of course, taking friendship to new heights by pretending to be a cater waiter, a job that got her through art school, but which she'd vowed never to do again. It was Pam who pointed Alex out to me.

"Hey, have you seen the woman in the purple blouse?" she said, swinging past with a tray of half-filled plastic wine glasses. "She keeps coming back to your stuff and she's asking about you."

I rubbernecked enough to get a look at her. "Wow. She's gorgeous."

"I know, right?" Pam said. "Get over there."

"I don't think so, Pammy… I'm done with straight girls."

"You don't have to sleep with her. Just find out if she brought her chequebook."

"Do you think she's buying?"

"Did you see her purse?"

"No."

"It's a Birkin bag. It costs more than your car. Get your ass over there." She thrust a glass of wine at me. "Here, go!"

I did as I was told, flogging myself with every step and trying to think of some clever opening line, but before I could open my mouth, the owner of the expensive handbag turned and skewered me with a look. "I love your skin," she said. "I just want to touch it."

I briefly forgot how to speak English. She seemed to find this charming, because she smiled, then reached over and took the wine from me. She took the tiniest sip, suppressed a frown, then gestured back at the canvas. "Your skin tones. They're just so lush and textured. Like Lucian Freud if he wasn't quite so pissed off."

"I love his work," I said. "But it can be a bit flinch-inducing."

"I saw his *Girl With A White Dog* at the Tate the last time I was in London. Made me want to crawl out of my skin." She peered more closely at *Nude No. 11.* "But *this.* This is… inviting. Great fabrics, too."

"Thanks," I said.

"Do you mostly do figures?"

"I do a bit of everything. Still lifes. Portraits."

"Do you work from photos or with a model?"

"A model whenever I can, but I don't always have access to one."

"I would take my clothes off for you any time you wanted," she said, and she pressed a card into my hand, managing to make it into a caress of cool fingertips. "Call me."

LATER, when I related our encounter to Pam, she had snorted and said, "Oh, Liv, you are so out of your league," but when I showed her the card, ("Alexandra Ingalls, Pratt and Newberry Designs,") she changed her tune. "You've got to call her. Pratt and Newberry is a very big deal. If she bought some of your work, it could really open doors for you. You might not have to work so hard at the day job."

But since the day job was substitute teaching and we were deep into flu season, I didn't have a chance to call her. And as it turned out, I didn't need to. She called me.

"I'm doing a loft that would be perfect for some of your work," she said. "Can I come to your studio and see some other pieces? We could have dinner after."

She loved my work, bought two pieces for herself and dinner ended up being pizza and red wine on her five hundred count sheets.

THIS IS what it's like to be with Alex: everything is a little brighter, a little more intense. She is incandescent and when she turns that brilliant light on you, it's like a drug. You are the only thing in the world that matters - you're fascinating and funny and sexy and smart and she can't get enough of you. The first six months were a cliché: there was sex, there was champagne, there was even a trip to Venice, for

God's sake, as if we were on some sort of permanent honeymoon. It was ridiculous and I was very happy.

And then I got offered a job and everything came to a crashing halt.

"High School Teacher" was not a label that Alex thought should apply to me. She saw me much more as "Artiste," and "Bohemian," whereas I found myself very attracted to "Pension Plan," and "Dental Benefits."

"The school is in the fucking *suburbs*," she'd said, as if she found such places personally offensive. We were sitting in a Starbucks, nursing seven dollar coffees and trying to hash out our future together. "You'll have to drive for hours."

"Lots of people have long commutes."

"But that's time that you could be painting."

"It's a foot in the door with this school board, something I've been trying to get for three years."

"I thought you were just teaching to pay the bills, so you could paint."

"I am. But I like teaching, and I really like teaching art. And this place has amazing facilities. There's even a ceramics studio and the other art teacher seems really cool. And anyway, I can still paint."

"I don't know. I don't think the timing is right."

"School starts in two weeks, so actually, the timing is pretty awesome," I said.

"No, I mean for us." She ran a finger around the rim of her tall white cup. "I'm thinking of making a change myself."

"What kind of change?"

"I've been wanting for a long time to start my own design business. In fact, I've got everything in place, I'm just waiting for the right moment to pull the trigger." Apparently the Pratt of "Pratt & Newberry" had been stealing the credit for Alex's work recently, denying her opportunities for advancement and hogging all the really lucrative clients for herself. This didn't really surprise me — the few times I'd met Lana Pratt, I hadn't exactly been struck by her bonhomie, and you don't usually climb to the top of the heap by being really nice to everyone on the way up. I knew Alex hated the old bat, but I'd had no idea she 'had everything in place,' for a big move.

"That's great," I'd said. "If that's what you want to do, I think you should do it." In hindsight, my encouragement may have been more than a little motivated by the fact that I wanted her to stop acting like I was selling out by taking a steady teaching assignment. But I honestly did want her to be happy.

So pull the trigger she did. "Ingalls Interiors" launched the same week that I joined the faculty of "Shady Creek Secondary School." Of course, there were the usual bumps in the road that one can expect when engaging in any new enterprise. I was stunned by the amount of paperwork that was required of me, as well as the amount of time I was expected to spend in meetings where nothing ever seemed to be decided. I was advised by Mr. Peck, the well-pressed principal, that it would reflect well on me as a new hire to join a lot of committees so I worked nearly every bake sale and car wash, I sold chocolate bars, wrapping paper and citrus fruit and in a moment of utter lunacy, agreed to help build sets for the spring musical. There was not a lot of time to paint. But I loved the kids, they seemed to love what I was teaching and even if I wasn't making much of my own art, I consoled myself with the fact that every day I had my hands on paint and clay and charcoal.

Unfortunately, Alex's road proved to be a bit bumpier. First, there was her inability to find a proper "space," which is to say, some sort of office/studio hybrid. "Without a space, you might as well just be an IKEA desk in the guest bedroom," she said. We had a spectacular fight when I pointed out that she *was* running the business from her guest bedroom, albeit on a very expensive French escritoire. It took nearly two months, but she finally found a spot that she liked, all the while having lunches/dinners/drinks, cultivating clients and spending whole days with her Blackberry clamped to her ear, and just when it looked like it might all come together — she was set to land a client who wanted to redo his corporate offices — Lana Pratt slammed Alex with a lawsuit. Non-competition, non-solicitation, and a whole bunch of damages from which the estimable Ms. Pratt was purported to be

THE KITCHEN SINK SUTRA

suffering. It was all bullshit - Alex had been completely above board when she'd left, hadn't taken so much as a piece of stationary with her and was taking the unenviable road of building a client base from scratch. But even bullshit can bankrupt you, which was what the fine lawyers hired by Pratt and Newberry had been instructed to do: bury Alex in paper, bleed her dry in legal fees…pick your metaphor, Lana Pratt was out to finish her.

Alex struggled on for a few months, but about the time that I started teaching summer school, the Sun Tzu of the decorating set pulled out her secret weapon. Within the space of a week, Alex lost almost every supplier she'd ever had. Every glass guy, countertop fellow, antique dealer, fancy lamp importer, art appraiser, tile man, painter, plumber and plasterer for five hundred miles suddenly decided that Alex was radioactive and it didn't matter that she'd worked with them for nearly ten years, that she had brought them hundreds of thousands of dollars of business, she was now dead to them.

Things became a little tense at home, too. We were both exhausted and the fat envelopes from Lana's lawyers that seemed to arrive daily in our mailbox started to send me into gasping panic attacks. Alex said not to worry, that everything was going to be just fine, she had it all under control - and then she promptly went to be fitted for one of those expensive orthodontic devices to keep her from grinding her teeth to nubs in her sleep.

And then there was the war over the Art Fair.

It seemed like such a good idea at the time. One day over lunch with Reggie Elliott, the other art teacher (a lovely, flamboyantly gay man who wore an ascot every day and who was three years away from retirement,) we were bemoaning the fact that everything at our high school was geared to jacking up the math and science scores. The arts in general, and the visual arts specifically, were virtually ignored - if there wasn't a standardized score to be published or a photo op for the principal with some robotics toy built by tenth graders, then it didn't exist. I don't remember which one of us suggested it but somehow we stumbled on the idea of holding a special event to showcase the amazing work that our artsy kids were doing and holding it the same night as the school science fair - partly as a symbolic protest, but also partly because we knew that at least some people would show up.

It was a load of work - first, convincing Mr. Peck that our kids deserved a tiny sliver of the spotlight and then once we'd secured his half-hearted support, organizing the event itself. Reggie and I wanted it to be as much like a real art show as possible, so we commandeered the wing of classrooms closest to the gymnasium where the science fair was going to be set up and divided up the kids' work by media. We got the students to design a catalogue for their work and they included the most hilariously serious artist bios I've ever read. It was weeks in the making and I poured myself into it, possibly in part to distract myself from my slowly imploding personal life.

Two days before the show, while I was supervising a team of kids who were printing and collating the catalogues we were going to hand out, I got a call from Alex.

"You're never going to believe who wants to meet you for drinks!" she said.

"Who?"

"Thomas Centella."

I admit, my heart skipped a beat. Thomas Centella owns several galleries here and in Europe and a show at a Centella gallery could make your career. Alex had been saying that I should pursue a meeting with him for as long as we'd been together, but I'd told her I had as much of a shot at meeting him as I did of swimming the English Channel. (Being Alex, she'd promptly offered to pay for swimming lessons and a plane ticket to London.)

"*The* Thomas Centella?" I said. "Are you serious?"

"Yes! I pulled every string I could and managed to get him to look at your portfolio and he's going to be in town this week for a few days and his assistant said he wants to meet you for drinks! Isn't that amazing?"

"Oh my God," I said. "Alex, that's huge!"

THE KITCHEN SINK SUTRA

"I know, I know!" she said. "But listen, she's on the other line, waiting to hear when you're available."

"Any night but Thursday," I said. "Because that's the night of the Art Fair."

It turned out that Mr. Centella would be delighted to meet me for drinks Friday evening at his swanky downtown hotel. Pam did a little dance when she heard and immediately began going through my wardrobe, rejecting every single item of clothing she laid her hands on, pronouncing each of them as "not Centella enough." Luckily, I was deluged with so many last minute details for the school show that I didn't have time to be nervous about meeting the great man.

The Art Fair, (or "The First Annual Art Fair," as Mr. Peck called it when he saw how many parents showed up for it,) was a howling success. It was worth every bit of work to get to see our kids so proud of themselves, talking to their families and peers about their use of colours and symbols and the meaning behind the media they'd chosen. A few pieces were even bid on, which was a bit surprising since nothing was actually for sale and we had to have one buyer agree to leave the piece with us until after report cards, but it was widely agreed that it was a marvellous event.

The only fly in the ointment was the fact that at seven o'clock, just as the doors were opening, Alex called in a panic to say that Mr. Centella's travel plans had changed, he was on a ten o'clock flight to Tokyo later tonight and could I drop what I was doing and hurry downtown to meet him for a really overpriced martini?

She literally would not take no for an answer and after an hour of haranguing calls and texts, I finally had to turn off my phone.

We didn't even fight when I got home that night, well after midnight. All she said was, "What I don't understand about you, Olivia, is why you are so very determined to be ordinary," and then she went to bed.

AND NOW I'M standing on a street in Stafford Falls on a cool September night with Ophelia, Mort and Lucy tugging at their leads, and Alex is on the phone from London, telling me that the guy who might be coming to "pick up the car," is actually a repo man because she's so far behind on the lease and by the way, she's got a job offer in London and she thinks it's "terrific timing" that I've lost my teaching job because now I'm free to come and join her.

And I can't think of a single thing to say.

CHAPTER 4

Tea and Sympathy

Another sleepless night, another too-early morning, another mob scene trying to walk the dogs. I streak through the shower again (note to self: buy cleaning supplies and scour this place) and I'm out the door by seven thirty, determined to find a place with decent coffee and still beat Angie to the hospital this morning, when I'm stopped short by the sight of a young man, standing in the driveway, his face pressed to the driver's side window of my car.

Shit, shit, shit.

"Oh, hello," he says, as if we're old friends who've just bumped into each other at the grocery store. "You wouldn't happen to be Alexandra Ingalls, would you?"

"No, but she told me to expect you," I say. "You're here to repossess the car, right?"

"Afraid so." He motions towards the street, where a big SUV with tinted windows is idling. "Me and Cliff. He has the paperwork, if you'd like to see it."

"Sure, I guess so," I say, descending the porch steps to the driveway. "Is there anything you need me to sign?"

He stands frozen for a second. "I don't know. Let me check with Cliff." He turns and jogs down the driveway to the SUV.

I unlock the door and gather up the CDs that are scattered around on the passenger seat, collect my sunglasses and lip balm, but decide to leave the napkins and extra sugar packets behind. It's while I'm doing a quick sweep of the glove box that it hits me - this gaping chasm of loss. It feels almost as if I've had all the blood drained out of my body, and I have to grip the car door to stay upright.

"Ma'am? Are you all right?"

"I don't even like this car," I say. "I never liked this car."

Repo Boy is at my elbow, looking worried. "Ma'am? Maybe you should sit down. You look a little -"

Mercifully, he stops there and doesn't tell me what I look like. I shut the car door and retreat to the porch steps, first dropping my sunglasses, then several of the CDs as I go. He scrambles along behind me, scooping things up as they fall out of my hands. He waits until I'm sitting on the steps to offer me the items.

Inside, the dogs, perhaps mindful of the drama unfolding in the driveway, begin to bark. Repo Boy casts a nervous eye at the house.

"I'm sorry -- what's your name?" I say.

"James."

"Nice to meet you, James, I'm Olivia," I say and we shake hands. "Don't worry about the dogs, they're all much too old to chase you. And I'm fine, really, I'm not going to faint on you or anything. I've just had a long couple of days."

"I'm glad to hear that — I mean about the not fainting. Cause this is my first time."

I have to chuckle. "It's my first time, too."

"Cliff says the paperwork is all done. I just need... uh, well, we need to ask you for the keys."

"Oh, right," I say and I detach the keys and fob from my key ring and hand them to him. I look at the remaining keys and realize that I forgot to give my school keys back, and that soon, I won't need the keys to Alex's condo anymore since she's putting it on the market this week. I start to feel oddly weightless myself, but it's not entirely unpleasant.

"James, I wonder if I can ask you a favour?"

I can see it's killing him not to trot back and ask Cliff if favours are all right, but then he steps up. "Um. Okay."

"I need a ride to the hospital to see my grandmother. Can you help me out?"

HE'S SO RELIEVED by the nature of the favour that he offers to ferry me, not just to the hospital, but out to the highway first so we can swing by the McDonalds to grab some breakfast — he's had first day nerves and wasn't able to stomach food this morning and now he's ravenous. I don't have much choice since he's my ride, and I'll do just about anything at this point to get some coffee, but he turns out to be pleasant company, regaling me with tales of his "Gamma" and how she's the only one who is allowed to call him "Jimmy," and how he still rakes her leaves every fall. Cliff tails us out of town to the Golden Arches and we make a little convoy through the drive-thru, where James insists on ordering an extra breakfast sandwich for Nana, which I accept because this kid has risked pissing off his boss on his first day just to help me out. He deposits me at the hospital and then drives off with a wave and a cheery toot of the horn of the car that Alex picked out, but apparently couldn't pay for.

I arrive at Nana's room to find not just Angie, but also Penny Clarke, both of whom seem a little dressed up for a hospital visit. Angie has brought a cheese omelet and fresh fruit cup for both Nana and me, but is worried that my omelet has gotten cold, since they expected me a little earlier.

"I had to do a thing first," I say.

They all look at me, happily expectant, waiting to hear what hijinks I've been up to on this fine morning.

"Anyone want an Egg McMuffin?" I say, holding up the grease stained bag, because I'm just not ready to explain Repo Boy to the room and I can't come up with anything else.

"Oh, pet, you remembered!" Nana says.

"Aren't you the thoughtful one!" Angie says and she takes the bag from me. Within seconds, Angie has carved the little sandwich into McThirds and is passing them out to Penny Clarke and Nana and they're nibbling on their tiny pieces and exclaiming as if I've brought them ambrosia. I plop down into a chair and take long sips of my coffee and try to figure out what it is that I have inadvertently remembered.

"Well, now it feels like a proper Sunday morning," Penny Clarke says, wiping off her fingers with napkins that Angie has made appear from her purse. "Angie, is Alf coming for you or do you want to ride with me to church?"

Church. Of course. It's Sunday. And on Sunday, the St. Martin's Altar Guild goes for their weekly guilty pleasure breakfast before attending to the all important tasks of changing the flowers, trimming the wicks and putting out the fresh linens.

"I can't believe you remembered," Nana says later, after the other two thirds of the Altar Guild have hustled out, with promises to return with all the news from the pews. And possibly scones.

"I'm glad you enjoyed it," I say. "Next time, I'll bring you each your own."

"Well, that will be a treat. But hopefully I won't still be stuck here next Sunday."

"Then we better get you moving," I say. "You're not going to get better lolling about like this."

"Do you fancy a stroll?" she asks.

"I thought you'd never ask," I say, and we both smile because this is the short form of joke we've had for ages — dropping full-barrelled hints until the other person gives in and offers what we've been angling to get. She pushes back her blankets. I help her into her housecoat and slippers and we set off down the hall, with our sights set on a full lap of the ward. She walks with her arm interlaced with mine and she needs to lean on me a bit, but we make good progress, considering the number of times we have to stop for her to introduce me to some nurse or custodian or random passerby. "This is my granddaughter, Olivia," she says each time, and she holds my hand while she talks and I remember a windy autumn day on Main Street, walking to the pharmacy or the grocer or someplace with her. I couldn't have been more than eight or nine and she reached for my hand as we started to cross the street. "Nana, I'm not a little kid," I'd said. "I don't need to hold your hand!"

"Of course you don't," she'd replied. "I need you to hold *mine*."

I'd rolled my eyes at the time, but now I wonder if she'd been speaking the truth.

She's pretty worn out by the time we finish our rounds and I have to take off her slippers for her and pull her blankets up. Home by next Sunday suddenly seems foolishly optimistic. I tuck her in, then grab her hand cream and I'm sitting on the bed with her, massaging lotion into the heels of her palms, when she blindsides me.

"So, pet, when are you going to tell me what's the matter?"

I freeze, her tiny warm hand resting in mine and I gape at her. What has she got, some kind of grandmother clairvoyance?

"Is it work?" she asks.

I move my head in a vague way. "Partly."

"Is it Alex?" Genuine concern now, even though I know that deep down, she's never been a big fan of Alex.

"Yes, it's Alex, too. And it's the condo. And now also the car."

Nana gives me her most attentive look. "All right, I think you'd better tell me everything."

It takes a surprisingly short time to explain how my entire life has unravelled in a little over forty eight hours. She listens with rapt attention, responding every so often with a chorus of "Oh, pet," and when I finish, I feel the tiniest bit better, partly because it's been hard concealing these things from her, but also because the look on her face confirms what I've been thinking and not been able to say: this is all pretty fucking awful.

"Well," she says, and she rearranges the front of her nightgown, and fusses with the blankets. "Well. I have to say, I'm very disappointed in Alex." This is an understatement of epic proportions, judging by the daggers in her eyes. "How could she just go off like that without you? With no regard for your feelings."

"She sees it as a chance to start over," I say. "She wants me to come with her."

"Well, what's done is done," she says, although clearly it's not, clearly she's got a few more rounds of vitriol for Alex, and also the school board, my former principal and probably even Cliff the Repo Guy. "No point in dwelling on it, though. The question is, what are you going to do now? Have you had time to think about it?"

I've had plenty of time, staring at the ceiling all last night, listening to the dogs snore and pass gas. I've had time to think what an idiot I've been, to ponder my complete lack of job prospects, to deliberate whether or not there's anything left to salvage with Alex, and to consider a couple dozen really great revenge scenarios. But none of this was particularly fruitful and I suddenly feel so very tired.

"I guess the first thing I have to do is find a new place to live," I say. "Actually, I'll have to move my things out right away because Alex said the realtor will be in this week with people to stage the place."

Nana takes my hand again and squeezes it. "Olivia, tell me honestly. In your heart, do you want to move to London?"

Actually, London sounds exciting and intriguing and absolutely perfect, except for the fact that Alex is there.

I say, "I don't know where I want to go, Nana," but even as the words are coming out of my mouth, I know they're not true. I know exactly where I want to go. "Would you mind if I stayed with you for a while?"

"I thought you'd never ask," she says.

It all catches up with me around two p.m. I hit that wasteland where no amount of coffee is going to be able to keep me upright and the stuff from the cafeteria is a biohazard and best avoided anyway. Nana announces that she's going to rest her eyes for a while and within seconds drops off into a serene nap. I think about slipping out to call Pam who doesn't even know what new indignities today has heaped on me, but the waiting room feels so far away and there's a slant of sunlight coming in Nana's window that's all but goading me to sleep. I scoot my chair closer to Nana's bed and lower my head to my arms for just a second.

Tapping awakens me — or rather, typing, somewhere nearby. My head weighs a hundred pounds, but I drag myself upright and there, across the bed, is Penny Clarke, her sleek little laptop set up on Nana's rolling tray, half-glasses perched on the tip of her nose.

"Olivia!" she says, brightly. "Good, you're awake!"

My face is hot and I can feel the waffle print that the hospital blanket has left on my cheek. The angle of the light has changed significantly and there are scones and a big teapot in a bright orange cozy on the bedside table, so Angie must be around here somewhere.

"Your grandmother is gone with Angie for a little walk," Penny Clarke says. "Very important not to lose muscle tone. Can I pour you some tea?"

"Uh, sure, thanks," I say and I swipe at my face to make sure there's no sleep drool lingering there.

She pours milk and tea into a styrofoam cup, doctors it with a liberal amount of sugar and passes it across the bed, then plops a scone on a napkin and hands me that as well. The tea is sweet and milky and it is the perfect remedy for heartbreak and frayed nerves.

"Rotten luck about your job," Penny Clarke says. "One can't help but wonder if anyone cares about arts education at all these days, but then with such a bunch of philistines running the school boards, it's no wonder." She peers at her screen and taps some more keys with great finality, then slips off her glasses and closes the laptop. "But, chin up. From what I've heard, you're an excellent teacher. You won't be without a position for long."

There doesn't seem to be a need for me to add much, so I just nod and nibble on my scone, which is some sort of cinnamon-brown sugar confection and is astonishingly good.

"As for Alex…" she says, but never gets to finish that thought because Angie and Nana round the corner.

"I thought we weren't saying anything about Alex," Angie says, and Nana widens her eyes and shakes her head vigorously at Angie, but Angie has already built up a head of steam. "But since we are, I don't mind saying that I never liked her. Not one little bit. Oh, she was all smiles and fancy clothes and no one could say she wasn't very pretty, but I told your grandmother, I did, I said, 'Violet, there's something about that girl. Mark my words, she's going to break our Olivia's heart.'"

"Angie, this isn't any of our business," Nana says, as Angie helps her back into bed.

"Yes, I'm sure Olivia feels bad enough without you conducting a post-mortem on it," Penny Clarke says.

"All right, all right, I'm just saying — I never liked her." Angie plucks another scone from the plate and hands it to me. "Here you go, dear. Something sweet to take your mind off it," she says, then she sets about pouring tea for Nana. "And anyway, a clean break is best, I always say."

"Olivia, your grandmother told us that you need to move out of your condo this week," Penny Clarke says.

There still doesn't seem to be a need for me to participate in this conversation, so I just nod again and nibble my second scone.

"I've made some inquiries on your behalf," Penny Clarke says and she passes me a page filled with her neat handwriting. "Here's a list of storage facilities not far from the condo. I read some of the online reviews and they all seemed good, but I phoned and spoke with someone at 'U-Store-It' and he seemed quite on the bit, so you might want to consider that one first." She passes me another paper. "These are the names of some moving companies. The one with the asterisk is the company that my brother and his wife used last year. Couldn't say enough nice things about them, they were especially careful with her Hummel figurines. Now, I'm quite happy to lend you my car Tuesday through Thursday, but I'm afraid I have an appointment that I can't reschedule on Friday. Would that give you enough time?"

I picture myself piloting Penny's dinosaur of a Chrysler through busy city streets with my worldly possessions in a tiny pile in the back seat and it's this picture — not looming homelessness, not unemployment, not Alex's sudden decampment — it's this pathetic scene that causes the dam to burst and tears to spring to my eyes. The cinnamon scone turns to ash in my mouth and I grab for my cup, but everything is blurry from the sudden tears and I knock it over and spill tea all over the floor.

Angie pounces with a wad of napkins to clean up the mess and Penny Clarke is saying something that's meant to be soothing or apologetic but Nana intervenes, and with a few quiet words, she clears the room.

I'm beyond embarrassed because I can't seem to make the tears stop.

"That's it, let it out," Nana says and this makes me cry harder because I'm supposed to be here to help Nana, and now there she is, handing me tissues with her good hand and murmuring comforting words.

"I'm sorry, pet, maybe I shouldn't have told them," she says.

"No, no, it's fine. They were going to hear the whole sad story eventually."

"Still. They can be a bit too much sometimes. They mean well, though."

"I appreciate the help, really, I do, it's just... it's all so real now, moving companies and storage spaces." Not to mention Penny Clarke's fucking Chrysler. I sniff and wipe my nose. "It's very kind of her to offer, but I really don't want to borrow her car, Nana."

"You don't have to then. You can rent something. A little van might be a good idea." She strokes my hair. "Maybe your friend Pam could help you pack. So you don't have to do it alone."

"I'll call her."

"Good then." She smoothes out the blankets, trying to look nonchalant and failing. "And when I'm home and things are more settled, we can look into finding you a car. The man who owns the dealership on the highway is on Alf's curling team, maybe he can help you find a good deal. And I would be happy to pay part."

"You're not buying me a car, Nana."

"Don't tell an old woman how to spend her money," she says. "And anyway, it would just be fair if I paid part because I'll be needing you to take me places. At least for a while."

"What 'places?' Where exactly are you planning on going?"

"Well, I'll have to go to physiotherapy. And I have a lot of meetings for my charities. And I like to go to Costco, sometimes. They have those butterscotch candies I like and they always have the best prices for cereal."

I picture my Nana rolling out of Costco with a hundred pound bag of butterscotch candies and a pallet of Raisin Bran, and it makes me smile.

"We can talk about a car when I get back," I say. "But I'm going to have to do something about a job first. Hey, if they're hiring at Costco, maybe I could get you a discount on those candies."

"Don't worry about that now. You go call Pam and tell her when to expect you. And send those two back in here, I want to have a word with them."

"Go easy on them, Nana. It's not their fault I'm a blubbering idiot today."

"Don't you worry about a few tears, my dear. Many's the time I've held Angie's hand over some horrible thing one of her kids has done to her. And you didn't hear it from me, but Miss Penny Clarke once took to her bed for a week over a handsome young doctor who didn't return her affections. They've had their share of broken hearts, too."

The idea of Penny Clarke struck down by anything, let alone unrequited love, is so foreign that it makes me pause halfway to the door.

"Nana?"

"Yes, pet?"

"I really did love Alex. And I feel sad because I thought she was the one, you know?"

"I know."

"But I think a bigger part of me feels terrible because I knew she wasn't, and I stayed anyway."

She nods, sagely. "It's all right."

"Nana, this is the opposite of all right. Absolutely nothing is all right."

"Well, at least you know where to start then, pet. Now go call Pam."

I'm completely out of other ideas, so I do as I'm told.

CHAPTER 5

And Just Like That

Tuesday morning, Penny Clarke insists on driving me to the car rental place to pick up the van I've rented for the move. She's also going to stay with the dogs and arrange for Nana's occupational therapy assessment, and what with daily visits from Anthony the Amazing Physiotherapist, and Angie delivering four course meals to the hospital, I pull out of Stafford Falls confident that Nana will be well taken care of in my absence. I've purloined *Pride and Prejudice* from Nana's vast audiobook library, and then it's just me, Jane Austen, a van that smells like old hamburgers and six hours of highway.

The feeling of optimism lasts for about three minutes.

The real problem with six hours of highway isn't the length of time you have to drive - it's the length of time you have to think about all the things that you'd rather not think about: What if Nana has another stroke? Did I remember to give Lucy her arthritis medication? Where did Alex and I go wrong? Is it time to finally cut my hair? I can't come to a satisfying conclusion on any of these questions and about the time I'm remembering what a pain in the ass Mrs. Bennet is, and wondering why Elizabeth doesn't just smack her, my mother calls.

It is a truth, universally acknowledged, that your mother knows exactly when you are at your most vulnerable and chooses that moment to phone.

"Hi, Mom."

"Where are you? Are you driving?"

"Yes, I'm driving."

"Do you have your headset on?"

"Yes, I have my headset on." This is not true.

"It's not safe to drive with a cell phone in your hand, Olivia."

"I've got you on speakerphone, Mom. I'm safe as houses."

"Are you certain? I can wait while you pull over and put your headset on."

"I'm good, Mom."

"Well, don't blame me if you're arrested for distracted driving or whatever."

"So, what's up?"

"I spoke to your grandmother this morning."

"She's doing well, don't you think?"

"Why on earth did you not tell me that you were fired?"

"For starters, because I wasn't fired. I was surplussed. That means they --"

"I know what it means. It means they have idiots managing their budgets and enrolment projections. And Alex? When were you going to tell me about Alex?"

"It just hadn't come up," I say, scanning the horizon for a police car who might obligingly pull me over for something. Anything.

"I thought you two were so good together," she says. "It's such a shame. Are you very upset?"

"Well. You know. It comes and goes." And when it comes, I feel like someone has sucked all the oxygen out of the room and I'm suffocating from the sheer weight of the sadness, but I'm not about to tell my mother that.

"I think I have the solution," she says.

"The solution? To what?"

"To your current predicament."

"Oh? And what would that be?"

"I think you should go back to school."

"I'd love to, Mom, but there aren't a lot of jobs right now."

"No, not to teach. To get your Phd."

Why is there never a cop around when you need one?

"Mom, I really don't want to go back to school right now." Or ever, actually.

"But think what you could do with a Phd! Museum work, auction houses, a professorship. The possibilities are tremendous."

"I'd rather paint or teach art. And I don't need a Phd to do either of those things."

"I can't help but feel you don't have a plan."

"A plan?"

"Yes, a plan."

"Well, today my plan is to drive for six hours and pack up everything I own. Tomorrow my plan is to watch the movers take most of what I own to a storage space, then drive six hours back to Stafford Falls. Thursday's plan involves meeting with Nana's doctors and arranging for the home care nurse. Friday, I plan to take an incredibly stubborn Boxer to the vet for her shots and clean Nana's house from top to bottom in case she gets out of the hospital this weekend. So as you can see Mom, I am not at all without plans."

"Olivia, I'm trying to help. Please be serious."

"My whole life blew up in my face four days ago. This is as serious as I can be right now. I'm going to take care of Nana for a few weeks, make sure she's okay and then I'll figure out what to do when the time comes."

"I hope you're not thinking of moving back to Stafford Falls. I grew up there, I know what it's like."

"I grew up there, too, Mom. And it's not that bad."

"If you're eighty five years old and you like to crochet. You're an artist, Olivia! You need to be in a cosmopolitan centre, surrounded by other artists. If you move back there, you will die creatively."

"I hardly think I'll die, Mom."

"I'm only thinking of what's best for you."

"I know."

"Let me make some calls. It wouldn't hurt to just look at some schools. I know the dean of a particularly good program in Italy."

Something feels ready to pop in my neck and I realize I'm gripping the steering wheel much tighter than is necessary, and I am just about to shriek, "*Italy?* Nana has just had a fucking stroke and you want me to go to *Italy?*" when it hits me. She really does think she's helping. This is her best answer, her most efficient solution, the way she fixes things: find a spot geographically as far away from the problem as possible, and enrol in a four year program of study.

"You know, Mom, I don't think the timing is right for me to move to Europe," I say and I manage to make my voice sound remarkably normal and not at all like I'm ready to hit someone.

"You need to think about your future. At least let me make some calls."

"You're right," I say, because otherwise this conversation is never going to end. "It can't hurt to consider it. Send me the information and I promise I will read it."

"Wonderful! You won't regret it!"

Of course I'll regret it, I'm regretting it already, but I'm desperate to get off the phone. "All right, then," I say. "Well. I should let you go. You've probably got a busy day."

"I have drinks with the Indian Minister of Corporate Affairs in a half hour. The man's as boring as blancmange but we need him to rubber stamp a new report about tariffs on polyester yarn, so off I go. I'll send you the information about the Phd programs as soon as I can."

"That'd be great."

"And I really am sorry about Alex."

"Thanks, Mom."

"Is there no chance you two might get back together?"

"She's moving to London, so no, I don't think so."

"That's too bad. I always liked Alex. She had such good taste."

"Good luck with the minister, Mom."

We hang up and it's a good twenty miles before I can unclench my shoulders and by then, Mrs. Bennet is lecturing her daughters on what a catch a single man with five thousand pounds a year is, and I'm grateful to listen to someone else's mother tell them what to do with their life.

I MAKE GOOD TIME, even including a twenty minute side of the road stop for a little picnic - Angie packed me a ham sandwich, two oatmeal cookies and an apple; I half expected a little note that said "Have a great day!" or "She never deserved you!" but there's just food in the little paper bag - and I roll into the largely deserted Shady Creek Secondary School parking lot around four. Two lifetimes have passed since I last strode across this asphalt and I'm especially glad that no one's around so I can get in and get out quickly. I do a walk-through of the classroom I was assigned, and I think of leaving a note for my students on the white board but someone's already covered it with a brilliant caricature of what I think is the vice-principal, judging by the crossed arms and over-sized forehead and I'm loathe to disturb such a great piece of satire. Most of my stuff is in the little cubby that serves as my office and I spend a fast hour jamming books and posters and files into boxes and then I'm back in the hamburger-scented van, slogging through rush hour, headed into downtown. It's raining and is just starting to get dark by the time I pull up outside our building and somehow this seems appropriate.

Pam is already there, sitting cross-legged outside our door, with a thick glossy magazine on her lap. She does not look happy.

"Ooh, is that art porn? What have you got?" I ask.

"September issue of *Art World Today*," she says. "I had to buy it because there is a feature article on Bianca Wren. Fucking horsey-faced poseur."

Well, this at least explains the look of thunderclouds on Pam's face.

Pam, Bianca and I were in the same Masters program together, and even though the average level of freakishness in any given art school is pretty high, I think all of us weirdos and refugees from the island of misfit artists agreed that Bianca Wren was a gigantic flake. Pam, for some reason, always seemed to take special offence and usually said her name with big gasps of breath and lots of emphasis on the final "ah," as in "Bee-Yonk-AHHHH." But the joke was on us because what Bianca understood, better than she grasped triadic colour theory or the influence of the surrealists on abstract expressionism, was the importance of self-promotion. She was probably the most commercially successful artist we knew and she was a media darling who constantly managed to swing big commissions and all sorts of artist in residence grants in cool European cities.

"She is quoted in this article as saying that her most recent work is about 'the unrelenting influence of gender politics and the shimmering divergence of hegemony in the modern world,'" Pam says.

"Yeah, but people eat that shit up," I say, dumping the pile of boxes I've lugged upstairs.

"She paints blurry squares and rectangles for Christ's sake!" Pam says as she tosses the magazine aside and shakes her head. "I used to do edgy stuff. Remember that? Remember when I was edgy? What happened?"

"I don't know. Breastfeeding, maybe?"

"No, I'll tell you what it is. It's living in a fucking shrine to Walt Disney. It wears you down. All those singing animals. All that *pink*. I'm so sick of pink I could vomit."

I pull out my ever diminishing key ring and unlock the door while Pam develops her theme, "The Destruction of Western Civilization by Disney Princesses," but when the door swings open, for just a moment I can't hear her anymore. I knew this was going to be hard, but I didn't realize it would all feel so foreign, so quickly. This isn't my home anymore.

Pam squeezes my shoulder. "Have you got booze?" she asks.

"I'm sure we can find something."

WE TRY to dig right in and get sorting and packing but what I don't count on is how upset Pam is that I'm leaving. There is such a cloud of melancholy clinging to the two of us that we break into the vodka before we eat anything and then things go pretty much the way you think they will. Hours later, very little is packed and we end up ordering all the dishes that we've never tried on the take out Thai menu, which might have been okay if so many of them hadn't contained some variety of fiendishly hot pepper, and we sort of scare the delivery boy because when he rings the bell, Pam has got Elvis Costello on so loud that the windows are rattling and she's dancing through the kitchen with the toilet brush and that's when I realize we need to sober up and get some food into our bellies because Pam can't stand Elvis Costello.

IT'S JUST before midnight and we're sitting in a red leather booth at the all night Greek diner around the corner, eating grilled cheese sandwiches and taking stock of our lives. The waitress, who looks like she's had a worse day than either of us, refills our coffee cups and drifts back to the counter.

Pam watches her go, then says, "Alex was always rude to waitresses. I hated that about her."

"It's good that we broke up then."

Pam snorts and dips the point of her grilled cheese into a little pool of ketchup. "I can't believe she let your car be repossessed. No, wait, I can totally believe it." She chews thoughtfully for a while. "Who is the new London job with anyway?"

"Someone who hates Lana Pratt even more than Alex does. I forget the name. I'm sure they're a big deal."

"Ah, the enemy of my enemy," Pam says. "What about the lawsuit?"

"I guess her lawyers have advised some sort of receivership so there won't be much left on the carcass for Lana to pick at."

"But you're okay, right? I mean, if you needed money, you'd ask, right?"

"Yeah, I'm fine for now. I'll have to get some sort of job though, to tide me over. And I'll have to do something about a car. You can walk most places in Stafford Falls, but I'm going to need a car to get Nana to her appointments."

Pam's gaze lingers on my face for just a second too long.

"What?" I say.

She shakes her head, reaches for her coffee cup.

"What is it?"

She shrugs and smiles sadly. "What am I gonna do without you?"

"Pammy, I'm not moving away."

"It feels like it."

"I'm just going to stay with Nana until she's back on her feet again — literally, because she's got this weird wobble when she walks right now — and then I'll be back."

"Will you?"

"My mother has already told me how I will be on creative life-support five minutes after I arrive, if that's what you're worried about. It's a tiny little town. There are no jobs, no galleries, there's nothing there for me."

"You can paint anywhere. All you need is good light. And there's not a whole lot holding you here right now, either."

"It'll just be for a few weeks. Two months, tops. I'm sure."

"So long as you're sure..." Pam says.

WE WRAP up the packing around four a.m., but Pam stays until the sky is lightening in the east because she swore she wouldn't let me spend my last night here alone. I send her off with a travel mug of strong coffee and the promise to call when things have settled down a bit. She threatens to visit with the girls and all their Barbie regalia if I'm really gone more than two months, so now I have that hanging over my head.

I pour myself a cup of coffee and drift back to the tiny room where I used to keep my painting supplies. My easel had been tucked away in storage for quite a while now - I'd given up the lease on my studio space when I'd started at Shady Creek because I couldn't justify the expense anymore, given how little time I was able to spend there - but

I'd tried to keep a couple of canvases and some paints here, just to say I was painting. Even though I never did, it seemed.

I sit on the floor and sip the first really good coffee I've had in days - Alex always insisted we buy an expensive roast - and I consider the fact that this is the only room in the place that looks noticeably different since I've packed up all my things. The living room, the kitchen, the bedroom, they all look like I might be away for the weekend, but this room is deserted: no work table, no paints, no canvases leaned against the wall. Just light and air. And I wonder, how long had I been shrinking like this? How long had I been making myself tiny enough to fit into this life with Alex? And how could I not have seen that before now?

IT IS A HELLISHLY long day even before I hit the highway. The movers get lost on the way to the storage unit and we exchange a series of snarky phone calls that make me wish I had listened to Penny Clarke and hired the movers who were so careful with her sister-in-law's Hummels instead of opting for the cheapest ones. Then the van blows a tire and I sit cooling my heels for an hour waiting for the roadside assistance guys, only to discover that they can't change the flat while my stuff is packed in the van, and that they are not allowed to touch the cargo for complicated liability reasons, so they sit in the cab of their tow truck eating chips while I take every box, bag and suitcase out and line them up on the side of the road. It is mid-afternoon before I start making any real headway back towards Stafford Falls but thankfully by then, I'm too tired to torment myself with existential questions about relationships, career choices or the future of my hair. I just drive and let the miles wash over me, following the yellow line on the asphalt until, many hours after the sun sets, I emerge from the woods and catch sight of the lights of Stafford Falls. I feel relief and disappointment in equal measure.

And hunger. It occurs to me that I haven't actually eaten anything since Pam and I wolfed down grilled cheese sandwiches, which technically was yesterday. Suddenly, I need something to eat like I need my next breath and I don't think there's much in Nana's fridge, because Angie has been feeding me since I arrived. And since the side-walks have already been rolled up, this being a weeknight in Stafford Falls, there's only one choice. I swing the van around and make my way to the lakefront, hoping that not too much has changed since I last lived here.

And sure enough, there it is, at the far end of the marina parking lot, an Airstream trailer up on blocks, festive Christmas lights wrapped around the sign on top that proclaims this to be "Burger's on Wheels: Stafford Fall's #1 Food Truck," which, punctuation peculiari-ties aside, isn't much of an honour, considering it is Stafford Falls' only food truck. Also, it's no longer on wheels. Nevertheless, there is the usual crowd at the picnic tables - a gaggle of teenagers, a couple on the world's cheapest date, and a guy about my age, by himself, reading a paperback. I park nearby and stagger on numb limbs to the little window to place my order (cheeseburger with fried onions and a black and white shake), and I am just considering whether I should have taken the young man up on his offer of fries, when I hear the guy with the paperback say, "Liv? Is that you?"

He's wearing a bright red windbreaker and a giant, infectious smile, and despite a few extra pounds and an earnest attempt at a goatee, I know immediately who this is.

"Eddie Spaghetti!" I say and he comes over and wraps me in a fierce hug.

Eddie Spaghetti, or Eduardo Angelino Spinella as his mother named him, was my first real friend in Stafford Falls. His family lived three doors down from Nana's and one of my earliest memories is playing Red Rover in his backyard at twilight with about a hundred of his brothers and sisters and cousins. We couldn't have been more than five and when I ended up on the sidelines with blood gushing out of my nose, he sat with me and held my hand until Nana came running with an ice bag and a handful of paper towels.

"I heard your Nana is in the hospital, I'm so sorry, how is she doing?" he says.

"She's holding her own. It'll take a while, but I think she'll be okay."

He holds me at arm's length to get a good look. "You look fantastic!"

"I've been moving boxes and driving all day, so I look like crap, but thanks."

"Are you moving back to the Falls?""

"Well, not moving exactly. I'm just staying with Nana for a while. You know, until she's doing better."

"And are you still painting? Living the exciting life of the 'artiste?'"

"More like the exciting life of the surplussed high school art teacher. But what have you been up to? Last I heard you were teaching phys ed over in Winchester, you big sell out."

Winchester is the next biggest town, forty minutes drive away, whose residents have always considered themselves so much more refined and worldly than the peasants of Stafford Falls. This has inspired a certain spirit of competitiveness in most things but especially sports, including a particularly vicious lawn bowling tournament some years ago.

"That's the first time I've ever heard you not call it 'Suckchester,'" he says, with a grin.

"Witness the new, mature me."

"I'm actually back in the Falls, now," he says. "I'm the vice principal at Stafford Falls Public School. Well, half time v.p. I also teach grade seven and eight."

"That's great! Good for you!"

"Who'd have thought, right? Maybe all those years I spent sitting in the vice principal's office I was actually preparing for the job."

"So when someone pulls the fire alarm, do you immediately suspect yourself?"

We're both cracking up over that one when Mr. Burger's on Wheels calls out that Eddie's order is ready. We amble over to the window and the guy passes Eddie a giant box of food with the largest order of chilli cheese fries I've ever seen.

"Your appetite is still good," I say.

"Most of this is for Connie," he says. "She's expecting. Twins, actually." He's managing to look proud, excited and terrified, all at once.

"Eddie, that's fantastic! Tell her I said congratulations."

"You should drop by! How long are you going to be here?"

"I don't know. A couple of months, maybe. But now that I know someone so high up in the school system, maybe you could throw some supply work my way."

I was only half-serious. I mostly said it as a joke, because I love to make Eddie Spaghetti laugh.

His eyes practically bug out. "Are you looking for a job?"

"Oh, I'm not sure how long I'll be here, I just need something to bridge the gap," I say, but he grabs my arm.

"I've got a half time teaching position that I need to fill."

"Starting when?"

"Now. Like last week."

"I don't know, Eddie. I don't have much experience with the really little kids."

"It's a support position, mostly small groups. And a few special kids."

"How special?"

"Some learning disabilities, and you know... different challenges. There's a teaching assistant to help, though and she's great."

"I don't know..." I say again, but I'm actually wondering how much supply work I would be able to get at the high school level. And then I'd be driving all over hell's half acre to schools, in a car that I don't currently have. Eddie's school is a twenty minute walk from Nana's house, and a half time position would give me time to get Nana to her appointments and take care of things for her. Also, supply teaching in a different school every day is a special kind of purgatory and I thought I'd already paid those particular dues. If it came to that, Costco would start to look pretty good.

Eddie senses my hesitation. "Olivia, at the moment, my best two candidates are a woman who is 108 years old and a really creepy dude who's a little too into taxidermy," he says.

"*Too* into taxidermy?"

"You know those tableaus that people used to make in the old days? Everybody standing around at a horse race or a tea party or something, wearing their fancy clothes, smoking pipes or whatever?"

"Yeah?"

"He recreates those with mice, Liv. Little stuffed mice. He showed me pictures. Please, just come in and talk to the principal. I'm sure she'll hire you for whatever length of time you're available."

I hesitate, mostly because I'm a little punch drunk from lack of sleep and highway hypnosis. Is this the best time to make a decision like this?

"I'll throw in an order of chilli cheese fries," he says and then I know it's the right thing to do.

LATER, after I've eaten, when I've got hamburger grease and chocolate syrup humming through my veins and the world feels like a safer, happier place, I turn the van towards Nana's house, deciding to take the long way around along the waterfront, then up Main Street and that's when I spot a familiar figure in colourful robes on the sidewalk. He's standing in front of the old bakery on the corner, and I see that the huge front windows are covered in brown paper. In big letters it says, "Opening Soon: The Second Chance Café."

It just comes over me, I don't think about it, I just crank down the window of the van and call out, "Hi, Tenzin!"

I can see the smile, even in the dim streetlight. "Hello, you!" he calls back and he waves, a big sweeping arc that makes his maroon sleeves flap like signal flags.

And just like that, I've moved back to Stafford Falls.

CHAPTER 6

There Are No Falls in Stafford Falls

A quick geography lesson: there are no waterfalls in Stafford Falls. I can see why you might think there are, but you would be wrong. And not only are there no waterfalls, there isn't even a lot of agreement on how a place with no quickly dropping water actually came to be called Stafford Falls. Some people say that Stafford Falls is actually a bastardization of Stafford "Fells," fells being a term generally used to describe an upland area that is barren or stony, and which is sometimes used for grazing. But since Stafford Falls is neither barren, nor is it stony, and there has never been much grazing going on here, that explanation seems unlikely. Granted, it's a little confusing for the tourists who are the lifeblood of the town three seasons of the year, but generally they get over their disappointment pretty quickly and then they seem happy to join in the little cartographic joke. A few years back somebody even made a tidy sum selling t-shirts that said "I Went Over the Falls at Stafford Falls," that had a cartoon of a guy bobbing along in a barrel towards a giant waterfall. Nana bought one and sent it to me.

Other things that Stafford Falls does *not* have: big box stores and fast food outlets, a multi-screen cinema (the town's movie theatre has one screen and it shows two movies each night for one week, seven o'clock and quarter past nine, and if you miss them when they're in town, then it looks like you're driving to Suckchester, doesn't it?) What Stafford Falls does have is water and sky and steeples and boats and trees and sunsets and colours. Oh God, such colours.

Stafford Falls also has a sailboat museum that used to be a sailboat factory, a florist, a tiny book store, one Chinese food restaurant, a butcher, a green grocer, a regular grocer (which now boasts an "international food" aisle which has soy sauce, taco seasoning and cans of coconut milk,) a pharmacy, a hardware store, four churches and three elementary schools. I am sitting in one of those schools now, Stafford Falls Public School, one of those great, solid, old schools that were built when red brick was plentiful and the architects liked to show off with tall windows and a big arch over the front doors.

Another Friday afternoon, another meeting with a principal.

I am clutching a file folder crammed with letters of recommendation, my glowing performance review from Shady Creek, a slightly out of date resumé and some sample lesson plans I'm hoping will dazzle the principal into hiring me on the spot. I'm wearing what I think is a conservative, yet flattering interview outfit: charcoal grey wool pants and blazer with white silky blouse, understated jewelry and minimal make up, all of which was fine when I put it on this morning to ride with Penny Clarke to see Nana at the hospital, but late September weather being what it is, now I'm on slow roast and the wool pants just feel damp and itchy and I wish I'd taken a minute to touch up my lipstick. And maybe my antiperspirant. I'm just about to ask Mrs. Demanksi, the school secretary, if I have time to slip off to the restroom when the door to the principal's office swings open and a tiny redhead emerges. Everything about her is clipped and tailored, like she's some sort of human bonsai. Her cream coloured suit is immaculate and I know for a fact that this unseasonably hot and humid afternoon is not making her sweat.

"Olivia Sutton?" she says.

"Mrs. Osgoode," I say, standing up and extending my hand. "Thank you for seeing me."

"Miss," she says.

"Pardon?"

"It's Miss Osgoode, not Mrs."

"Oh. I'm sorry. *Miss* Osgoode. Eddie Sp— uh, Mr. Spinella speaks very highly of you."

This is not entirely true. Eddie's exact words were, "She's not the worst principal I've ever worked for," but I'm willing to embellish after the "Mrs./Miss" debacle. Although I am starting to wonder how bad the other principals were.

"By any chance, is your mother Clara Sutton?" she asks and this should have been the tipoff, because no one in Stafford Falls ever asks if I'm my mother's daughter, partly because she hasn't lived here for over thirty years.

"Yes," I say, "my mother is Clara. Do you know her?"

"We went to school together," she says and something about that displeases her, but I can't put my finger on it. She ushers me into her office and motions vaguely at the straight-backed chair in front of her desk, so I sit. "Mr. Spinella wasn't able to provide me with a copy of your resumé, so I'm afraid I haven't had a chance to familiarize myself with it," she says, but the words are sort of hollow, because she's putting all her energy into studying me, scrutinizing my face as if she's committing it to memory or looking for something.

"I brought a copy with me," I say, and I actually find it hard to move, as if I'm pinned under the weight of her gaze. "I also have some letters of recommendation and some lessons that I've taught." I push the file folder across the vast expanse of desk and she takes a moment to put her reading glasses very precisely on her nose before opening the folder and beginning to read.

And read. And read. She reads every line on every page, slowly turning each paper over and laying it aside as she peruses the next. What feels like several hours later, she takes off her reading glasses and regards me with no discernible expression.

"I was under the impression that you had more classroom experience," she says.

"Well, I only have the one year on a full-time contract, but I do have three years of experience as a supply teacher — I've got letters from four principals in my file there, you probably noticed them. I also worked for two years as a teaching assistant when I was completing my Masters, so I feel quite at home in the classroom."

"That's a Masters of Fine Arts?" she says and she picks up my resumé and peers at it again. "In painting? You're a painter?"

"Yes. In addition to being a teacher."

"Of course. But I notice that there are several years between your Masters and when you got your teaching certificate."

How is she making that sound like an accusation? "Uh, yes, I did some different jobs," I say, "but mostly I was painting."

"I see. So, the painting didn't work out?"

"No. I mean, yes, it worked out. I just wanted to do more with my art. I was working as an instructor at a community centre, teaching life drawing and I really liked it and I realized that I enjoyed teaching art, so I thought I would take my career in that direction."

"You do realize that this is a special education position?"

"Mr. Spinella said it involved supporting students with learning disabilities and other challenges." Actually, now that I think of it, Mr. Spinella was not too forthcoming with the details.

"The CRC is a very important part of our school's special education program."

"CRC?"

"Community Resource Class. The teacher in charge of this class needs to be able to manage children with a variety of special needs, support the classroom teachers, help plan appropriate remedial interventions… it's quite a demanding position, actually."

Fine, by all means then, forget me and hire the guy who does the creepy stuffed mice tableaus, because I'm sure that'll work out well for you.

"I have qualifications in special education," I say. "I've taken all the required courses."

"But you have no real world experience."

"Well, I've done short term supply work in some special ed class-rooms…" I try to think of what else to say but come up empty.

"I'll be honest, Ms. Sutton, I was hoping for a more experienced teacher."

And I was hoping my girlfriend was kidding about the car being repossessed but we don't always get what we wish for, do we? Actually, fuck this.

"I understand," I say, and I get to my feet. "Well, thank you for your time, Miss Osgoode. I appreciate you seeing me."

"You don't look much like her," she says.

"I'm sorry?"

She leans back in her high backed faux leather chair, the better to study me. "Your mother. You don't resemble her very much."

What the hell is it with my mother and her? "People say I have her nose," I say, vaguely.

"I suppose," she says. "At any rate, see Mrs. Demanski on your way out. She'll have all the forms you need to fill out for the school board. Staff meetings are the first Thursday of every month. I believe Mr. Spinella has last period free, so he can show you to your classroom." She reaches for her glasses again and turns her attention to her computer screen.

I stand there for an awkwardly long time, parsing what she's just said, because it kind of sounds like she's hired me, but that can't possibly be how this conversation is going to conclude.

She finally looks up from her computer. "Is there something else?" she says.

I shake my head and slip out the door.

I am no longer surplus to the system.

EDDIE SPAGHETTI IS NOT available to show me to my classroom due to a cross country running practice that he is currently hosting, but Mrs. Demanski, who looks old enough to have been around the day they laid the cornerstone of this venerable school, gives me very detailed directions and sends me off with an armload of paperwork to be returned to her when I've filled in every blank. I wander down the hall to the very end as she instructed, every footstep creaking on the ancient wood floors but only find a set of stairs that seem to lead to the bowels of this fine old building, so I retrace my steps to the office and try a different hallway, to no avail. Finally, I come across a woman who is busy stapling yellow construction paper to a bulletin board and she smiles at me as I approach.

"Can I help you?" she asks.

"I'm looking for my classroom, actually," I say. "I'm Olivia Sutton. I'm the new CRC teacher. Very new. I was hired, like, five minutes ago."

So much passes across her face and none of it is good, but then she rallies.

"Carrie Bolton," she says and she sticks out her hand. "I'm grade five. Welcome to Stafford Falls Public School."

"Thanks," I say.

"I guess Frances isn't coming back, then."

"Frances?"

"Frances Holt, she was the last CRC teacher. She's not coming back?"

"I'm afraid I don't know."

She looks like she's going to say something, then thinks better of it.

"So, your room," she says. "I can show you where it is."

We backtrack the way I came, then head down the long hall with the creaky floor, to the top of the stairs that lead down into what appears to be darkness.

"Right down there, you can't miss it," she says. "It's the only classroom."

I can only assume that it's not "Punk the Newcomer Day" here at Stafford Falls Public School, and so I thank her and start down the stairs. I descend two full flights, all the way down into the gloaming. At the bottom, there are in fact two doors, one with a frosted glass window and a little nameplate that says "F. Holt, Community

Resource Class" and another that has the words "Boiler Room" painted on it. Being in possession of three university degrees, I choose the correct door on the first try.

There is a group of kids sitting around a table, and they all look up from their books when I open the door. Another child is sitting on the floor beside the only adult in the room, poring over what looks like some sort of antique map and humming.

"I'm sorry, I should have knocked," I say and I know I should introduce myself to the woman who seems to be in charge of this little gathering but I am overwhelmed by the claustrophobic feeling of this room. It is the most oppressive space I have ever seen. The windows are tiny and so grimy that the only sunlight they let in seems grey and there's a rickety set of steps that lead up to a blaze orange fire door, which appears to be the only other way to escape from this dungeon. But worst of all is the colour of the walls and the shelves and all the trim, which can only be described as the love child of Institutional Beige and Bilious Green. It's the colour I imagine oatmeal might turn if you left it out on the counter for six months. Just standing there looking at it is sucking the life juice out of me.

"Hey, everybody say hello to the new teacher!" the woman at the table says.

I wonder if it's too late to bolt.

IT TURNS out that the leader of this little group is Holly O'Hara and she is the teaching assistant assigned to the CRC class, which she takes pains to point out right after I introduce myself. It takes me a minute to catch on but then I get it: she wants me to know that she's here to assist the *class*, not necessarily the teacher. Particularly not such a wet-behind-the-ears, all-book-learning-and-no-street-smarts, why-do-they-keep-sending-me-rookies kind of teacher. She manages to communicate this quite clearly without actually saying it - it's there in the tilt of her chin, and in the way she keeps one hand protectively on the boy with the old-timey map. Somehow, despite this, I like her right away. She has deep smile lines, even though she's not smiling a whole lot right now, and she's quite a bit older than me, but it's hard to tell by how much because mainly she looks tired.

She escorts her reading posse back upstairs but when she comes back, her little friend is still with her. He sticks close to her, rocking a bit.

"How did you know that I was the new teacher?" I ask.

"Mr. Spaghetti said to expect you. He was fairly certain Miss Osgoode would hire you."

"Was that based on my suitability for the job or on the dearth of competition?"

"I'm sorry?" she says.

"It's nothing. I just didn't get the warmest feeling from Miss Osgoode."

A throaty chuckle escapes her. "There's a club you can join. We're thinking of getting t-shirts."

"Oh. It's that bad?"

"Don't worry, she sticks pretty close to her office. Mr. Spaghetti deals with the front lines stuff and he had nothing but nice things to say about you." She turns to the the little boy beside her. "Tobey, can you look at me?" she says in a light, pleasant voice.

The boy drags his gaze up to her face.

"Tobey, this is Ms. Sutton. She's the new teacher."

Tobey is all fine bones and delicate features and big, blue eyes. "She's the new teacher," he repeats, matter of factly.

"Can you say 'Hi, Ms. Sutton?" Holly says.

He rocks on the balls of his feet, looks down. "Hi, Ms. Sutton."

"Hi, Tobey," I say. "It's nice to meet you."

"Hades was the Greek god of the Underworld," he says to my shoes. "He was married to Persephone. When she returns to the Earth every year, she brings the spring and flowers with her."

"Wow, you know a lot about Greek mythology," I say.

"Yes," he says. "Who is your favourite god?"

"No one has ever asked me that before," I say. "I guess I'd probably pick Aphrodite. She's the goddess of -"

"Love and beauty," Tobey says, without ever looking up. "She is attended by the three graces."

There is something sweetly bird-like about Tobey, like he might be more at home perched in the high branches of an oak tree rather than here in this underground classroom.

"What about you?" I ask. "Who is your favourite god?"

"I like Poseidon. He's the god of the sea and also earthquakes," he says, and then, with great intensity, he adds, "The Greek alphabet only has 24 letters."

Miss Holly smiles at my slightly stunned expression. "We've been reading about ancient Greece today," she says. "Tobey is a big fan of *Professor Milo G. Hound's Race Through History* - you know the animated show?"

I nod knowingly, but in fact, I have never heard of this show and I realize I've got a lot to learn before I'm going to be able to speak Tobey.

"It's almost home time, kiddo," Miss Holly says to her little charge. "Let's get you back to your class. You can tell Ms. Sutton more about Greek mythology on Monday, okay?"

He's looking at his map now and doesn't answer.

"Tobey, can you say goodbye to Ms. Sutton?" That pleasant tone, again, as if it's the first time she's ever asked him to do anything.

"Goodbye, Ms. Sutton."

"See you later, alligator," I say.

Tobey's eyes flicker up towards my face, then away and he starts towards the door.

"I'll just run him up to his class and then if you have time, we can go over the schedule," Holly says. "I can tell you about our kids."

I nod eagerly. "That would be great." I watch them make their way up the stairs, side by side, and I unaccountably think of Pooh and Piglet walking through Hundred Acre Wood and I want to laugh, but more than anything I am so relieved because she just said "our" kids.

IT'S MUCH LATER when I finally make it to the hospital to see Nana.

She's without her usual entourage, although there is a little microwaveable plate with a lid on her bedside table, so Angie has been by with supper. Her glasses are low on her nose and she's frowning at a crossword puzzle, but she perks up when she spots me.

"How did the interview go?" she says.

"I got the job," I say.

"Oh pet, that's wonderful!" she says. "But you don't sound excited."

"I may be in over my head," I say. I start to describe my meeting with Holly and all the kids she's told me about but there are just so many little people we're supposed to be helping with their writing, reading, math, social skills and general outlook on life that I know I'm forgetting someone. No doubt a teacher with more experience would remember each of them and already have a plan. And possibly charts of some kind.

"Don't you worry. You'll work it out," Nana says, and even though she's my grandmother and is contractually obliged to say things like that, it still makes me feel better.

"I wish Miss Osgoode had that much confidence in me," I say.

"Do you mean Cynthia Osgoode?" Nana says. "Is she the principal?"

"Yes, and she said she went to school with Mom. Do you remember her?"

Nana suddenly seems very interested in smoothing out the creases in her folded up newspaper crossword puzzle. "Oh, yes, I remember her," she says. "I got to know her quite well when I worked at the library, actually. She was a regular in the evenings, doing her homework. Bit timid, but a smart little thing."

"What is her deal with Mom?"

Nana bobs her head from side to side, a funny expression on her face. "Well, I think there was a certain competitiveness between your mother and Cynthia."

"Competitiveness? As in, 'they spurred each other on to greatness?' Or as in, 'they hated each other's guts?'"

"You know how it can be in a small town. They always seemed to go out for the same activities - the musical, the debate society, the yearbook - and I don't think Cynthia had the easiest home life." For a moment, it looks like Nana is going to say something else, then changes her mind. "I'm sure it's all in the past. She's done well for herself. And she'll soon see that what a treasure she's found in you."

I try really hard to imagine any scenario where my mother's high school nemesis calls me a treasure but all I keep thinking is that the thing you usually do with treasure is bury it.

CHAPTER 7

The Deep Blue Depths

Nana comes home from the hospital on Monday morning. The nurses on the floor and even the ladies from housekeeping all come to say goodbye and wish her well and they seem genuinely sorry to see her go, although I suspect they're equally sorry to see the end of the boxes of baked goods that Angie was leaving at the nurse's station every time she dropped by. Nana rides home in the front seat of Penny Clarke's car, looking tiny and grey, and I am overcome with panic right there in the cavernous back seat because now it's all down to me, now I'm the nurse and the cook and the occupational therapist and what if Nana has another stroke? I don't think I even know all the symptoms of a stroke and so I start making frantic lists in my head:

#1 Ask Penny Clarke what the symptoms of a stroke are

#2 Buy a car immediately, (this morning if possible)

#3 Learn CPR

#4 Buy lots of fish to feed to Nana

#5 Ask Penny Clarke if fish is really that good for you

Just then, we pull up to Nana's and I spot Angie and Alf's little

Toyota neatly parked by the curb, so I add #6 Ask Alf for car buying advice to the list.

The dogs go berserk as Penny Clarke and I ferry Nana up the porch steps - they are hitting notes that the Viennese Boys' Choir would envy - and when Angie opens the door and releases them, I think that they're going to bowl us over and knock us all back down the steps - I foresee broken hips and chipped teeth - but the instant Nana leans down and says, "Good doggies, sit!" their furry little asses hit the porch boards like some sort of synchronized canine drill team.

"Oh, my puppies, I missed you," Nana coos as she strokes their heads and ears. Mortimer is trying to scoot a little closer to Nana, and Lucy Boxer fires him a dangerous look, but somehow Nana manages to give all of them enough attention that they feel like they're clearly her favourite and somehow, miraculously, we all get into the house without injury.

"I've just put the tea to steep," Angie says, and she's bustling around arranging cookies on plates. We settle Nana at the kitchen table, and the dogs mill around her like they're afraid she might disappear while she's busy peering out the picture window at her flowers. I still don't like her colour and I wonder if she'll ever regain the roses in her cheeks, but the look on her face right now is beatific. Nana is home with her dogs and her garden, and so all is right with the world.

"Alf!" Angie hollers up the stairs. "Alf! Come and have a cup of tea, dear!"

"What?" Alf's voice is muffled, like he's answering from the depths of a closet.

"TEA, Alf! There's TEA! Come down and have a CUP!"

"I didn't ask you to come up!" Alf hollers back. "Why would I ask you to come up?"

"I'll tell him the tea's ready," Penny Clarke says, and she climbs the stairs carrying Nana's overnight bag, with a secret smile that suggests she's possibly very glad she never married.

"Olivia, you must be excited," Angie says, between foraging in the fridge for milk and laying out napkins. "Your first day! I've told our

Max to look for you and to say hello and to make sure you feel welcome."

Max is Angie's twelve year old grandson. I doubt that rolling out the welcome wagon for me is high on his list of priorities for the day, but I thank Angie and tell her I'll make a point of watching for him.

"I'm sure you'll do a bang-up job," Angie says. "And I wouldn't worry a bit about Cynthia Osgoode if I were you."

I shoot Nana a look, but she's too busy glaring at Angie to notice. "Oh? And why shouldn't I worry, again?"

"Well, all that business with your mother and Cynthia and that boy... but that was ages ago," she says, as she picks up the teapot. "I'm sure she doesn't even remember it. And frankly, I don't think he turned out to be much of a prize, did he?"

"Who isn't a prize, now?" I ask, despite Nana's increasingly pinched expression.

Angie stops mid-pour, sensing that she's stepped in it. Her eyes flick back and forth between Nana and me. "Oh, it's not important," she says, airily. "Water under the bridge. I'm sure your grandmother's told you all about it."

"Apparently she left out the good parts. What boy?"

Angie won't look up from her tea pouring duties now. "Richard Puckett," she says, quietly.

The name sounds oddly familiar, and for a second, I can't place it. And then it hits me.

"Do you mean Dickie Puckett? The guy who drives the snow plow?" I can remember dozens of limericks about Dickie Puckett from my childhood, some of the best written by Eddie Spaghetti, who was so delighted that someone else had such a weirdly rhymable name, too. "Are you telling me that Mom and Miss Osgoode had a fight over Dickie Puckett?"

"I think he goes by Richard now," Nana says, as she pets Ophelia's big, black head, "and he's in charge of the Public Works department."

"He was such a good looking boy in high school," Angie says. "And of course he was in that band and he had that gorgeous hair."

It's been a long time since Dickie Puckett had any hair, so I find it hard to picture my mother and Miss Osgoode swooning over this guitar-wielding Lothario. Before I can ask for more details, Alf and Penny Clarke come tromping into the kitchen, deep in a discussion of the merits of chrome versus plastic grab bars for the bathtub. Not surprisingly, Alf is completely on the side of chrome.

"Hello, Olivia!" he says. "And Violet, welcome home. You're looking fighting fit." He accepts a cup of tea and a shortbread cookie from his wife and Mortimer immediately falls in beside him, eyes on the cookie. "I've finished putting up the grab bars in the tub and I've assembled your shower chair but I don't like the looks of the little plastic caps they've got to cover the feet. Worried it might scratch your enamel, so once I've had my tea, I'm off to the hardware store to find something in rubber."

Nana thanks Alf for his thoughtfulness and Angie's handing out tea cups and cookies and now all the dogs are angling for treats and the talk turns to the upcoming library fundraiser that apparently involves a German string quartet of some renown. I let it all wash over me, so very grateful that I am not in this alone, and so very distracted by the thought of my mother mooning over a boy. In a band.

ALL THE CHURCH bells are ringing their twelve o'clock refrains and I am hoofing it to school, wanting to be there early on my first day. Angie and Alf are going to spend the afternoon with Nana - Alf is tackling the job of assembling Nana's "rollator," the combination rolling walker/basket/convenient seat contraption that the sixteen year old occupational therapist suggested she use until her balance and stamina improve. I could tell that Nana wanted to tell her that such things were for old people, but instead she only asked if they came in British racing green. (Which apparently they do not, although Alf was able to secure one that's chilli pepper red and I told Nana I would paint flames on it if she liked.)

I make a quick stop at the corner store to buy a pack of cinnamon gum - I spotted a half-empty pack on the desk that Miss Holly has in that deplorable little hole of a classroom we now share and I'm hoping nothing says "I appreciate your support," quite like a first day treat of her favourite gum. After the two hours we spent going over the various needs of all our kids last Friday, I realize that her expertise and goodwill may be the only things standing between me and the words "Do you want fries with that?" so I am determined to win her over. I'm just leaving "Mel's," the little convenience store a few blocks from the school, which does a brisk business in candy and Mountain Dew every day starting around half past three, when the sound of a half-stifled guffaw reaches me, followed by the faint smell of cigarette smoke, wafting on the September breeze.

I stop and peer around the corner. There, in a tight little huddle, are four boys, about twelve or thirteen years old judging by their size. Like antelope on the savannah sensing the presence of a nearby lion, their heads all swivel to face me. Unfortunately, one of them looks achingly familiar.

"Hi, Max," I say.

"Shit!" says one of the others and he takes off down the alley like an Olympic sprinter. The other two boys trip over their own feet, then rocket off after the first one with equally impressive speed and I wonder to myself if Eddie Spaghetti has these guys on his cross country running team, because they are fast.

A war is playing itself out on Max's face, as if he's trying to decide if he should run or maybe just wet himself. Also, he's wheezing pretty badly.

"I don't know if you remember me, Max, I'm -"

"You're Mrs. Sutton's granddaughter," he says and this sparks a new look of defiance. "I have a note from my mom!"

"You have a note from your mom that says you're allowed to smoke?"

"No, that says I'm allowed to be off school grounds." He yanks a crumpled piece of paper from his pocket and thrusts it at me. There's a rattle in his breathing now.

I examine the note. "Huh," I say, "I would have thought that your mom would know how to spell 'permission.'" I nod to the cigarette pack that he's holding. "Dude, smoking is gross and I'm just guessing here but I also think it might be kind of hard on your asthma. Have you got your inhaler with you?"

He nods morosely in between gaspy breaths.

"You might want to take it now."

He pulls a little blue puffer out of the pocket of his cargo pants and takes two big gulps of medicine. "Are you going to tell my grandmother?" he asks, when he gets his first full breath.

"Nope," I say. "You're going to tell her, and if you're smart, you'll do it before your mom does. Now come on, it's my first day of school and I really don't want to be late."

I WANT to bring Max to Mr. Spaghetti, but he's nowhere to be found and so I drag his wheezing little ass with me to the office. Mrs. Demanski is still on her lunch break and Miss Osgoode's door is open, so I deposit Max in what is no doubt the bad kids' chair and step into her office.

"Miss Osgoode, I wonder if you have a minute?" I say.

She looks up from her computer screen and regards me with a lack of expression. "Yes, Ms. Sutton?"

I ease the door shut, but remain standing. "On my way to school just now, I found Max McInnis and three other boys behind Mel's and they were smoking," I say. "When I stopped to talk to them, the three other boys ran off, but I have Max here with me."

"You let them run away?"

At first I'm surprised by her question because I don't feel like I buried the lead in my news story - 'Kids! Smoking!' - but maybe she's trying to get all the details, so I go with it. "It happened very quickly. I know Max, and I assumed the other boys were his classmates but I didn't know their names. Before I could really say anything, they just...well, took off."

"A teacher from this school was addressing them and they turned their backs and ran away?" She's starting to look really pissed now, but I'm not entirely sure at what or whom exactly, which is a bit disorienting.

"Well, to be fair, they might not have known that I was a teacher here yet," I say.

"Regardless," she says and she's waving her hand in that same way my mother has when she's dismissing your argument. "Ms. Sutton, respect is one of the key values here at Stafford Falls Public School. If we fail to teach the children to treat us with respect, then we are failing the children." She pauses here and gives me a meaningful look.

"Okay," I say, because I have no idea where she's going with this, but I feel like she wants to me to agree.

"As you gain experience, you'll be able to look back on situations like this and see how you could have handled them differently. Now, I don't know what sort of problems you had with classroom management at your previous school -"

I have such an overwhelming compulsion to shout "Dickie Puckett! Dickie Puckett!" at this moment, that I fear I may have developed a case of Sudden Onset Tourette's.

"- but at this school, we have very high standards. Do you understand?"

I feel like she's expecting me to shout, "Yes, ma'am," and maybe throw in a snappy salute, but instead I say, "Would you like me to get Max now?"

She blinks and for a flash of a second, it looks like she may have forgotten about him. "Oh. Yes. Send him in."

I open the door and Max is still sitting there, a whole new shade of pale. I doubt it's going to take bright lights and a good cop/bad cop routine to make him cough up the names of his accomplices, and a tiny part of me is feeling bad that I'm going to abandon him to Miss Osgoode, but then that's just one more reason that smoking is bad for you.

I HAVE my first real students at 1:15 p.m., a remedial reading group made up of seven and eight year olds. Because I spent the weekend reviewing learning disabilities, the age-appropriate curriculum expectations, and theories of intelligence, I am armed with lists of sight words, flash cards, a fun ice-breaker game that involves identifying vowels and a great little story about a dog who can waterski, but the whole affair turns out to be a forty minute exercise in trying to get them to sit in their seats and look at the actual letters on the page. One kid yawns the entire time and even puts his head down on the table as if he might just catch a quick nap. The only thing that keeps me from quitting on the spot is Isabelle, who seems small even for seven years old, and who pats me on the arm and gives me a sympathetic look before she departs.

I'm still pondering what I can do tomorrow to capture their interest when the bell rings to signal the start of afternoon recess and I grab my jacket and race out to the playground because I'm on duty. It's a madhouse - a couple hundred kids racing around, screeching and yelling, drunk with the sheer pleasure of being outside. There are soccer balls flying like incoming mortar shells and so much colour and movement and noise that I stand there blinking for a few seconds, just trying to get my bearings. I spot another grown up - Carrie Bolton, the grade five teacher - and she seems to be supervising the part of the yard where the older kids are congregating, so I drift over towards the younger kids. A wave of little people is mounting some sort of attack on the play structure, swarming all over it like ants on a particularly delicious sandwich and I keep my gaze moving, trying to take it all in at once, watching for problems.

Of which there are plenty. I've just helped settle a dispute in the Grade One soccer game, (yes, the goalie can touch the ball with his hands, but no, he is not allowed to punch people), and I've just set a little girl back on her feet after an epic face plant during some intense double-dutch skipping when my eyes are pulled back to the play structure.

I see it all as if in slow motion, the boy on the platform at the top of the slide backing up, colliding with the little girl in the pink corduroy skirt. She teeters, loses her balance and then she's in mid-air, flailing as she falls. My feet won't move fast enough, it's like running in sand in a nightmare, although now that this whole unfortunate series of events is underway, I'm not sure what I think I'm going to be able to do to stop it. She lands hard and awkwardly and when she sits up, she is keening like a banshee and you don't have to be a doctor to know that the human arm is not supposed to bend that way.

THE ACCIDENT VICTIM'S name turns out to be Madeleine - I am informed of this by her concerned cohort of friends who take pains to point out that it's *Madeleine* and not *Maddie*, she really doesn't like to be called *Maddie* - but Madeleine is crying so hard that she's hiccoughing, and tears and snot are running down her face, so I'm not sure that she's too bothered by details like that right now. I want to scoop her up in my arms and run with her, but instead I force myself to speak calmly to her, gingerly help her to her feet and begin the long, long walk to the office.

Miss Osgoode blanches when she spots Madeleine's arm, but Mrs. Demanski, who is rifling through a filing cabinet that is nearly as tall as she is, simply says, "Oh, dear," and then she's in motion, guiding Madeleine to a seat, touching her arm with butterfly soft fingers, speaking in calming, musical tones to her. Madeleine's sobbing is downgraded to teary deep breaths, and by the time Miss Osgoode has Madeleine's mother on the phone, Mrs. Demanski has immobilized Madeleine's arm in a cardboard splint and is reading her a story to get her mind off her horrible, no-good day.

I'm about to leave - and wishing I'd thought to bring a tiny bottle of vodka in my lunch bag today - when Miss Osgoode says, "Ms. Sutton?" I turn back and see that she is holding a handful of paper. "Incident report," she says. "I'll need it by the end of the day."

I take the forms from her and make my way back to the schoolyard.

I'VE MADE it to last period, and I am sitting in the dungeon that is my classroom, filling out forms, waiting for my grade five math group to show up so that I can fill their heads with the wonders of the nine times table. Tobey is sitting on the floor beside me studying his map of Ancient Greece - as a rule, Tobey does not enjoy chairs, preferring to be able to sprawl and wiggle as he reads. Miss Holly has left him with me in order to sprint up to the bathroom, something which she has needed to do since ten o'clock this morning but hadn't quite been able to fit in until now.

I am trying to come up with a less sarcastic response to the last question on the incident report form, ("What could be done to prevent this accident from occurring again in the future?") So far I've got: "Tear down the fucking play structure and/or spread giant mattresses throughout the playground" - but I'm thinking I probably shouldn't actually write that down, no matter how much truth the thought might contain.

Tobey is reading names from his map in a quiet, sing-song voice and I'm just about to ask him to show me where Athens is, when the fire alarm goes off. At least I think the deafening sound emanating from somewhere above our heads is the fire alarm - given the ear-splitting, heart-thumping character of it, it may very well be one of the signs of the apocalypse but before I can decide either way, Tobey completely loses his shit. He clamps his thin little arms over his head and curls up into a tight ball, rocking back and forth, alternately flapping one hand and then the other and shrieking like someone is trying to take out his appendix with a butter knife, and that's when I remember Miss Holly telling me that Tobey's particular kind of autism comes with an excruciating sensitivity to sounds. Particularly loud ones.

I want more than anything to clamp my hands over my own ears and join Tobey on the floor, but I force myself to rally, and I rush out of the class to check the stairwell for my math group. There is no sign of them so I hurry back inside, close the door, then drop to my knees beside the writhing, screeching little creature that a few seconds ago was Tobias Green.

"Tobey," I say loudly, trying to be heard over the alarm and his cries, "Tobey, that's the fire alarm. We need to go outside, quickly. Will you come with me, please?"

This has no discernible effect on him.

"Tobey, you know what? It will be quieter outside. Let's go outside and get away from this noise."

I'm not even sure he can hear me at this point and I really want to get out of this building, given the possibility that something actually is on fire, but more than anything, I want to get him away from the thing that is causing him so much distress.

"Okay, Tobey, hang on!" I say. I wrap my arms around him, pick him up, and march up the rickety steps and out the orange fire door with strength I didn't know I had. He's actually not that heavy, elfin little boy that he is, but at the moment I have so much adrenaline coursing through me from the combined effects of the blaring alarm and Tobey's cries that I feel like I could bench press Penny Clarke's Chrysler.

We make our way down the walk towards the playground where all the other classes are gathering, congregating by grade, and the fire alarm is fading with every step I take and across the yard I see Miss Holly running in our direction. I stop and put Tobey down on his feet and for a moment, I think he might be calming down, but suddenly he ratchets the intensity back up and I can just make out that he's howling "Map!" over and over.

Miss Holly reaches us then and she pulls him to her, hugging him tightly to try to override the self-destruct signal that his nervous system is sending out. I feel beyond useless now and so decide to do the only thing I can think of that might help. I haul ass back through the tide of evacuating students to the fire exit, descend the steps to my subterranean classroom and find Tobey's precious scrap of paper, then reverse course, and speed walk to the yard where Miss Holly and Tobey are huddled together. I present Tobey with the map and he snatches it from me, then reburies his face in Miss Holly's shoulder, and finally his crying seems to subside a bit.

Just then, Miss Osgoode walks right by us with a stopwatch and bullhorn and it is all I can do not to trip her.

IT'S NEARLY five o'clock when I get home, after Incident Reports are completed and lessons are planned for tomorrow, and Angie and Nana are both quivering with excitement to hear about my big first day, but I can't even begin to describe how bad this day has been and I don't want to break it to Angie that her darling Max is trying to get an early start as a career chain-smoker, so I promise to tell them everything at supper - Angie has a pot roast in the oven for us - and I offer to take the dogs for a quick walk. I throw on sneakers and jeans and am out the door with three leashes gripped tightly in one hand before anyone can ask a question that I'm not ready to answer. To their credit, even the dogs seem to know not to mess with me and we charge along at a remarkable clip, to the end of Nana's street and then towards the lake. Stafford Falls doesn't have a dog park so much as it has a park along the waterfront where people sometimes take their dogs, but when we arrive, we have the place to ourselves. Out on the lake, a lone kayaker in a bright yellow boat is paddling serenely along, and the calm water and fading afternoon light make it all look like a postcard from some magical place where there are no broken bones or howling fire drills. There's a fence between us and the nearest road, so I unleash the dogs to let them transact their doggie business and I sit down on the bench of a picnic table to try to catch my breath.

And then my phone rings and it's Alex. Because apparently that's the kind of day it is.

"Olivia?" She sounds breathless, relieved when I answer. "I'm so glad I caught you. I really think we should talk…"

"*Now* you want to talk?" I say. "When I've moved out of our house and you're in another time zone with a new job, *now* you want to talk?"

"I know you're angry. And you're probably totally justified, but if you'll just hear me out, I think you'll feel -"

"No, Alex, you don't get to tell me how to feel." In the distance, a dog is barking, a repetitive, staccato drone and the sound is tap-dancing on my final nerve. "You don't get to make demands, or tell me what I think or make decisions for me anymore. You gave all that up when you decided to leave the fucking country."

"You're right. I should've talked with you before I made the move."

"No, you should have talked with me about whether or not you should *consider* making the move," I say, raising my voice to be heard over all the goddam barking. "And the fact that you can't see that is the reason that there's no point talking about this."

"Liv, are you okay? I know you're mad at me and everything, but you sound - are you okay?"

The tenderness in her tone nearly undoes me, I am a short step from bursting into the dreaded angry tears — and why in God's name is no one shutting that dog up? I spin around and scan the park for my three little charges.

Lucy is at the water's edge, barking a complicated tattoo of tattle-tale and alarm, Ophelia is frantically running back and forth on the beach and Mortimer - wait, where the hell is Mortimer?

And then I see him, or rather the top of his little white head and the wake it is leaving as he paddles directly out into the lake. He's maybe a hundred feet offshore and is headed out to the deep blue depths like a tiny, furry torpedo.

"Oh, shit," I say.

"What is it?" Alex says and I'm surprised to hear her voice because I'd forgotten I was holding my phone.

"Can Jack Russells swim?" I ask her.

"Jack who?"

"I gotta go," I say and I hang up and jog to the edge of the water.

Shit, shit, shit, he's really making good time now, his tiny head seems very far away.

"Mortimer!" I shout. "Mortimer, you come back here right now!" Either he chooses to ignore me, which is likely, or he can't hear me over Lucy's continuing protests, which is also entirely possible, because she's barking with her whole body now, broadcasting her disapproval out over the water. In any event, he just keeps on swimming, away from shore. And although he looks like one of those cute little sea otters you see on the nature shows, I know that he takes three kinds of medication for his heart and has a brain roughly the size of a lima bean, so he's perhaps not the best judge of his own limits.

"Goddammit, Mortimer!" I say as I kick off my sneakers and, yes, wade into the lake, because maybe I can't magically mend a little girl's broken arm, and maybe I can't protect poor Tobey from all the evil noises in the world - but there is no way my grandmother's ninety eight year old Jack Russell Terrier is drowning on my watch.

The water is bracingly cold and I only go a few steps before Ophelia bounds in after me - great, now she's decided to live up to her name and be a retriever. I've only gone a dozen feet and my jeans are feeling absurdly heavy and I'm still calling, fruitlessly, for Mortimer to come back when I feel Ophelia wrap her teeth gently around my wrist and pull me back towards the beach.

"Ophelia! Let go! Let go!" I say, but she won't let go and she's looking up at me with pleading eyes. The water is up to my thighs, and I'm wondering how much further I can walk before I have to dive and I'm noticing that the water is actually much colder than I first thought and that's when I realize that even Ophelia knows that this is a terrible idea.

I retrace my steps back to shore and then turn and peer out at the lake. I'm about to grab my phone - can you call 911 for a drowning terrier? - when I spot the bright yellow kayak slicing through the water, the figure in the cockpit paddling double time on an intercept course, headed straight for Mortimer's tiny bobbing head. A fancy bit of work with the paddle and the boat slows, then the occupant leans way out and plucks the Jack Russell with the dodgy heart out of the water. There's a bit of a scramble as Mortimer shakes and wiggles and the boat tips dangerously for a few seconds, but then the craft is righted and the paddler turns toward shore.

I want to jump up and down and applaud. I want to rush back out into the water and hug this person who is ferrying Mortimer back to me. And then the boat draws closer and I can see that Mortimer is standing with his front paws on the deck of the kayak, panting and looking oh so pleased with himself, and now I just want to go and wring his little neck.

"I'm guessing he belongs to you," the woman in the kayak says, when they reach the shallows. Mortimer takes the opportunity to hop out and splash his way back to the beach.

"Yeah, he's mine. Well, he's my grandmother's," I say. "Thank you so much. I think you may have saved my life because I was going to have to swim after him and I don't think that was going to end well."

The woman laughs and pops out of the cockpit. "The water's pretty cold, it's not a great day for a swim," she says as she hauls her boat up onto the sand a few feet away from the spot where Lucy, Mortimer and Ophelia are having a grand reunion. She's wearing a sleek black wetsuit and a yellow life vest and looks like she's just stepped out of an L.L. Bean catalogue or an ad for some miracle drug that makes you look wholesome and healthy. "I'm glad I could help. What's his name?"

"Mortimer. Although if you hadn't come along, it would have been Fish Bait."

She laughs again and crouches down. "Hey, Mortimer, come here, buddy," she calls out and instantly, he's there at her side, presenting his wet head for pets. "You're quite the long distance swimmer, aren't you?" she says, scratching him behind his sodden ears. Well, ear. Lucy and Ophelia instantly barge in, with swaying bums and friendly faces and she tries to pet them all. "I'm Julia, by the way," she says, over all their heads. "Julia Purcell."

"Olivia Sutton," I say. "Nice to meet you."

Lucy Boxer, who on principle distrusts pretty much everyone, has flopped over onto her back and is allowing Julia to rub her tummy. "What was Mortimer doing? Did he run away?" Julia asks.

"No, I was just distracted because I was on the phone with my ex and we were arguing, because she's moved to London and there was this little girl today who broke her arm and then the fire drill happened and — you know, I'm going to spare you the details. Suffice it to say that it was a pretty lousy day and I wasn't paying enough attention to the dogs."

"You don't have to spare me the details," she says and she has a glorious smile and the warmest eyes. "I'm not in any rush."

Something about this unexpected kindness touches me deeply. And then, to my tremendous embarrassment, I start to fill up and I have to take a deep breath to keep from crying.

"Okay," I say and I sniff and steady myself. "Uh, well, I'm feeling a little overwhelmed," I say to this complete stranger with the lovely smile. "I started a new job today and it didn't go well at all. There were fire alarms and broken bones and an awful lot of crying, but what I think is bothering me the most is that my grandmother had a stroke a little while ago and she just came home from the hospital today and I love her more than anything in the world and I'm supposed to be taking care of her but I have absolutely no idea what I'm doing. And as you can see, I can't even walk the dogs without courting catastrophe."

"Wow," Julia says. "That is a *lot*. Even without an ex-girlfriend thrown into the mix."

"It is," I say, "but now you've come along and kept the day from turning into an outright disaster. So, thank you."

She looks at my wet pants and smothers a smile. "Were you really going to swim after him?"

"My Nana *really* loves these dogs."

"Why don't I give you a ride home?" she says. Ophelia has nudged Lucy out of the way now and Julia is stroking her shining black head. "I loaned someone my van but he should be here in just a few minutes to pick me up."

I look at my three sand-covered companions and my own sagging, soaked jeans and decide that nobody needs us in their vehicle. "Thanks for the offer but I think we'd wreck your upholstery. And it's not that far."

"Are you sure? It's no trouble at all."

"Thanks, anyway. We'll be fine. If I can just find my shoes."

Julia spots them a little ways down the beach and she retrieves them for me while I snap leashes onto the three amigos.

"And thanks again, for saving Mortimer," I say, as I jam my wet, sandy feet back into my sneakers. "He means a lot to my Nana."

"It was my pleasure." That smile again, it illuminates her eyes. She plays with a strap on her yellow life vest for a moment, then says, "Look, I've just moved to town and I don't know many people here yet. Would you like to get together for a coffee sometime?"

"I would love to," I say, "but if you're new here, then I think it's my duty to warn you - it's not possible to get a decent cup of coffee in this town."

"Hopefully, that's going to change soon," she says. "I bought the old bakery on Main Street and I'm turning it into a coffee place."

"Oh my God, I saw your sign the other night! The Second Chance Café? That's you?"

"That's me. Right now there are more carpenters than baristas, but my espresso machine is supposed to be delivered next week."

My heart might actually have skipped a beat. "Your espresso machine?"

She nods. "A very fancy one. From Italy."

"You're going to make espressos? Right here in this town? Wow. Welcome to Stafford Falls."

"Well, thank you. It sounds like I'll be filling a need."

"More like saving some lives."

A chirpy set of honks interrupt us and we both turn to look towards the road. Tenzin, in full saffron regalia, is pulling up in a white van.

"There's my ride," Julia says. "Say, do you know Tenzin?"

"Doesn't everybody?" I say.

"Are you sure you don't want a ride? There's lots of room."

"No, we're good. Thanks for everything though."

She gives Mortimer a quick pet. "You stay on dry land, mister." She starts towards her kayak then turns back. "I'm glad I bumped into you, Olivia. And I really hope you'll come by for coffee soon."

Oh my God, that smile. Suddenly, I am much, much less angry with Mortimer.

WE MAKE OUR WAY HOME, sloshing and squishing with every footstep. Halfway to Nana's, a white van drives by and honks. Julia is at the wheel, but Tenzin is hanging out the window waving at me.

"Second day is always will be better!" he shouts.

God, I hope he's right.

CHAPTER 8

The Seventh Circle Needs a Coat of Paint

Reality rears its ugly head even before the sun rises on Tuesday, and when I hear the crash from the kitchen, I have my first inkling that today might not be the "is always better" day that Tenzin promised me. I bolt out of bed wearing nothing but a t-shirt, only to trip in the darkness over the obviously deaf Boxer who's curled up on the little rug beside my bed. The dresser conveniently breaks my fall and then I'm jamming my legs into my jeans as I stagger toward the hall, only realizing then that these are the jeans I went swimming in yesterday and that maybe if I'd hung them up they would have dried more thoroughly. Lucy is awake now and racing me for the stairs, and I trip over her again at the top of the steps, and so now I'm convinced that these dogs are secretly trying to kill me.

There's another crash and it's clearly from downstairs which means that someone must have broken into the house and is throwing the crockery around because surely that can't be Nana in the kitchen. Didn't we talk at length yesterday with Penny Clarke about how she is not to go up or down the stairs without assistance until her balance returns? Didn't the occupational therapist specifically warn us about the stairs and the potential falls and the catastrophic hip fractures that would result from a single unaccompanied trip down to the kitchen for a cup of tea?

"Nana?" I call, as I thunder down the stairs. I slip on the last two steps and nearly have a catastrophic fall myself, but I grab the banister to right myself, then charge down the hall to the kitchen, Lucy at my heels.

There, in the puddle of illumination cast by the light over the range, is Nana, looking both sheepish and annoyed. Her red rollator is on its side in the middle of the floor, its topmost wheel still spinning. At her feet are the pieces of what used to be a ceramic Quaker Oats cookie jar, the man in the black hat still smiling benignly despite his current predicament. Some of the shortbread cookies that Angie left for us are buried in the rubble and so naturally Mortimer is there, trying to snag himself an early breakfast treat.

"Oh, pet, I'm sorry I woke you," Nana says.

"Are you all right? What happened?" I say, pushing Mort out of the way with my foot because he's stomping all around the shards of broken cookie jar and I'm having visions of a trip to the vet to get his little paws stitched up.

"I'm so sorry, look at this mess! Only I wanted a cup of tea and I didn't want to bother you and now look what I've done."

"It's all right," I say. I bend down and start picking up the pieces, shoving Mortimer away again. "It's just a cookie jar. So long as you're not hurt."

"But you gave me that for Christmas! Remember all the box tops you saved to get it? You ate porridge every morning for six months to collect enough and I know how much you hate porridge."

"We can probably get another one on eBay," I say. "Mortimer, I swear to God, if you don't move…"

The kettle starts to whistle. I dump the biggest shards on the counter and turn off the element and the whistle fades and dies. The clock on the range informs me that it's 5:12 a.m., which explains why it's still so bloody dark out.

Nana is huffing and wringing her hands and muttering something that might have been "useless old woman," and seems way too upset about the damn cookie jar, but on reflection, I realize that I should have seen this coming. Dropping her cutlery all through supper last night as she tried to cut her food, sending peas rolling across the tablecloth and then the crowning indignity when she realized she couldn't help with the washing up after the meal - she was too tired and weak to stand at the counter - and so I washed all the dishes and dried most of them, while she sat at the table with a dishtowel waiting for me to bring her the odd cup and pot lid to wipe dry. By the time I helped her undress for bed, she was uncharacteristically quiet. I'd hoped a good sleep would help everyone but none of us are sleeping now and the precious cookie jar is in pieces on the kitchen floor and I honestly don't know what to do next.

"Why don't I make us a cup of tea?" I say. "You go sit in your chair and I'll bring it in."

This seems to ground her a little and there's even a flicker of a smile. I put the rollator back up on its wheels, push Mortimer away from the mess on the floor one more time and wait while she wheels her way out of the kitchen, the dogs following dutifully in her wake.

I bring the kettle back to the boil, then set the tea to steep and quickly sweep up the remains of the cookie jar. I cram the cups, spoons, milk, sugar bowl and teapot onto a tray and head for Nana's Flowery Room, wishing I'd taken time to change into dry pants and making a mental note to buy some damn pyjamas.

The Flowery Room, as I called it when I was a kid, is a sort of study off the kitchen, at the back of the house. It has a pair of French doors that open out into the garden and offer a spectacular view of Nana's hydrangeas. The sofa and wing back chair are splashed with pink and blue cabbage roses and the pillows are so cushy and over-stuffed that you sink when you sit on them. But what really makes the room are the bookcases; every wall and nook and corner is lined with white bookcases, floor to ceiling, crammed with Nana's favourite volumes. Her taste runs from Proust and Plato to Didion and Dahl and the whole room has an earthy paper smell, with the faintest undertone of Yardley's English Lavender. It has always felt like the safest place in the world to me, as if nothing bad could ever penetrate these book lined walls.

Nana is sitting in the wing back chair, looking tiny and frail, her housecoat wrapped tightly around her. The dogs are passed out around the room, but Mortimer lifts his head in case I've brought snacks.

"I've been thinking about your job," she says. "I'm sorry you had such a terrible time of it yesterday, pet."

I put the milk and sugar on the table beside her. "I'm sure everything will be fine, eventually."

"But that's just it. You shouldn't have to settle for fine. You should be off pursuing your dreams, painting and traveling. Not stuck here taking care of a broken down old woman."

"Hey, that's my Nana you're talking about, lady," I say as I pour her tea and place the cup and saucer beside her.

"You know what I mean. I don't want to hold you back."

"First of all, you're not broken down, you're convalescing. You just need to keep doing your rehab exercises and I'm sure you'll get your balance and everything back. Secondly, no one is holding me back from anything. I don't even know what I want to be doing anyway."

"I just don't want you to feel beholden to me."

"Beholden?" I plop down onto the sofa and reach for my tea. "Nana, I'm not here because I feel beholden to you, but if you want to get the ledgers out, then let's talk about all the things you've done for me in my life. Clothed me, fed me, took care of me. Didn't mock me the summer I dyed my hair blue."

This makes her chuckle. "Oh, and you were a sight, pet."

"You were a mother to me when my own mother left. I will always be grateful to you for that."

"I don't ever want you to think that it was an easy decision for your mother to leave you here with me," she says. She searches my eyes and smiles sadly. "It wasn't something she took lightly, believe you me. She loves you very much."

I sip my tea and try really hard not to roll my eyes. "I know, I know, she loves me. She just has strange ways of showing it."

"Oh, your mother can be a funny one, I'll grant you that," Nana says, and Ophelia comes over and plonks her big, blocky head in Nana's lap so she can stroke it. "I can't say that I always understand her. She's so much more like your grandfather, so analytical and focussed."

I would have gone with calculating and cold, but tomato, to-mah-to.

"It was a very difficult thing for her to do, you know." Nana reaches for her tea cup and it takes tremendous concentration to get it from the table, to her lips and back again. "Truth be told, I encouraged her to leave you with me, and I've always felt guilty for that. Like I stole you away from her."

"Well, I for one am very glad you did steal me away," I say. "I wouldn't have been happy traveling all over with Mom, never living in one place, her always working. And I don't think she would have been happy either."

"She was so close to getting her Phd when you were born and so I knew she couldn't stay here, but I just couldn't bear the thought of you leaving." She's getting misty now and Ophelia is watching her with big, anxious eyes. "You were like my second chance baby."

Nana had a baby when my mother was about five. His name was Robert Joseph Sutton and he lived for not quite two days. Nana was at the hospital with him for that whole time, holding him, singing to him, telling him what a beautiful boy he was. Then there were two miscarriages and finally the doctors told them they should stop trying.

I reach over and squeeze her hand. "Nana, I loved growing up here, living with you. I wouldn't change a thing. And I'm glad I'm here now."

"So am I, pet, and that's what I feel so terrible about. I hate what this stroke has done to me and I don't want you to have to take a job that doesn't make you happy, but underneath it all, I'm just so happy that you're here. Is that terrible?"

"I think you're allowed to feel happy that I'm home. But you know what you're not allowed to do?"

"What's that, pet?"

"Come down the stairs by yourself in the middle of the damn night."

"It's hardly the middle of the night."

"Promise me that from now on, you'll wake me up if you want to come down for a cup of tea."

"You need your sleep."

"Well, I'm certainly not going to get it if you're doing cartwheels down the stairs. Say, 'I promise.'"

"I promise."

"All right, then," I say. "Now, are you getting hungry?"

"I am feeling a bit peckish."

"Do you fancy some scrambled eggs?"

"I thought you'd never ask."

Outside, the sky is lightening from midnight blue to a deep sapphire.

IT'S A BUSY MORNING. Penny Clarke rolls in at eight o'clock to drive us to the hospital so I can meet with Nana's rehab team and learn how to help her with her exercises at home. Everything goes smoothly except just as we're leaving the hospital, Nana and Penny Clarke run into a lady from their church who also helps with the lunches in the church hall and they become embroiled in a conversation about the library fundraising concert that is so serious it seems to have Watergate undertones and so we hang about forever in the lobby, going over every detail of the canapés, the linens and the flowers. Then Penny Clarke has to make a quick stop at the grocers and I realize we need to do a major shop very soon and I really have to do something about getting a car, but most importantly, if we don't get a move on, I'm going to be late for work.

I roar out of Nana's just after noon. Penny Clarke is spending the afternoon with Nana and they're breaking out a jigsaw puzzle when I leave, although I extract a promise that Nana will at least try to take a nap (the rehab team impressed upon me the magical healing powers of sleep) and Penny Clarke has assured me that she will talk again with Nana about midnight strolls down the stairs. I wouldn't mind a nap myself right now or maybe a cup of coffee, which reminds me of Julia, her lovely smile and her soon-to-be-delivered espresso machine.

Maybe I'll take the dogs to the dog park after school today - although Mortimer is never, ever getting off his leash again - and maybe I'll walk us by the Second Chance Café on the way there. Just to see if she's around. Because it seemed to me that there was an extra sparkle in those gorgeous eyes (they're ultramarine, I'd say - the blue that Vermeer loved so much) and although I know I need another relationship right now like I need appendicitis, I could at least use a friend in Stafford Falls, preferably one with access to really good coffee.

It's just a bonus that she's so pleasant to look at.

I DESCEND to my subterranean classroom and see that the door is open but the lights are off, which means Miss Holly must be there with her ever present sidekick, Tobey, who is vexed by the hum that the fluorescent lights give off. The dynamic duo are not alone, though; Max McInnis is also there at a desk in the corner, looking even more tortured than when I left him sitting outside the principal's office. Around the room, at other desks that have been pulled as far away from each other as they can, are the three other boys whom I met oh so briefly behind Mel's yesterday. The wadded up remains of their lunches have been pushed to the corners of their desks and they each have a pencil and a piece of paper before them. They're all trying hard not to make eye contact with me.

Miss Holly looks up from her laptop when I enter the oppressive little room. "Hello, Ms. Sutton," she says brightly. "Tobey, say, 'Hello, Ms. Sutton.'"

Tobey's eyes stayed glued to his map. "Hello, Ms. Sutton," he says in a way that manages to sound both bright and distracted.

"Hi, Tobey," I say. "Uh, Miss Holly, I didn't know we were expecting company."

"Neither did I until the lunch bell rang, but I have to say, we've been having a lovely time together, haven't we guys?"

There is a dispirited mumble from one or two corners.

"Miss Osgoode sent them to have lunch in the CRC class for the next two weeks. We've just been reading through this really interesting article about some of the 4,800 chemicals that are found in cigarettes. Did you know that they put acetone in cigarettes?"

"Acetone? Isn't that nail polish remover?"

Miss Holly nods sagely as she scrolls through the list on her screen. "Yup. And also ammonia - that's in toilet bowl cleaners." She turns and fixes one of the boys with a sharp look. "Did you get that one, Adam? Ammonia. Double m." Adam reluctantly picks up his pencil and scratches something down on his paper. "We're going to have a little quiz later, to make sure we learned all the facts," she says to me.

It is becoming very hard to control my facial muscles. "I'll leave you to it," I say. "I need to go do some photocopying."

I can still hear her as I'm headed up the stairs.

"Oh, here's a good one, guys - arsenic. That's what they use in rat poison. You'd have to be pretty stupid to inhale rat poison, wouldn't you, Tobey?"

"Pretty stupid," Tobey says.

THE AFTERNOON UNFOLDS in much the same way as yesterday, minus the broken limb and the fire drill, two omissions for which I am deeply grateful. I see one group for math and give them a multiplication test, the results of which tell me that anything above the five times table is news to them. My Grade Three reading group rolls in next, although it might be more accurate to say drifts in like a slow-moving and somnambulant tide. The four of them drag themselves into chairs at the central work table. One of them, a boy named Davis, whose short hair has been styled into a little fauxhawk, yawns and looks at the table top and I can tell he is thinking about taking a nap again today.

"All right," I say, brightly. "I thought we'd try making up some sentences to read together. I've written a word on each of these cards and you can pick whatever cards you want to make up your sentence."

Three of them stare blankly back at me, and one of them, Wally, is looking at the ceiling.

"Let me show you," I say. "One of my favourite things to do is to draw so I'm going to make a sentence about that." I spread all my carefully printed flash cards out of the table and pluck out four of them, then line them up.

"See?" I say. "My sentence says, '*I like to draw.*'"

Isabelle smiles at me. "I like to draw, too. I'm a good artist."

"You're a terrible artist," Davis says.

"Davis, we're just going to say nice things to each other today, okay?" I say.

He shrugs. "She is," he says under his breath.

"You're not such a great artist, Davis," Kylie says. "You just draw guns. And stupid hockey sticks." Kylie is partial to pink leggings and today is wearing a long-sleeved t-shirt that informs me that she is a "Princess In Training."

Davis's face darkens and I can tell he wants to smack Kylie but she's got about twenty pounds on him and is absolutely going to hit him back so he takes a minute to reconsider his position.

"Okay," I say, "let's try one that's not so controversial. Does everybody like dogs?" I pull together four more cards. "*The dog is black,*" I read.

"I don't like black dogs, they're scary," Isabelle says.

"That's racist," Wally says. "You can't judge a dog by his colour."

"I bet you couldn't draw a dog," Kylie says to Davis. "Unless he had a hockey stick."

"Okay," I say, quickly holding up an arm to block Davis's fist, "Davis, this is a no-hitting room. Kylie, we're saying nice things or we're not saying anything, got it?"

They both mumble agreement but Kylie is trying to hide a smile.

Isabelle touches my arm. "I *am* a good artist," she says.

"I'll bet you are," I say. "How about you guys pick out the words you want and start on your sentences? If there are any other words you want that you don't see here, I can write them down for you on a blank card."

I spread them out on the table and Wally and Kylie help so enthusiastically that they end up knocking a bunch of cards onto the floor. "I'll get them!" Wally says and he bounces out of his seat like a jack in the box and disappears under the table.

"How about this word?" I say to Davis, holding up a card that says *game*. "Do you think you might want to use this word in your sentence?"

He shakes his head.

"Can you read this word for me?" I ask.

He doesn't look at the card, his eyes never leave my face. "Gate," he says.

"You've got the first two letters," I say. "Look at the other letters again."

"This is stupid," he says.

"Okay, you pick out a card you like and read it to me," I say. "Kylie, you too."

I notice that Isabelle has put three cards together. Her sentence reads, *"I like said."*

"Isabelle, you've got a sentence there, why don't you read me that?" I say.

"I like you, she said," Isabelle says.

"Good start," I say, "but you need to find *'you'* and *'she.'"*

Her smile fades. "I don't know what those look like," she says.

I grab a blank card and print *'you'* for her. "This says *'you,'"* I tell her. "Go find one that looks just like it."

She begins hunting through the cards, her little brow furrowed in concentration.

I realize that Wally is still AWOL and so I lean down and peer under the table. He is busy building a little house of flash cards and has actually gotten to a second level. I'm so impressed, I'm tempted to let him continue, but decide that Miss Osgoode would not be as impressed as I am if she walked in.

"Hey, Wally, can you come back up to the table and write me a sentence?" I say.

"Oh, sure," he says, as if the activity that was going on over his head had just slipped his mind. "Are there any Star Wars words?"

"I'll write you some," I say and I reach for my marker.

Thirty minutes later we have successfully written and read four sentences:

"Yoda is green and funny."

"I do not eat apples."

"I like you, she said."

And *"He got game."* This last one is from Davis who, when I pointed out the incorrect grammar, argued that he'd heard it in a song. Since he'd remembered how to read the word *game*, I let him keep it and called it a win.

When they leave, Isabelle pats my arm again but today it seems less like encouragement and more like consolation.

I sit in the ringing silence of my own personal little Underworld and survey the room after they've left. There isn't even a chalkboard in this classroom, which seems to me to exclude it from the very definition of classroom. That fact, coupled with its cozy proximity to the boiler room, makes me wonder if this isn't actually the room where the custodian used to keep the floor polish and rolls of brown paper towels.

Be that as it may, now it's my classroom. It's *our* classroom, Tobey's and Isabelle's and Wally's.

And we all deserve better.

I set off to find the custodian. I have paint questions.

TWO SURPRISES AWAIT me when I get home. The first is tucked behind Penny Clarke's giant car - it's a little Jeep of some kind that is a yellow so bright it almost makes your eyes water and I can't for the life of me figure out which of Nana's friends would drive such an odd vehicle.

I have barely put down my schoolbag and am still being swarmed by dogs when Penny Clarke hotfoots it through the kitchen to meet me, Nana rolling along in her wake. They're both beaming.

"What do you think of my new car, pet?" Nana says.

"Your new car?"

"Didn't you see it in the driveway on your way in?"

"Do you mean the Jeep?"

"Yes," she says and she's nearly giggling with glee. "It's something called a 'Wrangler,' and it has a few miles on it but Alf knows the mechanic at the dealership and he said it's in very good shape and Penny Clarke got them to throw in the first two oil changes. I think it will be just the perfect little thing for getting around town in."

"That sounds great, Nana," I say. "Just one thing, though - and correct me if I'm wrong - but I don't think you've ever had a driver's license."

"Yes, but with my eyes, that's probably best, don't you think, pet?"

"Nana, I said you shouldn't buy me a car."

"I didn't buy you a car. I bought *us* a car. It just so happens that I'll need a little help driving it."

"When I left for school, you were breaking out a thousand piece puzzle of the Taj Mahal and promising to take a nap. How exactly did that turn into, 'Hey, let's go buy a bright yellow Jeep?'"

"Isn't it a marvellous colour? I thought it would be safer because it would be so visible."

She's so obviously delighted that I can't bring myself to tell her that the colour borders on obnoxious, and just then a sudden image of off-roading in the banana yellow Jeep, Nana in the shotgun seat gripping the chicken bar, flashes through my mind and I can't help but smile.

"It's great. Thank you for getting it," I say.

"Do you really like it, pet?"

"I do," I say. "Listen, I need to go to the hardware store. Why don't we take it for a test drive?"

"Let me just get a CD," Nana says, wheeling her rollator around to head back into the kitchen. "The young man at the dealership said it had a CD player and I'd like to hear what it sounds like."

THE KITCHEN SINK SUTRA 105

Penny Clarke picks up a Fed Ex envelope that's sitting on the table by the front door. "This came this afternoon for you," she says, her expression a weird mix of sympathy and something else. "It's from London."

This halts the conversation abruptly and for a little while, we both stand there and stare at the cardboard envelope, as if it might have something to contribute. Eventually, Penny Clarke pats my arm in a way that reminds me of Isabelle, then sets off to help Nana with her musical selections.

NANA BRINGS two CDs on our little drive, one from each end of her musical library it seems, and I am treated to multiple renditions of *Dancing Queen* and *Ride of the Valkyries* on the way to and from the hardware store. Nana pronounces the sound system as more than adequate - she particularly approves of the robust bass - and despite the fact that I think we must look like a rolling overripe piece of tropical fruit, the Jeep handles nicely and I even catch myself singing along which makes Nana smile.

I make us leftover pot roast sandwiches for supper and the lack of cutlery makes everything a little easier for Nana, although she knocks over the salt shaker and later spills a bit of milk when she's doctoring her after dinner tea. She wheels herself into the Flowery Room, all three dogs following close behind, and I bring in her tea, then go back to the kitchen to clean up. For once, I don't lament the lack of a dishwasher because it gives me a few minutes to think without young and old alike interrupting me. I can hear the laugh track of some T.V. show punctuated from time to time by Nana's own quiet chuckles or a word or two to Mort and Lucy who are having a territorial spat over a dog bed and after, when I know the kitchen will meet her exacting standards, I peer into the Flowery Room and see that she's asleep in her chair, surrounded by dogs.

And then I can't delay the inevitable any longer. I drift back to the kitchen, sit down heavily at the table and tear open the Fed Ex envelope. Inside is a single piece of ivory paper, so thick and heavy it feels like fabric. I can see her writing this with her favourite Mont Blanc and it occurs to me that anyone else would have just sent an email, but Alex international couriers a fifty dollar piece of paper, written with a three hundred dollar pen.

Liv-

I don't know where to start - this is my third draft of this letter - I had a whole speech prepared for when I spoke to you on the phone last night, but now it all seems kind of artificial, so I will distill it down to the basics.

I miss you. I need you. I don't want to give up on us. I want you to come to London - eventually to stay, but for now at least to visit, so we can sit face to face and talk about how to make us work again. Say the word and I will courier you a plane ticket.

You are my best thing, Liv. Believe that.

All my love,

Alex

MY FIRST THOUGHT is to call Pam and read this to her so I can rant and feel all self-righteous but then I realize that mainly I just feel sad. What kind of fairy tale was I living in? And how is it that she thinks that I could up and leave Nana and my job? I keep thinking about how "our" condo looked when I'd packed up all my things - as if I'd never even been there. If Alex had been the one to move out, all that would've been left was an easel and and a couple of travel mugs. Yet, how is my present situation different? I am currently living in my childhood bedroom with most of what I own in boxes stacked against the wall, driving a lemon-coloured Jeep that is owned by my seventy eight year old grandmother.

Now I definitely need to call Pam.

There is such a crescendo of screams on Pam's end when she answers that it sounds like someone is slaughtering her children - possibly Pam herself by the sound of her voice.

"Oh my God, is everything okay?" I ask.

"Just giving the spawn of Satan their baths," she says. I hear her bellow for Jason to come and there are muffled instructions and quick thumping footsteps. A door slams and then there's blessed silence.

"You still there?" Pam asks.

"I am. Where are you that's so quiet?"

"The garage. I've been spending a lot of time out here lately. It's quite nice actually. I'm thinking of hanging some art. So, what's up?"

"I got a call from Alex yesterday and a little note today, basically telling me she can't live without me and asking me to come to London."

"Wow. She's got nerve, I'll say that for her."

"She says she doesn't want to give up on us."

"She picked a strange way of showing that. You know, leaving the country and selling your home. You're not thinking of going, are you?"

"No, it's not that. It's just...Nana really needs me and I think I'm going to be here a little longer than I originally thought. And I picked up a half time teaching position so I'm committed to that now..."

"That's great, though, isn't it? Regular work? You've got to pay the bills."

"I suppose."

"Olivia, what's the matter?"

"I think I just feel sad. Like I lost something wonderful, only I know it wasn't. And that maybe I'm moving backwards by coming here. That, and my boss hates me. Well, she hates my mother."

"That's nice. You have something in common."

"No, she *really* hates my mother. Like, 'stomp-on-the-accelerator-if-she-saw-her-crossing-the-street' hates her.'"

"What did your mother do to her?"

"A bunch of stuff, but I think it was mostly about a snow plow driver who was in a band."

"Oh, well, that makes sense then. What are you gonna tell Alex?"

"That at the moment, I have a life here."

"Well, there you go," Pam says. Suddenly, there's a high-pitched, but muffled beeping in the background. "Gotta run. I think something's on fire."

We hang up. I peek in on Nana again, but she's snoring softly, so I tiptoe out of the Flowery Room. I go find my laptop and set it up at the kitchen table.

It takes a surprisingly long time to write such a short email.

Alex,

Thank you for the lovely words. It was an incredible couple of years and I hope you know I love you, too, but I'm not sure how much of our life together was real. And since you decided to move to another continent without so much as discussing it with me, I can't help but think that maybe we weren't on the same page about a lot of things. It's very sad but if I'm honest, I think we've run our course.

Good luck in London - you're talented and amazing. I wish you every happiness and success.

Olivia.

WHEN I'M DONE WRITING, it's very dark out and I can see my reflection in the picture window. Ophelia wanders into the kitchen to check on me and ends up lying down beside my chair, her chin a comforting weight on my foot.

CHAPTER 9

Plums in the Icebox

I t's later that week when I hear the first snarky CRC comment.
Because I feel partly responsible for Miss Holly having been
saddled with extra lunch duty, specifically the management of Max
and his smoking colleagues, I offer to come in early every other day
and supervise them so that she can actually take her full lunch half-
hour, sans Tobey. She is surprised but delighted by my offer and I
don't need to make it twice. But by Friday, I don't think I can take one
more hour of the anti-smoking program, (although we did look at
some pretty startling photos of mouth tumours on Wednesday,
photos that made Max's friend Daniel blanch so I think we may be
wearing them down.) I opt instead for a combined educational and
useful skills approach.

I get Tobey settled with his dog-eared copy of *Professor Milo G.
Hound's Big Book of Greek Mythology,* and then say, "All right, men, I
have an assignment for you today."

"You can't give us an assignment," Adam says. "You're not our
teacher."

Adam is that kid that they never tell you about when you're

studying to get your Bachelor of Education, when in fact, there should be whole seminars taught on the topic of managing the Adams of the world. But I've been a substitute teacher in high school classes where the inmates towered over me and were veritable virtuosos of shitty attitudes, so Adam's going to have to try harder than that to get my goat.

"Actually, I *am* your teacher right now, Adam, and more to the point, I'm the person who gets to decide when you leave, so you might want to keep that in mind," I say. "And I should add that whoever successfully completes the assignment gets to leave early today. All you have to do is calculate the surface area of the walls of this classroom."

"What for?" Daniel asks.

"I'm going to paint and I need to know how much paint to buy."

"For real?" Max says.

"For real."

I put tape measures, paper and a couple of calculators on the work table in the centre of the room. "I need to see your calculations and I need you to be as precise as possible," I say and I go settle in with Tobey to read about Apollo and Artemis.

Max and Daniel pounce on the supplies, but Adam and Zack remain rooted in their seats and are so busy assuming postures of studied casualness I think they might sprain something.

Max and Daniel hustle around the class for quite some time, trying to appear confident and in charge of the situation. They lay the measuring tape out in various places, whispering numbers to each other, all the while shooting worried looks back over their shoulders at the two inmates who are on strike.

I let them huddle and discuss their strategy for a few minutes, then I say, "You guys know the formula to calculate surface area, right?"

They assure me in quasi-insulted tones that they do in fact know all about height times width, but less than a minute later Max wanders over to where Tobey and I are sitting.

"What colour are you going to paint things?" Max asks.

I show him a picture of the island of Santorini in Tobey's book, with its lush mediterranean blues and its clean, stark whites. "Kind of like this," I say. "And then maybe we can add some columns, like the Acropolis."

While Max studies the picture, Tobey pipes up. "The Minotaur was a monster who lived in a labyrinth," he says to Max, with a certain detached intensity. "He was half-man and half-bull."

Max gives Tobey a puzzled look for this massive non-sequitur and I am about to explain how sometimes Tobey likes to repeat phrases he remembers from things he's read or seen on tv and how it's helping him to learn to talk to people, but before I can, I hear a snort from the other side of the room, and then Adam says, just loud enough that I can hear, "More like half-boy, half-retard."

And that is when I catch sight of Miss Holly, standing in the door-way, with murder in her eyes.

"Miss Holly," I say, "Adam and I need to talk. Would you take Tobey and those guys back to their classrooms?"

She hesitates for a heartbeat but then says, "Come on, Tobey. Don't forget your book."

Tobey toddles off after her, immune to the supercharged feeling in the room, but Max, Daniel and Zack hurl themselves out the door.

When their footsteps have receded up the staircase, I go over and pull a chair closer to Adam's desk. He is less deflated by the departure of his audience than I'd hoped.

"Retard? Did I hear that right, Adam?"

He shrugs and doesn't look at me, but it's not out of shame or embarrassment, it's more like he's trying to bait me into telling him to look at me.

"I'm going to assume you don't know much about autism and assume that by calling Tobey a retard, you were trying to imply that he's stupid, which, I assure you is not the case. He's a very smart little boy actually. It's just that parts of his brain have trouble communicating with each other so sometimes noises really bug him or sometimes he's not sure how to say what he wants to say so he repeats something he's heard on tv."

Adam feigns utter disinterest. He is really good at it, and it's my guess that he practices a lot.

"Adam, we don't know each other very well yet, but -"

"Oh, but do you think we could be friends some day?" he says, firing on all smartass cylinders now.

"I doubt it," I say. "Unless you have a hidden fondness for Abstract Expressionists." Fortunately, my voice does not sound nearly as pissed off as I am. "Look, bottom line: you don't have to like me, but you do have to treat everybody in my classroom with a basic amount of respect. I will not allow you to make Tobey or any other student in my class feel bad. Am I being clear?"

We teeter in that moment and I can see him making internal calculations and then the mask of adolescent smugness slides into place.

"You know what everybody calls this class, don't you?" he says. "The Clueless Retard Class. CRC, get it?"

"Well, Adam, all I know is that right now, there's only one kid in the CRC class, and that's you. And if you ever want to get out of here, you'd better get measuring the walls because that assignment wasn't optional."

I get up and go to my work table and start organizing my notes for my afternoon lessons. Adam sits in his desk until the bell rings to signal the end of the lunch hour and then he leaves.

Odious little toad.

Next time I'm going to let Miss Holly chew on his neck.

I HAVE bus duty at dismissal, which is a bit like standing hip deep in a river during a particularly frantic salmon run, but once the last little fish is safely on the bus, I head to the staff bathroom to change my clothes, then set about unloading the tarps and cans of paint from my excessively cheerful Jeep. I've got the fire door and the tiny windows propped open for ventilation, I've just had a good chuckle at Max and Daniel's surface area calculations and I'm about to make the all important boom box music selection when Eddie Spaghetti pokes his head in the door.

"Is this a private party?" he says.

"So you do actually work here!" I say. "I was beginning to wonder if it was just a rumour."

"I know, crazy week. But I brought beer," he says with a grin, holding up a pair of beer bottles.

"In that case, you can come in."

He cracks open the bottles and hands me one, then plops himself down on a chair. "Sorry I haven't been down before now," he says.

"No, you're not," I say. "You've just been too afraid to come down here and face me, you big coward. 'A few special needs,' you said. You didn't tell me I was going to be running the county jail."

"I wasn't counting on you breaking up an illegal tobacco ring, now was I?" he says. "Actually, I'm kind of surprised that Cynthia sent those boys to you. She usually gives me those kinds of detentions to supervise."

"Well, *Cynthia* isn't my biggest fan. Or my mother's."

"What does your mother have to do with anything?"

"Long story. Involves Dickie Puckett of all people, I'll tell you later. And what is that kid Adam's deal?"

"Ah, Adam. We've spent many happy hours together, Adam and I. Well, maybe not happy, but many hours, anyway."

"He called Tobey a retard and while I was lecturing him on the power of word choice, he informed me that my class is commonly known at the 'Clueless Retard Class.' Right to my face he said that."

"I'd heard 'Completely Retarded Crowd.' Real bunch of Dorothy Parkers, aren't they?"

We both take long draws from our green bottles and silently ponder the sad future of mankind.

"It's so great Cynthia said you could paint your room," Eddie says.

I drink my beer and study the ceiling tiles.

"You did ask Cynthia, right? I mean you cleared this with her?" He's looking kind of nervous now and I suspect he's going to revert to calling her Miss Osgoode at any moment.

"I cleared it with Stan," I say.

"Stan? You mean Stan, the custodian?"

I nod. "We had an excellent chat about water-based versus oil-based acrylic paint. He knows his paint, that Stan. Has some strong feelings about the whole volatile organic compounds situation going on with oil-based paints and suggested that unless I felt strongly about gloss - which I do not - I was much better off with that new water-based stuff."

"You didn't even ask Cynthia, did you?"

"I thought this was one of those situations where it might be better to beg for forgiveness than to ask for permission. So if you need plausible deniability, you should go now. But please leave the beer."

He groans and rolls his eyes. "You're killing me, Liv."

"Don't whine, it's not an attractive quality in a man."

"And nice Jeep, by the way," he says. "Love the colour."

"Watch what you say there, Mr. Spaghetti - my Nana picked it out. She said she wanted something that was visible."

"From space?"

"I forgot how funny you are," I say and I slap him on the back. "So...roller or brush?"

A long suffering sigh. "Roller," he says.

And we're off.

Two hours in and we're making good progress in our Sickly Beige Eradication Program and despite the paint fumes, the new colour scheme is making it feel more spacious down here, like you can actually breathe. Unfortunately, Eddie Spaghetti has seriously underestimated the amount of beer we'd need so he's set off in search of more refreshments while I hang off a ladder and tackle a tricky bit of moulding. I'm just pondering the possibility of stencilling some clouds onto the ceiling when I hear a tapping at the fire door, and a voice says, "Hello, hello!"

I twist around on the ladder and see a gaggle of beaming faces in the doorway.

"Hello, pet! We wanted to see how you were getting on and we brought you some supper," Nana says, and then Alf is giving her his arm to help her down the rickety steps, with Angie and Penny Clarke right behind, toting a picnic basket and grocery bags that look like they contain enough food for the 101st Airborne. "Oh my goodness, I see what you mean about the colour," Nana says, scanning the unpainted walls. "It could put you off your feed, couldn't it?"

Within minutes, there is a sandwich bar set up on the centre work table, with buns, a variety of cold cuts, two kinds of mustard, several mason jars of pickles, and a selection of soft drinks. Someone, probably Angie, has also put down a tablecloth and laid out paper plates with matching napkins.

The place is a total shambles, with paint cans and tarps everywhere and now there are four senior citizens all trying to be helpful - Alf is telling me about this special brush that he likes to use for painting trim, and offers to nip home to get it for me, while Penny Clarke and Nana do a slow tour of the room, quizzing me on what sort of curtains I have in mind for the little street level windows - and it takes on an even more festive air when Eddie Spaghetti bounds down the fire door steps, swinging a six pack of beer. "Nana Sutton!" he says and he rushes over to hug my grandmother, and it's like a little party has broken out down here in this half-painted Underworld. Alf is helping himself to a bottle of beer and Angie is lecturing him about his blood pressure and Nana is asking Eddie Spaghetti if she can fix him a sandwich and this is when I spot Miss Osgoode, standing at the door to the classroom.

She is wearing a trench coat and has her briefcase and purse with her, as if we'd just caught her leaving. Her expression is a little frightening because it's such a mixture of things: one part shock and one part thunderclouds, with a generous sprinkling of outrage, possibly at the notion that so many people are having fun in her school. For just a second, everybody freezes, including Alf, who even though he's as deaf as a post, has picked up on the sharp change in air pressure that just blew through the room.

As usual, Nana saves the day. "Cynthia Osgoode!" she exclaims. "How wonderful to see you!" She starts rolling her way across the room to greet her.

"Mrs. Sutton," Miss Osgoode says, and now she's genuinely flustered. "I'd heard you were ill. How are you?"

"I need this ridiculous contraption to get around, but I'm getting my sea legs back, slowly but surely," Nana says. "Do come in and join our little picnic, we're just about to make sandwiches."

Miss Osgoode is shaking her head and backing away. "No, no, thank you."

"Are you sure?" Nana says. "We have plenty and Angie brought some of her home made pickles."

"Thank you, but I can't stay." She really looks like she wants to flee now and I'm sincerely hoping she will, but instead she forces herself to step into the classroom and pins Eddie with a look. "I just wanted to tell you to make sure to finish up before eleven because that's when the night janitor's shift finishes."

"Sure," Eddie says. "We won't keep him late."

"All right, then," she says. "Have a good evening." She turns and leaves, but Nana goes rolling after her.

Eddie sidles up to me and says under his breath, "I wonder if that guy who does the taxidermy mice has found himself a job yet? There might be a couple of openings here for him."

"Sorry, Eddie, I didn't mean for you to be in the poo with me." I'm watching Nana talk with Miss Osgoode at the foot of the stairs, out of earshot. Miss Osgoode is listening intently to what Nana is saying and then she smiles and touches Nana's arm. That tiny gesture, her hand on my grandmother's arm, is fraught with meaning.

Eddie drifts off to find a beer and claim the sandwich that Angie has prepared for him and I watch Nana wheel her way back into the room.

"What did you say to her?" I ask Nana, when she rolls back in.

Nana's smile is somehow sad. "I told her I'd seen her mother a few weeks ago, when I was over at Birch Haven. You know, the nursing home in Winchester? I just wanted to tell her how well she looked."

"Her mother is in a nursing home?"

"She has Alzheimer's. She's had it for years, the poor thing. But when I saw her she'd just had her hair done and she looked so happy.

She didn't remember me of course, but we had a lovely little chat about the nice girls who come in to do the residents' hair. I just wanted Cynthia to know that she seemed happy."

I give her a quick peck on the cheek. "Thank you, Nana."

"What for?"

"You might just have saved my job. And Eddie's."

"All God's creatures have their burdens to carry, pet. Never forget that. Now, let's make you a sandwich and talk about some curtains."

And because she distracts me with smoked turkey and finials, I forget to ask what she was doing at Birch Haven.

I HAVE NEVER BEEN SO glad to see a weekend in my life. We all have a bit of a lie in on Saturday morning, then devote the rest of the day to cleaning the house, walking the dogs and getting in a load of groceries. Sunday morning Nana does her exercises, both the rehab calisthenic variety and the kind that involve using her weak hand to do things like squeeze a rubber ball. She does this last one sitting in a lawn chair in the garden in the sunshine, Ophelia at her feet, throwing the ball for Mortimer and Lucy Boxer to chase when her hand gets tired. I bring her out a cup of tea and the phone, just in time to watch Lucy hip check Mortimer and send him flying ass over teakettle into the rosebushes as they scrap over the ball.

"It's Angie," I say, handing her the receiver. "She's got all the church news for you." She chats with Angie while I go check to see if Mortimer is bleeding from his close encounter with all those thorns. He only has one little scratch on his snout but he has a beady look of revenge for Lucy, who is already back sitting primly beside Nana, waiting for her to throw the ball again.

"Well, good luck tomorrow with the lawyer," I hear Nana say. "Call and tell us how it went."

I wait until she hangs up. "The lawyer? That's never good news, is it?"

"Poor Angie," she says. "All these problems with Alf's pension."

"How bad is it?"

"It's not good. They're seeing a lawyer who's starting up a class action suit but..." Nana waggles her head back and forth. "They're talking about having to sell the house."

I look out across the garden, and further away down to the shining lake. The trees have mellowed since I arrived in Stafford Falls, there are golden and crimson patches amidst the green now, and the air this morning feels thinner, cooler.

"Is there anything that needs doing in the garden today, Nana? Pruning or wrapping or something? I could do it for you, if you gave me directions."

"Oh, I think you deserve a day off, don't you? You've been working like a galley slave, we should do something to enjoy the day." She pets Lucy's head meditatively for a while, then brightens. "What would you think about driving over to the farmer's market in Winchester? They'll have all the apples in now. We could make a pie."

"Are you sure you're up to it? It'll be a lot of walking."

"When I get tired, I'll sit. It will be good exercise."

"In that case, call Penny Clarke, see if she wants to come with us."

PENNY CLARKE JUMPS at the chance to go to the Winchester farmer's market and she insists that we take the new Jeep - she's always wanted to ride in one she says, and she has been thinking about maybe trading in her Chrysler, a car that I'm pretty sure pre-dates the 1973 oil crisis. She's even considering getting an SUV and this would give her a chance to compare the rides.

She seems a bit less impressed, though, when she's crammed into the backseat, between Nana's folded up rollator and Mortimer, whom Nana decided we should bring along on the off-chance he decided to act out some revenge plan on Lucy. "Not a lot of cargo room, is there?" Penny Clarke says, casting an appraising eye around the tiny compartment.

"No, but the young man told me that you can take the top and the doors off in the summertime," Nana says.

"Oh, Olivia, you mustn't do that," Penny Clarke says. "That doesn't sound safe at all,"

I'm mainly thinking that taking the top and doors off might make it all a little less yellow, but I assure Penny Clarke that I will play it safe.

We make good time but Suckchester is busy and there's a lot of jockeying for parking. I let Nana, Penny Clarke and Mortimer off at the entrance to the park where they hold the farmer's market and go find a safe place to leave the jeep. By the time I meet up with them, they've already procured little paper cups of cider and are chatting up the man at the cider stall. He's telling them about all his organic farming methods and we've bought a jug of cider and two dozen Honeycrisps before I can drag them away.

The market is amazing. There's a huge number of stalls, and dozens of little white tents set up under the sprawling branches of old oak trees and we wander past baskets and baskets of carrots, beets, cabbages, onions and garlic. Mortimer sniffs everything, scores a few choice bits of food that have fallen from people's hands and happily endures the petting of everyone under the age of ten. There's a woman selling honey and beeswax candles and Penny Clarke has a long conversation with her about alfalfa versus buckwheat honey before buying a jar of the buckwheat variety. I tell her that it looks like molasses and am treated to a lecture on the power of antioxidants as we stroll along.

There's a whole section of the market that has grass fed beef and artisanal cheeses and sausages made from what look like really happy, well-adjusted pigs. Suckchester is embracing the whole foodie thing apparently and I've sidled up to the sausage stall and I'm just angling my way towards the tray with free samples when someone nearby says, "I know that sweet face!" I feel a tug on Mortimer's leash and turn to see that he is jumping up on a woman whose stunning smile is also familiar to me.

"Julia!" I say, and I feel suddenly, stupidly shy.

"Olivia! Hi!" she says, and then she stoops down to give Mortimer a thorough ear scratch. "You should bring old Mort here by the guy who's selling the organic dog biscuits. The peanut butter and oatmeal ones smelled so good, I was tempted to try one."

"If Mortimer doesn't sniff those out, I'm sure my grandmother will," I say.

"Have you tried one of these sausages yet?"

"I was just going to snag one," I say, and I'm trying to juggle the bags of apples into one arm and untangle Mortimer's leash to free up a hand, but Julia says, "Oh, you've got to try this one," and she picks up a little toothpick-speared piece of sausage and feeds it to me.

"Isn't that amazing?" she says, and she's standing so close to me that I can see the patterns of grey-blue in her irises as she peers at me, waiting for my reaction. Definitely ultramarine, I decide. "Don't you love the flavour of the fennel seeds?" she says.

It *is* delicious and I nod eagerly and make appreciative noises but in reality, it is the intimacy of the moment that has left me gobsmacked - her hand didn't linger, she didn't wipe my greasy lips with a teasing index finger, but somehow, I feel almost like I've just been kissed. And the kiss tastes like liquorice and humanely-raised pork.

It's not at all unpleasant but I have to snap out of it because Nana is at my elbow now and so I make introductions.

"Mrs. Sutton, how nice to meet you," Julia says, as she shakes Nana's hand.

"I understand I have you to thank for rescuing Mortimer from certain death in the lake," Nana says and she pats Julia's hand. "I'm very grateful, my dear."

"Actually, I think it might have been Olivia I saved," Julia says, "because she was determined to swim after him. Either way, it was my pleasure."

"Olivia tells me that you've bought the Olson bakery and that you're going to turn it into a café. When are you opening?"

"I'm hoping to be open in about a month, but there always seems to be some delay with the construction. One day it's plumbing, the next day it's electrical - but I've got my fingers crossed for early November."

"Any news on your world traveling espresso maker?" I ask.

"It's been held up at customs but it's still on schedule for a delivery early this week," Julia says. "I have lots of other ways of making coffee, though. You should come by."

Just then, Penny Clarke yoo-hoos to Nana from a stall where someone is selling goat milk soap so we have to move on.

"Here, let me give you my number," Julia says, and then she rummages in her bag and produces a business card that is the creamy mocha colour of a good latte She whips out a pen and scribbles on the back before she gives it to me.

"I'm so glad to see you, again," she says.

"I am, too," I say. "And there's the added bonus that I'm wearing dry clothes this time."

She laughs. "So… give me a call. Or just drop by. I'm almost always there."

"I will," I say.

She gives Mortimer a final pat, then waves and disappears into the crowd around the artisanal cheese maker.

Nana squeezes my arm and then we head off to sniff samples of goat soap.

I officially love the farmer's market.

By the time we get home, Nana says that she is knackered and so once I have installed her in her bed for a nap with her three furry guardians, I head down to the kitchen to put away the produce and other stuff we bought. I stash things in the fridge and consider getting a start on the apple pie we'd talked about making, but first I empty the little carton of plums we bought into a white bowl and put them on the kitchen table. They're damson plums, slender and ovoid but still plump and ready to burst their skins from a full summer of sun and rain. There are so many violets and purples on their surfaces, broken up with patches of faint, fine dust, that I stand there, studying their shapes and their colours, and then my eye is drawn to the bluish puddles of shadows that fall on the white bowl they're in. I am reminded of a hundred boring still lifes I produced in school and not one of them ever looked as good as this bowl of plums, sitting on the kitchen table, illuminated by the cool afternoon sun.

I have to paint them.

I tiptoe up to my room and silently tear through a half a dozen of the boxes that are stacked there. The really good paints and brushes and my easel are out in Nana's garage, so I just grab watercolours and oil pastels and an armload of paper and hurry back down to the kitchen as if it's Christmas morning and Santa just went back up the chimney.

I feel stiff and awkward at first, and the charcoal feels foreign in my hand and I try to remember the last time I just sat down and drew something and I can't. I switch to pencil and I pause and just let my eyes travel the geography of the plums, the bowl, the shadows and I trace the lines and don't look at the paper and finally, like releasing a too long-held breath, it starts to flow.

I draw and discard, shape and shade, and half-finished sketches start to pile up on the floor at my feet. Then I try to reproduce the plummy purples with watercolours, but they feel too slow and flimsy, I want body and texture and colour that jumps off the page, so I switch to the pastels and start to build up thick, greasy layers. I rub the blocks and swirls of pastels together but what I really need is my palette knife and big gobs of viscous paints that I can smear on a huge canvas and it occurs to me that this still life has more life in it than the last dozen portraits I've attempted.

The sound of dog claws on kitchen tiles jars me from my thoughts and when I look up, Nana and her puppy posse are making their way across the kitchen.

"Can't you sleep?" I say.

"I slept for ages," Nana says and when I look at the clock, I see that two hours have passed.

"I'm sorry, I lost track of time. I was going to start the pie," I say.

"Oh, pet, these are marvellous," Nana says, picking up a few discarded sheets from the floor and studying my sketches with a critical eye. "Your purples are so rich, I feel like I could taste them," she says. "They make me think of that poem about the plums. You know, the one about the plums in the refrigerator. Oh, how does it go again?" She taps her fingers on the grip of her rollator. "Well, this is going to drive me to distraction. I have to look it up."

"You look it up and I'll start the pastry," I say.

"I'll just be a minute, then I'll come and help." She rolls off towards the Flowery Room and her canine escorts fall in behind her.

I survey the mess of paper and art supplies that are spread across the table and the floor. I'm not at all satisfied with any of the sketches - I'm rusty and I know it - but it just feels so good to have *made* something.

We eat nothing but apple pie for supper, with thick curls of smokey cheddar on the side and it's delicious.

CHAPTER 10

Control-Top, Sheer-Toe Blues

It is worth every dollar I spent on paint, every minute I hung off the ladder and every ounce of grief that Miss Osgoode is no doubt going to rain down on my head, when Miss Holly and Tobey walk into the classroom on Monday afternoon. They both stop in the doorway and just stare, as if they can't take it all in. They have the same expression on their faces - wide, unbelieving eyes, mouths open in little ohs.

"Athena is the goddess of wisdom," Tobey says, and he points at my sketched-in Parthenon mural. "That was her temple."

"Oh my God," Miss Holly says. She takes a few tentative steps into the room, still gaping at the sight of it all.

And to be fair, it is quite a sight. We threw down base coats of cerulean and ultramarine to suggest those incredible Mediterranean sky and sea blues, then slapped in stark white accents around the room, which I am currently filling with tiny murals of houses and colourful fishing boats and of course, on a hill in the corner, the Parthenon.

"You did this?" Miss Holly says.

"Mr. Spaghetti and I did it, although you might want to downplay his involvement if Miss Osgoode is within earshot. And there was a catering service involved, but otherwise, yeah."

She does a slow turn in the middle of the room. "It's fantastic. I can't believe how much it - oh! is that wall a chalkboard?"

"It's chalkboard paint, but we can use it just like a regular chalk-board," I say. I peeled the painter's tape off just a few minutes ago and the edges are crisp and straight and the surface is just begging to be written on. "And over here," I say, leading Miss Holly to the corner furthest removed from the door, "I was thinking we could make a little space for Tobey, you know, a little rug, some pillows. Maybe hang some fairy lights. Some friends of my Nana are fixing up a little child sized rocking chair that they had in their attic and we could see if he likes sitting in it. Maybe rocking would give his wiggles a bit of an outlet."

"I've been wanting to bring in one of those big exercise balls to see if we could get him to sit on that - I suggested it to Mrs. Holt but she wasn't keen on the idea."

"I'm as keen as they come, so bring it in, we'll try it out," I say. "I was also thinking about looking around for some lamps, so we could turn off the overhead fluorescents and still have light, but it would be a warmer light, you know?"

"I might have something at home," she says. "If not, we can hit the thrift store."

"There are a few more things I'd like to find. Do you know, is there a room in the school where they put the stuff nobody else wants?"

Miss Holly throws back her head and laughs. "You're standing in it, honey," she says.

We laugh together at the absurdity of our boiler-adjacent classroom.

"What is it you need?" she says. "Maybe I can scout around."

"A bookcase."

"A bookcase?"

"Yup. We're starting a book club."

NANA WAITS until Wednesday morning on the way to physio in the world's yellowest Jeep to casually bring up Julia.

"That lovely young woman we saw at the farmer's market, pet - what was her name again?"

I look over at her in the shotgun seat, sitting there feigning innocence, clutching her handbag in her lap. "You mean the woman who 'rescued Mortimer from certain death,' as I believe you put it?"

"Yes."

"Her name is Julia."

I'm finding it hard to believe that Nana doesn't remember her name. Unless this is one of those personality-change, memory-loss stroke side effects.

"Julia who?" she asks.

"Julia Purcell."

Nana nods as if she's savouring the words. "And where is she from?"

Ah. It's not brain damage. It's a fishing expedition.

"I don't know where she's from, Nana. We've only met twice and one of those times I was a bit distracted by having nearly drowned myself trying to save your dog."

We ride on, the dulcet tones of Frank Sinatra and some swinging, brassy group filling the little Jeep. Nana picked the music this morning again and I'm thinking I might have to institute a policy of taking turns being the DJ, but then I remember that technically, it's her car.

"And you say she's a friend of Tenzin's?" Nana says.

"She knows him well enough to have loaned him her van."

I can almost hear her sitting there, scanning her network of friends and informants, looking for a dependable source of intelligence, little pins and tumblers falling into place.

"It will be nice to have a real café in town," I say, in an effort to distract her from her mission.

"Oh, won't it, though? I can't remember the last time I had a really good cappuccino," she says. "Do you know the very first time I ever had a cappuccino was on my honeymoon with your grandfather?"

"You're kidding."

"No. We stayed in Rome for a week and every morning we'd go to Caffé Grecco and your Poppa would have a triple espresso and I would have a cappuccino and we would look at the paintings and watch the people come and go."

"That must have been before Poppa had heart problems, because a triple espresso is a lot of caffeine."

"Oh, he needed it, pet. We weren't getting a lot of sleep."

"God, Nana! Please don't tell me things like that."

She chuckles. "You know, Goethe drank espressos at the Caffé Grecco in Rome. And Keats and Shelley. Or maybe they drank cappuccinos or lattés I'm not sure. But they were all patrons at one point or another."

"So how did you enjoy your first ever cappuccino?"

"I thought it was the most exotic, delicious thing I'd ever tasted."

"Well, we'll have to go to Julia's café when she opens and see how hers compare."

Nana gives me a sidelong look and smiles a tiny smile.

I turn up the music and we sing along with Ol' Blue Eyes so we don't have to discuss anyone's love life anymore.

IT IS a momentous day because this is the first day that I'm leaving Nana alone for part of the afternoon and I'm nervous. This decision came at the end of a protracted discussion in which I was informed by Nana that there was nothing any of us could do to prevent her from having another stroke and that the constant hovering and babysitting was making her feel like a burden, and "for heaven's sake, pet, surely I can sit in my own home for just a few hours without supervision." I only gave in after a quick call to Penny Clarke who backed Nana, but who also agreed to pop in around three o'clock, just to say hi and have a quick cup of tea.

I make Nana's lunch and set her up in the Flowery Room with the phone, her cell phone (a device that I'm not entirely sure she knows how to operate,) the TV remote control, a pile of books and a canine honour guard, and I extract a solemn promise that she will not climb the stairs by herself and that she will call me if she so much as sneezes.

So when my cell phone rings just after I dismiss the kids for afternoon recess, I leap out of my chair as if it's on fire and hurl myself in the direction of my bag to answer it. In my haste, I don't bother to look at the number.

"Nana! Is everything all right?" I say, and my heart is pounding in my chest.

"Olivia, that's no way to answer a phone call," my mother says.

Jesus, Mary and Joseph Christ.

"Sorry, I thought you were Nana," I say, and I take a deep breath to try to slow my heart. "I left her alone for the first time today."

"I know, I was just talking to her. Why on earth did you not call me to tell me you'd taken a teaching job in that town? I know you don't care what I think but you could have at least had the decency to let me know, so that I didn't look like an idiot talking to the dean of that fine arts program in Florence."

"Did he say he thought you were an idiot?"

"Well, no."

"Then probably he doesn't."

"Did you even read the brochures about the Phd courses that I sent you?"

"I did."

"And what did you think?"

I think they make a very colourful pile on my dresser, but that's probably not what she's looking for. "They're lovely, Mom, but the timing is just not right. Nana is still using a walker, she needs my help and it's going to be a little while yet. That's why I got a job."

"If it's about money, Olivia, I can send you money."

"Thank you for the offer, Mom, but I'm good."

"You're going to get stuck there, that's what's going to happen, do you know that? Mired down in that place, never to escape."

"It's only been a few weeks."

"Are you even painting?"

I look around at my classroom, at the sea and sky and my almost finished Parthenon.

"As a matter of fact, Mom, I have been painting tons. Real classical stuff." My phone buzzes. "Just a sec," I say and I whip the phone around to peer at the screen. It's a text from Nana.

All is well here, pet.

Your mother might phone you.

XO, Nana

A day late and a dollar short, but apparently Nana does know how to use her cell phone, so that's good.

I AM HOPING that Nana has had a perfectly pleasant afternoon, reading and catching up on *Coronation Street,* but when I get home from school, I find Nana, Penny Clarke and Angie in a high flutter. Apparently Penny Clarke and Angie rolled in around three with news that the wheels had come off the Very Big Deal library fundraiser that they've been planning for six months. And although my Nana has at one point or another supported nearly every charitable cause on the planet, from a women's shelter in Suckchester to South American earthquake victims, none are as close to her heart as the Stafford Falls Public Library.

"What's the matter?" I say, when I catch sight of the command centre that's been set up in the Flowery Room.

"We've lost the caterers," Nana says. "Angie phoned to confirm this afternoon and long story short, they've very suddenly gone out of business - I think someone made off with the cash register - and now we've got two hundred tickets sold and not a morsel to feed them."

"Oh, no, that's terrible," I say. "But couldn't you guys do it? You know, your church luncheon group?"

They all stop and look at me like I've just suggested they serve botulism petit fours and salmonella salad.

"Olivia, this is a very fancy affair," Penny Clarke says. "The Deschauer String Quartet is an internationally renown ensemble.

We're charging an arm and a leg for these tickets. We can't just give people ham sandwiches and a few of Angie's date squares."

I remember hearing a story about a fistfight at a church picnic over the last one of Angie's date squares but pointing that out right now doesn't seem helpful.

"I knew this was going to happen," Angie says. "The price he offered us was too good to be true. We should never have trusted that Jean-Georges fellow. There was something just a bit off about him." She huffs and shakes her head. "I'll bet his name isn't even Jean-Georges."

"We'll find somebody," Penny Clarke says. She's simultaneously peering at her laptop screen and dialling the phone.

"Not at this late hour," Angie says. "We'll have to cancel."

"We can't cancel. We'll lose our deposit on the hall and we have to pay the quartet," Nana said.

"When is it?" I ask.

"Two weeks from Saturday," Nana says. "Penny, what about your brother? Would he know of anybody in the city?"

"I'll ask, but once you add on the travel time to Stafford Falls, I doubt we'd break even."

Nana flips through some pages. "Have we tried 'An Affair to Remember?'"

"They're booked," Angie says.

"What about 'Edna's Edibles?'"

"She doesn't do drinks or serve, so we'd have to get the liquor licence ourselves and hire a bartender and wait staff," Penny Clarke says.

"What would that cost us?"

They all hunker down over their papers.

"Is there anything I can do?" I say.

"I wouldn't say no to a cup of tea," Penny Clarke says.

"Oh, let me help you, Olivia," Angie says, hoisting herself to her feet. "I'm rubbish with numbers anyway."

The dogs are torn between guarding Nana and the possibility of treats in the kitchen, and in the end, Ophelia stays at Nana's side and Mortimer and Lucy trail Angie and I into the kitchen.

"It's ironic," Angie says, as she fills the kettle. "All the years that Alf worked the floor at Stirling Marine and here I am trying to put on a concert there. That's how he lost his hearing you know, from the noise of the machines. The poor man's as deaf as a stone and now I'm dragging him to listen to a bloody string quartet there. If it weren't so tragic, I'd laugh."

"How did it go at the lawyer's?" I ask.

"It sounds like we're all going to be referred to some sort of fellow who specializes in pensions and benefits litigation," she says. "Alf says the problem is that if it goes to court, even if we do recover some of his pension, the legal fees are going to be very high because the other side has such long trousers, or something like that."

"You mean deep pockets?"

"Yes, that's it."

"I'm sorry, Angie," I say. "That's really lousy."

She shrugs, but I can see what it's costing her to try to let on that everything's okay. "Well, it's a hard knock life, to be sure. I mostly feel bad for Alf, though. He's such a proud man, you know, and he worked so hard his whole life to provide for us."

Just then, Penny Clarke pops her head around the corner. "Angie, do you know where our copy of the rental agreement with the museum is? I can't seem to lay my hands on it."

"Oh, I just saw it, give me one second," Angie says and she scurries back to the Flowery Room.

I catch Penny Clarke's eye. "You're not tiring Nana out too much, are you?" I say. "Because she had physio this morning and she didn't nap today and you know how she feels about anything to do with the library - she won't rest until she's fixed this."

Penny Clarke seems to find something I've said tremendously amusing. "Don't worry, I'm keeping my eye on her," she says.

"What? What are you smiling at?" I say.

"I'm smiling at you, the dutiful granddaughter," she says. "May I just say, it's rather nice to see."

"Is there really nothing I can do to help?" I say.

"Not unless you have a secret contact in the world of discount smoked salmon."

"I may not be an expert but even I know that you probably shouldn't buy salmon that's been discounted," I say.

She laughs and heads back to the Flowery Room and I am left with Mortimer and Lucy, both of whom are giving me the evil eye because I have been in the kitchen for more than sixty seconds and have not provided them with some of the organic peanut butter and oatmeal dog biscuits that we got at the farmer's market.

Which reminds me.

"Hey, do you guys want to go for a *walk?*" I say.

Their ears twitch in unison at the word and for once they agree on something.

I AM NOT a person who has the talent of being able to appear casual at will but my efforts are certainly not helped by the three yanking, straining, panting dogs who are dragging me down Main Street. If they were all at least pulling me in the same direction we might make some progress but most of the time, my arms are splayed out front and back because someone is always trying to stop and sniff something on the sidewalk while someone else has suddenly decided to explore their genetic heritage as a sled dog and haul us all full steam ahead, and despite arthritic hips, heart conditions and pure old age, these dogs are *strong*. I wonder again how on earth Nana ever walked them.

A half block from the Second Chance Café, I start to reconsider - maybe I should have called first, maybe I shouldn't have brought the three stooges with me - and I've pretty much decided to turn tail and head back to Nana's when a small group steps out of the café and onto the sidewalk. There's an older man and woman, then Tenzin, then Julia herself. The woman has just given Julia a hug when Mortimer spots his beloved rescuer and races forward. Lucy, never one to let Mortimer get anywhere ahead of her, charges after him.

The sudden movement startles Ophelia who senses she's missed some alarm and she gives a deep-chested bark and bounds ahead too, and that's how the three of them manage to drag me squarely into a parking meter.

Exactly the elegant, insouciant entrance I was hoping for.

"Oh my God, are you all right?" Julia says, as she rushes over.

It's knocked the wind out of me and I can't speak, so I nod vigorously and flap my hand in the affirmative. I'm bent over, hands on my knees, trying to focus all my efforts on pulling in a breath when I suddenly realize that I have let go of all three leashes and have inadvertently released the hounds in downtown Stafford Falls.

I straighten up in a panic, only to see all the dogs gathered around Tenzin, who is speaking what I'm guessing is Tibetan to them. They are staring up at him adoringly.

"Olivia?" Julia's hand is on my arm and her voice is nearby but foggy somehow and I realize it is becoming imperative to get some air into my lungs. I direct every ounce of concentration I have on just taking one slow breath and the world starts to sharpen up around me again.

"You're really pale, you need to come and sit down," Julia says and she ushers me through the doors and into the café.

The place is dim because the tall front windows are papered over and it all looks a bit like a war zone. There's scaffolding against one wall, tarps flung over everything and although there's not a workman in sight, there are enough power tools scattered about to equip an army of contractors.

"Here, let me clear off a chair," the older woman says and she hastily pulls back a tarp and then yanks the plastic wrap off a fancy wingback chair.

Within seconds, I'm sitting with my feet elevated on a cardboard box, trying to reassure everyone that I'm fine. Julia has disappeared deeper into the café to fetch me a glass of water.

"Really," I say for the third time. "Now that I can breathe, I'm okay. Mainly I think I hurt my pride." This is only partly true - my pride *is* deeply wounded but my sternum is aching pretty fiercely, too. Not that it's an area to which I feel I can apply an ice pack in polite company. That might have to wait until I'm home.

"I'm Bea Wiseman, by the way," the older woman says to me. She's tiny and roundish and has very short salt and pepper hair that might look harsh on anyone else, but which comes off more as carefree on her. She is wearing chunky jewelry and has what can only be described as a matronly bosom. "This is my husband, Murray," she says. "We're working with Julia and Tenzin on Six Perfections. You know, the retreat center?"

"It's nice to meet you," I say. "I'm sorry if I'm interrupting a meeting or something."

"Not at all, we were just leaving," Murray says. He is tall and balding, with glasses that make him look a bit owlish as he peers down at me. "Are you sure you're all right, though? I could swear I heard something crack when you hit that parking meter."

Julia saves me from another round of I'm-fine-reallys by showing up with a glass of water. "Sorry I took so long but I couldn't find any ice. This isn't very cold, I hope that's okay."

"You shouldn't give a person in shock ice water," Murray says. "It's very hard on the circulatory system."

"For heaven's sakes, Murray, she's not in shock," Bea says. "She's just a little shaken up."

The front door to the café opens just then. Tenzin has taken the dogs for a quick trip around the block - apparently he finds them as charming and fascinating as they find him - and they're so well behaved on their leads when he reappears with them, that I start to wonder if they behave for everyone but me. He marches the dogs over to where I'm sitting, says a few curt words to them and they all sit.

The little traitors.

"I am hoping you are recovered?" he says to me and gives me one of his beaming smiles and I find myself smiling along with him, despite the throbbing pain in my chest.

"I'm much better, thank you."

"We are not making our acquaintance personally before now," he says. "I am Tenzin." He puts his palms together and bows his head.

Close up like this, it's hard to tell how old he is, maybe forty, maybe sixty.

"I'm Olivia."

"Olivia," he says as if he's trying the word on for size. "It is very musical, your name. But, Olivia, I must be telling you something."

"What's that?" I say.

"This one here," he says and he points at Mortimer. "He is very big problem. Big troublemaker. What is his name, please?"

"He's Mortimer," I say. "He's my grandmother's dog."

"Very big troublemaker," he says and he laughs, a short barking laugh. "But also very wise."

I look over at Mortimer sitting there all nonchalant, and wonder, if he's so wise, how come he hasn't still got two whole ears?

"All right then, we should be off," Murray says. "Miles to go, promises to keep and all that."

"I hope we'll see you again, Olivia," Bea says and there's something in her smile that reminds me of Tenzin's, but it's tempered somehow, as if she's seen some things. She pats my hand and then follows Murray and Tenzin through the debris in the café to the door. Julia sees them out, then comes back and pulls another wing back chair out from under a canvas tarp and sits down.

"I'm so glad you came," she says. "Sorry about the whole parking meter thing, though."

"Yes, and best never mentioned again, please," I say.

"But you're here, and that's wonderful," she says.

"Bea said that you're working on the retreat centre too? How many hours do you have in your day?"

"Just the usual number at the moment, but I'm hoping to add on a couple in the spring when the construction at Six Perfections gets started. That's when it's going to get crazy."

"Tenzin spoke to my Nana's church group about what they were planning to do. She and her friends thought he was marvellous."

"Isn't he? Bea was very lucky to get him. He's an important teacher in his lineage."

"His lineage?"

"In Buddhism, they trace the transmission of knowledge back through each successive teacher to the Buddha himself," she says. "Hey, I know I got you here on the promise of a cup of coffee, but now I'm thinking I'd rather have a glass of wine. What do you think?"

"The sun is over the yardarm somewhere," I say. Also, it might make the parking meter shaped ache in my chest subside a bit.

She disappears into the back again, then reemerges a little while later with a bottle of wine, a couple of glasses and a big stainless steel bowl of water. She puts the water down on the floor for the dogs and pours us both wine. It's a nice Australian white, well-chilled, and we sip and watch the dogs all try to jam their heads together to get a drink from the bowl.

"So, are you Buddhist, then?" I ask.

"I'm more Buddhish than Buddhist," she says. "I meditate and I read a lot but I'm not an expert or anything. Not like Tenzin or Bea. Bea is a meditation teacher and psychologist and she's written several books, too. She's really the person behind Six Perfections, I'm just admin and finance."

"I had wondered what drew you to our little berg," I say. "Stafford Falls is kind of off the beaten path."

"I came here with Bea and Murray to look at the property for the retreat centre and I just loved the town from the moment I saw it. I mean, there was just so much sky! And then I saw this bakery for sale and well... I realize how corny this sounds, but I just *knew*. I'd been looking for a way to escape from my life for a while and when I saw this town, I just knew that this was what I wanted."

"Escape from your life? Wow. That sounds serious."

"I'd had a couple of truly lousy years. And I loathed my job."

"Which was what?"

"I was an accountant. I think I only ever did it to please my dad. He was one of the partners in the firm and it was always just assumed that I would follow in his footsteps, but I finally had to admit that it just wasn't for me."

"Why not?"

"Well, for one thing, I hated nearly every minute of it. I mean, I love the elegance of numbers and it definitely appeals to the part of me that likes to control everything, but I'm just not cut out for corporate culture. And of course there was that one other issue that made it impossible for me to continue."

"What was that?"

"I really, *really* hate pantyhose," she says, and she smiles.

"Sing it, sister," I say and I lift my glass and we toast our mutual dislike of all things nylon.

I look around at the work in progress that is the Second Chance Café. "So what does your dad think of this project?"

She smiles. "He didn't think much of it, at first, but now he's an investor. A kind of 'I-wish-he'd-be-more-silent' partner."

"What caused his change of heart?"

"We both sort of had epiphanies, I guess. My older sister died a few years ago and I think it really made us all look at the world a little differently."

"Oh, I'm sorry," I say. "She must've been very young."

"Yeah, she was thirty six," she says. "It was very unexpected. Rebecca was one of those people who ran marathons and could talk for half an hour about fish oil supplements, you know? And then one morning she found a lump under her arm. Eleven months and nine days later she was gone."

"Julia, that's awful. I'm so sorry."

Lucy goes over to Julia and nuzzles her hand to get some pets. Julia obliges her and Lucy makes a little grumble of pleasure.

"Yeah, it was an awful time, especially for her husband and her boys, but it really made me think about how I was choosing to spend twelve hours a day doing something I hated."

"And wearing pantyhose to do it."

"Exactly."

I think of my bowl of plums and how the afternoon had passed in slow motion while I drew and shaded, like I'd stepped outside of time for a little while.

"Anyway, it was actually Rebecca who introduced me to Bea. She'd read some of Bea's books about meditation and then had some sessions with her and Bea really helped her not be so afraid and angry all the time. She was there the day Rebecca died, with all of us." Julia abruptly stops petting Lucy. "Wow. I'm sorry. This is becoming a really heavy first date. Oh, and I wasn't going to use the word date, in case this wasn't one. Although I'm kind of hoping it is."

Is it the wine that's making me feel so warm? Or is it the way she's looking at me? I really do need an ice pack now.

"Let's see how it goes," I say. "We can always name it later."

"I have another confession to make," she says, and she looks adorably contrite somehow.

"What's that?"

"I googled you."

"Me? Why?"

"I'd heard you were an artist."

"Where did you hear that?"

She cocks her head and gives me a look. "Olivia, this is Stafford Falls."

"Point taken," I say.

"Anyway, I was wondering if any of your portfolio was online, because I was intrigued and wanted to see some of your paintings."

This is when I remember that I'd been thinking that my website needed a complete overhaul because it was looking old and dated, and also that I was supposed to renew my contract with my web host but had been putting it off because money was so tight. But before I can start making excuses, Julia says, "Oh my God, your work is amazing!" and she impulsively reaches over and squeezes my arm. "Your portraits - well, they're more than portraits, they're like little short stories. It's like you've captured these moments that tell you everything about the people in them. And so many of them have the sense that something is just about to happen. That series called *Thresholds* - it was remarkable."

"Thank you," I say and I think I may actually be blushing. "That's what I was trying to do. Show the moment before something happens, how everything is coiled and ready and poised right on the edge of change."

"Look, I know this is not the time, today possibly being a 'date' and all, but some other time, I'd like to talk to you about renting or buying a piece to hang in the café," she says.

"We can definitely do that," I say.

"But for now, we need more wine," she says, "and I should probably feed you something if I'm going to ply you with booze. I'd offer cheese and crackers, but I don't think I've got crackers. Actually, now that I think of it, I'm not sure I have any cheese, either. I do have more wine, though."

"Let me just check in with my Nana," I say, searching my pockets for my phone. "When I left, she was in full crisis mode."

"She's not ill, is she?"

"No, no, nothing like that. It's actually a catering crisis. It's for this big deal concert in a couple of weeks, a fundraiser for the library that she's been organizing for months."

"The string quartet concert? I saw a sign for that at the town hall and I tried to get a ticket but it was sold out."

"They found out today that their caterer has gone out of business and they can't seem to find anybody to fill in on such short notice."

"What do they need? Drinks and canapés? Desserts and coffee afterwards?"

"I think so."

"Probably a cash bar?"

"I don't know."

"How many people?"

"Two hundred, I think."

"What's the venue?"

"The sailboat museum."

She bites her lip and looks into the middle distance for a few seconds. "I can probably do it for the cost of the food, if I can call in some favours," she says. "That many people, we'll want two people on the bar and I'll need three staff, but I bet you look great in black, so we'd only have to scare up a couple more people."

"I'm sorry? What?"

"My mom was an event planner for twenty years but she started as a caterer. By the time I was twelve I could assemble twenty mushroom *vol au vents* with garnish in under a minute. Call your Nana and tell her she's got a caterer."

"Wait, I have to ask you a very important question," I say. "Do you know where to get discount smoked salmon?"

"Ew," she says and she wrinkles up her face. "You don't want to serve anybody discounted salmon."

"I think you've got the job."

JULIA DRIVES us all back to Nana's in her van, with Mortimer riding in my lap. Within minutes of our arrival, Julia is talking menus with Angie, and Penny Clarke is dialling the number of someone who might be able to expedite a liquor license for us. Apparently the smoked salmon is going to be on tiny sesame crisps with a dollop of wasabi cream and minced chives and Julia is saying she thinks she can sweet talk the guy at the farmer's market into giving her a good price on some chèvre because she has a great recipe for chèvre profiteroles with a honey glaze. The concert is definitely back on and everybody is excited and Julia's mom thinks she can get one of her cronies to courier us a samovar and enough silver trays to pull it all off and then, while I'm on hold with someone who can rent us linens, Julia brings me an ice pack wrapped in a tea towel and gives me a little knowing smile.

"Ice it," she says. "It will feel better."

I gratefully hold the ice pack to my chest. "Why are you doing all of this?" I ask.

My question makes her pause, phone to her ear. "What do you mean?"

"You've already got two jobs and a major renovation to supervise and now you've taken on a huge catering gig that you're not even getting paid for. Some people might say that's crazy."

She smiles at me like I'm an adorable child who's just said something clever. "Olivia, I didn't come to Stafford Falls to make a big living. I came here to have a big life. But…full disclosure?"

I nod.

"I really want you to like me," she says.

Now I'm the one smiling. Penny Clarke calls to her just then, a question about Prosecco and Julia drifts away to consult on this weighty topic.

Yeah, it was totally a date.

CHAPTER 11

Barbies Love Beethoven

It's three days and counting to the library benefit concert and early indications are that we're actually going to pull it off. I'm sitting in the waiting area at the hospital, down the hall from the physiotherapy room, reading texts from Pam about how much laundry she has to get done before she can begin packing the two tons of clothing, toys and assorted equipment that are required to take her offspring on their upcoming road trip to Stafford Falls. Despite the amount of work involved and the fact that Martha might be coming down with a cold, Pam is totally pumped to drive for six hours to come to our little podunk town and hand out hors d'oeuvres all night, which makes me wonder what her social life has been like since I left town, and I resolve to get her good and drunk one night while she's here.

so how's julia? she asks and I can hear the smile in the text.

Fine, but busy. And I'm not even sure it's a thing so back off.

Julia's been really busy, actually, what with trying to build a café *and* getting a retreat centre off the ground *and* catering the Stafford Falls cultural event of the year so we haven't had a chance to get together again except for discussions that centre on things like whether or not we want those little doilies for the silver serving trays, and meetings on the fly that are almost always chaperoned by old women anyway. Two weeks of shotgun emails, long to do lists and daily trips for physio have made our late afternoon interlude seem far away and just a bit imaginary. Even the bruises on my sternum have disappeared, but I'm pretty sure it all happened and she really did say that thing about it being a date and how she wanted me to like her.

Which I think I do.

Somebody in hospital scrubs pushes an elderly man in a wheelchair past me, towards the physio treatment room. He's leaning to one side in the chair, a blanket covering his legs, and his hands are useless claws in his lap and I am struck once again by how much worse Nana's stroke could have been, how lucky she was.

How lucky I was.

Can't wait to see you, I've missed you guys I type to Pammy.

i can't wait to meet julia, she replies.

A few minutes later, I spot Nana rolling her way down the hall and she's making that face she makes when something hasn't gone her way. It's not a pout so much as it is an expression of stoney determination and I know two things for sure - first, that Anthony has shot down her request to switch from her rollator to a cane for the night of the concert, and second, that Anthony, although he might be young, is one tough customer, because it is very hard to say no to my grandmother when her mind is made up. I meet her halfway down the hall and hold her coat for her to slip into.

"He said no, huh?"

"He said, 'we'll see,' as if I don't know what that means."

"There's still two more days," I say.

"He's as bad as Penny Clarke," she says, and she's trying to knot her silk scarf and her left hand is giving her trouble. I've noticed that it's worse when she's tired, like after an hour and a half of physio, or late at night, when I'm helping her undress.

"They both have your best interests in mind," I say, and that sounds lame even to my ears because Penny Clarke does come on like a thunderstorm sometimes and everybody's been a bit stressed as the big day draws near.

I decide to unleash my secret weapon.

"I was just talking with Pam and she said the girls are very excited to come to visit."

Her face lightens. "Did you tell her again that I would gladly send them train tickets? It's such a long way to drive."

"Pam says they'll be fine. She's got movies for them and the girls think it's a big adventure. They're bringing their Hallowe'en costumes to show you."

We make our way out of the hospital and the change in the air is a cool relief, sweet October air that makes you breathe deeper and stop and look at the clouds.

"Do we have time to make a stop at the grocery store on the way home?" Nana asks as we roll along towards our happy little Jeep.

"Sure, what do we need?"

"I want to look for some little paper cups for cupcakes," she says. "I think they have some with Disney characters on them. The girls might like that." She passes me her rollator as she boosts herself into the Jeep. "And some food colouring so we can make pink icing."

And we're back.

It's a big day down in the basement of Stafford Falls Public School, because today is the day I'm going to launch "The Just Make Something Book Club," a little project I've been slowly putting together over the past couple of weeks for my reading groups. Part of the problem for these kids, I've come to think, is that they don't *love* books yet, although who can blame them? Books are difficult for them right now, hacking away at each new word until they figure it out and then trying to remember what the first damn word was when they get to the end of a sentence. It's slow, taxing work and there's very little joy in the process.

I realized this a few weeks ago while sitting in Nana's Flowery Room, drinking tea and putting off doing the dishes after supper. I'd

asked her what the library fundraising money was earmarked for and
Nana explained that it's going towards improving the children's
services at the library. Apparently their collection is outdated and
they need lots of new books, but they're also desperate for fresh paint,
a new carpet and some child-sized furniture.

"It has to be an inviting place," Nana said, "a place that's every bit
as exciting to them as a toy store." Her big dream, she tells me, is to
build an addition onto the existing library, a whole wing just for kids,
with giant windows to let in the daylight and a puppet theatre and a
full-time children's librarian, but for now, she's concerned with
sprucing up what they've got and getting more volumes on the
shelves.

I'd looked around at the hundreds of books on Nana's own shelves
and realized that this was the very room where I learned to love
books, at first by being read to before bed, in my pyjamas, usually
with a cup of cocoa, then later, on my own, although still usually in
my pyjamas and with a beverage close at hand. Pooh, Aslan, Jane Eyre,
Philip Pirrip and Kinsey Millhone - I'd met them all right here in this
very room.

And that's what I want to try to give to Tobey, Isabelle, Wally, Kylie
and Davis.

I've assembled a broad selection of books from the school library
and I've mainly chosen books with lots of photos or illustrations and
minimal text, barely a sentence per page in some cases. There are
books about bats, books about dump trucks, books about mice, birds,
cars, stars, trees, cats, dogs, gardening, and my personal favourite, a
book with nothing more than close up photographs of owl pellets,
each with labels identifying the various bits of fur, bones, feathers and
other indigestible bits that owls have puked up. I think Wally is going
to love that one.

I've also amassed an impressive array of materials with which to
make things: construction paper, cardboard, markers, crayons, paint,
glue, scissors, bits of fabric, ribbon, magazines, pipe cleaners,
modelling clay and even googley eyes. I have just finished laying it all

out in bins and boxes around the room when Miss Holly, Tobey and the four amigos arrive.

Kylie is telling Miss Holly that she saw Davis picking his nose while they were at the water fountain.

"If he did, I'm sure he knows to use a tissue next time," Miss Holly says, "but really, Kylie, Davis's nose is his business, not yours."

The Princess In Training is not satisfied with this answer but is so busy grinding out a pouty face that she does not see Miss Holly surreptitiously pass Davis a tissue.

"How come he's here?" Wally asks, nodding his chin in Tobey's direction.

"Same reason we're all here," I say. "To work on our reading."

"He can read?" Davis says, but I'm not sure whether he's impressed or threatened by this new bit of knowledge.

"Tobey's a pretty good reader but we can all use practice, right?"

Davis gives me a noncommittal nod and seems to chew on this new bit knowledge. Isabelle, in the mean time, is swaying back and forth, bending herself into contortions trying to get her face into Tobey's line of sight. Finally, Miss Holly says, "Tobey, can you look at Isabelle?"

Tobey drags his gaze up from the floor and his eyes light on Isabelle for a second.

"Hi, Tobey," Isabelle says, with a million dollar smile.

"Hi," Tobey says, and then he adds, "Socrates was one of the founders of Western Philosophy."

When I've got them all in their chairs, including Tobey who sort of squat-kneels on his chair, I explain that twice a week from now on instead of worksheets and flash cards, we're going to have a meeting of "The Just Make Something Book Club."

"There are only two rules in our book club. First you have to read something, then you have to make something," I say. "You can pick the book, and you can use whatever materials you can find in the class-room." I give them the quickie tour of the art supplies I've collected and then set them loose to choose their first book.

It does not go how I'd hoped.

First, there's the shoving match that takes place in front of the bookcase - Kylie swears she didn't touch him, but Wally's rolling around on the floor holding his knee, howling, which sets off Tobey who has to go out in the hall with Miss Holly for a minute to compose himself. Davis smirks at Kylie while I'm telling her she needs to be more careful around other people, and this is too much for her, especially since no one took her accusation of nose picking very seriously and when she thinks I'm not looking she makes a gesture to Davis that suggests he'd better be careful at recess.

Eventually, I get a book into each child's hands and send them to disparate corners of the room to read.

Isabelle has chosen a book about birds and I watch her turn the pages slowly, carefully looking at each picture. Then she shuts it and smiles at me.

"You have to read the words, too," I say.

This piece of news seems to disappoint her.

"How about I help you sound out the hard words," I say.

It takes a bit of time and quite a lot of effort, but between us, Miss Holly and I ensure that each of the club members has in fact, read one book.

"All right," I say. "Now you can go ahead and make something about your book."

"Do you mean like a drawing?" Wally says.

"Sure, you could make a drawing. Or anything else you can think of," I say.

"Like what?" Kylie says.

"Well, let's see. You read a book about cats, right? You could make a model of a cat. Or a cat puppet. Or a scientific diagram showing the parts of a cat. Or a comic book about a cat."

Kylie ponders this for a moment, then shrugs. "I guess I'll make a drawing," she says, and she drags herself over to the bin with the paper and markers.

Wally, who as I'd anticipated has chosen the book about owl pellets, has already procured himself a big sheet of paper and is scribbling a giant, dense cloud in the middle, at top speed. He rips through three pieces of paper before I can coax him to ease up a bit. "See?" he says, when he holds his successful fourth try up for me to inspect. "See? It's a giant owl pellet that an owl threw up."

"That's great. Can you add some labels, like in your book?" I say.

"Labels?"

"Of what's in the owl pellet. Like feathers, or claws or beaks or whatever."

"But I don't know how to spell those words."

"You could copy them down from your book."

The look on his face tells me he's dubious that such a crazy plan could work, but he goes to retrieve the book from the shelf anyway.

Isabelle appears at my side and holds up a mostly blank page for me to inspect. "I'm finished," she says.

I take the paper from her and study it. In the far left lower corner, there is a microscopic drawing of a stick-bird. At least I think it's a bird. It has a beak, anyway.

"It's not very good, is it?" she says.

"It's an excellent start," I say. "Could I make a suggestion, though?"

She nods.

"Picture it in your mind before you start and use all the space on the paper," I say. "Here, let me show you." We sit together at the table and I wrap my hand around hers, encircling the tiny fist that is clutching the pencil. "Just keep your arm loose," I say and I move her hand in a graceful bird shaped arc across the paper. I sweep her hand back and forth on the paper, her pencil leaving a grey trail and sketch out the roughest outline of a bird. "Now you try," I say and slide her a fresh piece of paper. She spends the rest of our time together trying to imitate the motion and leaving pencils marks all over the table.

When our time is done, Miss Holly rounds them up to escort them back to their classroom. I stand there, sifting through their meagre output - although Tobey's made a good start on a map of Greece - and I must look as discouraged as I feel because Miss Holly stops in the doorway and calls my name.

I look up.

"You know what accounts for seventy five percent of special ed?" she says.

"What?"

"Showing up the next day."

I laugh, in spite of myself. "And the other twenty five percent?"

"Paperwork," she says, and she shrugs. "They're not thinking as far out of the box as you'd like, but don't worry. It was a good start." Tobey tugs at her hand then and she leaves, but a moment later I hear her voice in the stairwell. "Davis, hands to yourself, mister," she says.

FRIDAY IS A BLUR OF ACTIVITY. I drop Nana off at her physio appointment, then haul ass to Suckchester to pick up an extra pastry bag for Julia and three boxes of some fancy sparkling wine that apparently cannot be obtained for love nor money in Stafford Falls. It all takes longer than I expect and I roar back into the hospital and speed walk my way to the rehab wing to find Nana sitting in the waiting room, her rollator parked nearby, a beaming smile on her face, and a cane across her lap.

"Anthony said yes?" I say.

"He said yes for Saturday night. Next week, we're going to practice with it but he said I could take it for a test drive at the concert."

We celebrate by grabbing lunch from 'Burger's on Wheels: Stafford Fall's #1 Food Truck,' and Nana awes me by not only ordering a chilli dog, but by consuming the entire thing with a complicated set of napkin manoeuvres that keep her cream coloured blouse pristine. Clearly, the physio is helping.

I make it to school with five minutes to spare, and enjoy an afternoon of phonics, flash cards and mini-lectures about Aristotle and Socrates from Tobey. When I roll in to Nana's at four o'clock, Pam has already arrived with the girls. She and Nana are sitting at the kitchen table, drinking tea and the girls are ensconced in a fort made of TV tables and blankets in the Flowery Room. They are watching a movie on Pam's laptop and Mortimer is snuggled in between them on a pillow, his eyes riveted to Martha's tiny bowl of goldfish crackers.

"Hey, Tater Tots!" I say and I crawl into the fort to plant kisses on the girls' foreheads but am scolded and quickly turned out because I've come between them and the singing teapot in a movie they've seen roughly five hundred times.

Pam is much happier to see me and gives me a longish hug.

"I see Martha's fear of dogs does not extend to elderly Jack Russell terriers," I say to Pam.

"She's a little better about the whole dog thing. She even petted Ophelia," Pam says. "Hey, I met your girlfriend."

"She's not my girlfriend, we haven't even had a proper date, yet," I say.

"Well, she's been by a couple times this afternoon to drop stuff off and update your Nana," she says, "and I like her. And speaking of people who aren't your girlfriend, have you heard back from Alex?"

"A couple of very airy, this-is-what-I'm-up-to emails, so apparently we're going to be friends."

"Ugh. Friends with your ex. What could possibly go wrong with that plan?" Pam says.

Nana comes back into the kitchen, having refilled the girls' snack bowls. "Pam, I was thinking since we're going to be so busy with making the sesame crisps, maybe we could order a pizza for supper. Do the girls like pizza? Because if they don't, we also bought some of those frozen chicken nuggets. I doubt they have any nutritional value whatsoever but Angie says all her grandkids loved them and anyway, it's a special treat."

"You're one to give lectures on nutrition," I say. "Chilli dog for lunch, pizza for supper?"

"I'm fortifying myself for tomorrow," Nana says. "What do they call it? Carbo loading?"

"They'd love pizza," Pam says.

"It's settled then. Let me just get something to write with and I'll find out what everyone wants. Olivia, call Julia and tell her we're getting pizza and that she should come by because that poor girl is running like a chicken with her head cut off today and she needs to eat." She rolls off in search of a pen.

Pam watches her go and shakes her head. "Oh, she's good," she says.

JULIA TURNS out to be dining with Penny Clarke tonight, if tuna sand-wiches can be called dining, so that they can churn out a few hundred profiterole shells as well as big batches of wasabi cream cheese, chèvre pastry cream, and some sort of feta cheese and sun-dried tomato concoction that will be piped onto fancy cucumber slices. She's also running between Penny Clarke's and Angie's house, which has been set up as the dessert station. Julia and Angie tweaked some of Angie's traditional recipes to make them a little fancier and then miniaturized them, which by definition I guess also makes them fancier, not to mention easier to eat in one or two bites. Julia tells me to thank Nana for the invitation and assure her that she is not going without supper and then she has to go because her honey glaze is in danger of scorching.

All of these jobs have been carefully assigned so that Nana can participate but not have an overwhelming amount to do - the concert itself tomorrow night is going to tire her out, and I'm prepared to muscle her out of the way tonight and roll, cut and bake several hundred damn sesame crackers on my own if necessary.

Pam and I get a rhythm going pretty quickly though and Penny Clarke's pasta machine emerges as the star of the day because I have no idea how else we would have gotten such fiddly dough thin enough to bake up like crackers. The trick is finding enough space to cool things before we slap them into plastic bins, and eventually every flat surface of the downstairs is covered with cookie sheets, and we have to keep a close eye on the dogs because they're finding these crackers to be as delicious as their farmer's market organic biscuits.

Nana starts out toasting the sesame seeds, but that involves endless standing at the range and her rollator keeps getting in the way, so she switches to measuring ingredients for each new batch of dough and I can tell she's feeling a little useless because Pam and I are doing all the real work. But then the girls work their magic by showing up in the kitchen and pleading with Nana to come and play Candyland with them and for the rest of the evening, as we bake sheet after sheet of crackers, we hear the three of them in the Flowery Room, laughing and playing games, so that's pretty good.

SATURDAY DAWNS a little earlier than I'd like and from the time my feet hit the floor, I am juggling a giant to do list that includes, among many other things, another trip to Suckchester for an extra samovar, because evidently you can't have enough samovars. I get back to find that Nana has talked the girls out of breakfast at McDonald's by suggesting that they could help her make breakfast for everyone at home and quite some time later we all sit down to pancakes which look exactly like you'd think pancakes made by a recovering stroke victim and two very small girls would look like.

"They're letters," Rose tells me. "Yours is a Q. It was supposed to be an O, but it dripped."

Mortimer ends up with a bit of pancake batter on his head and Martha is feeding Lucy Boxer bits of her bacon when her mother isn't watching so it seems she's completely over her dog phobia, which is nice, especially for Lucy, who spends the rest of the day tailing her like a squat, brown shadow, waiting for food to fall from her hands.

I INSIST that Nana take a little rest in the afternoon, which sends Rose and Martha into hysterics because they think they're going to have to go down for a nap, too. Nana acquiesces with grace, and I'm not sure if it's because she's actually tired or because she doesn't want to make a fuss in front of the girls. Either way, I count it as a win and use the time to shower, dress and let Pam do my hair.

The real fun starts after Nana gets up from her siesta and begins to dress for the concert and suddenly, my pragmatic, Middle-English speaking, suffragette of a grandmother turns into a vain teenager who can't decide what to wear. The indecision goes on for nearly an hour ("Does this brooch go with this dress? Is this hem too long? Does this cane make my ass look big?") until both Pam and I, as well as Martha and Rose, have assured her that she will be the belle of the ball. It's only as we're leaving that I realize she's wearing the first outfit she tried on.

The young single mom who lives next door to Angie and Alf has been drafted to babysit Rose and Martha and she (and her adorable eleven month old son) are warmly welcomed by the girls when they arrive - it helps that she comes bearing colouring books depicting all the Disney princesses in their various impractical, bosom-enhancing outfits. There's a tricky moment as we're all leaving when Rose starts to cry because her Barbie has just told her that she really wants to go hear a string quartet, but then the World's Best Babysitter, (who is also sometimes known as Samantha) handles it with a deft hand, suggesting they dress up and have their own concert in the Flowery Room and Rose has stopped crying and is having buckets of fun before the Jeep has backed out of the driveway.

WE ARRIVE at the sailboat museum to find Julia running the place like a drill sergeant, albeit a blonde and adorable one in a knockout little black dress. There are bins and trays laid out on every counter and she is methodically and rapidly assembling canapés and dispensing instructions to anyone foolish enough to come within earshot. She stops long enough to tell Nana that she looks fantastic, which makes me love her just a little bit more, but we're all so busy doing the final prep that I don't get a chance to say it. Penny Clarke arrives with three quarters of the Deschauer String Quartet in tow, then quickly departs again to return to the B & B to pick up the cellist and his instrument because she was unable to get all four of them and all their kit into her giant backseat. Eddie Spaghetti cruises through, lugging a flat of glassware out to the bar, which he is manning for us because he was pretty much the only person any of us knew who had experience serving booze - he bartended his way through university - and I'm very grateful to him but at the same time I can't resist teasing him about the little black bow tie that he's sporting.

"I thought you said that under no circumstance would you wear a bow tie. I think you said something about bow ties and losers."

"Your Nana asked me to wear it," he says, "and shut up or I'm not giving you any wine."

I apologize by helping him to carry the last two boxes of wine glasses out to the bar because he's such a good guy to do this, plus, I really, really want some wine. At the bar, I meet Drew, who is serious and earnest and more than a little boy-scouty and unlike Eddie Spaghetti, somehow he looks like he was born wearing his bow tie. Eddie introduces us and it turns out that he's another neighbour of Angie and Alf's, which makes me start to suspect that their house is the nexus around which Stafford Falls is built. I thank him for coming to help out tonight, but I secretly wonder what Angie could possibly have on this kid to have blackmailed him into volunteering for this.

Back in the kitchen, Pam has fallen into rhythm with Julia, artfully piping tiny pyramids of whipped feta cheese onto little sculpted cucumber slices and they're trading catering horror stories as they work ("Oh my God, shrimp salad, don't get me started on shrimp salad...") and it occurs to me that almost everybody, including Penny bloody Clarke, has gotten to spend more time with Julia than I have and although this seems very wrong to me, I don't have time to think about it because just then Angie pops her head in to say that they're about to open the doors.

The main hall of the sailboat museum is huge, with cathedral ceilings and open beams that are a warm honey colour. Most of the wall that faces the lake is floor to ceiling windows, and the setting sun, combined with all the dozens of flickering tea lights that Julia has set out, are giving the whole place a golden glow. The museum exhibits that chronicle the rise and fall of sailboat building in Stafford Falls are nice if you like that kind of thing, but this room, Stirling Hall, is the jewel of the place and as such, it is the site of a constant stream of receptions and parties. People even come here from far away to have their weddings, just so they can have this room and the lake in their wedding pictures and tonight, I can see why.

I attempt to head out onto the floor with my first tray - heirloom

cherry tomatoes and miniature balls of buffalo mozzarella on tiny
skewers - but am relieved of it within steps by Pam, who doesn't trust
me to teeter around the room with a bowl of pesto dip balanced at
shoulder height, and so I make my virgin trip out into the hall with a
couple dozen salmon sesame crisps held proudly aloft, only to come
face to face with Cynthia Osgoode.

"Oh. Hello, Ms. Sutton. How nice to see you," she says and it's clear
that it's anything but nice to see me, but I give her a thousand candle
watt smile and offer her a canapé, because this is my Nana's party and
the children need new books. Thankfully, next I run into Eddie's
Spaghetti's lovely and extremely pregnant wife Connie and I ply her
with salmon and point her in the direction of the profiteroles.

The wine flows and we're all swept off our feet, at a dead run back
to the prep area to reload our trays every few minutes and either these
canapés are the best these people have ever tasted or most of them
haven't eaten in days because they are hoovering them up. Just when I
start to panic that the supplies in the kitchen are looking thin, somebody dims the lights a few times and Penny Clarke's voice comes over
the PA system, asking people to start taking their seats. Pam, Eddie
and I congregate in the kitchen, looking for a break, but Julia has
already started artfully arranging tiny espresso brownies and minus-
cule raspberry tarts on silver trays and she dispatches Eddie to haul
samovars to and fro.

And then the music starts, with a series of strident and breath-
taking chords that suddenly fill the hall, and it seems impossible that a
space that was designed to build fancy boats could have such perfect
acoustics, but those four little wooden instruments are making the
room expand and suffusing it with a melancholic warmth. We all put
down what we're doing and drift out into the hall to listen, hypno-
tized. Julia comes up beside me and slips her hand into mine, and we
stand there, swimming together in the Beethoven's String Quartet
Number 12, letting it flow over us and I could stand here all night.

AFTER THE ECSTASY, the dishes.

It's all a howling success and half the people are pressing cheques into Nana's hand and the other half are lined up outside the swinging door to the kitchen trying to find out the name of the caterers and Julia actually runs out of business cards, but finally the place clears out and the clean up begins. Nana looks utterly done in but is beaming with pride and, I think, doing quick calculations in her head. Pam offers to take her home and before I can even answer, Julia says to Pam, "Go ahead, I can drive Olivia home when we're done."

Eddie Spaghetti catches Nana just before she leaves and I see the two of them, heads bent together, Eddie clutching the wad of bills that have been piling up as tips on the bar. Nana gives him a secretive little nod and as I'm making my way back to the kitchen with a tray of cups, I see Eddie Spaghetti give the handful of cash to Drew, who looks shocked and shakes his head adamantly. But then, after a few quiet words and a friendly clap on the back from Mr. Spaghetti, Drew takes the money and looks a bit like he's going to cry. Now I really want to know what's going on with this skinny kid in the bow tie, and I make a mental note to squeeze the info out of Angie at the next available opportunity.

We start the long process of hosing down the glassware in the sink before packing it into the big plastic trays to go back to the rental company but when we're down to the last couple of flats, Eddie pops by to say he's got to get Connie home because her ankles are swelling at an alarming rate and he's offered Drew a ride, so then it's down to the two of us. I prepare to start toting a flat in the general direction of her van, but Julia hands me a styrofoam cup of sparkling wine and pulls me through the kitchen door back out to the hall, where the lights are dim.

"We deserve a break," she says, and she slips out of her pumps and sits down. "Plus, this bottle was open, so we can't return it."

Never one to waste good wine or the opportunity to sit beside a beautiful woman, I plunk myself down nearby and take a long sip of creamy bubbles.

It is intensely quiet, the sound of violins not even a faint memory in the beams now.

"So, this ex-girlfriend you mentioned a few weeks ago," Julia says, "she's definitely an ex, is she?"

"She is," I say and I tell her about London, and the lawsuit, and the condo and after she refills my styrofoam cup, I even describe James the Repo Boy and our trip to McDonalds, which makes her smile.

"You've had a really lousy couple of months," she says.

"Things are looking up," I say. "How about you? Any recent exes hanging around?"

She shakes her head. "My most recent ex just moved to New Zealand, where she'll probably be very happy. Amy's very athletic, very into extreme sporty stuff."

"So, she was all earthy and freckled and outdoorsy?" I say.

"No, she was more like all gortexy and rock-climby. Very driven."

"Rock climby?" I say. "Wow. That does sound a bit driven."

"She was always training for those adventure races, you know the ones that are five days long and you raft and bike and kill grizzly bears with your bare hands and things like that," she says.

"Would it surprise you to know that I've never once even considered doing something like that?"

"Placing you squarely amongst us sane people."

"Well, that remains to be seen," I say. "So what happened? Why did you break up?"

"She met someone - one of her adventure race teammates actually. Amy was really attracted to her and I was in the midst of deciding to leave my job…" She shrugs.

"So you didn't have driven in common any more."

"We tried to work it out, but in the end… I guess she just wanted to be with that other woman more."

"I'm sorry," I say. "I didn't mean to make you feel sad."

She pours the dregs of the wine into our cups and touches hers to mine in a silent styrofoam toast. "I'm not sad," she says. "Not now."

It's quite a while later when we finally get back to the dishes.

CHAPTER 12

Bathing the Baby Buddha

There are so many things I love about my Nana - her compassion, her intelligence, her meatloaf, to name just a few - but if I am completely honest, I could probably do without her perennial need to dress up her dogs in Hallowe'en costumes. It's not like I'm worried that it might humiliate them in front of their canine peers, it's just that I've always felt that it takes such a lot of time and energy that could be used for something more useful. This particular Hallowe'en for instance, it takes two trips to the pet store in Suckchester to get the right size pirate costume for Lucy Boxer (she's spreading a little in the chest,) and a series of fittings with Penny Clarke to turn Ophelia into a Jack-o-Lantern (complete with a jaunty orange and green cap that Ophelia tries to paw off every time Nana is out of the room.) But despite my initial lack of enthusiasm for the idea, every bit of effort is rewarded when I first lay eyes on Mortimer, who this year will be greeting the trick or treaters on Nana's porch dressed as a pissed off little hot dog, complete with puffy bun and yellow felt mustard running down his back. I take several dozen snapshots of him in his outfit to enjoy later, and in every photo, he is giving me a death glare that makes me suspect that at some point, he's going to pay me back for inflicting this indignity on him.

The post-Hallowe'en sugar shock hits the kids at school hard and they are crabby and listless and generally useless for a week, but gradually as the November cold settles in, they come back to their senses. Then, overnight, all the fall colours disappear and the sky and lake turn an angry shade of pewter and it begins to rain a cold, hard rain. The kind of rain that makes you want to buy more wool sweaters, the kind of rain that makes you wish there was a warm café nearby with a wingback chair by the window and a steaming mug of hot coffee with your name on it.

Which there will be soon.

Work on the café has definitely sped up since Julia's espresso machine arrived, which I think is because she is now keeping all the workers on site in an optimally caffeinated state by serving them round after round of lattés, cappuccinos and espressos. She says it's just so that she can practice pulling espresso shots and steaming milk to perfect her technique but I think she's discovered the perfect formula for keeping productivity high: every time the guys' energy starts flagging, she just goes around the place with a tray of drinks and suddenly, flooring is being laid at twice the normal speed, light fixtures are hung in a trice and the painter's assistants are flying to and fro with buckets of semi-gloss.

The only drawback is that everyone's become a bit of a self-appointed critic. At first, they were hesitant to even try her fancy espresso drinks - the coffee from the food truck was perfectly fine for them, thank you very much - but now they're all like, 'Julia, the foam on my cappuccino was a little thin,' or 'Julia, I think you got the tamp better on the first round of macchiatos.' But the place doesn't look like a bomb just went off anymore, so I think it's working out in her favour.

She's also started to hire some staff - Drew, the volunteer cater waiter, to be precise - but early indications are that she chose extremely well. Drew is recently returned from university - a little earlier than he'd planned and without a degree - and the circumstances are a little murky but I heard that his mom has been sick, although I don't think that's the whole story. Apparently he's been working something like nine part time jobs - pizza delivery, stocking at the grocery store, painting, raking, cleaning gutters - anything to make a little money, and even though Julia can only offer him minimum wage to start, he's over the moon at the idea of something approaching full time work. He's also quite the coffee connoisseur and Julia told me that a sizeable chunk of his interview was taken up by a spirited debate with her on the merits of central versus south American coffee beans.

Almost every day after school, rain or shine - and to be clear, there is a lot more rain than shine right now - I take the dogs for a walk and we stop in at the café for a visit and a hot drink. When she can spare the time, Julia comes walking with us and she holds Mortimer's leash which makes him all dewey eyed, but also saves me from walking into parking meters and things, so that's nice. It's so lovely, this slow, getting to know each other process. So far we've covered ex-girl-friends (one major heartbreak, but no stalkers,) coming out stories (she was fifteen, her father choked on his martini and her mother said, 'I'm sure it's just a phase, darling,' so overall, not too bad,) favourite music (Beatles over the Stones, although she also purports to know all the words to that Gilbert and Sullivan song about the Modern Major-General, but only after sufficient shots of bourbon,) and of course, movies (she confessed a certain fascination for the oeuvre of Patrick Swayze, but I think I still like her anyway.)

A couple of weeks after the library gala, the dogs and I arrive to find Drew wrestling with the controls of the espresso machine and grimacing. He is not wearing a bow tie, but somehow looks like he should be.

"Hi Drew," I say.

He looks up, startled. "Oh. Hi, Olivia."

"How's it going there?"

"Good. Fine," he says. "I just can't seem to get this nozzle to-"

There is a sudden whoosh of steam and a noise that sounds like the coffee machine is trying to launch itself into orbit.

Drew steps back quickly, eyes wide.

"Don't worry," I say. "It used to do that to Julia at first, too."

"It did?"

"Yeah, there was one day she actually got milk on the ceiling."

Drew is still processing that visual when Julia walks in from the back, phone to her ear. "I realize that," she says to whoever is on the other end of the line, "but it's just that you told me *last* week that I would be receiving them *this* week." She spots me and there is a change in her face, a brightening, that makes me feel warm and gooey inside. As she passes by, she presses a button on the espresso machine, spins a dial and then pats Drew on the back and nods for him to try again. Drew steps up and a perfect hiss of steam comes out of the nozzle.

"Wow," he says.

"I know," I say. "It's like she's magic."

"All right, well, please call me if you hear anything," Julia says and then she slips her phone into her pocket as she rejoins us, but I can't help but notice that she looks a bit frazzled today - which means that there's a tiny crease in her forehead.

"Was that about the cups or the furniture?" I ask.

"That was the cups, but I also found out today that my table tops and table legs are in two different places, neither of which, as you can see, is here, and then to top it all off, they delivered the wrong chairs this morning and I practically had to arm wrestle the guy to take them back." She shakes her head. "I can't open without cups. And the reporter from the Winchester paper is coming tomorrow to take pictures and write a feature for the Stafford Falls section and we're not nearly set up."

"There's still time for the cups and everything to show up before you actually open," I say. "That's not for, what, three more days? And just ply the reporter with some really good coffee and he'll be eating out of your hand. He'll write about how great his cappuccino was, not that the tables aren't here yet."

"I suppose," Julia says. "But I need them to run a good picture, that's what people will notice."

"What if we took the couple of armchairs you do have and set them up by the front window? That would make a nice picture, with your logo on the glass."

Julia bites her lip as she thinks. "That *would* look good," she says. "Maybe with a little table. There must be something upstairs that I could use."

"I'll make you some coffees while you go look, if you want," Drew says. "Olivia, your usual?"

"Yes, please."

"Extra hot double shot lactose-free latté, coming up," he says. "Anything for you boss?"

"I'll have the same," Julia says, and she bends down and pets Mortimer who has been sitting at her feet, waiting to be noticed. "You guys come and help me sniff out a table upstairs."

The dogs and I follow her behind the counter and through to the back and it occurs to me that the dogs are going to miss coming in to visit when she actually opens, because probably the health inspectors take a dim view of people traipsing through food prep areas with flatulent Boxers and scavenging little Jack Russell terriers. We might be able to pass Ophelia off as a seeing-eye dog, but still, I think our days of backstage access are limited.

We follow Julia up the back steps to the little apartment above the café where she's been living, Lucy stomping and wheezing, Mort struggling to get ahead of her, and Ophelia, as always, guarding our back, and then at the top of the stairs, Julia suddenly turns, slips one hand behind my neck and kisses me - a long, sweet kiss that makes me stop breathing for a moment. It's surprising and insistent and the touch of her fingers on the back of my neck makes me shiver.

When she pulls away, she's smiling. "I'm really glad you came by today," she says.

I want to say something clever and witty, but find I can only grin like an idiot. She doesn't seem to mind, because she kisses me again and it's at least as good as the first one.

"So," she says, when she's done making my heart race, "do you see anything you like?" My head is still feeling a little spinny so it takes me a minute to figure out that she's talking about furniture and by then, she's started to wander around, sizing up every flat surface for something that could pass for coffee house chic in the Suckchester Gazette.

I haven't been up here before, although she'd told me that she was using the space as living quarters and I'd pictured something dusty and drab, but it's really more like a loft. There's the same reclaimed brick wall that's a focal point downstairs and big windows at both ends which make it bright and airy. There's a beautiful Japanese screen, behind which I see the edge of a bed with a starkly white and very puffy duvet and a little dining table and a couple of chairs, but the main feature of the room is a big desk that's stacked with papers and binders and files, and I can't help but wonder where she lived before she moved her things in here, and what exactly she gave up to come to Stafford Falls.

"What about this one?" she says. It's a little end table in a very dark wood with clean lines and I can immediately picture a tiny espresso cup on it. If she had any espresso cups.

"It's perfect. We should try it with the chairs, but I think it's the right size," I say.

She gets a dishcloth from the sink and gives the little table a quick wipe down. "All right," she says as she hoists it onto one hip, "Let's go see how Drew is doing with the coffees. Sometimes he needs a little help with his milk frothing."

I hesitate and she stops at the stairs and looks back at me. "What's the matter?"

"We need to have a proper date," I say, and it comes out a little more vehemently than I mean it to, but I'm on a roll now and there's no going back. "Preferably one that doesn't include my Nana or any of her friends. Much as I love her, I'd like some alone time with you."

"I like your Nana, too," Julia says. "But okay, for the purposes of a proper date, she's not invited. How about dinner out, someplace a little fancy?"

"We may have to drive to Suckchester for that," I say, "but I agree in principle."

She puts the table down and comes back to where I'm standing, surrounded by dogs. "Thankfully, we've got all that first kiss tension out of the way, so we won't have to worry about that."

"Yeah, that's a load off my mind. Thanks."

"Are you sure it was okay though?" she says, and she's standing very close to me again, and I can smell the soapy fruity smell of her hair, mangoes maybe. "It's been a while for me. I was worried that I might be a little rusty."

"I didn't think you were rusty at all, but if you want to try again..."

We practice until Drew yells up that the coffees are getting cold.

THURSDAY IS A PERFECTLY average day at Stafford Falls Public School - Tobey greets me with some inscrutable quote about Greek mythology, Kylie pitches a fit while we're doing phonics flash cards because she says Davis is making faces at her, (which he probably is, but damned if I can catch him at it,) and Miss Osgoode manages to convey a whole buffet of disapproval with one curt, "Good afternoon, Ms. Sutton."

And then at recess, while I'm on yard duty, everything goes pear-shaped. (Is there some expression that indicates a condition that is worse than 'pear-shaped?' For instance, 'ass-shaped?' Or 'steaming pile of dog shit-shaped?' Because there should be.)

The first indication that something is amiss is when I spot the giant circle of seventh and eighth graders forming up — it's never good when they travel in packs - and moments later I hear the universal chant of schoolyard bloodlust echo across the playground.

"Fight! Fight! Fight!..."

Carrie Bolton is usually stationed with the older kids, leaving me to run interference among the rug rats, but clearly something big is going down over at that end of the yard, so I abandon my post by the play structure and jog across the grass to the growing mob scene. I have to push my way in to the centre of the circle, shouting for everybody to break it up and back away. I might as well be spitting into a hurricane for all the good it does but I finally manage to break through the knot of kids and spot the two combatants. I'm not at all surprised to see Adam, but I am absolutely floored by the fact that Max McInnis is straddling Adam's stomach and whaling the crap out of him. Adam is splayed out on his back on the ground, blood gushing from his nose, and he doesn't even seem to be fighting back. Daniel is there, too, trying in vain to pull Max off Adam, but he's unable to even slow down Max's flailing arms. Strangest of all, though, is the fact that Max is administering this beating while crying - big, chest-heaving sobs.

"Max!" I shout. "Stop it!" I bound forward, grabbing blindly, only managing to get hold of his shoulder, and as he whirls around, he nails me in the mouth with an elbow. I stagger backwards, one hand reflexively clamped to my face, my eyes tearing up from the sting of the blow. Max is every bit as shocked as I am and we gape at each other for a few stunned seconds before he scrambles to his feet, shoves his way through the phalanx of spectators and disappears.

I consider running after Max but then I realize that Adam is moaning and rolling from side to side, holding his belly and I figure I should see if he's all right. This is when Carrie shows up, finally having tunnelled her way through the assembled mob, so I leave her to take care of Adam and I collar Daniel who's trying to fade back into the crowd.

"What happened?" I say, and maybe it's my tone of voice, or maybe it's the blood dribbling down my lip but Daniel is very forthcoming with details. Evidently there'd been an incident in class just before the kids were dismissed for recess. Zack's iPod had gone missing and someone said that they'd seen Max in the coatroom. The teacher asked Max to show her the contents of his backpack and sure enough, there was Zack's shiny little music player and his headphones. According to Daniel, Max had turned purple and started crying and had sworn that he hadn't taken it, and the teacher had taken him to the office at recess so she could call his mom. Instead of waiting around for the axe to fall, he slipped out to the yard, found Adam, tackled him and, in Daniel's words, "went bananas."

Carrie's broken up the crowd now and is helping Adam to his feet. I'm just about to tell her that I'm going to frogmarch Daniel to the office when I realize that Adam is looking right at me and he's smiling.

IT'S AN HOUR LATER, and Max is nowhere to be found.

Mr. Spaghetti and Miss Holly lead a class to class search, having a quiet word with each teacher as they go but it doesn't take long to realize that Max has vanished. Miss Osgoode stops chastising me about losing a student long enough to put in a quick call to the police and within minutes, a cruiser pulls up. I feel better just seeing the big guy in a cop uniform stroll in the front door, but I am a little surprised when he stops to greet Miss Holly with a peck on the cheek. Then I see the name on his jacket - "Mike O'Hara," - and I remember that this is Stafford Falls, so of course the town constable is the husband of my teaching assistant.

Mike the Cop runs down a quick list of things to do and places to look and it suddenly occurs to me that maybe Max went to his grandparents' house. I excuse myself and speed walk back down to the catacombs to my classroom so I can give Angie a quick call. I'm fiddling with the lock on my classroom door and hoping I can get her on the line before a police car pulls up in front of her house, when I hear a sniffle. I pause in the dim light and listen with my whole body. There is a faint wheeze coming from the dark space, way back under the stairs. I take a few steps in that direction.

"Max?" I say.

Another sniff.

"Max, are you all right? Everybody's really worried about you."

"I didn't mean to hit you," he says.

This makes me smile, which causes the little cut on my lip to sting, but I'm so relieved to have found him that I really don't care. "I know you didn't. It was an accident. I need you to come out and talk to me, though."

"I didn't take Zack's iPod," he says and his voice is flat and I realize that he doesn't expect me to believe him. And if I hadn't seen Adam's arrogant little grin, I probably wouldn't.

"I know," I say. "But right now, there are police cars out looking for you and one of them is going to your grandmother's house and if she thinks something has happened to you, it's going to scare the life out of her, so you need to come with me to the office so we can tell everybody you're okay."

There is a wheezy silence while he considers this.

"My mother is going to kill me," he says. "She said if I got into trouble one more time this year she's going to take away everything."

"She's just going to be relieved that you're safe," I say and he actually chuckles tearfully at this.

"She's going to kill me," he says, with finality.

I wait a little while, and then I can hear him weeping softly again. God, it's a lot of work being a twelve year old boy. "Max, come on out now," I say.

"Adam holds my head in the toilet almost every day," he says. "He dared me to steal Zack's iPod and I said I wouldn't and so every day he sticks my head in the toilet. I hate him. I hate him so much."

"You need to tell your side of the story, Max," I say. "I'll stay with you, if you want."

He cries a little bit more and then finally I hear him push some boxes out of the way and he emerges from the shadows. We trudge up the stairs in silence, side by side.

At least we've found him. The worst is over.

And then everybody's parents arrive and I realize just how wrong I can be.

I'VE KNOWN VALERIE BUTLER, Max's mother, since she started dating Angie and Alf's youngest son and I've never much cared for her. Even Nana, who rarely speaks ill of anyone, has been known to mutter darkly about her. She's loud and brash and I've always hated the way she speaks to Angie, criticizing every thing she says and belittling her for never having had a career. (Valerie is the "head receptionist" at a dental clinic in Suckchester and she always takes great pains to emphasize the heavy mantle of responsibility she bears - to hear her tell it, the oral hygiene of the entire city of Suckchester rests on her bony shoulders.) I don't like her for a whole host of reasons, but today, the fact that she marches straight into Miss Osgoode's office and pauses only long enough to give her son a withering look makes me long to slap her.

"What's he done now?" she says, and before Miss Osgoode or I can even open our mouths to answer, she swivels her gaze back to Max, who is slumped in a chair. "Do you know how busy I am this after-noon? Do you have any idea how hard it is for me to leave work in the middle of the day like this?"

If Max knows the answers to either of those questions, he's smart enough not to answer, and he continues to stare at his running shoes.

Miss Osgoode starts to explain that there was a problem in the classroom this afternoon, but Valerie cuts her off again to tell Max - completely without irony - to sit up and listen to the principal. Miss Osgoode tries to continue, but when she gets to the part about the iPod being found in Max's bag, Valerie turns on him again.

"You *stole* that kid's iPod?" she says, and I can only assume that the screechy notes in her voice are meant to underline her outrage.

"I *didn't*," Max says, but it comes out as more of a plea than a defence and he's starting to look like a cat that's being carried to the river in a burlap bag.

"Then what was it doing in your goddam knapsack?" she says.

"Mrs. McInnis," Miss Osgoode says, and even her soothing tones are sounding taxed, "it might be best if -"

"That's it!" Valerie says to Max. "That's it, you're out of hockey, I'm cancelling Christmas and that new computer you wanted? You can just forget it, mister!"

Miss Osgoode makes eye contact with me, shifts her gaze to Max and then to the door. I don't need a decoder ring to figure out what she means, or a push to get me going.

"Hey, Max," I say, "why don't you come with me and we'll…uh,… well, just come with me." I lead him out into the reception area and close the office door.

We sit in the bad kids chairs, listening to the only slightly muffled voices on the other side of the door. Mrs. Demanski stops typing long enough to wordlessly offer Max a tissue. He blows long and hard, then tucks the used tissue into his jeans pocket.

"I'm telling the truth," he says to me.

"I know," I say.

"Nobody else believes me," he says. "Why do you?"

Because our Nanas are best friends. Because there'd be no reason to attack Adam if he were guilty. Because this is exactly the sort of Machiavellian plan that Adam would dream up.

"I just do," I say.

There are staccato footsteps in the hallway - determined, Type A footsteps, the footsteps of someone on a mission.

We all look up to see a very tall, very angular man in a dark coat sweep into the office. He is impeccably dressed - double breasted suit, colourful tie and Italian loafers that probably cost more than my last paycheque.

"Hello, Mr. Prescott," Mrs. Demanski says.

"Where is my son?" he says.

Mrs. Demanski summons up a smile. "He's with Mr. Spinella. I'll just send for him." She picks up the intercom handset, says a few quiet words and hangs up. "He'll be here in just a minute."

"I would like to have a word with Mrs. Osgoode," he says.

"I'll let her know you're here," Mrs. Demanski says.

He glares at her, then looks pointedly at his watch, and quietly fumes. Max and I are pretty much taking up all the available seats in the office, so he stands there by Mrs. Demanski's desk as she picks up the intercom handset in slow motion to notify Miss Osgoode of her most recent visitor. Max is trying to make himself as small as possible, but I am busy searching this man's face for some resemblance to Adam and wondering exactly what sort of parenting style produced this particular chip off the old block.

Finally, Mrs. Demanski hangs up the intercom. "Please go right in, Mr. Prescott," she says and he marches into Miss Osgoode's office.

Mrs. Demanski, who is rising in my estimation by the minute, meets my gaze and rolls her eyes.

The next half hour is a medley of loud voices, recriminations, vague legal threats and assorted bickering. Eddie shows up with Adam in tow - he's making quite a show of holding his ribs, and is affecting a bit of a limp - and everything seems to get worse for a few minutes. A little later, Miss Osgoode's door opens and Adam's dad stalks out.

"I'll be taking this up with the superintendent," he says, pushing Adam ahead of him towards the exit. "And you," he says, stabbing a finger at Max, "you stay away from my kid, or I will have you charged and locked up. Do you hear me?"

Max goes pale and looks like he might wet himself, but seconds after Adam and his dad have left the office, Valerie McInnis stomps out, grabs Max by the arm and drags him out, too.

I try to think of something encouraging to say to Max as he leaves but I've got nothing.

And then -

"Ms. Sutton, could you come in here for a moment, please?"

Mrs. Demanski offers me a sympathetic little smile as I pull myself to my feet and trudge into the principal's office. Eddie is sitting down across from her, looking serious and not making eye contact.

"I'm giving Max an in-school suspension for three days," Miss Osgoode says. "Mr. Spinella will have him here in the office for the morning, but I'll need you to supervise him in the afternoons. I'd like you to see his teachers to arrange for him to have work."

"What about Adam?" I say.

"What about him?"

"Are you suspending him, too?"

"For what?"

"For bullying Max. For threatening him and sticking his head in the toilet. I know what Max did was wrong, and he should be punished but -"

"Ms. Sutton, I have approximately three hundred witnesses who saw Max tackle and repeatedly punch Adam," she says. "And I've got exactly zero witnesses who have ever seen or heard Adam threaten Max in any way, and before today, Max has never once reported this behaviour to a teacher."

"Max is scared of him. And speaking of witnesses, you've also got exactly zero witnesses who saw Max take the iPod."

"I'm not suspending him for stealing, I'm suspending him for his aggressive behaviour."

"But Max has done exactly what we're always telling the kids to do if they're bullied - tell a teacher. And now you don't believe him?"

"I didn't say that," she says. "But I can only act on complaints and incidents that have been observed by a credible witness."

I can tell from the rising colour in her cheeks that she's not enjoying having this conversation with me, but I'm in for a penny now. "Are you afraid of a lawsuit?" I say.

"Olivia, it's an in-school suspension," Eddie says. "He's not even going to miss any time. Under the circumstances, this is a very lenient decision."

I swing my gaze around to rest on Eddie Spaghetti, the boy who cried every day as we walked home from the first week of high school because someone in the boys' locker room had pointed out to everyone while they were changing that he had little man boobs. And I suddenly feel like I don't know him at all.

"It doesn't matter if it's lenient," I say. "Who's going to protect Max?"

"I am, Ms. Sutton," Miss Osgoode says. "I'm the principal. And as long as I sit in this chair, it is my job to protect all of the children. I don't have the luxury of playing favourites."

I am about to argue that it's not playing favourites to make sure that a twelve year old boy can pee without being assaulted, but even I can hear how pointless this debate has become. "Fine," I say. "I'll make sure Max has work. Is there anything else?"

"Not at the moment," Miss Osgoode says. "Could you please close the door on your way out?"

I am happy to oblige, even if I close it a little harder than it needs.

A string of muttered curse words is on the tip of my tongue, but I bite them back when I notice that Mrs. Demanski is still at her desk, watching me. I try to force a smile.

Mrs. Demanski offers me a little cellophane wrapped candy, and then gives me a stack of paper.

"Incident report," she says.

THE SUN IS WELL and truly set when I emerge from the school. There's a fingernail of moon and a few over-achieving stars making their appearances, and I can see my breath as I trudge out to my Jeep. It smells like snow is coming - that steely, clean smell that the air gets before the flakes start to fall. I've just unlocked the car door when I hear footsteps and Eddie Spaghetti calls out, "Olivia, wait up!"

Even filling out an entire ream of paperwork hasn't made me cool off much, and I just want to go home and wash this day off of me, but I wait while Eddie jogs over from his car.

"I didn't have a chance to ask you, is your lip okay? That's a nasty cut," he says.

"You should see the other guy," I say. "You know, the one you suspended."

"Why are you mad at me? This isn't my fault."

"I'm mad at you because you went along with it. You should've stood up for Max."

"I should have stood up for *you*, you mean," he says. "My God, Olivia, not everything Cynthia does is a personal vendetta against you, you know."

"This isn't about me," I start to say and then I falter. "Okay, it's a little bit about me because I can't help but think if Max had told anyone else but me that Adam was sticking his head in the toilet, she would have done something about it. But what I'm really pissed about is the fact that this kid is scared, Eddie - he's legitimately afraid of Adam - and you're not willing to cross Cynthia Osgoode to help him out."

"Jesus, give me some credit," he says. "I didn't just fall off the turnip truck yesterday. Do you really think I'm not going to be on top of this? I will be Adam's shadow until I catch him at something I can prove. But since you bring it up, yes, Cynthia Osgoode is my boss. I live and die based on her recommendation to the school board. It's easy when you're only going to be here for a few months to be all cavalier and piss her off at every possible opportunity, but this is my career."

Something about this really stings, and suddenly my lip is throbbing and I just really want to leave. I open the door to my sunshiny Jeep and heave my schoolbag across to the passenger seat. "I've gotta go," I say. I get in and start the engine, but he's got one hand on the door.

"Liv!" he says. "Come on! Let me buy you a beer."

"I've got to get home," I say.

I can see he's debating how far to push this. "All right," he says. "I'll see you tomorrow, okay?"

"Not if I see you first," I say and I pull the door closed.

NANA IS WARMING up a pot of soup when I arrive home and she calls out a cheery greeting, but when I come into the kitchen and she catches sight of me, her face falls.

"Oh my goodness, are you all right?"

"I was breaking up a fight in the schoolyard," I say. "It's not a big deal, I'm fine."

She regards me with a measuring gaze and what I've said apparently comes up short, because she starts shuffling around the kitchen with her cane. "You sit down," she says and in a series of trips, she brings me a couple of aspirin, some ice for my lip and a bowl of hot soup.

We eat our soup together and I sketch out the highlights of the day.

"Poor Max," she says, when I finish.

"Yeah, but don't say anything to Angie unless she brings it up, okay? I'm probably not supposed to talk about it outside of school and Adam's father sues people for sport."

"I know what will make you feel better," Nana says. "You should take the dogs for a walk."

My heart sinks in my chest. "Nana, I just want to take a bath and go to bed," I say.

She gives me a smile and then teeters off to get the leashes. "Oh pet, just go and see Julia," she says.

THE SECOND CHANCE Café is like a shining jewel in the night. Someone's taken the brown paper down from the windows and the golden light is streaming out like honey. Inside, I see Tenzin, a saffron beacon against the chocolate walls, and he's laughing and carrying around a big cardboard box. Julia is hovering over Drew who is squatting by the pieces of a little round table, wrestling with a power tool of some sort. He does not look like someone who knows his way around a tool box, and so it's probably good that Julia is pointing and giving instructions the way she is.

I want to just stand there in the shadows and watch everything going on for a while, but Mort will not be separated from the great love of his life, and so he bounds ahead and starts scrabbling at the glass with his little terrier paws. Julia looks up at the sound and then smiles when she sees who it is - my God, could you ever grow tired of that smile? - and she hurries to let us in. Her eyes widen when she spots my puffy lip but she ushers me in without a question and the feeling of her hand on the small of my back is at once comforting and disarming. For just a second, the weight of the day presses in on me so heavily that I think I might crumple. Luckily, I am distracted at that moment by Tenzin who is clapping his hands in delight at the sight of my three furry companions. I drop their leashes and they fly to him, Lucy's tough guy image forever shattered as she wags her stub of a tail and snuffles and snorts and tries to lick Tenzin's face.

Julia squeezes my hand. "Do you want to talk about it or do you want a glass of medicinal grape juice?"

"Grape juice, please," I say.

She nods approvingly and disappears into the back to procure what I really hope is wine.

It's only then that I realize that every flat surface of the café is covered in white ceramic glassware of varying sizes. They all have "Second Chance Café" in a lazy script, under a stylized black line drawing of a sunrise.

"You've got cups!" I say, when Julia returns.

"Isn't it great? *And* tables," she says, waving her hand at the assorted table tops and legs that are scattered around the cafe. "No chairs yet, but I'm feeling lucky."

Just then the drill that Drew is using to assemble the tables makes a shuddering, shrieking sound and he drops it as if it just shocked him. Which it might have.

"Drew, can I give you a hand?" Julia says and she puts her wine glass down and gets on her knees beside him to help brace things while he cautiously picks up the drill again.

The dogs have disappeared so I drift into the back to find them and end up in the kitchen with Tenzin who is standing at the big utility sink, wearing rubber gloves, up to his elbows in soap bubbles. There are tidy pyramids of espresso cups stacked to his left and several open boxes nearby.

"Dishwasher pipes broken," he says, with a sunny smile, as if this is a terrific development. "So, I am washing the new cups for Julia."

"Let me find a towel," I say. "I'll dry for you."

"I would be very much appreciative," he says. "In return, to thank you, I will teach you the secret to great happiness."

"Well, that sounds like a good deal," I say. I fortify myself with a swig of medicinal grape juice, grab a dish towel from a stack on the counter and take a tiny cup off the peak of one pyramid. "Okay, I'm ready. Hit me."

"The first step," he says, "is in washing the dishes."

I give him a look. "Seriously? That's your big Tibetan secret? Washing the dishes?"

He nods sagely as he dips a sudsy cup into the flow of water from the tap to rinse it and something about the way he does it reminds me of all the hours that Nana and I have spent together doing the washing up. Helping with the dishes was one of my first jobs - standing on a chair beside her at the sink, holding glasses and plates under the running water to get off all the soap. She would tell me stories while we worked and sometimes we sang show tunes, which is why I am one of the few people my age who knows the entire Cole Porter songbook.

"You know, I think my Nana would agree with you," I say. "She's always refused to get a dishwasher, even though I've begged her for the last twenty five years to buy one."

"I am thinking that your Nana is very wise," he says.

"So, the first step to great happiness is to wash the dishes. What's the second step?"

"Second step in secret of great happiness is this - when you wash the dishes, you must wash every cup, every spoon with the care that you would give as if you were bathing the baby Buddha himself," he says.

The image makes me smile - Tenzin, with his bright yellow rubber gloves giving a tiny newborn a bath, right here in the kitchen of the Second Chance Café.

"It must take you an awfully long time to clean up after a dinner party, Tenzin," I say.

This strikes Tenzin as spectacularly funny and he laughs so hard and long that Julia pops her head in to see what's going on.

"Everybody all right?" she asks.

"We are most fine," Tenzin says. "Most truly excellent."

"Tenzin is teaching me Buddhist secrets," I say.

"Enlightenment at the kitchen sink," he says and he laughs some more, a belly shaking laugh that floats up into the room like bursting soap bubbles.

CHAPTER 13

O Night Divine

Stafford Falls loves Christmas the way some towns love football.
If there was such a thing as a competitive Christmas league,
Stafford Falls would be ranked on the national level, that's how much
we love Christmas in the Falls. It starts during the first week of
December, when the local high school puts on a play, usually a musical, (this year it's *Annie*, and there have been posters of optimistic,
button-eyed redheads in all the shop windows for weeks) and then
there are spaghetti suppers and pancake breakfasts at one or the other
of the churches every week for the rest of the month to raise money
for toy drives and baskets of food for people who need a helping
hand. Naturally, there's some serious tree decorating - huge evergreens are set up all through downtown and local businesses sponsor
the cost of decorating the trees. There are ecumenical carol services
that rotate through the various churches and one year we even tried
our hand at a Living Nativity Scene but ended up having some significant livestock challenges — the firefighters were eventually able to
round up the donkey and the cow but by all accounts, there's still a

couple of rogue sheep on the loose somewhere between here and Suckchester.

But by far my favourite event has always been Stafford Falls' nod to our pagan friends, the Solstice Bonfire. Every year, there's a huge bonfire in the park down by the lake and there's drumming and music and food stalls and it's really just a great excuse to be outside on the longest night of the year, drinking heavily spiked hot drinks. I've only ever missed three Solstice Bonfires in my entire life: the year I had chicken pox and a fever of 104, the year my mother insisted on taking me to Rome for the school holidays (chicken pox was marginally more fun,) and my one and only Christmas with Alex, so I am pumped to be able to attend this year.

Life has been moving on at its usual petty pace. The Just Make Something Book Club, although not exactly blossoming, is perhaps at least budding - everybody except Kylie has moved on to using other media to make artistic representations of what they've just read. Wally is currently into clay and made a pretty ferocious grizzly bear the other day after reading a book about animals that hibernate. Unfortunately, Kylie bumped the shelf the bear was displayed on and now it looks more like a grizzly who's angry about having to wait to hear about getting prosthetic limbs. Wally handled it pretty well though, which infuriated Kylie as it seems to be her sworn duty to send at least one person into hysterics each day. The real champion though is Tobey, who, in addition to reading and writing like a pro, is now drawing elaborate family trees of the Greek gods in precise and colourful lines on the chalkboard. Even the other kids have started to notice and admire his work, but when they compliment him, he usually says, "He who is wisest, knows that he knows nothing," which, unfortunately, is a bit of a conversation killer.

Even Miss Holly seems happier, although it may just be the cappuccinos I'm bringing her everyday at lunch time, so she may not actually be more filled with joy, just more heavily caffeinated. Either way, it's a win because there's a spring in her step and she's keeping up with Tobey, who most days has got so much energy, it's like he's nuclear powered.

The only blot on this happy landscape is poor old Max who looks pale and tired a lot of the time and won't talk to me, almost as if he's been told specifically not to. I take Eddie at his word that he's shadowing Adam et al, but every day I find a dozen excuses to loiter near where the seventh grade boys congregate, just so that they all know that I'm paying attention.

The Second Chance Café has opened, if not to dramatic results, then certainly to a steady trickle. It might take a while for the denizens of Stafford Falls to truly appreciate the awesomeness that Julia is pouring into cups, but it has been busy enough that she's had to hire another staff member already, in the person of Samantha, the lovely, young single mom who babysat Pam's girls when they were here for the concert, and who is just so happy to be out of the house that she vibrates with a quiet zeal the whole time she's taking your money and ringing up the sale.

To Julia's great relief, the chairs did arrive, although only the night before she opened, and they proved so hard to put together that an emergency call had to be dispatched to Alf for help with the damn things. Alf, whose speciality for years was handcrafting teak decks for obscenely expensive sailboats, slapped them together in no time. Of course he refused payment of any kind from Julia, but did allow that he'd always wanted to try an espresso, and even though Angie keeps him on a strict decaf diet at home, Julia pulled him a shot and so now Alf spends a lot of time devising elaborate ways to sneak out to the Second Chance Café to have a tiny cup of very strong coffee with Julia.

Julia and I have had two official dates: one, a good old fashioned "go to the movies and hold hands in the dark" date, and one a fancy dinner out, although we nearly lost the reservation at Suckchester's best Italian restaurant because I made the mistake of going up to Julia's loft to pick her up and she looked so unbelievably gorgeous that one thing led to another and we had to drive pretty fast to Suckchester to be only a little late, but no complaints.

One of the nicest developments of the season is that Nana has re-instituted Sunday family dinners, a tradition that was a pillar of my childhood and that until now, I don't think I fully appreciated. There's usually a giant roasted piece of meat that keeps us in sandwiches for days, mashed potatoes, two veg with a proper dessert and, much to my grown up delight, some really good wine. It takes both of us to prepare it - that much peeling and polishing is still outside of Nana's abilities - and we get out the good china and the silverware and the linen napkins and it requires an insane amount of cleaning up after, but we take our time and enjoy the day. Julia has become a regular fixture at these dinners at Nana's insistence ("The poor lamb has no family here," she says,) and Penny Clarke often comes (she is the purveyor of the really good wine - she has strong opinions about French Burgundies and I am willing to listen to every single one of them for a glass of what she produces from her handbag,) and sometimes Angie and Alf drop by, usually with an elaborately iced cake that Angie just "whipped up" that afternoon. Lately Nana has been making noises about wanting to have Miss Holly over with her husband, Mike the Cop, and their two great, galumphing teenage boys. Nana remembers Mike the Cop fondly from when he was ten years old and used to come to the library and scour the shelves for Hardy Boys mysteries, but we haven't gotten around to inviting them, yet. I did, however, flatly refuse to have Mr. Spaghetti and his lovely wife Connie over for Sunday dinner - Eddie and I are back on speaking terms, but I'm still not thrilled with him. He has been making a point of dropping by my classroom a lot more though, and we all know it's not like it's on the way to somewhere, so I know he's trying, but I'm still annoyed with him.

I think what I like best about the Sunday dinners though is that it shows how much better Nana seems to be feeling. She's been able to reduce her physio appointments to three times a week, freeing up two blessed weekday mornings. Nana has insisted that for at least one of them, we have a civilized morning, so we take books and go to the cafe to sit and sip coffee and read. Sometimes I draw in my sketchbook, and Julia always comes and sits with us for a bit and when I watch Nana and Julia talking and giggling together, it's almost as if Julia has breathed new life into Nana, too.

She has not recovered a lot of dexterity with her left hand, but she's a trooper, practicing every day with her rubber bands and putty, doing all her fine motor exercises - lately she's working on shuffling cards, including fancy two handed ripple shuffles, most of which get away from her and send cards spraying everywhere much to Mort's delight, but she keeps at it because she can't wait to get back to her bridge club and is self-conscious about having to play Fifty-Two Pick Up when it's her turn to deal.

Her walking is much improved and she's managing quite well with her cane - it's hard to imagine her ever needing the rollator but she still seems a little frail to me, in comparison to the Nana from my memory - she of the quick, tireless strides in her sensible shoes. We walked everywhere when I was a kid, partly because she didn't drive, partly because it was Stafford Falls so you *could* walk everywhere you needed to, but also I realize now, partly because it meant time for us to talk, time to visit with the neighbours and admire their gardens; time to have a life.

IT IS BITTERLY cold for the first two weeks of December, far too cold to snow, but the lake freezes over and for one day it's a stunning, grey mirror. And then it warms slightly and the snow comes and suddenly it's as if the volume knob of the whole world gets turned down and everything is puffy and clean and softer somehow. It's also romantic and I catch myself daydreaming about long walks in the snow with Julia - there are cute red mittens involved and I'm wearing a hat that doesn't make me look like an escaped mental patient which hats tend to do to me, but hey, it's my daydream so I get to look good in my hat.

There's a nice snowy layer in place by the time the Solstice Bonfire rolls around, enough that I'm worried about Nana losing her footing down at the park, and I insist that we take her mothballed rollator with us, just in case. It is testament to how much she wants to go that she agrees without debate, so I load it and her into our lemony Jeep

and we head off for an evening of standing around in the cold, cele-
brating midwinter.

The place is a mob scene - Christmas fever is running high and
most of the town has shown up to see the fire chief light the huge
fire and then watch the orange flames licking at the velvety black
sky. We make slow progress once we arrive, because everybody we
meet wants to stop and chat with Nana but finally, we make it to
the Second Chance Café booth. Julia's stall is pumping out hot
chocolate that she's spiking with peppermint syrup, or for the really
adventurous, a slightly sweet chilli pepper syrup, as well as mulled
cider and plain old coffee. The smells coming from the area
surrounding her little piece of the park are enough to make your
brain explode with pleasure and there's a big lineup when Nana and
I arrive, but Julia herself is nowhere to be seen. Drew is there,
though, and he's run off his feet trying to keep up with the orders. I
move us to the front of the line, set up Nana's rollator and sit
her down.

"Hey, Drew," I say. "Do you need a hand?"

"Olivia! Yeah, that would be great. Julia had to take a phone call
and I'm getting slammed here."

I've handed out a couple dozen hot chocolates (to my surprise, the
chilli pepper syrup is selling well) when the crowd parts and I spot
Julia making her way back towards us. She looks sad somehow, even
as she's greeting the people in the line up for her stall, but she
brightens a little when she sees Nana. They talk for a while, or more
specifically, Julia talks, with a fair bit of exasperated arm waving and
matching facial expressions, and Nana is doing that slow nodding
thing she does whenever I'm ranting about something and she's
encouraging me to tell her all about what's wrong. This little exchange
goes on for some time, particularly considering the fact that half the
population of the Falls is standing in line, dying to get something hot
to drink, but by the end, Julia looks happier. She's smiling when she
arrives at the stall and sees me.

"Hey," Julia says, and she kisses my cheek. "Are you on the payroll
now, too?"

"Yes, but the good news is that I will work for hot chocolate," I say. "Is everything okay? You looked upset."

She bends down and rifles through a box, emerging with a long sleeve of white plastic cup lids. "I just got off the phone with my mother," she says. "My brother-in-law has decided at the last minute to take the boys to Scotland to see his family for Christmas and my parents are going, too, and my mother has just informed me that I'm being selfish because I won't drop everything and join them."

"Don't you want to go?"

"Sure, I'd love to see everyone but for crying out loud, I've just opened a business - I can't leave town for two weeks."

We're pretty busy for the next while, so much so that there isn't really time for conversation but it's gratifying to see so many people walking around with Second Chance Café cups. Nana insists on trying the chilli pepper hot chocolate and pronounces it delightful, then appoints herself as official greeter, sitting there on her rollator seat at the front of the line, telling everybody Solstice Facts while they wait for their hot drinks. She's just starting in on how the Roman feast of Saturnalia was related to the originally Germanic festival of Yule and is getting up quite a head of steam when I interrupt and take her aside for a quiet word.

"Nana, I want to ask you something," I say.

"Of course, pet, but first I wanted to tell you, I've invited Julia to join us for Christmas. The poor lamb's family is going away without her and so I told her to bring her things and that she'll spend it with us. Anyway, she seemed quite pleased to be invited, so I hope that's okay with you. Now what did you want to say?"

"I was going to say, is it okay with you if I invite Julia to come for Christmas, but as usual, you're one step ahead of me."

She pats my hand and gives me a sly smile. "Good for you, pet. Faint heart never won fair lady," she says. "Now, let's go see when the school band is going to play. I want to be in the front row."

IT IS such a relief to have some holidays from school - two weeks of not having to sound cheerful and positive about another phonics lesson, two weeks of not having to shrug off the heavy mantel of Miss Osgoode's disapproval - it is, in a word, sublime. And then comes my favourite day of the entire year, Christmas Eve, and Nana and I are both up early so that we can enjoy every single minute. We spend a long time lounging in the Flowery Room in our pyjamas listening to Ella Fitzgerald sing carols and talking about Christmases past - Nana tells me about when she was a little girl and money was in very short supply, how every single gift was handmade and how she cried with happiness the year that her parents bought her a doll from the catalogue. It was the most beautiful thing she had ever seen, with a china head and painted-on Delft blue eyes, and she's as excited as a little girl as she tells me about it.

We've got one or two last minute things to pick up at the grocery store and Nana buys a huge ham on impulse because Penny Clarke's brother and sister-in-law have gone on a cruise for their holiday and so Penny Clarke is having Christmas dinner with us and apparently the gigantic turkey that's brining away in the basement isn't going to be enough to feed the four of us, but I keep these thoughts to myself and tote the damn ham out to the Jeep for her. We spend much of the afternoon preparing the vegetables and stuffing for tomorrow's feast and making a couple of pies in case Julia doesn't care for Christmas Pudding, although how someone could not like a dessert that incorporates that much booze is beyond me, but I just do as I'm told, rolling pastry and carrying stuff up from the cold cellar in the basement.

The plan is to head over to the church for the Christmas eve service and have drinks and nibbles afterwards. The six o'clock service is Nana's favourite because it's the one where the kids do the Nativity story and you can always count on at least one magi who throws up half way through or a Virgin Mother who drops the baby Jesus. (The year I was eight and I played a shepherd, the whole cardboard manger backdrop came down on all our heads and everyone still thought it was a brilliant production.) Julia was hoping to close up shop around five and join us at church because I have assured her that it will be very entertaining, but the doorbell rings at four-thirty, sending the dogs into paroxysms of barking, and there she is, loaded down with shopping bags, snowflakes in her hair, smiling that smile that I am well on the way to finding irresistible. She just looks so happy to be here and in this moment, I am so grateful to her brother-in-law for jetting off to Scotland with the kids that I want to send him a thank you note.

"I hope it's okay I'm early," she says. "The café was deserted so I closed up."

"Come in! Come in!" Nana says as she wades through the tide of dogs to get to Julia and gives her a quick hug, then relieves her of one of her shopping bags. "Olivia, take Julia's coat, and Mortimer, you get down, you naughty rascal!"

There is so much wagging and sniffing of bags and furry bodies in the way that it's impossible to get Julia inside and out of her coat and finally Nana has to go shake the treat jar in the kitchen to lure all the dogs away, but finally we get Julia in and unpacked. She's brought the ingredients to make some fancy baked artichoke dip, a bottle of champagne, presents for under the tree, and of course three bags of organic dog biscuits, each with a different coloured little bow. Within minutes, she's been folded into the festivities, and Julia is telling us how, in her family, no Christmas Eve is complete without a viewing of *It's a Wonderful Life*, and Nana is confessing a life long crush on Jimmy Stewart and this is turning out to be the best Christmas Eve, ever.

THE ST. MARTIN'S Nativity pageant does not disappoint - one of the heavenly host spends most of the play with his index finger up his nose, despite the frantic waves of his mother from the third row, and two of the wise men get the giggles right before they are introduced to the Messiah, but the manger stays standing this year, so that's good. It's snowing harder when we leave the church, and everybody cheerfully trudges through the snow to their cars. Penny Clarke is coming over for drinks and she follows us in her car as we slowly make our way through the town on barely plowed streets, but luckily our bright yellow Jeep is really good on the slippery roads. We're just pulling into the driveway, and Nana is telling us how she can't wait to try the arti- choke dip and that she might even have a little thimble of champagne, when Julia says, from the backseat, "Are you expecting anyone?" and she points towards the house.

Someone is standing on the porch with what looks like an awful lot of luggage, but the light is dim and the curtain of snow is so heavy that I can't make out who it is. I open the door to get a better look.

Her voice cuts through the snow like a blowtorch.

"Where on earth have you been?" my mother says. "I've been waiting for hours!"

JULIA TURNS out to have yet another remarkable talent - she mixes a superb vodka martini with lemon twist - and I'm availing myself of the second one in what is probably too short a time, to help myself fully appreciate the awesome Christmas surprise that my mother has just delivered by showing up. Julia and Penny Clarke take over the catering duties while my mother regales us with tales of nearly missed connecting flights and sprints through airports with armloads of presents (of which I do not believe a word - my mother has never *sprinted* for anything in her life, especially not in Ferragamos, and the last time she carried her own luggage, I was in utero.) At one point, she compares her KLM flight to a cattle car, (she had to fly economy because she wasn't able to bully the girl at the ticket counter into an upgrade no matter how many fancy platinum cards she waved at her,) so then Penny Clarke tells us in a good-natured way about the 19 hour train trip she took from Jaipur when she was in India training surgical nurses and how it actually *was* a converted cattle car and how there were even people riding on top and chickens walking up and down the aisle, and for once, my mother has the grace to agree that that does sound worse than her watery gin and tonic and narrow seat.

Nana is clearly so delighted to see my mother that she's even a little weepy when they first embrace, and later, I catch my mother looking at Nana with an expression of such affection that if I didn't know better, I'd say my mother's tiny heart had grown a few sizes since last I'd seen her. Nothing like a cerebrovascular event to make you stop and take stock, I guess.

There's a dicey moment when my mother yanks me into the dining room and hisses, "I really wish you'd told me you were seeing someone!" but our little heart to heart is interrupted by Penny Clarke, who pops her head in to ask if I know where Nana keeps her soup tureen and even though there's no reason for anyone to need a soup tureen tonight, I hang off a step ladder to get it down from the top shelf of the cupboards, and it's only later when Nana winks at me that I realize she was trying to save me from a protracted interrogation on the topic of my love life.

And eventually, all the candles and the falling snow and the martinis conspire to make everybody just mellow enough for this to work and we are passing a semi-lovely evening, sipping and nibbling, and listening to Bing tell us how he'll be home for Christmas, when the doorbell rings. The dogs are baying like a pack of wolves at the front door and I have to shush them and shoo them away to actually get the door open, and that is when I catch sight of Alex standing there in the halo of the porch light, her cheeks red from the cold, a beaming smile on her face.

"Merry Christmas!" she says and she throws her arms around me and kisses me.

"What are you doing here?" I say, when I can disentangle myself from her. "You're supposed to be in London."

"You always told me how amazing Christmas in Stafford Falls is, so I came to see for myself," she says. "Look at you, you look fantastic! God, I must look a mess, I've been on a plane since - Christ, I don't even know what day it is. And my driver was a complete moron, we got lost twice between here and the airport."

"But, you're supposed to be in London," I say again, and this is probably not a good sign, this repeating myself.

"Olivia?" Nana calls from the kitchen. "Who's at the door?"

And all I can do is stand there and stare at Alex, because I can't make the words come. We've exchanged exactly three emails since she left for London, one of which was me confirming that we were in fact broken up, the other ones light, fluffy "I-am-busy-but-fine" missives that certainly would not lead you to believe that you were invited to come and visit. On Christmas Eve.

"Aren't you going to invite me in?" she says with a laugh, and I still don't answer because I hadn't actually realized that I had a choice, when suddenly, Nana is at my side.

"Good heavens, Alex, what a surprise!" Nana says.

"Merry Christmas, Mrs. Sutton," Alex says, a little too loudly, which is how she has always talked to my grandmother, as if she were a bit dim and more than a little deaf. "You're looking well!"

"Thank you, dear," Nana says. "Please, come in out of the cold!"

So Alex crosses the threshold, but it takes a couple of trips because she's got a lot of luggage and while she's ferrying her stuff from the porch into the house, Nana takes me aside and whispers, "Did you know she was coming?"

"If I'd known she was coming, don't you think I would have mentioned it?" I whisper back.

But for better or worse, my Nana is not someone who would turn you away on Christmas Eve, so Alex is welcomed into the fold and food and drink are thrust at her. She seems more interested in the drink, but at this point so am I, and thank God Penny Clarke picks up the martini making slack because Julia is looking more than a little perplexed by recent developments. Everybody knows each other, except for Julia and Alex, and Nana makes that introduction before I get a chance to, and thankfully she avoids going into titles and explanations that I don't want to discuss at the moment, such as, "Let me introduce Alex, Olivia's ex-girlfriend who let their car be repossessed and who decamped to another continent," or "This is Julia, a woman whom we're all absolutely smitten with and whom we wish Olivia would just call her girlfriend already."

We try to go back to our festive sipping and nibbling (although to be fair, some of us are taking bigger sips than others and wishing we could get refills, like, five minutes ago,) but the dynamics are just a little off now because Julia's being kind of quiet and Penny Clarke's eyes are darting around the room as if she's waiting to see who's going to blow first and my mother and Alex seem cozy, which really should have set off alarm bells.

And then someone mentions presents and this seems like a brilliant idea and so does another pitcher of martinis, and I volunteer to mix this batch because I'm going to sample the hell out of it while I'm alone in the kitchen and I'm just starting to think that maybe we're going to actually get through this clusterfuck of an evening - one ex-girlfriend, one meddling mother and a partridge in a pear tree - when Alex comes to join me.

Before I even know what she's doing, she slips an arm around my waist, buries her face in my neck and says, "It's so good to finally see you, Liv, I've missed you so much," and because she presses her lips against my ear and literally purrs these words to me, I jump a little and knock over the bottle of vodka that I was reaching for and a puddle of booze spills onto the counter. Then I'm bobbing and weaving, trying to free myself from her tentacles, but she's having none of it, it's like she's got three sets of hands and she just keeps saying, "Liv, listen to me, please just listen, we have to talk-"

"No," I say, and finally I manage to grab her by the forearms and push her back a step. "Trust me, Alex, we really don't."

"Please! I flew across an ocean to come and tell you this."

This jars me into a momentary silence. It's not just that I can't remember the last time that I heard Alex use the word please, it's the slightly unhinged look she has in her eyes which I don't think is just the result of too many trans-Atlantic drinks.

"All right," I say, and I cross my arms. "Say what you came to say."

She takes a moment to draw herself together, as if she's rehearsed these words and wants to get them right. "I've done a lot of thinking about where we went wrong," she says, "and I have come to the realization that it was largely my fault. You see, I think you were the first person I have ever been with who loved for me who I am, not for what I could give them or what I could do for them. You only ever wanted *me*, but I didn't know how to handle that and I ruined everything. And I'm sorry, Liv, I'm *so* sorry, but losing you has made me realize that I did not have my shit together and that's why I have been keeping my distance for these past months, because you deserve to be with someone who has her shit together. And now that's me. So I've come here on Christmas Eve to ask you to please come home with me."

"Come home with you?" I say.

She nods and her eyes are sparkling with anticipation.

"Alex, I am home," I say. "This is my home."

"I know, but not forever, right? Obviously your Nana still needs you but pretty soon, she'll be better and when she is and you're ready to come to London, I just wanted you to know that I've got everything set up. I've already got us a flat - it's in Notting Hill, but it's not too fancy."

"Alex, I'm not -"

"Wait, let me finish!" she says. "Liv, you need to be painting and I want to be able to give that back to you and so just before I left, I signed a lease on a studio space for you. It's absolutely gorgeous - big and airy and it's got brilliant light - you will be able to paint amazing things in this studio. And I've shown some of your work to a dealer who has a gallery in the East End and he is dying to see more. I think he might want to represent you and --"

Alex keeps talking and her words are coming faster and faster, as if she's some giant snowball that's rolling downhill but I can't hear her anymore because I am so distracted by the absolute lack of sound that's coming from the other room - Rosemary Clooney is no longer imploring us to fall on our knees and hear the angels' voices, and so I'm guessing the CD has stopped playing and there is a sucking vacuum of quiet now and I start to think about how the absence of noise can actually be louder than noise itself, and how every word of this slightly hysterical conversation is being broadcast into the Flowery Room and all of a sudden, I feel very, very sober.

"That's it," I say and I grab Alex's arm and drag her down the hall, out the front door and onto the porch.

"What the hell is wrong with you?" I say and even the heavy snow that continues to fall can't muffle my words. "That woman you just met tonight? Julia? We've been seeing each other for a couple of months now and I'm crazy about her and I'm very much hoping she feels the same way about me. And now you bust in here, uninvited, and go on and on about Notting Hill and studio space without even bothering to ask what I think about any of it and you think that means you've got your shit together?"

"But your mother said that you'd been - "

"I'm sorry, what?" I say and I hold up my hand to stop the tide of her words and I can feel the beat of my pulse in my temples. "Did you just say, '*your mother said?*'"

"Yes, we talked about it and she thought that you should -"

"Are you fucking kidding me? You wanted to convince me of something so you called my *mother*? Have you ever listened to anything I've ever said?"

And that's when Alex starts to cry and I freeze because I've never seen Alex cry, not in all the time we were together, not when she was being sued, not when her favourite aunt died, not when she had a kidney stone and actually passed out on the way to the hospital - emotional and physical pain were no match for her steely determination and her equally steely tear ducts. But now she's bawling like a little kid, covering her face with her hands.

"Nothing works anymore," she says, in between deep sobs, "nothing feels right."

"You're going to be fine, Alex. You just have to give it some time."

"I don't know anymore," she says. "I used to always know, but I just don't anymore. If you would just come back to London with me I could start -"

Fortunately, that half-assed thought is interrupted by the front door opening and my mother marching out onto the porch, because apparently she wants one more opportunity to share her opinions, but Nana is close behind her, insisting that she leave us alone to sort out whatever it is between ourselves, and of course right behind Nana is Penny Clarke, who is telling Nana to slow down and be careful not to slip on the snow on the porch. This little parade comes to an abrupt halt when they spot Alex and her tear-streaked face. My mother gives me one of her "What did you do now?" looks and actually tuts at me, but Nana is already on the case, shuffling across to Alex and putting an arm around her.

"You come inside with me, my dear, before you catch a chill. I'll make you a cup of tea," Nana says and then the three of them huddle up around Alex and hustle her back into the house. It is testament to Alex's weakened state that she allows them.

And then it's just me and the echoes in my head of this ridiculous conversation we've been having and I'm at the point where I'm beginning to wonder how much gas is in the sunny little Jeep and how far I could get on it, when the door creaks open again and out comes Julia, in her big puffy parka, with my coat over her arm. She crosses the porch to where I'm standing, and holds the coat for me to put on and then we both just stand there for a while, looking out at the falling snow which is coming down in fist-sized popcorn balls now.

After a while she says, "So, your ex-girlfriend is a bit intense," and it makes me laugh and loosens something that had become tightly knotted in my chest.

"I'm sorry," I say. "I didn't realize that tonight would be so crazy. I understand if you don't want to stay."

"Oh, I'm not going anywhere," she says. "It takes more than a little crazy to chase me away."

She reaches over and takes my hand in hers and it feels warm and comforting.

THINGS DON'T GET REALLY UGLY until Christmas dinner.

It's a perfectly lovely day, or at least I think it is - maybe I'm just giddy from the novelty of getting to spend an entire day with Julia. Alex is gone - Penny Clarke, who has a huge rambling old house and has secretly always wanted to run a B and B, dragged Alex home with her to spend the night in one of her guest rooms and the next morning, by the time we're pulling the tray of cinnamon buns out of the oven, Alex is already winging it back over the Atlantic. Everyone seems to have tacitly agreed not to mention the whole unfortunate affair, although Nana looks like she's biting her tongue a lot and is definitely keeping a sharp eye on my mother.

We all sleep late on Christmas morning, partly because we put away so many martinis, but also because we stayed up well past midnight to watch Clarence get his wings and George Bailey get his second chance. Everyone seems delighted with their gifts - Nana especially loves the Quaker Oats cookie jar which I found online and for which I did not have to eat a single spoonful of porridge. It's anyone's guess what my mother thinks I will do with a fuchsia sari, but I do like the little bronze statue that she's brought me - it's the figure of a man, dancing in the middle of a ring of little flames. He has more than the usual number of arms, which I think must be very helpful, and a really self-satisfied smile on his face. Nana tells me that it's a statue of Shiva the Destroyer, but I never get a chance to ask her what exactly it is that he destroys and why he's looking so smug about it.

The day passes blissfully and slowly, the hours marked mainly by the ringing of the doorbell and the resulting ballistic barking of the dogs as they rush to answer it. Mrs. Cameron from next door drops by for a quick shot of sherry and later Angie and Alf stop in on their way to Suckchester - they're delivering fruit cakes that Angie has spent the last six weeks marinading in booze - and finally Penny Clarke arrives with not one, but two bottles of wine - a red and a white, because, as she tells me, turkey is a tough call and not everybody appreciates the subtleties of a sauvignon blanc, but everybody always loves a good Beaujolais. I take her word for it and have both bottles safely stashed away before she can take off her coat.

The dogs follow Julia around as if she was wearing some sort of dog biscuit perfume, and Lucy even lets her tie a big red bow to her collar which makes her look quite festive. By mid afternoon, my mother, who is staggering a little from the jet lag, sneaks off for a nap and we break out the Scrabble board, which is great fun until Penny Clarke starts slamming down words like "caziques" on triple word squares and then it's down to her and Nana. Convoluted discussions erupt over the etymology of certain words, which is not an argument that you can win with someone who can read Middle English and speak with authority about things like 'the Northumbrian dialect,' but Penny Clarke gives it a go anyway.

I nip into the kitchen to check on the turkey and as I'm closing the oven door, Julia sidles up behind me, slips her arms around my waist and rests her chin on my shoulder.

"Did you know that zymurgy is the branch of chemistry that deals with fermentation in wine and beer?"

"As a matter of fact, I did, because my Nana is a rock star among Scrabble players," I say, and I turn and wrap my arms around her. "Are you having a nice Christmas? Apart from being trounced at board games?"

"I'm having a wonderful Christmas," she says, and she gives me a little squeeze and we stand there together, just feeling the heat of each other's body until my mother wanders in, up from her nap and desperate for a gin and tonic. Apparently, the sight of Julia and I canoodling in the kitchen does nothing to improve her mood which can best be described as prickly, but she says little and retreats to the Flowery Room with the drink I make her and doesn't reappear until the turkey hits the table.

Dinner is a minor masterpiece, served on Nana's best china. We've even broken out the Waterford crystal and every goblet catches the candlelight and makes the room sparkle. I feel foolishly, optimistically happy, and I am so lulled by obscene amounts of turkey, stuffing and wine that I don't even see it coming.

"It's a pity that Alex didn't stay," my mother says, and it's not so much the actual words she speaks as it is her blatantly faux casual tone that makes everyone pause, cutlery suspended over their plates.

"She's certainly missing a spectacular meal," Penny Clarke says. "Olivia, this turkey is a revelation."

"It's the brining process," Nana says. "I was skeptical, but Olivia had read about it in a cooking magazine."

"Alex always had so much ambition," my mother says, picking up her discourse as if we'd all begged her to continue. "I'm not surprised she moved to London, really. I can't help but think that the tastes of her clients here weren't evolved enough for her. The Europeans are a much better fit for someone with her kind of style."

I'm not sure which part of this little sermon is most out of touch with reality, the part where Alex leaves the country because she's too good for all the lowly peasants who want a bathroom reno, or the part where my mother has all these positive feelings about Alex, because she never expressed a single pleasant thought about her the whole time we were together.

There is a momentary strained silence, and then Nana says, "Olivia, would you pass the gravy, please?" and her words break the spell and for just a second, I think we're going to get past it, I think that we're actually going to get this train back on the tracks and continue having a nice time. But then my mother keeps talking.

"I think the thing that I most admire about Alex is her fearless-ness," my mother says. "Imagine the courage it takes, heading off to another country like that, to start up your own venture. It must be very exciting for her."

And that's enough.

"She's not starting up her own venture," I say. "She's been hired by some decorator who hates Alex's old boss. And it wasn't fearlessness, it was going into receivership and running away."

"I'm sorry, my darling, I shouldn't have brought it up," my mother says and she makes a face that is at once sympathetic and victorious. "Obviously, Alex is still a sore spot for you."

I open my mouth to reply but Nana beats me to it. "Clara," she says, a trifle sharply, "you must try the stuffing. It's quite delicious."

"No, thank you, Mummy, I'm not eating carbs these days," my mother says.

Penny Clarke says, "Julia, where in Scotland is your family spending Christmas?"

"My brother-in-law's family is in Edinburgh, actually, but they're going to do a little travelling in the new year," Julia says. "My nephews were pretty excited about going to Loch Ness. When I last spoke to them, they were hatching a plan to capture the monster."

"I love Scotland," Nana says and she and Penny Clarke start to reminisce about the trip they took a few years back to the U.K. and they are deep into a rapturous recounting of their tour of the gardens at Balmoral Castle when my mother turns to me and says, "Olivia, tell me - have you done much painting since you've been here?"

For a moment, I wonder how much she's had to drink, but then I remember that she's so convinced that the world would be a better place if people would just bow down and do her bidding that it probably doesn't matter how much gin she's guzzled, because she would probably behave this way stone cold sober.

"Not a lot," I say. "I've been pretty busy with school."

"Ah, yes, school. Have they offered you a contract yet, dear?"

"Well, not a permanent contract."

"So it's not a steady job."

"It's five days a week, so it's pretty steady," I say.

"But it's only part-time and it's supply work, isn't it? What's going to happen in June? Will you just be let go again?"

"Well, that's six months away, so -"

"I don't know why you accepted that position in the first place," she says. "Not only is it taking up valuable time that you could be using to paint, it's not even teaching *art*, which is what you profess to want to do. It's not taking you at all in the direction you want."

"No, Mom, I think it's not taking me in the direction *you* want. I'm quite happy."

"Well, forgive me for caring, my dear, but I can't just sit back and watch you just wander aimlessly through your life. You haven't got a steady job, you're not painting - what exactly is your plan, Olivia?"

At this exact moment, my plan involves jabbing a silver-plated pickle fork into her right eye, but I'm not sure I should share that with everyone, because it might ruin the festive feeling.

"My plan," I say, pushing back my chair and standing up, "is to go and heat the brandy for the Christmas Pudding. Can I get anyone anything while I'm up? More wine, maybe? I know I'd like some."

I gather up the empty plates and head to the kitchen, with my canine bodyguards trailing along behind. I've taken a series of deep breaths, counted to ten three times and am breaking up bits of turkey to give to the dogs when my mother appears, carrying her empty wine glass.

"I know you're angry with me," she says. "But I have such high hopes for you, don't you see that? It's only because I love you that I bring up these things."

"Look, I know it's not prestigious and world-changing, but I'm doing good work at that school, Mom. And I've helped Nana at a time when she's needed me. I've even met a really wonderful woman. What is so wrong with any of that?"

"What's wrong is that you're not thinking ahead, Olivia. Your grandmother isn't going to need your help forever - if it comes to that, she's not going to *live* forever - and then you'll have to decide what to do next. You are wasting your life in this one-horse town and you need to start thinking about where you are going to go after Stafford Falls." She locates the bottle of Beaujolais and pours herself some more. "And as for your new girlfriend, leaving aside the fact that she was crazy enough to walk away from such a lucrative job in order to come and serve coffee to the sad inhabitants of this little berg, the last thing you need is to get involved with someone who plans to actually stay here."

"That's enough," I say, and I close the fridge door so hard, I hear the contents rattle. "*I* will take your crap because I don't want to upset Nana on Christmas Day, but don't you dare say a thing about Julia. You don't even know her."

My mother appears utterly unperturbed by my snarly tone, which somehow makes me angrier. I'm just choosing my next salvo from a long list of things I'm probably going to regret saying when suddenly, there's Nana, shuffling in from the dining room.

"You know, I'm so full from supper, I think I need to take a little pause before we serve the pudding," she says and her tone is light and airy but she is staring daggers at my mother. "Olivia, you worked so hard to make dinner, why don't you and Julia go for a little walk? Your mother and I can do the washing up."

What's funniest about this - even funnier than the look on my mother's face - is that Nana still can't really do the dishes yet because she can't stand at the sink for that long without her cane, and most nights I do the cleaning up and she dries a few things and takes lots of breaks, so basically Nana has just declared that she's about to punish my mother by making her do chores. This is a delightful development and I'm about to ask if I can stay to listen to the lecture that my grandmother is no doubt about to give my mother while she watches her wash the good china, but then I spot Julia in the hall, and she's holding up my coat and scarf and giving me that smile that I can't resist.

"Thanks, Nana," I say and I kiss her on the cheek and Julia and I fly out the door.

And so I get my walk in the snow with Julia, and she does have red mittens which are adorable, and I do wear a hat that probably makes me look like an idiot but Julia doesn't seem to mind because she holds my hand as we walk through the snowy night.

And then she says, "Can I ask you something?"

"What's that?"

"How long has it been that you haven't been painting?"

She's so earnest and sweet and she's only asking because she really wants to know.

"Almost two years," I say and suddenly, I feel like I want to cry.

"Oh, sweetie," she says, and she wraps her arms around me and we stand there together in a pool of street light for a long time.

CHAPTER 14

Pointing at the Moon

Thankfully my mother has a better offer for New Years, so she's gone by the 29th which is a great blessing because we're all really feeling the close quarters by then and even Nana seems to be getting exasperated with my mother's prima donna behaviour - the last straw is when she makes a disparaging comment about Lucy's flatulence and voices are raised and people have to go to different rooms for a while to cool off.

And then in a blink, holidays are over, school is back in session, and we begin that long slog through those months when it seems like Mother Nature might be trying to do us all in. It's remarkably, bitterly cold for a ten day stretch in January and it is during this portentous bit of weather that the Spaghetti twins decide to be born. They're a tiny bit early, but according to Eddie's mom, whom we meet at the post office, the way they eat, they'll be caught up in no time. Once mother and children are home from the hospital, Nana and Angie and Penny Clarke prepare a big box of frozen casseroles and stews and muffins for me to take to the happy family so they don't have to worry about meals for the first little while and can focus on diapering, burping and sleep deprivation. Nana makes me deliver the care package even though Penny Clarke repeatedly offers to, because Nana knows that Eddie and I need to bury the hatchet - or as she said to me, "It's time to let it go, pet. He's your friend." And of course she's right and when I show up on their doorstep with boxes of food and two hand-stitched baby quilts, ol' Eddie Spaghetti gets a little misty-eyed, and frankly so do I, and it's not long before I've been invited in and am holding the tiniest human beings I've ever seen. Eddie even laughs when I ask which one is called Bolognese and which one is called Carbonara, so I think we're going to be all right again.

But the greatest godsend in this miserable winter is the Second Chance Café, which pumps out an unending supply of comfort in the form of hot, caffeinated beverages and a place to sit out of the blistering cold. Business is definitely booming since the Solstice Bonfire - people are still talking about the chilli pepper hot chocolate and there was such a demand in the weeks after Christmas that Julia has added it to the menu for the foreseeable future. When Nana's physiotherapy is reduced to two mornings a week, we immediately institute a second "coffee house morning" as Nana has taken to calling them, and it's not long before she's holding salon hours and hosting her extended circle of friends there, and is even involved in behind the scenes machinations to get the library board to permanently move its monthly meeting to "her" table at the café.

This particular morning, we've all settled in with our drinks, and Nana and Penny Clarke are discussing some irregularity in the scheduling of the jobs at the church luncheons - Penny Clarke suspects that this is the first shot being fired in a move by "that sneaky Charlotte Ramsay," to take over the chair of the Luncheon Committee, which has been Penny Clarke's purview since time immemorial. Angie is recommending some sort of scorched earth approach but Nana's advocating a more moderate, wait-and-see strategy. I'm only half listening, alternately scanning the horizon for Julia and leafing through a copy of *The Journal of Reading Education* that came for Mrs. Holt and got handed down to me - I'm skimming through "Gender

Differences and Self-Esteem in Reading Achievement," which I think proves how desperate I am for a good idea.

Essentially, the problem is that my reading group kids seem to have gotten a little bored with the "Just Make Something Book Club." The initial excitement to create things has faded and they're kind of phoning it in now - except for Kylie, who was already phoning it in, so now she's pretty much drooling and staring at the ceiling. I'm trying to think of something that will spark their interest again but I just don't know how to compete with SuperZombieVision in 3D or whatever Disney/Pixar digital hullabaloo that has just come out that week. I'm just the mean lady who wants them to memorize their spelling lists and who forces them to read words with more than three letters, because I think that might be a useful job skill someday.

"That looks like very serious reading," Angie says to me, when there is a break in the war council. "Is it for school?"

I tell her it is and I sketch out the problem I'm having getting the kids interested in reading.

"It's a miracle they have any attention span at all," Angie says. "They're just always plugged into a screen. Do you know that the vans they sell now have television screens in the back seat?"

"I suppose the parents like it because it would keep them quiet in the car," Nana says. "But really, when do they have a chance to read or daydream?"

"Our Max spent the weekend with us last week and the battery ran out on the little video game that he plays and he'd forgotten the charger at home," Angie says. "Well! You'd think the world was coming to an end! Finally, Alf made him come out to his workshop and they built a little bookcase together. Do you know he enjoyed himself so much that now he's constantly asking Alf what they can build next? Yesterday Max was trying to convince him to draw up some plans for bunk beds."

Penny Clarke launches into an "in my day" sort of speech, the kind that involves reminiscing about walking ten miles uphill and barefoot in a snowstorm to school, but I'm not listening because I'm thinking about Max and Alf and how there's nothing like the excitement of getting your hands dirty and how doing something in real life is a thousand times better than reading about it and how I can possibly use that fact to make my kids want to read.

Which is how, two weeks later, I find myself driving to work with Nana and Mortimer to launch "Anything Can Happen Day." Mortimer has had a bath and is wearing the new collar that Nana insisted we buy him for the occasion - it's a jaunty red plaid that even I have to admit looks nice against the brown spots on his back. I am having second thoughts about all of this, but especially about our choice of canine ambassador - I thought we should bring Ophelia, who, despite her constant worried expression, strikes me as the most steady and reliable of Nana's three dogs and therefore the best choice to visit small children who are likely to accidentally poke her in the eye, but Nana insists that Mortimer is the man for the job. He's shameless and will do literally anything for a biscuit - including wearing his Hallowe'en hot dog costume, which Nana has stashed in a shopping bag, to break out in case things get dull. And to give Mortimer his due, he genuinely does seem to enjoy kids. He's very good about stopping to let them pet him whenever we're out walking - by comparison, Lucy Boxer just glares at the kids until they slink away and Ophelia is always too busy scanning the street for highwaymen and other potential dangers to just enjoy the attention the kids give her.

Also, and perhaps most definitively, Isabelle reminds me that she is afraid of black dogs, so Mort it is.

The brainstorming session in which Isabelle expressed an interest in dogs ("My mommy said we can't have a dog because she's allergic and she says they eat their own poo and they're disgusting, but I would still like a dog and I would teach him tricks,") yielded some fascinating results. Spurred on by Isabelle's dog request, Davis allowed that he'd always wanted to ride a horse and since I know that Penny Clarke has some contacts in the equestrian world, I put that on the list, too. Miss Holly says she's always wanted to learn how to bake bread and that seems doable and might be an eye-opening experience for them, a sort of "slow food" thing, so I write that on our big chart of fondest wishes. Then I tell everyone that I've always wanted to learn to meditate - I've been reading a book on meditation for kids that Julia found for me and I'm so desperate to try to get them to focus that at this point I'll try nearly anything, up to and including standing on my head - and they all seem a little underwhelmed by that. But then Kylie gets us back in the spirit by saying she wants to know more about Jacques Cousteau, which at first seems a little eccentric but eventually I figure out that she's after something in the neighbourhood of marine biology and I decide to go with that.

As usual, Tobey is a little more cryptic. When it's his turn to contribute, Tobey, who lately has been watching a lot of *Professor Milo G. Hound's Race Through History* says, "Cassandra warned the people of Troy not to let in the big wooden horse," so I write down that he'd like to make something related to Ancient Greece, and we decide to work out the details later.

Wally is much more specific. "I want to learn about things that explode," he says.

"You mean, like, rockets?" I say.

"Do they explode?" he asks.

"Sort of. When they take off."

"Okay then, rockets. So long as they explode."

"I'll see what I can do."

But for today, for our first "Anything Can Happen Day," I have a (hopefully) non-exploding dog and my grandmother, who may very well be more excited than the kids.

It's snowing again today and maybe that makes the room feel so cozy, or maybe it's the warm light from the funky lamps that Miss Holly found at the thrift store or the cocoa coloured carpet that Penny Clarke gave us for the kids to sit on at circle time, but whatever it is, all that's missing is a crackling fire in the hearth. And, I suppose, a hearth.

We've come a long way from Institutional Beige and cracked linoleum.

The kids are bouncing like ping pong balls when they arrive and only get more wound up when they spot Mortimer, who, to his everlasting credit, stays seated beside Nana and just watches them, his shiny black eyes scanning them for the possibility of treats. Eventually, though, Miss Holly and I get them all seated on the carpet in front of Nana's rocking chair.

"Everyone, I'd like to introduce my grandmother to you," I say.

"*You* have a grandmother?" Kylie says. "But you're old."

"Everybody has a grandmother, stupid," Davis tells her.

"Davis, let's use nice words today," I say, "and yes, Kylie, even though I'm very old, I have a grandmother."

"My grandmother lives in Florida," Wally says.

"Good for her," I say. "So, this is my grandmother, Mrs. Sutton, and her dog, Mortimer."

Isabelle's hand shoots into the air.

"Yes, Isabelle?"

"Mortimer is a Jack Russell Terrier," she says.

Mortimer's ears, such as they are, twitch up at the mention of his name.

"Ew, what happened to his ears?" Kylie says.

"I found Mortimer hiding under my porch on a very cold night," Nana says. "He was very thin and I'm not sure how many nights he'd spent outside, the poor little fellow. So I took him to the veterinarian right away but he had been in the cold so long that he had frostbite on his ears. Do you know what frostbite is?"

"It's like when your fingers freeze off," Kylie says.

"Yes, it's like that, and the vet had to operate on his ears to save them." Nana strokes Mort's head as she talks, and Mort closes his eyes in bliss. "But let me tell you, he sure didn't like wearing bandages on his ears after his operation. He was always trying to take them off with his paws." Nana makes little swiping gestures near her ears and the kids laugh a bit and then Wally pipes up: "I wouldn't like to wear bandages on my ears either!"

"I think he looks kind of cool with his ears like that," Davis says. "It makes him look special."

"Did it hurt? What the vet did to him?" Kylie asks.

"Probably a bit," Nana says, "but thankfully the vet also gave me some medicine to give to him to make him feel better. And now he's a very happy dog, aren't you, Mortimer?" She looks down at Mort and makes a twirling motion with her finger and suddenly Mortimer is up on his back legs and dancing in a little circle. The kids are delighted at his little doggie two-step and they laugh and applaud. Another sign from Nana and he sits again like a proper little gentleman and she slips him a treat.

It is not at all lost on me that this is the same creature whom I can barely walk on a leash and who frequently drinks out of my coffee mug when he thinks I am looking the other way.

"Now, I was told someone had a report to give," Nana says.

Isabelle is on her feet in a flash, and she comes to stand beside Nana, clutching a huge piece of construction paper. It took her two days to choose the colour - was brown more of a 'dog colour' than blue? Would Mortimer mind if she picked pink, her favourite colour, even though he was a boy? Eventually she decided that green was a good compromise, green being sufficiently "doggish" and "masculine" I guess and now she holds it up to show everyone her work. The poster is entitled *Things You Ned To Do To Tak Car Of Yur Dog*, and she has cut out photos from magazines and pet store flyers of leashes, dog bowls, dog beds and tennis balls as well as a whole passel of very happy pups, who are clearly enjoying being well taken care of. The poster is divided into four boxes which she has labelled Food, Exercise, Sleeping and Love, which covers it nicely I guess, but what's most impressive is that she's written a sentence or two in each box, to explain what you need to do do have a well-adjusted dog, including my favourite, "*You shud walk your dog three time a day. So he dose not poop in the house.*" But since she's the girl who couldn't read the word "you" the first week we met, I have decided to be completely blind to her creative spelling and I'm totally putting this one in the win column.

After Isabelle has read us all the sentences on her poster, everyone claps for her and she flushes with pride, then Nana enlists Isabelle to help put Mort through his paces. He sits on command, he rolls over, he jumps in the air, the little ham even gives Isabelle a high five and of course the crowd goes wild. Then Nana asks if they would like to hear

a story and the kids think that's the best idea *anyone* has *ever* had, so
Nana pulls out a picture book called *Gavin Finds His Forever Home*,
which is about a dog that nobody wants to adopt and who has to wait
for a long time at a shelter while all his friends go home with little
boys and girls. Mortimer settles himself in the middle of the pack of
kids while Nana reads and he is petted ferociously the entire time. We
even go overtime and when the bell rings to signal the start of recess,
nobody moves, because they're still so busy questioning Nana about
Mortimer's likes and dislikes and looking at pictures of Lucy and
Ophelia that they can't be bothered to go out to play.

Finally, I have to put an end to it because they have to go back to
their regular classroom and I'm worried that Nana will be tired out,
not that she's showing any signs of slowing down. Everyone shakes
Mortimer's paw before they leave and beg both me and Nana to allow
him to return again.

Tobey is the last to get moving and he stays on his knees on the
carpet for a long time, petting Mortimer. Eventually, at Miss Holly's
prodding, he stands up, but instead of following Miss Holly to the
door, he walks towards Nana as if he's drawn there by a string. He
leans against the arm of the rocking chair, eyes downcast, then
reaches out to touch Nana's hand. His tiny fingers trace the map of
wrinkles and veins on the back of her hand as if he is touching something fascinating and precious and then he leans his head a little
closer and says, "Socrates says that the unexamined life is not worth
living."

"I couldn't agree more," Nana says.

FOR THE NEXT WEEK, every single person we meet - at the grocery
store, at physio, even random pedestrians in the street - has to stop
and hear the story of Nana and Mortimer's visit to the Community
Resource Class, as told by Nana, with special emphasis on Isabelle's
exceptional presentation and all the children's impeccable behaviour.
It is testament either to the kindness of the people of Stafford Falls, or
at least to the high esteem in which they hold my grandmother, that

every single one of them listens intently and appears charmed and delighted. Meanwhile, at school, I am barraged daily by the kids to "please, please, please let Mrs. Sutton and Mortimer come back again." Even Miss Holly weighs in, suggesting that it might be a good thing for Tobey, since not only did Mort seem to have a calming effect on him, but without prompting, Tobey had engaged Nana in conversation, something which rarely happened. "I don't know, maybe it's some sort of special grandmother vibe," Miss Holly says, and that clinches it - it is decided that once a week, Mort and Nana will come to read a story. Of course the person who is most excited to hear this news is Nana and she immediately begins planning out what books she'd like to read to the kids and dreaming up thematic costumes for Mort to wear.

IT'S mid-February and it feels like it's been quite a while since Julia and I have been able to sneak off for a real date - between the demands of school, shovelling the damn driveway (which I seem to have to do three times a day) and things getting busier for Julia at the café, it's been hard to find a time when we're both (a) free (b) alone and (c) awake. I express this frustration to Nana one morning as I'm fixing us breakfast.

"Then you have to make the time," she says as shuffles across the kitchen, cane in one hand and a brooch she'd like me to help her pin on her sweater in the other. "Call her right now and see if she can go out tonight."

"She's probably busy. She's had a lot of retreat centre stuff lately," I say.

Nana gives me that look she used to give me when I was a teenager and she wasn't buying my bullshit, a sort of grandmotherly gimlet eye. "Call her," she says. "Even if she's too busy, she'll know that you wanted to see her and that will count for something, won't it?"

I can't argue with that sort of logic, especially before I've had any coffee, so I pin on her brooch - it's a pretty amethyst number because she always likes to look nice for physio - and she takes the spatula from me to man the stove while I go find my phone. It's a couple of rings before Julia answers so I know I'm calling in the middle of the commuter rush, but when she answers I can hear in her voice that she's glad I've called.

"I won't keep you long," I say, "but I really want to see you and I wondered if you could sneak away from your piles of work tonight."

"I can't," she says. "Bea is coming this afternoon and we're meeting one of the investors out at the retreat centre to go over some numbers." There's a pause and I can hear the clatter of glassware and the whoosh and gurgle of milk that's being frothed. "Hey! Why don't you come with us?"

"I'm not sure how much help I would be going over the numbers," I say. "I doubt I can count as high as you can, since I haven't had any of that fancy accountant training."

She actually laughs at that and for a moment, I realize how lucky I am to have met this woman.

"No, really, you should come," she says. "Tenzin is back from New Mexico and he's been asking about you. He could give you a little tour of the place while I have my meeting, and then Bea is staying over out there, so we can drive back to town together and if it's not too late, we could stop by my place for a while." I can hear the smile in her voice. "I'm prepared to throw in a latté, to sweeten the deal."

"Is that your plan? To seduce me with delicious espresso drinks? Because I'm a little ashamed to admit how effective such a plan might be."

She laughs. I love that sound.

"We'll pick you up at five," she says. "And dress warmly. They still haven't installed the new furnace in the main cabin."

I'm grinning like the love sick fool that I obviously am when I return to the kitchen. Nana's face lights up when she spots my smile.

"I take it you're going out this evening," she says.

"I am. We're taking Bea out to Six Perfections so they can meet with some investor," I say as I get the plates from the cupboard and bring them to the stove to load them with our breakfasts. "I'm gonna hang with Tenzin, but then I think I'll get Julia to myself."

"Well, the first part doesn't sound as romantic as I was imagining, but the second part has promise." Nana slides an egg and some bacon onto each plate then gives me a sly smile. "Try to stay out late, would you?"

"I'll do my best."

"I think I'll call Angie and see if she wants to come over for tea and a chat tonight," Nana says. "She's been feeling a bit down, lately, I think."

"Any news about Alf's pension?"

"None that's good, I'm afraid."

I make my way through the wall of wagging dogs to the table with our plates. "I feel bad for them," I say. "They worked really hard their whole lives, they deserve to get to take it easy now."

"They do," she says, as she settles into her chair across from me and pours cream into her coffee. "And something will work out, but in the meantime, we have to keep their spirits up."

I ponder her words for a moment, but before I can ask if she has any specific spirit-lifting plans in mind, I am distracted by the gallery of yearning faces lined up beside the table.

"No," I tell the dogs. "I'm not sharing my bacon today."

They stare back, the three saddest dogs in the world, right here in our kitchen.

"Really. I'm eating all of it myself," I say.

Giant drool bubbles begin to form at the corners of Lucy's mouth, and Ophelia somehow manages to look disappointed and worried at the same time. Mort just stares laser beams at me.

I cave and give them each a little morsel of bacon, then try not to make eye contact with Nana.

"And people say I'm the soft touch," she says.

IT TURNS out that the anti-freeze line in the Second Chance Café van is, in actual fact, frozen ("I know," Julia tells me, "I've had the mechanic explain it three times and I don't get it either,") which prompts a flurry of late afternoon phone calls and in the end, I'm the one picking people up in my sunny little Jeep. Bea is dressed as if she is headed on an Arctic expedition and Julia insists that Bea sit up front which is good because I'm not sure that both Bea and all of her parka would fit in the tiny backseat of the Jeep.

Six Perfections is outside of Stafford Falls, a thirty minute drive on twisty roads that follow the contours of the lake. Bea, a lifelong city dweller, thinks this is a terribly exciting thing, driving out of our tiny town and into the woods that surround Stafford Falls and even though it's dark, she spends most of the drive peering out the windows, exclaiming at the snow-draped evergreens and the glimpses of the frozen lake. It's strange and lovely to see Stafford Falls through the eyes of someone who didn't grow up here, someone who doesn't know the gritty underbelly of our little Arcadia and it makes me wonder which one of us has a more accurate picture of the place.

However, she does seem at once very interested in questioning me about myself and yet quite well informed about various aspects of my life and this suggests to me that Julia has been talking about me. Suddenly I'm very curious and I want to find out what Julia might have said, but since I'm busy driving and this isn't high school, I refrain from passing her a note that says "Does Julia like me? Check yes or no."

"So who is it you're meeting with?" I ask.

"His name is Jamie Buckley. You're going to love him, he's a great guy," Bea says.

"And he's financing the retreat centre?"

"His foundation is the major backer," Julia says.

"He has a foundation?" I say. "Just how rich is he?"

"His business cards say, 'Internet Gamer and Bajillionaire,' but I'm not sure that's a precise figure," Julia says. "Although it's probably not far off. He made a lot of his money in video games. You know, the ones that let you be a knight or a wizard and you run around killing dragons or whatever."

"And how did he come to be interested in your retreat centre?"

"It was his idea, actually," Bea said. "He came to see me a few years ago, he was having terrible panic attacks, the poor guy - it had become a daily thing. He contacted me and I did some sessions with him. Eventually he joined my meditation group and now, as he says, he's all 'Buddhisty.'" Bea is grinning as she says this, the way you might smile when recalling a particularly naughty but endearing child.

"Oh, Bea, that makes me think of the first time that we met," Julia says and the two of them burst into peels of laughter.

"I'm sorry to laugh, honey," Bea says. "I know it was a tough day for you."

"Go ahead, laugh," Julia says. "It was pretty ridiculous."

"Oh, but you were suffering!"

"Okay, now you have to tell me," I say. "How did you two meet?"

"We met at the hospital while my sister was getting one of her marathon chemo sessions," Julia says. "She was in this clinical trial for an experimental drug but it required whole days of treatment, so we made up a schedule, you know, so that there would always be someone there with her. I had pulled a middle shift that day, so I had snuck out of the office for a few hours and brought her some lunch. Then, right about the time that I was supposed to go back to work, my heart started to race and I was sweating and I couldn't catch my breath - it was awful."

I can see her face in the rear view mirror and there is a strange mix of sadness and amusement there.

"Anyway, I didn't want Rebecca to know that I was having a heart attack or whatever, so I tore off to the bathroom and barricaded myself in a stall, to try to pull myself together. And then I hear the door open and a little voice says, 'Julia? Are you okay?' It was Bea, who had just arrived and Rebecca had sent her after me. But of course, I can't answer her because I'm hyperventilating and tears are streaming down my face and that's when it actually hits me - I'm not freaking out because I am sitting with my sister who is slowly dying from a terrible disease. I'm freaking out because I have to go back to the office."

"You poor dear," Bea says.

"Do you remember what you said to me?" Julia says, and she leans forward and puts her hand on Bea's shoulder.

"I do," Bea says and pats Julia's hand in a way that makes me think of Nana, and the two of them smile. "I said, 'My darling girl, is this the life that you want to be living?'"

"I'm so glad we met," Julia says.

So am I.

THE ENTRANCE to the old Boy Scout camp is a bit tricky to spot in the dark but when the Jeep's headlights wash over the Tibetan prayer flags that are strung among the bare branches of the trees like brightly coloured laundry, I know we've found the spot. The driveway is long but thankfully well plowed and soon we emerge from the trees into a clearing. There's a very fancy car parked nearby but it's the huge log cabin structure ahead of us that really steals the scene. It's clearly old but really well preserved and more than anything, it's just big - more of a lodge than a cabin, really. I can't imagine how many trees were felled to build it and it's got two storeys and a huge field stone chimney from which is emanating the welcoming smell of woodsmoke.

The door opens and out steps Tenzin, waving and sporting a fine New Mexico tan. "Hello!" he hollers at us and then he giggles in sheer delight. "Welcome to Six Perfections!"

I NEEDN'T HAVE DRESSED QUITE SO warmly because it's sweltering - Tenzin has half a tree burning in the hearth - and so we all spend the first while peeling off layers until we can stand the heat. Jamie is on his phone in another room when we arrive, so we have time to hear about Tenzin's trip to his home monastery in the mountains near Santa Fe, although he feels the best part of the trip was the mother and baby he shared seats with on his flight back. The baby was fussy and the mother obviously exhausted because halfway through the flight, she finally just passed her mewling infant off to Tenzin, who made amusing animal noises for him for the rest of the trip, until the baby fell asleep in his arms, drooling blissfully all over his monk's robes.

And then Jamie is finished with his call and he comes to greet us. He's not what I expected a bajillionaire to look like, but the expression of adoration on his face when he wraps Bea up in a hug makes me like him immediately. He's a weird mix of boyishness and greying computer nerd, and he keeps one arm protectively wrapped around Bea as Julia makes introductions.

"So *you're* Julia's artist," he says and he shakes my hand with enthusiasm, and somehow that title makes me a feel more than a little bit pleased. "I'd love to look at your work sometime. I've been trying to learn about art and I'd like to start seriously collecting." He tells me about some of the pieces that he's recently acquired and it sounds like he's getting some good advice on buying. It also sounds like he has an absurd amount of money. "I was also wondering if I could pick your brain about developing some sort of an artistic vision for this place," he says.

Tenzin waves his hands to interrupt. "There will be no brain picking until we have had our supper," he says. "The picking of brains is very bad for digestion."

Tenzin is very excited about serving us supper it turns out, because he has brought back a load of dried chilies and special corn flour and a whole host of ingredients that aren't easy to find outside of New Mexico and has spent the day slaving in the kitchen, and soon we're all seated around a huge harvest table digging into trays of enchiladas that are smokey and gooey and I think might be the harbinger of some sort of new and unanticipated style of fusion cuisine: Tibetan-Mexican.

Shop talk inevitably intrudes, even as we shovel food into our mouths, but I don't mind because I'm starting to see the size and scope of what Six Perfections is going to be, and it's going to be amazing. Bea and Jamie have a vision for the place that extends well beyond what I'd imagined - which to be fair, was pretty much a bunch of tree-huggers sitting on meditation cushions, ohmming their way into mellowness. This is going to be a multi-faceted place and they're foreseeing hosting corporate team-building sessions, having yoga and tai chi camps and writer's colonies and stress management courses.

"It's ambitious," Bea says, "but it's also exciting. There's a real need for a place like this. A sort of hub for learning and wellness. I think it's a really wonderful idea." She pats Jamie on the arm and the bajillionaire actually blushes a little.

"It's going to have quite an impact on the town, too," Julia says, to me. "It will create some jobs, naturally, but also lots more visitors. It could extend the tourist season to year round traffic."

"Fortunately, there'll be a place in town for all those people to get fantastic coffees," Jamie says.

"There won't be if you don't hire a proper accounting firm, soon," Julia says. "You and this project are seriously cutting into my barista hours, mister."

"But I like working with you," Jamie says. "You always seem to know what I want before I want it."

"And that's exactly the kind of job description that I left my last job to avoid," Julia says. "This week, I'm sending you the names of three firms I recommend. You need to choose one."

"What if I double your paycheque?" Jamie says, and there's a sparkle in his eye, but I'm not entirely sure he's kidding around.

"You can triple it if you want, but I've still got better things to do with my time, James." She says this with a sweet smile, and for just a second, I wonder how many people there are in the world who ever say no to this man and his terrific piles of money.

Thankfully, Bea steers the conversation back around to the plans for building and soon they're all talking about the eco-friendliness of the upcoming construction and I learn more about wastewater, sustainable landscaping and preserving groundwater aquifers than, strictly speaking, I really need to. This leads to Julia and Jamie both pulling out their laptops and they're just getting into a fine game of duelling spread sheets, when Tenzin turns to me and says, "I am wondering, Olivia, if you would like to see the bees?"

"Isn't it a little cold for bees right now?" I say.

"Oh, the bees are sleeping. But they will not mind if we peek at them," he says with a conspiratorial grin.

I could use a walk in the fresh air, having recently eaten half my body weight in enchiladas, but as Tenzin and I pull on our boots and coats, it suddenly occurs to me that he's wearing some pretty flimsy robes for a stroll in the depths of a Stafford Falls winter.

"Tenzin, will you be warm enough without - well, you know, pants?" I say.

He grins and pulls the hem of his maroon robe up his shin a little to expose a few inches of waffle fabric.

"Thermal underwear," he says. "Very clever. Very warm."

He struggles into his parka and then he pulls a jaunty little toque over his bald head - a red and blue striped number with a puff ball on top that looks exactly like one that Angie might have knitted for Max - and the outfit is complete.

We holler goodbye to the board of directors who are deep into a conversation about the comparative costs of rainwater harvesting systems, and then we step out into the night.

It's the kind of still, clear cold that hits you in the lungs and it's so quiet, you can hear yourself breathe. The forest all around us is naked and dead and silent. The moon is a sliver short of being full and there are bluish shadows on the snow where it's casting its cool light. It's haunting and peaceful and I want to stand there and somehow draw it all inside of me.

It takes a little while to strap on the snowshoes, and a little longer still to get our strides - Tenzin takes a spectacular tumble when he gets the hem of his robes tangled in his snowshoes - and then of course he has to recover from the gales of laughter that accompany his fall - but soon enough we're on our way, shuffling through the drifts, following a path through the woods. We pass a couple of smaller cabins as we go, and he points out where things are going to go - the meditation hall, the guest cabins, the meeting rooms, the gardens - he is particularly excited about the prospect of raspberries. The property is huge and varied and there are forests to walk through and big sloping lawns that lead to gorgeous views of the lake.

"Natural setting is very good for learning and healing," Tenzin says to me as we puff our way up a hill to a little ridge. "Helps to focus the mind."

At the top of the ridge, we pause and Tenzin indicates the empty field of snow before us with tremendous pride. It doesn't look like much - about a dozen hives are lined up at the edge of the field and each one is a wearing a little snow hat, but Tenzin beams at the sight of them, so very fond of his slumbering bees. The lights of Stafford Falls are way off in the distance, little twinkles, maybe imaginary.

We look up at the blanket of stars. Tenzin points a gloved finger at the moon, which is bright and clear and close.

"Tomorrow is full moon," he says. "Very auspicious day. We will open Six Perfections on a day of full moon. Much luck. Much positivity."

I can't remember the last time I've heard this kind of quiet. There is a contagiousness to it, and it makes everything inside me very still.

CHAPTER 15

It's a Small, Small World

It's lunchtime and I'm sitting in my cozy little Mediterranean themed classroom, keeping Tobey company while he eats his sandwich, a process that involves methodically taking apart all the constituent pieces of bread, ham and cheese, laying them out on a napkin and eating them in a complicated order that I have not yet deciphered. I'm simultaneously trying to engage him in conversation and scrolling through pictures of fish tanks on a site named something like CheapAssFishTanks.com, and I'm just beginning to seriously rethink this whole aquarium-in-the-classroom idea because who knew that a big glass box could cost that much, when Eddie pops his head in the door.

"Oh, so you're here," he says and he sounds vaguely disappointed.

"Nice to see you, too, Mr. Spaghetti," I say. "Tobey, look, it's Mr. Spaghetti. Can you say hi to him?"

"Hi, Mr. Spaghetti," he says and then he puts a tiny piece of ham into his mouth and chews thoughtfully.

"Good to see you, Tobey," Eddie says, and he collapses into a chair at the table with us.

"To what do I owe the pleasure of such an underwhelming greeting?" I ask.

"I was hoping you weren't here yet," he says. "I was going to call you and ask you to bring me a quadruple espresso from Julia's when you came in."

"You've still got twenty minutes before the afternoon bell. You could make it to the café and back in that time."

"There is an excellent chance that I would fall asleep at the wheel," he says, and he lays his head down on his crossed arms.

"Who's keeping you up, Bolognese or Carbonara?"

He lifts his head to give me an incredulous look. "They never sleep, Liv. They just never sleep. I mean, one of them will sleep, sure, for like fifteen minutes, but as soon as one drifts off, the other one wakes up. I love them more than life itself, but it's like they're a tag team who are trying to kill me with sleep deprivation and really foul poop." He lowers his head. "And I think I did a stupid thing this morning."

"Probably. What did you do?"

"I might have said something to Connie about how it must be nice to be able to stay home all day and not have to go to work."

"Oh, Eddie," I say. "You didn't."

"Yeah, I did," he says. He sits up and rubs his face with his hands, as if he wishes he could wash away the memory of it. "Except I didn't mean it the way it sounded. I meant it like, you know, it's good that she's home and maybe she could get some rest."

"You said that to the mother of your two month old twins?"

"In my own defence, I was really, really tired at the time."

"Wow. You are such an idiot."

"I know."

"It might be smart to show up with flowers, when you go home," I say. "And not the kind from the grocery store. The real kind."

"Good tip," he says. "Hey, do you think Julia would make an espresso delivery? Just this once? There are serious extenuating circumstances."

"Oh, yeah," I say, "I'm sure she'll drop everything during the lunch hour rush and scream over here with some coffee for you because you're a bit tired. You should totally call her."

"I bet she'd do it if you called," he says, and he grins and does this eyebrow waggling thing that makes me want to smack him in the face with a big book. "Hey, are you looking at aquariums?" he says, angling my laptop towards him so he can check out the screen.

"Yeah, Kylie wanted to know more about Jacques Cousteau and scuba diving, so I'm going to set up an aquarium and we're all going to research fish. Except I didn't realize it was all so complicated. Maybe I'll just get a big glass bowl and spring for a goldfish instead."

"You can't do that," he says. "That's a terrible environment for a fish."

"I beg your pardon?"

"If you're going to get fish, you have to take care of them properly."

"Okay, mom," I say. "I promise to take them for walks every day."

He seems to be choosing not to hear me because he carries on as if I haven't spoken. "I can hook you up with a used tank - I recently upgraded to a fifty gallon salt water tank so I don't really need my little twenty gallon one anymore." He spins the laptop around to face him and starts typing and scrolling. "I've got a spare heater and I think I've got some extra gravel hanging around somewhere, but we're going to need to find you a filter system -"

He completely loses me for a while here because he's extolling the virtues of something I think is called the Shit-Skimmer 2000 and how it's worlds ahead of the old Shit-Skimmer 1000, but then he turns back to me and says, with great earnestness, "What did you have in mind in terms of plants?"

"I wasn't going to bother with plants," I say.

"You have to have plants," he says, as if I'd just suggested I jump out the airplane without my parachute. "You need it for the water chemistry and to give the fish shelter and a sense of security."

"Well, I certainly wouldn't want to make the fish feel insecure," I say. "But couldn't I just get a little treasure chest or something? Surely the little devils could hide behind that when they feel the need for some alone time."

He shoots me a look that says he'd really appreciate it if I would please take this more seriously, and then he begins to lecture me on the role of plants in the aquarium's ecosystem and soon is in quite a lather over phosphates and nitrates, and what will happen if I let the latter take advantage of the former and how it will all result in rogue bands of algae staging a revolution in the tank.

"But if you buy your fish from Phil, I can probably get him to throw in a few plants to get you started," he says, at the end of this little botanical diatribe.

"I'm sorry, who's Phil?"

"My fish guy. In Winchester."

"Oh, of course, Phil the Winchester Fish Guy," I say. "Tell me one thing, though."

"What's that?"

"How is it that I've known you this long and still, I had no idea that you were a gigantic fish nerd?"

"Perhaps instead of making fun of people with fascinating hobbies who are about to do you huge favours, you should be dialling your little phone there and seeing how fast your girlfriend can get some really strong coffee to the front office."

Out of the blue, Tobey laughs and we both turn to look at him, surprised. "Fish nerd," he says, then he laughs again and picks up a little square of cheese and nibbles the edges to a perfect circle.

THE WINTER SUN is low on the horizon by the time I'm strolling down the sidewalk to the Second Chance Café and it's giving everything long, cool shadows. I'd forgotten what winter in Stafford Falls was like, how cold it was and how much snow there was, but also how beautiful it could be. It's anything but stark, especially in the timeless twilights - those stretched out moments after the sun has set and all the orange has finally leaked out of the sky, and what's left is a water-colour wash of deepening blues: cobalt, ultramarine, indigo. It's as if the whole world has just stopped and given a giant, cosmic sigh and I love to stand at the picture window in Nana's kitchen and just look at the sky on days like this. I suddenly wonder what Tenzin would have to say on the subject of twilight, and as I swing open the door to the café and take my first hit of coffee bean infused air, I resolve to ask him next time I see him.

The café is half full - the comfy furniture is occupied by a quartet of young guys who could best be described as proto-hipsters, and who have been showing up a couple times a week to play what look like ridiculously elaborate board games and drink syrupy espresso drinks. They're friends of Drew's - he sometimes joins them to play when he's not working, and when he is working, he's often hovering at their table in between customers, telling them "Guys, you can't just sit here for hours, you've got to order more stuff!" Apparently, they come all the way from Winchester to hang out at the café and play games and they imbibe so much caffeine that I'm surprised they don't fly home.

In another corner, I spot Nana with Mrs. Skipper, who is the head librarian at the Stafford Falls Public Library and if Mrs. Skipper has a first name, I don't know what it is. As long as I've known her, I've only ever heard anyone call her Mrs. Skipper, including her husband, Mr. Skipper. There are stacks of colourful catalogues on the table between them and judging by the looks of delight on their faces they're spending more of the money that the string quarter concert raised. I give Nana a wave and make my way to the counter to see Julia, leaving them to their happy shopping.

Julia, on the other hand, looks less than pleased. She's leaning on the counter, her delicate little chin cupped in her perfect little hand, watching Drew's gamer friends, and looking decidedly glum.

"What's the matter?" I say.

"I'm having a pastry crisis," she says.

"I'm sorry, a what?"

"They don't like my baked goods."

"Who doesn't like your baked goods?"

"Those guys. Drew's friends."

"But they always order cookies and things, don't they?"

"Only because Drew forces them to. But they never finish anything they order. And today, I brought them over a plate of muffins, on the house, and it's still sitting there. They haven't even touched them." She shakes her head. "They're 20 year old boys. They'd eat asbestos if you put frosting on it, but they won't touch my muffins?"

Several licentious and witty comments spring to my mind, but the look of distress on her face causes me for once to pass on the clever joke and try to just be a sensitive listener.

"If I'm ever going to expand into sandwiches or even little breakfasts," she says, "I need the food to stand on its own and I'm afraid that the stuff I'm serving is not good enough."

"Okay, so you might be having a pastry situation," I say, "but you did make an exhausted new father very happy today. Not to mention most of the staff of my school. Thanks for sending Samantha with the coffee and treats for everybody. That was way beyond the call."

She waves away my words. "It's just good advertising in a small town," she says.

"Well, it was a big hit. Everybody talked about it all afternoon - some of them even mentioned it to me and most of them can't give me the time of day."

"Did anyone mention what they thought of the pastries, though? Because I think the the bakery is over baking the cookies and that's why they're dry. And the muffins are sort of crumbly, they should have more-"

I reach across the counter, take her hands in mine and make her look at me.

"You're obsessing a bit," I say.

"I don't want to be known as the woman with the substandard pastries."

"I think you're known as 'the woman that saved us with her lattés.' Isn't that enough?"

"Olivia, I'm serious," she says, but there's a twinkle of a smile lurking there, because apparently I'm irresistible. "But since it looks like your Nana is pretty busy with that guy, do you want to come upstairs for a while and help me take my mind off my baked goods?"

"What guy?" I say and I turn to look and see a man hovering over Nana's table. He's about my age and is wearing a very fancy overcoat which immediately makes him stand out in this town because that coat says, "I don't spend a lot of time in the cold," whereas most people in the Falls are dressed as if they're just on their way to the lake to do a little overnight ice fishing. He's smiling at Nana, all pearly white teeth, and holding her hand as if he just shook it but now is refusing to let it go.

"Wait, I know that guy," I say.

"Of course you do," Julia says. "That's Tyler Cooke with an 'e.' At least that's what it says on all his real estate signs."

A dim recollection of seeing his business card tickles at the edge of my brain but before I can put my finger on it, Nana spots me watching them and starts to look decidedly uncomfortable.

"Just a second," I tell Julia and I weave my way through the tables and chairs to Nana and her slippery new friend.

"Olivia!" Nana says as I approach, and is it my imagination or are her eyes darting around as if she's looking for an escape route?

"Hi," I say and I stick out my hand. "I'm the granddaughter."

Tyler Cooke with an 'e' swivels to face me and graces me with a smile so bright, it's a wonder I don't get a sunburn. "Of course, the granddaughter! I've heard so much about you!" he says and he does one of those two-handed handshake manoeuvres where his right hand is doing the shaking and his left hand is gripping my bicep with such affection it's as if it's all he can do to keep from flinging his arms around me and hugging me. I can't help but notice that he has meticulously manicured hands that are unbelievably soft and part of me wants to ask him what sort of moisturizer he uses. The other part of me wants him to get away from my grandmother though, and I decide to go with that part.

It's as if I've telepathically communicated this to Nana because even before I can say a word, she's ripping catalogues out of Mrs. Skipper's hands and jamming them into her public broadcasting tote bag.

"Well then, I must be off. We can finish up tomorrow, if you don't mind, Mrs. Skipper," Nana says, but she doesn't actually wait to hear whether or not Mrs. Skipper minds because she's already on her feet, yanking on her coat and searching for her cane. I haven't seen my grandmother move this fast since the time I stepped on the wasp's nest when I was seven. "It was lovely to see you, Mr. Cooke," she says and then she's in motion, headed for the door. I have to scurry to keep up and we're half way to the door before I can wrestle the tote bag away from her to carry it, but then she slips her arm through mine and we step out into the cold night.

"I was going to bring the Jeep around for you," I say.

"A little walk will do me good," she says.

"Well, watch your step, it's icy," I say. "Nana, was that guy bothering you? Do you want me to tell him to leave you alone?"

There is a strange mixture of amusement and something I can't quite place in her expression and then I feel a little silly for having suggested that she might need protecting. This is, after all, the woman who stared down an entire church hall full of her "narrow-minded neighbours" (her words) when the first woman vicar was appointed to St. Martin's. My grandmother stood up and told her friends and neighbours in no uncertain terms that anyone who didn't like the situation was invited to leave and that she would be right there at the back of the church, happily holding open the door for them.

"Oh, you know how real estate agents are," she says. "They're always trying to drum up business, I suppose."

"I guess so. But don't let him pester you if you're not interested."

"Oh, pet, look at that sky!" she says. "Isn't it beautiful?"

"It is."

"How was your day? Did you give Wally that book about knights that I found?"

And then she starts telling me about how she thought she might have the kids make little puppets to act out the story she's reading to them the next time she comes to my classroom, and how she saw a flyer advertising a sale on sirloin tip roasts and that we should pick an extra one up for Angie, and long before we get home, Tyler Cooke with an 'e' is forgotten.

LATER, just as I'm finishing up the dishes and I'm deep into a train of thought about Julia and pastries and oddly enough, what fish need privacy for, the doorbell rings. The dogs tear through the house in their never-ending competition to be first at the door, and a deft move on Mortimer's part sends Lucy sliding on one butt cheek into the dining room chairs and then angry dog words are exchanged and I need to take a minute to break that up, so it's quite a while before I actually get the door open, which is when I discover Alf standing there, his tartan cap in hand.

"Alf?" I say, and it's just so strange to see him without Angie. He seems incomplete somehow.

"Evening, Olivia," he says. "I'm sorry to drop in unannounced. I hope I haven't disturbed your supper."

"No, not at all, I was just cleaning up," I say and I nudge Mortimer back into the house with one foot. "Is everything all right?"

He ponders this for a moment, fingering his cap and frowning slightly. "Truth be told, I need some advice."

"Come on in, I'll get Nana," I say.

"Uh, well, it's your advice I'd like, actually."

"Oh," I say and this surprises me about as much as if he'd asked if I'd like to go ballroom dancing with him, but I try to rally. "Come on in."

Nana shuffles into the hall as I take Alf's coat and they exchange pleasantries while the dogs sniff his pant legs with as much enthusiasm as if he was wearing meat trousers. Nana shoots me a questioning look as she shepherds Alf towards the kitchen but I don't know what's up either so all I can do is shrug.

"Can I get you a cup of tea, Alf?" Nana says, and when he hesitates, she's quick to add, "or maybe something stronger, to warm you up?"

"I suppose I could have a wee drop, Violet," he says. "If it's no trouble."

Nothing is too much trouble for this man who single-handedly keeps Nana's house in repair and Nana pulls out the really good stuff

that she keeps in the cabinet in the dining room and I am dispatched
to find the lowball glasses, but soon enough, the three of us are seated
around the kitchen table, sipping miraculously good Irish whiskey
(from the Sod itself and rumoured to have been made by angels or at
least monks) and Alf is telling us that Angie thinks he's at the curling
rink.

This is when I know it's really serious because Alf has come here
on his curling night and he would rather cut off his right arm than
miss curling. Also, he's taking quite a risk not being upfront with
Angie because by noon tomorrow, at least ten people will have called
her to ask if Alf is okay because he missed curling.

"I feel terrible doing this behind Angie's back and all, and I'm
breaking my promise talking to you but I've thought about it and I
really think it's the right thing to do," he says. "The lad needs help and
I'm not sure how to help him."

"Which lad?" I ask.

"Our Max," Alf says.

"Is he okay?"

"Oh, he's not ill, but I'm very worried for him. Only it seems the
situation at school has gotten quite bad. That boy Adam has made
things pretty miserable for him."

My heart sinks at his words. I've been trying to keep an eye out for
Adam and his posse but short of setting up a guard post in the boys'
lavatory - which I have seriously considered - it's been almost impossible to single-handedly guarantee Max's safety. The fact is, I've hardly
seen Max in the past few weeks and I'm pretty sure he's been actively
avoiding me.

"He didn't want to tell me," Alf says, "even though it's been
apparent for months that he's not himself. I've been making a point of
having him over to work in the shop with me, you know, to build
some things, maybe take his mind off his troubles." He heaves a big
sigh. "Well, it took some doing, but I finally pried it out of him and it
seems that it's just become a fairly constant stream of harassment."

"What did Max say was happening?" I ask.

Alf looks down at his hands and it suddenly occurs to me how much like his grandson he is. "A certain amount of it is just boys being boys, you know, name-calling and talking with their fists. But some of it seems…well, a bit abusive, if you ask me, like they're trying to humiliate him. Someone squashed ketchup packets in the pages of his textbooks and another time someone peed in his winter boots. Most days someone steals his lunch he says, but once, they'd put dog turds in his sandwich." Alf takes a sip of his whiskey, as if to fortify himself. "Some of it is happening on the walk home, which I understand is outside of the school's authority, but still. Last week, apparently they hit him in the kidneys so hard, their was blood in his urine that night."

"Oh, the poor child," Nana says.

"Ordinarily, I'd teach the boy how to throw a good punch, because there's nothing a bully dislikes so much as the sight of his own blood, but Max is terrified to fight back because this boy Adam's father is a lawyer and apparently he's convinced Max that if Max so much as touches him again, not only will he be sent to some sort of children's prison, but Adam's father will make sure Peter loses his job."

"And Max believes him?" I say.

"Completely. Although to be fair, Adam's father is the town solicitor and Peter's computer business has several contracts with the town, so I suppose it's not outside the realm of possibility."

"Alf, I'm so sorry," I say. "I had no idea it was so bad. I'd been trying to keep tabs on things but I guess I've been missing a lot."

"Oh, it's not your fault, Olivia. Max is trying to cover it up because he doesn't want anyone to know. But the thing is, I'm worried for him. A person can only stand so much abuse and I'm afraid he's going to do himself a harm." Alf is looking pretty miserable himself right now, absently rubbing his thumb on his glass. "He only talked to me because I promised him I'd keep it to myself and now I've gone and betrayed his confidence. I don't know if he'll ever trust me again. I just didn't know what to do and so I thought I'd ask your opinion, Olivia."

My opinion is that the lunatics are running the asylum, and that it's high time that the adults in this situation put a stop to that.

"I think we need to call in the big guns, Alf," I say.

I make a quick phone call and find out that, as a matter of fact,

Holly O'Hara isn't busy at all and would love to come over for a glass of Nana's finest Irish whiskey.

VERY EARLY THE NEXT MORNING, Miss Holly and I are sitting in our subterranean classroom, sipping cappuccinos from the Second Chance Café and nibbling on the blueberry scones that Julia insisted we try, even though it means there will be an inquisition later regarding our impressions of the scones's moistness or lack thereof and their relative strengths and weaknesses as a pastry experience, but I'm in love and will do nearly anything to put a smile on that sweet face, so I bought a half dozen damn scones.

"So, you really painted that painting in the café?" Miss Holly says. "That's by you?"

The whole time I was ordering our coffees, Miss Holly had stood in front of *The Studio*, the painting that Julia had picked from my portfolio to hang in the café, studying it like there was going to be a test later. *The Studio* is a view, not surprisingly, of a studio where I'd worked a few years back, in the great tradition of just painting what's in front of you. I'd done it in exaggerated cool tones, melancholy blues and greys and it contrasted the golden glow of the café quite nicely.

"Yes, that's one of mine." I dole out little butter and jam packets for our scones, which are, I'm sorry to say, a bit dry.

Miss Holly looks at me as if she's just seeing me for the first time. "If I could pick up a paintbrush and make something that looks like that, I don't think I'd do anything else all day long but paint."

"The painting part is a lot of fun," I say. "It's the 'selling things' part that's a pain in the ass. But if you ever wanted to give painting a try, I'd be happy to teach you some stuff."

"Oh, I can't draw," she says. "Even my stick people are pathetic."

"People always say that, but it's not true," I say. "Anybody who can learn to write in cursive lettering can learn to draw. You just need a little instruction and some practice and you'd probably be amazed at what you can do."

"I don't know," she says. "I don't think I could make something that looks like what you did."

Just then, we hear heavy footsteps in the stairs and a moment later, Mr. Spaghetti appears in the doorway, grim-faced and red-cheeked from the pre-dawn cold. He peels off his coat and throws himself down in a chair. I slide a cup of coffee and a scone towards him the way one might offer a fresh carcass to a particularly cranky carnivore, but Miss Holly just laughs at him.

"I'd ask if you got up on the wrong side of the bed, except you don't look like you've gone to bed yet," she says. "Rough night?"

He takes a long drink of coffee and then fixes her with a stare. "They do eventually start to sleep through the night, right? I mean, someday?"

"They do," she says. "But then they start teething. And then there's toilet training and chicken pox and monsters under the bed and broken arms and then you can't sleep because you're wondering how you're going to pay for the braces they need and then there's university tuition to think about and then they start driving..."

He gives her a hard look. "When can I expect to get a full night's sleep again?"

"I'll let you know as soon as I have one."

"You're not helping," he says and he takes another long pull on his coffee "Okay, what's so important that I had to come meet you this early? Because I could still be sneaking a nap in the shower right now."

Miss Holly looks at me expectantly.

"I had a visitor last night," I say and I tell Eddie Spaghetti everything Alf told me, and to his credit and despite his extreme fatigue, Eddie listens carefully to every word, systematically munching his way through a pair of scones as he does so. He even winces a little at some of the choicer bits that I recount.

"That poor kid," Eddie says. "I didn't realize. I'd been trying to keep an eye on Adam, but..."

"I'll say this for Adam," Miss Holly says. "He's very good at what he does."

"Yeah, he's a bit of an evil genius, isn't he?" Eddie says and he starts to slather butter and jam on another scone. "Okay, so first we're going to have to have Max's parents in and talk to Cynthia."

It takes Eddie a moment to interpret the resounding silence that comes in the wake of that last statement. He looks from Miss Holly to me and back again. "Guys," he says. "We have to talk to Cynthia."

"Of course we do," Miss Holly says, "but you and I both know what's going to happen, Eddie. We'll have a week of assemblies where she gives speeches about how "Stafford Falls Public School Stands Up to Bullying," and she'll send some teachers for special bully support training at the school board and then we'll probably have a poster contest for the best anti-bullying slogan, but the fact of the matter is that while we're doing all of that, Max will still be peeing blood and eating dog-shit sandwiches."

At this moment, I am so grateful to have Miss Holly on my side that I resolve to bring her a cappuccino every day for the rest of her natural life. Eddie looks less delighted with her, but I notice that he's not contradicting her.

"What do you suggest?" he says, finally.

"We need to close the gaps," she says. "All of this stuff is happening at unstructured times of day - recess, lunch, on the way home. We need to set it up so that we've got Max covered. If we can catch Adam and his little gang at work, all the better, but mainly, we have to keep Max safe."

"I'm going to go out for all the afternoon recesses," I say, "so I can keep an eye on things. And we're going to start a little lunch club for Tobey - it's too loud and over-stimulating for him in his regular class so he usually eats here, but it's not good for him to be alone all the time, so we'll invite three or four boys to hang with him. Max will be our first volunteer."

"I'll supervise that time," Miss Holly says, "and I'll make it known in seventh grade that I'll find it extremely suspicious and will have to investigate if anybody shows up without their lunch."

Eddie slurps some more coffee while he considers this. "I could cover some extra morning recesses. And Max could keep his book bag and boots and things in my office. Nobody's going to touch his stuff there."

"As for after school, Nana is going to hire Max two days a week to shovel and walk the dogs and do little jobs for her and if he's not at her front door fifteen minutes after dismissal, she will probably call Mike the Cop."

"Who knows?" Miss Holly says. "Mike may just start taking his afternoon coffee breaks in the cruiser down the street from the school. It's not like he's got international drug cartels to break up every day at half past three."

Even Eddie has to smile at that. "I'm holding basketball tryouts this week," he says. "Being on a team might give him a little confidence boost."

"Alf told me that any day we can't cover, he would be glad to come and pick Max up and have some special grandpa bonding time," I say.

"It sounds like you've got almost all the angles covered," Eddie says.

"Yes, but we wanted to know what you thought," I say.

Eddie snorts and reaches for another scone. "No you didn't. You'd hatched this whole plan and you just wanted to sell me on it so I'll talk to Cynthia for you."

"What did you do to her to make her hate you so much?" Miss Holly asks me, but before I can answer Eddie says, "It's about a boy who was in a band."

"Must have been quite the boy," Miss Holly says.

"My goodness, you're all here early," Miss Osgoode says from the doorway.

I almost drop my coffee and Eddie actually coughs up a bit of scone at the sound of Cynthia Osgoode's voice. I swear to God that woman moves on little cat feet. Even Tobey, who can't weigh more than sixty pounds sounds like a stampede coming down those decrepit stairs, yet I hadn't heard so much as a creak from the stairway before she materialized.

"Good morning, Miss Osgoode," Miss Holly says, the smoothest and least ruffled of our little trio. "We'd offer you a scone but I think Mr. Spaghetti has just polished off the last one."

"That's quite all right," she says. "Mr. Spinella, when you're done here, could you drop by my office, for a word, please?"

He nods vigourously as he chugs more coffee, trying to choke down the rest of the scone.

Miss Osgoode gives us a pinched little smile and then is gone.

Jacques Cousteau day turns out to be a lot of fun. The week before the big day, Mr. Spaghetti gets Max to help him lug the aquarium down to our room and fill it with water and set up the filters and everything so that the tank can "cycle" before we add fish - I eventually have to stop listening to Eddie's lectures on water chemistry but Max seems fascinated by the whole process, particularly the part where you stick little test strips in and study the colours they turn and soon Max has taken over this job and the two of them spend a lot of time standing, looking into the fish-less tank, and discussing pH numbers and other such fascinating things. This is particularly gratifying because poor old Max looks a bit like a weary refugee these days and it's good to see him interested in anything.

We decide to have refreshments for Jacques Cousteau Day and Davis suggests fish sticks but Kylie won't hear of it because that would be cruel, all of us sitting around eating cod, while not six feet away their little cousins dart innocently around the aquarium. We settle on goldfish crackers and juice, although Wally wonders aloud if goldfish crackers are actually made of goldfish and that's a bit upsetting for a while, but thankfully Miss Holly looks up the ingredients on the Internet and everyone is satisfied that the crackers are indeed goldfish-free.

The biggest surprise of the day though is when Kylie's father appears at the door of the class at lunch time. He is a giant of a man who is decked out in heavy outdoor work clothes and he is holding a package of frosted sugar cookies, which he sheepishly hands to me.

"Sorry they're from the grocery store," he says. "I'm not much of a baker."

"The kids will love them," I say.

"Thanks for doing this," he says, and he has the same coffee brown eyes that Kylie has, only shyer. "She's been really excited." And then he's gone before I can even say anything.

Nana and Mortimer arrive and that causes quite a stir, and then Mr. Spaghetti comes after lunch with a big plastic bag full of water that contains a half dozen little stripy fish. Kiley tells everyone that theses are zebra danios and that they like fresh water and that they don't usually attack other fish, but that they love to eat. She also informs us that although she thinks that danios are generally nice fish, her favourite fish, what she hopes we will get next, is a couple of Siamese Fighting Fish.

This does not surprise anyone.

Then Kylie helps Mr. Spaghetti release the danios into the tank and everyone claps when they start to dart around and check out their new digs. They like the plants a lot and immediately try to eat them. We eat cookies and crackers and grape juice and Mr. Spaghetti talks a lot about his own fish tank and shows us pictures from the time he went scuba diving on the Great Barrier Reef, which Kylie says looks exactly like *Finding Nemo*. Nana reads everyone *Arty the Smarty*, an oldie but goodie about a fish named Arty who swims to the beat of his own drum, which I think is the last thing that Kylie needs to hear, but Nana insists that there's a good lesson in it and for good measure, she has Mortimer wear a shark fin and run back and forth during the exciting parts, so it's actually kind of fun.

Later, after the kids have left and the classroom is quiet except for the gentle burble of the fish tank, my phone beeps and there is a message from Pam: a photo of her with Martha and Rose, their tiny arms linked with two astonishingly photogenic young women who I think are Snow White and Cinderella. The iconic Magic Kingdom castle is in the background and the accompanying text says, "*I. Am. In. Hell.*"

I laugh out loud.

At least it's warm, I reply, and I go back to picking bits of ground up sugar cookie out of the carpet.

Another beep.

phone me asap, the text says. *Bianca fucking Wren wants to give you a solo exhibition.*

CHAPTER 16

Wide Open Heart

T alking on the phone to Bianca Wren is a little like trying to funnel the output of a fire hose through a drinking straw - only a very small percentage of the water actually gets through and it's very hard on the straw. I know I'm missing out on so much - the gestures, the clothes, the jewelry, the hair - and of course I have to hear about her most recent gig as artist in residence in Berlin, her new boy toy (Scottie) and all the challenges and difficulties of the European art scene, which in essence can be boiled down to 'so many dance clubs, so little time.'

While she talks, I have time to drink not one, but two espressos, brought to me by Julia, who keeps circling back to the table to give me encouraging looks, but I really don't mind listening to Bianca pontificate because it gives me a chance to think about the whole situation.

On the one hand, a solo show at a gallery associated with Bianca Wren is very exciting. As Pam pointed out, her name alone will ensure the attendance of a large number of critics, curators and collectors (plus associated hangers-on and wanna-bes) and half the battle of a successful show is getting people in the door. Pam also pointed out that it's been a while since I've showed my work and if I don't put myself out there, I'm never going to get any new opportunities and then I'll end up cooking chicken nuggets six nights a week and trying to find ways to hide broccoli in my children's food, and then one day when I'm folding yet another load of pink laundry, I'll catch myself humming something from *Mary Poppins*, and then I'll realize that any chance I ever had to be a legitimate artist is gone and all that's left to do is to wait for death.

I'm not sure Pam is enjoying her family holiday very much.

On the other hand, this all just feels so foreign, like maybe I'm not an artist anymore. And to be fair, if an artist is someone who makes art, then it's been a good long time since I've been one. Since about the time I moved in with Alex, started teaching high school and gave up my studio.

But if I'm not an artist, then who am I?

Thankfully, I'm saved from the cliff of despair that comes after *that* thought, because just then, Bianca finally wraps up the overture to the "The Bianca Wren Show" and gets down to business.

"So, darling, you're not very easy to track down," she says. "Your website link isn't working and I couldn't locate you at any of the galleries. Thank the gods that Pam's contact info was still current, because I don't know how else I would have found you."

"Well, I'm glad you did," I say. "And thanks for letting me know that my website is down. I'll check into that." And, you know, renew my contract with my internet host. "I'm not sure Pam had the dates right, though. Do you really want to open in two weeks?"

"Seventeen days to be precise," Bianca says. "I know it's insanely last minute. The truth is that this is a brand new gallery and we had someone lined up but there was a whole legal drama - I won't bore you with the details. We have someone for six weeks hence - Louise Lawlor, do you know her? She does the most marvellous mixed-media work - but what with the bills piling up - gods, darling, you would not believe the overhead, and well, long story short, we need to open."

"To be honest, Bianca, I would think that you'd want to show some of your own work," I say. "Your name would attract a much bigger crowd than mine."

"The fact is, darling, I'm not spending much time in the studio. Almost everything's already sold and I'm so busy travelling and advising that I couldn't pull together a show in such a short time. Also," she says, and she lowers her voice conspiratorially here, "just between you and me, I'm beginning to rethink the whole paradigm of the painter as someone who actually applies paint to canvas."

Far away, in Florida, I imagine Pam's head exploding.

"But still, why me?" I say.

"Cards on the table, darling?" she says. "You're one of the few people I know with such a backlog of unsold works."

It almost feels likes she's reached through the phone and slapped me.

"But that's only part of the reason why I'm calling you," she adds, quickly. "The other part is that I think your work is very good and you're the kind of artist that our - well, Scottie's gallery wants to represent. Your work is fresh, it's technically excellent, it's got wide appeal but best of all, it's still good enough to satisfy the snobs. You're one of the best painters I know, Olivia, and I don't understand why you're not selling like mad. I realize that this is not how things are usually done and no, you weren't our first choice, but you're a very good choice and you'd be a solid opening for the gallery." She laughs a little, her trademark trill. "And you should trust me on this, because you know what, darling?"

"What?"

"I'm very good at spotting the next big thing."

Actually, she's very good at *promoting* the next big thing, but since I'm going to be the big thing she's promoting, I'm willing to let the distinction go.

"Look, I won't kid you," she says, "it will be tight. But I've got all the scaffolding in place, all I need is for you to sign the contracts and we'll put it all in motion. I'll even bring the paperwork to you myself!"

"Well, that's the thing," I say. "I'm in Stafford Falls."

"Stafford Falls!" she says, with something between fascination and awe. "That sounds positively delicious! Where is that exactly?"

I describe exactly where our delicious little town is - six hours drive through near wilderness, an hour from the nearest train station, within shouting distance of the middle of nowhere - and she quickly decides that we can probably work this all out with emails, phone calls and some intrepid courier service.

We quickly agree to terms - the usual financial split, plus they'll contribute to crating and transportation costs and she's even quite amenable to me advising on the installation, although that's going to be a battle royale because she's probably going to want fountains and neon and dancers and I'm going to want clean white space and good lighting. The pressing concern is getting a catalogue printed and circulated, which means making decisions on what pieces to include.

"I can delay the printers for about 48 hours, but no longer, so I need you to get on that right away. And for Christ's sake, Olivia, get your website up and running. It's the 21st century."

"Yeah, I'd heard," I say, as I scribble notes on a Second Chance Café napkin.

"So, do we have a deal?" she says.

I look across the café and catch Julia's eye. She gives me a thumbs up and a questioning look.

"I'm in," I say.

My heart is beating a little bit faster and for the first time in a long time, it's not the coffee.

NANA IS over the moon when she hears, and Pam starts texting me pictures of outfits that she thinks I should wear to the opening and while I'm panicking to Julia about my defunct website, Drew pipes up that one of his D&D friends is a real whiz at websites and he could ask him to have a look at it for me if I wanted, so it's all coming together rather nicely, until the next day when I go to see Miss Osgoode to explain that I need to take a day off. I don't anticipate it's going to be a problem as it's now March and since September, I have not missed a single day of fun and games in the basement, but the look on her face tells me that I have miscalculated. Or possibly tracked something smelly into her office.

"So," she says and somehow she's managing to look disappointed and vindicated at the same time. "You want time off, so soon after March break?"

Actually March break, which is next week, is the linchpin upon which the entire plan in riding. I am leaving Nana in Penny Clarke and Angie's care for most of that week so that I can go to the city and bulldoze through everything that has to be done, (uncrating, installing, pricing, fighting off Bianca's more absurd suggestions and God help us all, finding something to wear) but I absolutely need the extra day the following week because on the Friday, I have three (three!) interviews with some half-way decently regarded publications and Bianca is dropping hints that there might be a possible radio interview, as well. And anyway, none of this is Cynthia Osgoode's business.

"Just one day. The Friday," I say.

"I suppose this is for your show," she says, and somehow she manages to make it sound like my 'show' involves a pole and a lot of sticky dollar bills.

I smile and nod, not trusting myself to actually open my mouth at this point.

"Well, if you absolutely have to," she says. "See Mrs. Demanski for the paperwork." And then she sighs in a very put-upon way and casts her gaze back to her laptop.

And of all the tiny indignities of the past six months, of all the pissy tones of voice, of all the slights and injustices, it's this sigh, this huffy little 'the-things-I-put-up-with' expulsion of breath that finally pushes me over the edge and I hear myself saying, "Miss Osgoode, is there a problem with the way I've been performing my job?"

I instantly regret opening my mouth. My Poppa always said the first rule of debate is never to ask a question you don't already know the answer to, and I already know the answer to this question, but now it's out there and I can't take it back.

Cynthia Osgoode takes the time to sit back in her chair and fold her hands together before she answers. "No, there isn't 'a problem,' as you put it. You've been discharging your duties fairly competently."

"Then what is it exactly that I've done that's made you dislike me so much?" I ask.

"I don't dislike you, Ms Sutton," she says. "I just don't think we see the world in the same way."

"Oh. And how do we see it so differently, you and I?"

She regards me with an icy stare and I can see that she's every bit as angry as I am. "I think you see the world very much the way your mother saw it - from a position of privilege. She always thought that she was entitled to special treatment because of who she was, when the fact of the matter is that she was a manipulative, attention-seeking snob, who constantly flaunted her family's wealth."

And now the gloves are finally off, except I can't really argue with anything she's said because although I didn't know my mother when she was sixteen, that description sounds about right. Except for the flaunting part - I think Nana would've put an end to any flaunting in short order and I'm about to tell her this when she delivers her final judgement.

"And you're just like her," she says.

"I'm *nothing* like her," I say, and I'm a little surprised at how hot my face is feeling.

"You think you're too good for this job," she says.

"That's not true."

"Teaching has always been your second choice and now that you've got a gallery show, you're giving that priority over your duties here. You have no respect for authority and you change whatever aspect of the CRC program you like on a whim."

"I have not been changing the program on a whim. I'm trying to engage the kids, I'm trying to make the process of learning fun. What's wrong with that?"

"Life isn't fun, Ms Sutton, and we're not doing the children any favours by leading them to believe otherwise. Now, I'm very busy, so is there anything else?"

I suppose this isn't the time to tell her that the day after tomorrow, I've invited a Buddhist monk to come to my class to teach us all how to meditate, so I just say, "No, thanks, that's everything," and seize the opportunity to get the hell out of there.

BUT OF COURSE, this conversation dogs me all afternoon. I carry it around like a bone and gnaw on it for hours, the way Lucy does when Nana brings her a treat from the butcher's. I think I'm doing a good job of keeping it to myself but after dismissal, when I'm sitting down at my desk to begin wading through the detritus of paperwork that always seems to breed there, Miss Holly sticks her head in the door and says, "Is everything okay?"

"Yeah, everything's fine," I say.

"Are you sure?" she says. "Only you seemed kind of preoccupied this afternoon."

"Oh. Well. I had a little chat with Miss Osgoode," I say.

Miss Holly nods sagely, then she shuts the door, takes off her coat and pulls a chair up to my desk. "All right, what did she say?" she says.

"Let's see...she told me she thinks I'm not committed to teaching and that I've changed the CRC program too drastically. Oh, and that I view the world from a position of privilege."

"So it wasn't a pep talk," she says.

"I didn't feel very peppy afterwards, so no, I guess not."

"Look, you know she's wrong about the teaching thing, don't you? You're doing a great job down here. The kids adore you and they're learning. This place has needed shaking up for years and you've been a breath of fresh air. I mean, Olivia, look around you."

Which I do. And I see colourful posters the kids have made about dogs and scuba diving and fish and birds, I see Tobey's most recent chalk wall map of the Peloponnesian War, into which we've incorporated his spelling words, I see clay horses and knights that are acting out a scene from a story that Wally is reading. I see a happy, busy place that kids are glad to come to.

"They are learning, aren't they?" I say.

"But I don't think that's what's bothering you," she says. "What else did our fearless leader say?"

"She said that I act as if I feel that I'm too good for this job."

Miss Holly's head waggles back and forth as if she's weighing this notion. "Well," she says, "she's almost right about that."

I am so gobsmacked by her words that I feel my face getting hot again. "You think I act like I'm too good for this job?"

"No, I think you *are* too good for this job," she says. "But I don't think you know that."

"What are you talking about?"

"Olivia, every time I go to the café and look at your artwork, I think to myself, why the hell is this woman not painting every hour of every day? And I know, I know, it's the commerce side that's tough and sometimes you need a day job because canvases and paintbrushes and whatever aren't free. I get it - everybody's got bills, and really, the only reason you and I are sitting here today is because your grand-mother got sick and needed you to take care of her. But this isn't where you'd be if that hadn't happened."

She's right of course - I hadn't planned to be in Stafford Falls, in our cozy little basement room, coercing reluctant students to read and investigating the social needs of tropical fish. But when it came to that, where would I be? Because I also hadn't planned to lose my high school job or my girlfriend, either. If Nana hadn't gotten sick, would I have gone to London with Alex? Or would I be in the city, alone, substitute teaching, eating expired yogurt and struggling to come up with the money to rent studio space?

I think Miss Holly mistakes my sudden silence for hurt feelings because she's quick to add, "Look, I'm no expert on art, but apparently some people think you're good enough to have a show, so you prob-ably need to think about that. As for Miss Osgoode, I think she's just a jealous cow."

"Jealous? Of what?"

"You've got a ticket out of Stafford Falls. You get to play in the big leagues, not unlike your mom. Cynthia Osgoode has risen as high as she's ever likely to go and you're a big deal artist whose star might just be beginning to rise."

"I'm not a big deal artist," I say.

"So you say. But here's the thing: it's your life, kid. What are you going to do with it?"

I honestly don't know what to say.

"Look, I gotta go. Mikey Jr. has a hockey game in Winchester at five." She leans forward and pats my hand. "You'll figure it out."

And then she's out the door.

THE NEXT MORNING, the Great Pastry Crisis comes to an unexpected head.

Nana is hosting her regular Thursday morning salon at the Second Chance Café and in addition to the usual suspects, Nana has invited Mrs. Skipper, the librarian, and Charlotte Ramsay, who has either stopped being sneaky and trying to take over the church luncheon scheduling from Penny Clarke, or who is being lured into the fold in a clever attempt to keep one's enemies very close indeed. They're sitting beneath *The Studio* - Nana has decided that that's her table - and they are deep in conversation on topics as diverse as the New Vicar (the Reverend Archie Lewis - he's young, but we like him,) Mrs. So-and-so's new hair colour (who does she think she's fooling?) and the possibility of the town hosting some sort of sailing regatta in the summer (it sounds like a great idea, unless Jimmy Dunhill, the dolt of a mayor, decides to run the event himself, in which case it is guaranteed to be a fiasco.)

I'm at my own table, across the café, and I've been passing a lovely half hour alternately making lists of things I need to do for the show and sketching Nana and her friends - quick gesture sketches which are interrupted at regular intervals by phone calls from Bianca Wren, needing to ask my preferences on a variety of subjects and demanding to know if I've got a title for the show yet. Which I do not, because I'm still trying to wrap my mind around the fact that there is a show. The thing is, titles always stump me and this time I'm virtually paralyzed

trying to come up with a name because it's got to be arty and preten-
tious yet descriptive and commercial while also being intriguing but
accessible, and frankly that's way too much pressure to put on three
or four words.

Julia comes to sit with me when there's a lull, and she beams at
my little ink sketches, studying each one as if they were precious and
clever, and she tells me that she loves to watch me draw, which is
sweet but also a bit of a turn on and I'm just about to ask her if
Samantha is around and could she cover the counter for a few
minutes so we could slip up to her apartment, when Julia spots
something across the room that makes her face fall. I twist in my
chair to try to see what it could possibly be that's upset this darling
angel, but her gaze seems to be fixed on my Nana and her cronies,
who aren't doing much more than sipping cappuccinos and nibbling
on cookies.

Before I can ask her what's wrong, she's on her feet and marching
across the café. She comes to an abrupt halt at their table and stands
there, hands on her hips, staring at this group of startled old women. I
scramble after her and arrive just in time to hear her say, in an oddly
quavering voice, "Are you enjoying your cookies?"

Her words have pinned poor Mrs. Skipper in place - it's as if she's
frozen in time, one of the offending cookies partway to her mouth.
No one seems to want to make eye contact with Julia but nobody is
looking guiltier than Angie and it's only then that I realize that the
cookies in question are not from Julia's pretty glass pastry case.

"You brought those from home?" Julia says, and her voice still
sounds funny and it takes us all a second to realize that she's not mad,
she's hurt, which is much, much worse. And then the emotional dam
bursts and I think Julia might actually cry and Angie is spewing apolo-
gies and shoving cookies into her purse and Penny Clarke is saying, "I
told you this was going to happen, Angie!" and Charlotte Ramsay
looks like she's very sorry she ever accepted Nana's invitation to
coffee. Samantha the barista arrives on the run just then, with a cloth
and soda water, probably assuming that the giant fuss going on in the
corner must involve a gallon of spilled coffee, but then she just stands

there, looking scared and blinking, while Nana tuts and tries to soothe Julia.

After a while, once Julia has been convinced to sit down with them and Angie has apologized a dozen times and Nana has told Penny Clarke to stop saying 'I told you so' because it's not helpful, they get deep into baked goods analytics.

"No one wants a muffin, dear," Angie says. "They order a muffin because they think it's healthy, they think it's not cake but the problem is that it's bland, crumby cake, usually with hard little bits of dried up fruit in it - basically, it's bad cake. And life's too short to eat bad cake, I say."

"For my money, you can't beat a good coffee cake," Mrs. Skipper says.

"Now, a coffee cake, that's a whole different animal," Angie says, "because a good coffee cake has got sour cream in the recipe so there's a moisture and a richness there, plus you've got a streusel or a glaze on top and that makes it a real treat."

"You should have a coffee cake on the menu, dear," Penny Clarke says. "You could sell slices or even little individual ones and probably charge more for them."

Samantha, who has just arrived with a tray full of the next round of cappuccinos says, "Actually, I think a lot of people would buy a whole coffee cake to take home," and everyone sort of stares at her, a little startled, because she so rarely speaks.

"It's true," Nana says. "There's been a real void since Olson's closed the bakery. The ones at the supermarket aren't really very good. They taste like they were made in a factory."

"Which, I'm sorry to say dear, is what your pastries taste like," Penny Clarke says, and when Nana gives her a look, she adds, "We're just trying to help, Violet. The girl knows that the pastries aren't selling."

"But they're not made in a factory," Julia says. "I'm getting all my baked goods from a bakery in Winchester."

"Which one?" Charlotte Ramsay asks.

"Jake's Cakes," Julia says.

"Oh," everyone at the table murmurs, in the sort of tone people usually reserve for biopsy results.

"What?" Julia asks, looking around at all the downcast faces.

"Well, there's your problem," Angie says. "That Jake fellow cuts corners on his ingredients. He buys lots of mixes and uses cheap shortenings. It seems like all the bakeries do, these days. Nobody takes the time to do it from scratch, but you can taste the difference, you really can. What you need, dear, is one of those - oh, what do you call it, Violet, like the people at the farmer's market?"

"Artisanal bakers," Nana says.

"What she needs is you, Angie," Penny Clarke says, and everyone stops talking and looks at Angie.

"Oh, I couldn't - I mean, that would be too —" Angie says but it's as if a giant clockwork has been set in motion and everyone at the table is thinking some variation of the same thing, and then they all start to talk at once.

"You could work right out of your own kitchen."

"You've baked enough to fill ten bakeries for church functions this year alone, Ange."

"Do you need a business license to start something like that in your house?"

And then everyone is silenced by a plea that seems to soar over all the other voices.

"I want to help!" Samantha the barista cries.

For the second time that day, everyone stares at her.

"Sam?" Julia says.

"Mrs. McInnis, I've always wanted to know how to bake and my mother never taught me, and Julia, you can only afford to give me part time hours, but I need more to do and if someone could just give me a chance, I know I could be very good at baking and I would still work the hours you gave me, Julia, but I just really need somebody to give me a chance, so, please, Mrs. McInnis... if you decide to do this, I want to help."

All eyes swing round to look at Angie, who seems more than a little befuddled by the whole scene that's unfolding around her, but she summons a smile for Samantha, who is wringing her hands and shifting nervously from foot to foot and says, "Well, dear, if you're going to be my first employee, then I think you had better start calling me Angie."

THE REST of the day is spent in serious negotiations at the table in the front window. Julia and Angie come armed with the tools of their respective trades - spreadsheets and recipe books - and Alf drops by for a part of it and he seems more excited than anyone and is quickly dispatched to the town hall to enquire about licenses, health inspections and other such things. Julia walks Angie through the benefits of different forms of incorporating, getting a small business loan, various kinds of liability insurance and some clever tax moves. There is significant and passionate debate on the subject of cupcakes (Julia thinks they're a passing trend and Angie has strong feelings about the frosting situation) and they finally have to agree to table that clearly divisive topic until the next meeting. Angie goes through three chai lattés before it's over, but when it is, there are handshakes and big smiles all round and "Angie's Artisanal Baked Goods, LLC" is born.

"Well. I'm going to be a corporation," Angie says. "Fancy that."

THE LAST DAY before March break is probably not the best day to have a guest come to the CRC, especially one who's supposed to teach us all how to be calm because the kids are drunk with the idea of a week off and are bouncing around like so many little pinballs, but the school year is marching on and we have quite a wish list of projects to work our way through. I delicately suggest to Nana that it might not be the best day for her and Mort to visit because the last thing we need, while we're all lying around on gym mats trying to be still and mindful, is a nosy little Jack Russell terrier, darting around licking everyone's face.

After lunch, Miss Holly, Tobey and Davis station themselves at the front door of the school to watch for Tenzin and shortly after the bell rings to begin afternoon classes, this unlikely quartet comes ambling down the creaky stairs - Davis, in front, carrying a box for our guest and Tobey, taking up the rear and holding Tenzin's hand, the sight of which makes Miss Holly and I exchange looks of amazement.

Everyone crowds around Tenzin the instant he steps into the room and a couple of the kids actually touch his arm as if they're trying to make sure he's real, and this shouldn't surprise me because he's got to be the most exotic thing they're ever seen in Stafford Falls. The questions are already pouring out of them, (Kylie asks him why he is wearing a dress and Davis wants to know if they play hockey in Tibet and if so, which is his favourite team?) but before I can wrangle them onto their assigned spots on the carpet, Eddie Spaghetti slides in the door, a big grin on his face.

"You really do have a Buddhist monk in your class," he says.

"I know, he's pretty cool, isn't he?"

"Very cool," he says. "Uh, so… Cynthia has asked me to come and remind you that this is a public school and that there shouldn't be any overtly religious, um…stuff."

"Oh, please. You're not here to scold me for her, are you?"

"Nope. I'm just delivering the message because she told me to, and now I'm going to check on the fish."

"For heaven's sake, he's just going to teach them to sit still for thirty continuous seconds which might help them to, oh, I don't know… learn to read?"

"Personally, I think it's a great idea," Eddie says. "Phil Jackson attributes his eleven NBA championship titles in part to the practice of Zen Buddhism. He says it gives the players focus and mental discipline."

"NBA - that's baseball, right?"

He stares at me. "Sometimes it's like I don't even know you."

I smile. "Just yanking your chain, Mr. Spaghetti. You're welcome to join us if you want."

"Really?"

"Pull up a mat."

And to my great surprise, he does. He sits cross legged on the floor with the kids while Tenzin unpacks his box of marvellous things and Davis and Wally both scoot as close as they can to Eddie, obviously delighted to have the Vice Principal sitting amongst them like a mere mortal. When Tenzin has settled himself on the floor too, and adjusted his robes around him, he casts his beaming gaze out at the little group and the whole place falls into a hush.

"Thank you enormously for inviting me to come to your class-room," he says and he looks at each of the kids' faces in turn and seems to give them their own personal, radiant smile. "I am very excited to come here to teach you how to breathe."

"Breathe?" Kylie says. "We already know how to breathe!"

"You do?" Tenzin says and he affects a look of utter amazement. "Show me this breathing that you know how to do!"

And so they they all start sucking in deep breaths and puffing out their cheeks like a convention of hyperventilating asthmatics.

Tenzin shakes his head and grins. "Oh, no! No, no, no! I have much bad news for you, my new friends! So many years you are doing the breathing all wrong! When you were little babies, you did the breathing correctly, but now you are all wrong! I think you have forgotten!"

The kids think this is hilarious, that they've forgotten something they knew when they were infants but they've never been chastised by someone who smiles as much as Tenzin does, so they take this news quite cheerfully.

"How can we be breathing wrong?" Kylie says. "If we were breathing wrong, we'd be dead!"

"That is not for me to say," Tenzin says, "but I can see, plain as your face, that you are all doing the breathing wrong because, my silly friends, you are doing the breathing with your lungs."

"That's what you're supposed to breathe with," Kylie says and she pulls a long, whistley breath in through her nose, as if to illustrate her point. "See? That's breathing."

Tenzin shakes his head as if he finds her adorable, then says, "Would you like to see a picture of the place where I was born?"

Of course everyone does, so he takes out some photos and hands them out to the kids who study them with the sort of concentration that they use when they're trying to locate Waldo. The photos show a colourful, rocky place, which he explains is Dharmsala, in northern India - it turns out that our Tibetan monk has never actually been to Tibet, although he hopes one day to visit it - and then he passes around pictures of his monastery in Santa Fe, some of which contain pictures of his brother monks sitting in meditation or working in the monastery's gardens.

Kylie, though, is having none of it. "But you're supposed to breathe with your lungs," she says, when we're done passing the pictures around. "That's how you do it."

"And who is this person who told you to breathe with your lungs?" Tenzin asks her.

"No one told me. That's just how you breathe."

Tenzin nods, as if he's considering what she's said, but then he says, "I wonder if you have ever seen a singing bowl?"

"Bowls can't sing," Davis says, but there's a look of uncertainty on his face because until today, he was pretty sure that you used your lungs for breathing.

"Magic bowls can sing," Isabelle says.

"There's no such thing as -" Kylie starts to say but then Tenzin pulls a purple silk cloth off the most beautiful thing I've ever seen. It's a bowl, about as big as a basketball, made of shining, hammered bronze, and it is covered in curling patterns and flowing script that have been painted on by the finest of hands. It's a little work of art and even the kids are wowed by the sight of it. They ooh and ahh and Tenzin lets everybody touch the bowl before he takes out a little wooden mallet.

"Listen to the bowl," he says, "listen as far as your ears will take you."

And he strikes the bowl with the mallet and the most remarkable sound starts to fill the room. It's a long, undulating tone that seems to stretch out to infinity and it makes me think of ripples racing across the surface of a still pond. The kids are frozen the whole time, fixed in place, straining to hear the very last syllable of sound as it circles and then finally dies away.

"Do it again!" Wally says and he claps his hands.

"This time, listen with your whole body, not just your ears," Tenzin says and he strikes the bowl and the guttural bong it makes rolls around the room again for almost a full minute, the sound ebbing and flowing, like a sluggish pendulum. When it finally fades past the threshold of perception, the kids stir a little and I realize that for the past thirty seconds, they have been perfectly still, mouths open, attending to nothing but the sound of the bowl.

"This time," Tenzin says, and his voice is very quiet now, just a whisper, "lie down, close your eyes and listen with your heart."

Everyone lies down on the mats, without talking or shoving or muttering threats to each other, which is in itself a minor miracle, and when everyone is settled, Tenzin strikes the bowl again and the sound is different this time - it seems slower and richer as if it's actually travelling around our little class touching everything it encounters, washing over all of us and suddenly I am struck by the strongest memory - standing at a huge blank canvas in my studio, brilliant winter sunlight flooding the room, the earthy, flat smell of fresh paint on my palette, paintbrush in my hand. I feel —

It's not happiness, really, or peace, it's more like flow or presence or awareness or something but whatever you want to call it, I'm just there, completely, exquisitely there in the moment, in the painting.

"Now you are breathing correctly," Tenzin says and without even seeing his face, I can tell he is smiling. "Now you are not doing the breathing with your noses or lungs. Now you are doing the breathing with your heart wide open."

And we are. All of us. Together.

"You must do everything with a wide open heart," Tenzin tells us, as we lie there. "You must do your reading and draw your pictures with a wide open heart. You must play your hockey and eat your broccoli with a wide open heart. Always, always, a wide open heart."

There's a lovely peaceful pause as we all take this in and I can feel how relaxed the kids are and that's the exact moment when Eddie Spaghetti starts to snore - a quiet, back of the throat, low rumble of a snore, but a snore nevertheless and we all prop ourselves up on our elbows to look at him. The kids start to giggle but Miss Holly hushes them and puts a finger to her lips and then we all get up very quietly and make our way to the work table where Tenzin has brought pictures of mandalas for us to colour. We pass a lovely half hour together, sharing markers and making art and whispering to each other while Mr. Spaghetti sleeps the sleep of the innocent and exhausted.

And when they've all gone out for recess and I've helped Tenzin pack up his singing bowl and pictures, just before I wake Eddie up to send him to his next class, I take out my phone and send Bianca a quick text:

I know the name of the show now.

CHAPTER 17

The Secret to Scones

The first time I see The Scott Levinson Gallery, I feel like I'm going to throw up. This is not so much a reflection on the gallery - which is shiny and gorgeous - as it is the result of a long drive, a sleepless night in Rose's Cinderella bed, which was designed for a much shorter princess than I, and just possibly, a teensy bit of nerves. This is the first show I've had in several years and arguably the most important one of my career thus far and since I've spent the last seven months surrounded by arthritic dogs, old women and small people who pick their noses, I'm not sure what shape my "cool art show" chops are in. Actually, to be completely honest, I'm not sure I ever had "cool art show" chops.

Thankfully, Pam is there to cut through all these complicated emotional and psychological issues with her usual pragmatism. "Stop being such a fucking baby," she says and she grabs my arm and drags me towards the gallery. "We have pictures to hang."

We're barely through the door when Bianca comes to meet us, arms spread wide in a dramatic gesture of welcome. "Oh, my darlings," she says, and many air kisses are exchanged and there is a great deal of hugging that doesn't involve a lot of touching. "Oh, it's so good to see you in the flesh! It's like old times at school, isn't it?"

I'm not sure what old school times she's referring to because I'm pretty sure she called me Susan for most of the first year of the fine arts program but I go along with it. Also, since I have made Pam pinky-swear that she will be nice to Bianca, which includes not rolling her eyes or making gagging gestures behind her back, I feel a certain pressure to set a good example.

"Let me just get us some espresso and then I'll show you around," Bianca says, then she turns and croons, "Giancarlo! *Abbiamo bisogno di tre espressi, per favore!*"

A very young, eager and stunning young man appears from nowhere - he has melted chocolate brown eyes and looks like he's just stepped away from his day job modelling boxer briefs. His smile, which lingers for a few breathless seconds on Pam, tells us that nothing in the world would make him happier than to bring us tiny coffees.

"Isn't he precious?" Bianca says to Pam, who is flat out staring at Giancarlo's retreating backside. "And he's invaluable. Scottie and I don't know what we'd do without him."

I can tell Pam is thinking about what she'd like to do *with* him, so I slip my arm through hers and say, "Focus. We have pictures to hang, remember?"

"Right," Pam says. "Pictures."

Bianca gives us a tour of the space, pointing out changes they've made since they took over, then leads us to her desk - a glass and steel number that looks like it could be an art installation of its own - and I see that Bianca has been looking at my new and improved website - her laptop is open and there's my glowing face, smiling back at me from the computer screen. I look remarkably self-confident for someone with so much unsold work.

"I love the website, darling," Bianca says. "Who is your web designer?"

I don't actually want to say, "Drew's D&D friend, Pete," so I mumble something about how he's a new guy I've just discovered. I also don't mention that I was relieved when I saw that the finished product didn't involve elves, magical swords or mythical animals that breathed fire.

"I love it," Bianca says. "It's clean and lean and very inviting. Really showcases the work."

Soon Giancarlo is back with little silver espresso cups for all of us, but then a phone rings somewhere and he disappears to answer it, much to Pam's dismay.

We sip our coffees (they're almost as good as Julia's but not quite, and that makes me miss her and wish she was here sharing this) and then Bianca gets down to business and starts showing us her ideas for the install and the opening and there is remarkably little that I disagree with - the only proposal I veto is the one that involves video screens with loops of me talking about my work because (a) I don't think I could stand to be in a room with that many versions of myself all talking at once and (b) it just sounds silly. Bianca acquiesces with grace, but does insist that there be some sort of multi-media display with a "Getting to Know the Artist" theme and I give in on this point, unless it involves providing baby pictures.

Scott Levinson himself drops by partway through our negotiations and he turns out to be much older than I expected - partly because Bianca calls him "Scottie," but also because if I remember correctly, Bianca likes to keep at least a good ten years between herself and her current boy toy and Scottie is clearly much older than we are. His carefully-styled black hair is shot through with silver and he's got a whole George Clooney, stubbly, metrosexual thing going and of course he's lovely to us. He says lots of nice things about my work and tells us how delighted he is to be representing me, then he kisses Bianca on the cheek and disappears, possibly for a man spa appointment.

And then we get down to work. The bulk of the day is spent uncrating the twenty one pieces of art that comprise my show, and it turns out to be a really joyous and emotional thing. I feel so oddly, disproportionately happy to see each of these paintings as I free them from their wooden boxes - it's almost as if it's a reunion with good friends who've been away for too long on a trip and I find I have to keep prompting myself to continue measuring, hammering and hanging because I just want to stand back and gaze at them, get to know them again.

By four o'clock, a good chunk of the show is up but I'm faint from hunger and Pam looks like she might start snacking on Giancarlo at any moment, so I tell Giancarlo we're stepping out for a bit and I drag Pam out of the gallery to the closest restaurant I can find which turns out to be some sort of upscale gastropub where we order very expensive burgers and equally expensive microbrew cream ales with clever, punny names. We are waiting for our meals and inhaling a bowl of bar snacks when I finally notice that Pam is uncharacteristically quiet.

"What's the matter?" I say.

A big sigh. "I'm just finding this all a little…well, honestly, I'm a little jealous," she says. "But don't get me wrong, I'm delighted for you - you deserve this and I'm so happy you're getting this show. It's just… it's kind of reminding me of what I gave up, you know? What I'm missing."

"You could have it again," I say. "You always said that when the girls were in school you'd be able to devote more time to painting."

"That was before I knew how much laundry there'd be. And that there'd be ballet lessons and soccer and endless fucking car pools… but, no, you're right. I just need to make the time and get back to it." She sips her beer and regards me with a measuring gaze. "Actually, I'd been thinking…" she says, but then she shakes her head.

"What?"

"No, never mind, this is probably not a good time to talk about it."

"Jesus, Pammy, don't make me drag it out of you. I have to save some energy to fight with Bianca about my video autobiography. And, you know, eventually drive home."

"Well, that's just the thing," Pam says. "Where is your home these days?"

"What do you mean?"

"I'm wondering when you might be coming back to live here," she says. "Because I can't work in the basement anymore, the light is crap and the place is filled with toys - I'm like the mayor of Barbietown down there and I need some place away from my house and my husband and my kids. And I know it's corny, but I'm really inspired by you getting a show and all. And I was just thinking that if maybe you knew when you were going to move back to the city and if you were going to get back into your work in a more full time kind of way, maybe we could rent some studio space together."

Something about how she's saying this is making me feel sad and I realize that in a very real way, I abandoned poor old Pammy when I left to take care of Nana. But it's not like these tiny little issues of 'home' and 'the future' haven't been on my mind - in fact, I have had to actively put all those thoughts aside lately, all the more often since Miss Holly reminded me that I was never supposed to be in Stafford Falls at this point in my life. But there's Nana's welfare to think about and now there's Julia, too, except I don't want to put too much pressure on that relationship because it's lovely and fresh and new and it feels like making too many decisions about it at this point would be like stomping on a seedling.

But Pam is looking at me like her puppy died and oh my God, she's right, I need to make some decisions, or at least start thinking about making decisions because even though it's March, June is not that far behind and June means no job and I need a studio but who will take care of Nana? And then it's not a very long trip back to Julia and I assume she feels the same way but what if she -

Pam grabs my hand and snaps me out of it. "Stop it. You're coming unspooled, I can see it in your eyes."

"Yeah, a little bit," I say.

"It's okay. You don't have to decide the rest of your life this very minute," Pam says. "I just wanted to throw out the idea of sharing studio space."

"I would love that," I say. "Although I'm not sure how much work we'd get done."

"Oh, obviously we'd have to have some rules. And only a little bit of wine."

"I've really missed you, Pammy."

"I've missed you more," she says and maybe it's the low blood sugar or the sheer giddiness of being out on the town in the middle of the day without her children, but Pam starts to tear up and then I get a lump in my throat, too. Mercifully, before we can both turn into sniffly messes, our high class burgers arrive and we tear into them and for a little while we just eat and think our own thoughts and then Pam says, "So, do you think Bianca is sleeping with Giancarlo?"

I snort. "I think Scottie might be sleeping with Giancarlo."

"God, I hope someone is sleeping with Giancarlo," Pam says, "because otherwise that would be such a terrible waste of man meat."

IT FEELS like March break is over in a heartbeat - it takes three days to install the show in a way that pleases both Bianca and me, and then before I know it, I'm back in Stafford Falls and back to the grind of dogs, kids and toting Nana to physio. Anthony thinks Nana is doing well in almost all areas but balance and it galls her that she still needs the cane and she's worried that she's losing muscle tone because she can't stride about with the same speed and conviction that she used to. Lately, she's been talking about getting a stationary bike and Penny Clarke has been trying to convince her that they should start doing water aerobics together. Angie thinks she might join in too, especially if they can have a good soak in the hot tub after because it really helps her arthritis, but she's pretty busy churning out test batches of coffee cakes, scones and banana breads for Julia, so it might have to wait until spring actually arrives, an event that seems unlikely given the amount of snow still on the ground.

Fortunately though, the CEO of "Angie's Artisanal Baked Goods" does make the time to show up at school the first Wednesday after the break to fulfill Miss Holly's Anything Can Happen wish, which originally was to learn how to bake bread but which has been amended to 'learn how to bake something delicious,' because we realized we'd have a bit of trouble fitting bread baking into an afternoon, what with the kneading and the time the loaves would need to rise, so lemon scones it is.

We've taken over the staff room because that's where the oven and the fridge are located and Angie is running the place like General MacArthur with a wooden spoon. Max has dropped by and is helping Nana dry the mason jars that are going to be part of the butter making station, although we've also brought the food processor to hedge our bets in case all the jar shaking doesn't yield enough butter for our delicious scones. Tobey greets Max like a long lost brother - they've been having lunch together for a couple of weeks now and Tobey has taken to Max in an uncharacteristically clingy way, which may have something to do with the fact that Max understands most of Tobey's obscure Ancient Greece references. For his part, Tobey thinks Max is some sort of hero, his own personal Theseus, which is nice for Max because he's not used to being top of the heap, and right now Tobey is attempting to assist Max, although mostly what he's doing is holding the dripping jars up in the air to carefully study the prisms of colour that the sunlight makes as it streams through the glass.

Meanwhile, Angie supervises an extensive washing of hands, then everyone dons one of the aprons that she's brought (Wally and Davis have a bit of a shoving match over the apron that has a big red lobster on it,) and then we all crowd around Angie and get down to business.

"All right," Angie says and she produces some index cards from her apron pocket. "There are three secrets to making a delicious scone. Who's going to read the first one?"

All of their hands shoot up into the air, and they emit eager little noises that make them sound like puppies.

Angie gives the first card to Wally who reads, albeit a little haltingly, "The butter must be very cold."

Angie sends Max to get the butter, milk and the mixing bowls out of the fridge, while she tells everyone that she actually chills all the ingredients so that everything will stay cold while she makes the dough. She recruits Isabelle to help her measure flour, and Isabelle proceeds to spill not one but two cups of flour all over the table and the floor, and so while Miss Holly intervenes to help her, I go for the broom and dustpan, which is good because while I'm gone, someone knocks over the whole bag of flour. But, no harm no foul and soon enough, the spilled flour is cleaned up, a new bag of flour is procured and then everybody is busy breaking up the butter and flour into little bits in their mixing bowls. This goes quite smoothly until Wally sneezes into his bowl and wipes his nose on the back of his hand, and then I have to take him to the sink for a good nose blow and a re-washing of his hands, while Miss Holly gets him a new bowl of butter and flour to mix.

Davis is given the vaunted job of grating the lemon zest with what turns out to be a terrifically sharp citrus zester and so then I spend quite a bit of time washing lemon juice out of his cuts and applying bandaids to his little knuckles, while he winces and dances from foot to foot. We give it another go, this time together, my hand over his, carefully harvesting the fragrant rind and it's going well until I squirt lemon oil into my eye and then I have to stop myself from cursing, loudly. Davis thinks the look on my face is quite hilarious until a few minutes later when it happens to him and then it's as if he's been tear-gassed and he's basically rolling on the floor and clawing at his eyes. Nana takes over as head zester then which is probably for the best, because Davis and I need to go and splash cold water on our faces.

Then Angie has Isabelle read the second secret to scones, which is the somewhat cryptic message, "Less is more."

"When we add the wet ingredients," Angie says, "we're going to mix it all up in five stirs, no more. You shouldn't over stir your dough, because your scones will come out like hockey pucks."

Davis and Wally suggest that it would be great to bake some hockey pucks, and could they make theirs like that, please? But then they quail under Angie's dark look and dutifully count out their stirs like everybody else.

The third secret of scones, which Kylie reads and which turns out to the be most challenging of all is, "Let the dough rest for at least fifteen minutes."

"Sometimes," Angie says, "you just have to let things *be*. That's what they need."

We use the resting time to get the baking sheets ready and while we do that, Max tells everyone about the cherry jam that Angie makes.

The cherries in the jam, he tells us rather proudly, come from a tree in Angie and Alf's back yard and he regales us all with tales of his grandfather's perennial war with the local fauna to keep them away from these precious cherries - apparently, Alf uses nets to keep the birds off in the early season and then homemade traps for the squirrels later on, but Alf and Max always drive out into the woods to release the squirrels and apparently Alf leaves them with a little care package of peanut butter and bird seed for their first night in the wild, the old softie.

This prompts everyone to start telling stories about their grandparents, and the kids are all trying to talk to Nana and Angie at once and the March sunshine that's streaming through the wall of windows in the staff room is making it so bright and hot and stuffy and the kids are all so loud and I'm so tired...

And that's when Kylie pushes a button on the food processor to see what it will do, and since it is holding six cups of heavy cream and doesn't have a lid on it, what it does is launch a giant cream tornado many feet into the air. It's beautiful really, a big, white, graceful wave and for a second, everyone in the room, including me, is frozen in place, eyes up, mouths open in little ohs of wonder and surprise.

And then it all lands on our heads.

MUCH, much later, after Kylie has tearfully apologized and I've mopped the staff room floor and washed down all the cupboards and made a mental note to never, ever cook with children again, when I've gone home, burned my clothes and washed my hair twice, I emerge from the shower to find Nana, Penny Clarke and all the dogs waiting for me. Nana has packed me an overnight bag, and informs me that Penny Clarke will be staying over with her, if I'd like to go spend a little time with Julia, which she really thinks might do me some good. Twenty minutes after that, I'm on Julia's doorstep.

"I'm sorry if I still smell a bit like sour milk, but my grandmother just kicked me out and basically told me not to come home until I'd gotten myself laid," I say.

She smiles and takes my hand. " I can help you with that," she says and she pulls me inside.

'WIDE OPEN HEART:' An Exhibition of Paintings by Olivia Sutton, opens three nights later and it is, for the most part, totally awesome.

The opening of a solo exhibition is a strange cross between a birthday party and a beauty pageant - people you love and respect are congratulating you, while relative strangers stand around discussing your merit as (a) an artist and (b) a human being. Thankfully there is no swimsuit category, but for good or ill and for just a little while, you are the most important person in the world and everybody wants a little piece of you.

Also, there's lots of booze, which never hurts.

And since this whole situation - everything from the tequila shrimp canapés and the jazz trio in the main room to the crowd of truly beautiful people that Bianca has invited (it's like she sent a memo to central casting for a flock of hip, artsy extras) - since all of it landed in my lap like some gigantic gift from the gods of art (or possibly the gods of commerce, because I've noticed that Scottie and Bianca have priced my work at about 25% more than I'd ever be able to ask for with a straight face,) I decide to just enjoy the ride.

And it's a pretty good ride. I sip my glass of champagne, accept hugs and best wishes from all, and field questions about my work from people who seem to actually want to know why, oh why had I used Prussian blue and not ultramarine on a particular piece, and was I consciously aware that I used negative space as a character in my portraits?

And the thing is: I can talk about that stuff all night. Not bullshit talk, not the fanciful tale you spin about your subconscious connections, most of which are basically designed to loosen the customer's grip on their chequebooks, but legitimate issues of art: light, line, colour, composition. I could talk about the cool, muted tint of Prussian blue until the cows come home, about how it becomes breathtakingly beautiful when it's thin and transparent, how buttery it feels on your palette knife when it's thick; about how negative space is the actual point of almost all of my compositions because it represents air and light and time and the heartbreaking absence of something else.

And I haven't talked about these things to anyone for months - maybe years - and it feels really, really good. So good, that occasionally, Bianca casually stops by to take me by the arm and point me towards another cluster of breathless fans and potential buyers. This is not her first rodeo, that's for sure, and she works the room like she's playing a finely tuned musical instrument - a greeting, a touch, a trill of a laugh at just the right moment - it is her very own brand of performance art and she has assembled a huge audience for it.

Mostly though, I'm thrilled to see familiar faces in the crowd and I'm incredibly touched that some of them have travelled so far to be here for my show. Eddie Spaghetti and his wife Connie have even come all the way from Stafford Falls and it's a really good thing because Eddie saves Jason, whom Pam has dragged with her, from actually dying of boredom. The two of them spend the lion's share of the evening holding up the walls and talking sports and trading assorted lies. Connie doesn't even seem to mind, because this is her first real night on the town since the twins were born - Bolognese and Carbonara are with their grandmothers who are tag team babysitting and Connie's phoned them about a hundred times to check that everything is okay, which of course it is. Eddie's arranged for a nice hotel for the night, and I think Connie pretty much feels like Cinderella at the ball, so that's lovely.

Bianca has set up a little sitting area with comfortable sofas because I was worried about tiring Nana out, and Nana and Penny Clarke are ensconced there with Bea and Murray Wiseman, holding court and accepting congratulations by proxy. Julia, who is dividing her time between tending to Nana and drifting from room to room, gazing intently at my work, tells me that Nana is regaling everyone with stories about me as a child, most of which highlight my precocious talent for painting, and only a few of which are actually mortifying. Nana looks so happy, sitting there in a new dress, holding her champagne flute carefully in her lap, and I have a sudden, unbidden memory of her propped up in her hospital bed, looking tiny and frail. Thankfully, that image is blasted out of my head by a booming greeting and bone-crushing hug from Reggie Elliott, my former art teacher colleague from Shady Creek Secondary School.

"Oh my God, look at you, you're gorgeous," he says. "All that time I worked with you and I never knew you had those legs!"

I fight the urge to do a little twirl for him and then he quickly catches me up on all of the SCSS gossip - including a few choice bits involving who went home with whom at the last staff party, but then he turns serious and grabs my arm and pulls me in for a quiet word.

"Listen, I wanted to tell you - you know I had two more years until retirement? Well, the school board is trying to get rid of some of the dead weight, I guess, because they're offering an early retirement incentive this year and I've decided to take it."

"Good for you!" I say. "Have you got plans?"

"We're going to travel," he says. "We've already booked a cruise through the Greek islands in September that's going to be marvellous, but that's not important. The reason I bring it up is because they're going to need someone to replace me and Mr. Peck has already started pestering me about getting in touch with you and I think the job is yours, if you want it." He grins, and waves his hand at the scene around us. "Although why you'd trade *this* for life at a suburban high school is beyond me."

I'm a little bit stunned. Shady Creek feels so far away in space and time that it might as well have been someone else's life. Before I can summon up an answer, Bianca is at my elbow.

"Olivia, darling, I'm so sorry to interrupt, but I've got the director of the Northrop School of Design waiting to talk to you," she says. "I've been telling him about your background as an educator, and he wants to talk to you about reinvigorating their first year drawing program." She lowers her voice and leans closer. "I think he's looking for faculty."

I refrain from telling her that my most recent experience as an "educator" involves a lot of standing by the play structure trying to convince kids not to jump on top of each other, and instead tell Reggie I'll see him in a bit and let myself be led to my next conversation.

The guy from Northrop *is* looking for faculty and after we talk at length about how so many design programs are lacking a good foundation in drawing basics and I explain how I would go about teaching it, he gives me his card and asks me to phone to set up an interview, so now it's officially raining jobs.

I'm still standing there, clutching the card and staring at it, more than a little astonished when Julia and Pam appear beside me. Julia slips an arm around my waist and gives me a little squeeze and I tuck the card away.

"You've already sold nine pieces," Pam says. She's glowing but I'm hard pressed to say how much is glee and how much is free booze.

"Really?" I say.

"And I just saw Jamie's agent and he's got his eye on at least two pieces," Julia says.

"Jamie Buckley sent a buyer to *my* show?" I say.

Julia nods. "He had to fly to New Zealand this week, but he didn't want to miss out on a chance to snap up an original Sutton."

"He didn't have to do that," I say. "I only included him on the invitation list because I thought it would impress Bianca. I didn't expect him to come."

"Trust me, Jamie only does things because they are a lot of fun, or because they will make him a lot of money," Julia says.

"You know, as life philosophies go," Pam says, "that's not a bad one. But, speaking of invitations, out of curiosity, Liv, did you invite your mother?"

"I did, but she's in China right now so I'm safe."

Pam waggles her head and makes a face. "Maybe not as safe as you thought."

She's looking at something over my shoulder and I turn and follow her gaze directly to my mother, who is barrelling across the crowded gallery towards me, with Bianca in tow.

"Surprise, darling!" she says and she throws her arms around me in a theatrical embrace.

"Mom," I say, as I have the daylights hugged out of me. "You're here! I really didn't think you'd be able to make it. You know, all the way from China."

"You didn't think I was going to miss this, did you? My daughter's exhibition at a gallery of this calibre?" she says.

Bianca's beaming and signalling the cater waiters to get my mother some champagne pronto, obviously pleased to be curating this mother and child reunion, but my mother is so busy scanning the crowd, trying to pick out who might be "somebody" that it takes her a minute to notice that Julia and Pam are actually standing beside me. When she does, she says "Oh, hello Paula," to Pam, and gives Julia a tepid smile.

"Have you seen Nana yet?" I say, but she's already redirected her laser focus onto Bianca, and they are discussing the percentage of the show that's sold, the provenance of the shrimp, and whether or not that handsome little Italian boy could procure my mother a gin and tonic. Then, thank God, Bianca spots someone she wants to introduce my mother to, so the pair of them flounce off.

We wait for the manic eddies they leave in their wake to clear and then Pam says, "Okay, but it was still nice that she came."

"Shut up, Paula," I say.

"Olivia?" a quiet voice says. I turn and there's Connie, with a somewhat reluctant looking Eddie Spaghetti.

"Hey, you guys!" I say. "Sorry I haven't had much of a chance to hang out with you."

"We won't keep you long because you probably need to make the rounds and all but we just wanted to say thanks for inviting us," Eddie says. "It was nice of you to include us."

"I'm so grateful that you came," I say. "I know it's a long way to drive but it means a lot to me that you're here."

"Oh, it's been a wonderful night," Connie says. "I had no idea being a painter was so glamorous!"

"Yeah, well, most of the time, it's just me in a t-shirt covered in paint, drinking cold coffee and listening to NPR, so this is kind of a step up."

They laugh but then they start casting sidelong glances at each other and having one of those conversations that married people seem to be able to have simply by changing the angle of their eyebrows in meaningful ways. Pam and Julia wisely choose this moment to go get more champagne.

"Is everything all right?" I say, when I can't take the suspense any longer.

"Oh, everything's fine," Eddie says. "We were just going to - well, initially, we thought we would, but now that we're here and we've seen all your work and everything…" He looks at Connie again and they do more arguing without speaking.

"Oh my God, you guys. What is it?" I say.

"We wanted to ask you if you would paint a portrait of the twins," Connie says.

"Of course we would pay you," Eddie says, quickly. "But we didn't know how to figure out what the going rate was and really, we had no idea how beautiful your work was…I mean, I thought you were good, but I had no idea…anyway, I don't know if it's something you'd consider -"

Connie looks like she's about to strangle him with his own tie just to shut him up so I jump in.

"I would be delighted to do a portrait," I say. "On two conditions. First, I will do it for the cost of the paint."

"Oh, but Liv-"

"And second, it will be a family portrait. I want to paint the four of you, together."

They are so utterly delighted by this news that Connie squeals and throws her arms around me, while Eddie Spaghetti just stands by, beaming and blinking a lot, like he's got something in his eye.

It is a glorious night. I see Nana and Penny Clarke off around eleven and mercifully Nana convinces my mother to leave with them but not before my mother gives me an impassioned and slightly tipsy speech about how this is all she's ever wanted for me, this kind of recognition and success. "Do you see?" she says, as both Julia and Pam help her into her coat, "You leave that podunk little town for one night and you sell dozens of paintings and get a job offer. I was right, Olivia. This is where you belong."

"Thanks for coming, Mom," I say, as Julia and Pam hustle her out to the taxi where Nana and Penny Clarke are already waiting.

The crowd doesn't start to thin until midnight. After the jazz group has packed up and the last straggler has left around one o'clock, Julia, Pam, Bianca and I all collapse on the plush sofas while Scottie and Giancarlo break out the really good stuff to celebrate the fact that of the twenty one pieces that make up *Wide Open Heart*, only three remain unsold, and Bianca is certain that they will be snapped up in the next week or so.

Scottie distributes glasses and Bianca offers a toast to me, the first person officially represented by The Scott Levinson Gallery and the woman who put them in the black. I've never tasted Dom Perignon before and I'm not at all surprised to find that it tastes like sunshine and success.

"So," Bianca says, "you have a lot less unsold work than you did yesterday at this time and you know what that means, don't you?"

"My cheques aren't going to bounce for a while?" I say.

Bianca allows a tolerant smile. "I suppose so, but more importantly, it means that you need to get back to your easel, my darling."

And except for sneaking off with Julia to the fancy hotel that she has booked us for the night, I can't think of anything I'd rather do.

CHAPTER 18

Greeks Bearing Gifts

T.S. Eliot once famously said that April is the cruellest month - some depressing thing about dirt and lilacs, I think - but Eliot has obviously never spent a winter someplace like Stafford Falls because April is such a relief when it finally comes, you almost want to weep. First, you can take off your winter boots and heavy coats and all your sweaters and you begin to feel light and buoyant; then the warmth comes creeping back, tentatively like a shy animal, as if it's not quite sure whether or not it will stay; and then the very quality of the air changes - it becomes softer, more like a caress than a slap, and the whole world smells of mud and trees and melting, growing things. Suddenly, life is full of potential.

A little too much potential, actually.

People keep offering me jobs - really good jobs, with nice perks like studio space and eager young art students who will hang on my every word and business contacts and flexible schedules and things like that. There's the job at the Northrop School of Design, (called N-Sod by those in the know,) but there's also a position teaching drawing at a fashion design school and then there's a potential contract at my alma mater (a shitty night class schedule, but still, it was flattering to get the offer,) and of course, there's the head (which is to say, only) art teacher position at Shady Creek Secondary School. Mr. Peck called me himself and went so far as to say that he should never have let me go. In addition, two galleries have called me to ask if I'm happy with The Scott Levinson Gallery, and, if not, when might it be convenient for them to view some of my work?

My cup is not only running over, it's spilling all over the table and the problem with that is that I'm feeling more than a little paralyzed in the face of so much choice. That and every single one of these offers shares the same deal-breaking drawback.

They're not in Stafford Falls.

But Julia and Nana are.

So it's a problem. And as usual I'm dealing with this problem the only way I can think of - by putting off making any decisions at all and distracting myself from thinking about it by keeping very, very busy: every surface of Nana's house is shining and spotless, my school paperwork is up to date through next month, and the dogs are walked so frequently that now when I pick up their leashes, they all scurry away like they just remembered that they're late for an appointment in the other room.

Not that all my busyness and denial is stopping everyone else from constantly bringing up the topic, as I discovered last week at Sunday dinner. Alf, who was only dissuaded from a third helping of Nana's scalloped potatoes by a pointed look from Angie, thought I should investigate the pension benefits of all the jobs before I made any decisions. Angie said that she thought that the most important consideration for me should be whatever job gave me the greatest chance to advance to other positions and then she asked where Nana had gotten such a lovely leg of ham, and was there apricot jam in the glaze? Nana and Julia both thought the primary criteria should be whatever job gave me the most time to paint and they also agreed that the carrot cake Angie had made for dessert might have to make it onto the Second Chance Café menu. Only Penny Clarke was silent on the entire matter of my future, but did wonder aloud whether she should have brought a bottle of Gewürztraminer to better complement the ham, because she was finding the Riesling she'd settled on a little uninspiring.

It's weird - it's only been a few weeks since my show but that celebratory glass of Dom is starting to feel like something I saw in a movie once. I will admit to having bought multiple copies of the national newspaper that ran the positive review of my show ("*...a painter with vision, whose canvases are at once brooding and luminescent...*") and, under duress, I would possibly confess to carrying around a clipping of the aforementioned review in my bag, so that I can take it out and read it from time to time. At the moment, it's the only tangible proof I have that the whole event actually happened.

The most exciting development, though, is that I've set up a studio. Well, a space where I can paint, anyway. It's actually the sunporch of Penny Clarke's venerable, rambling house, but it's roomy and it's got a wall of north facing windows that overlook the manicured garden that is her back yard. I have a little space heater to cut the morning chill and it's got a great starving artist garret feeling about it. I'm there almost every morning - Penny Clarke has even started ferrying Nana to some of her physiotherapy appointments so that I can get in extra time at the easel. The birds at her bird feeders sing for me, and sometimes I listen to the radio, but mostly I am so absorbed in simply putting paint on canvas that Penny Clarke has started setting a really loud alarm clock in the kitchen before she goes out so that I remember to clean myself up and get to school by noon.

The best days are the ones when Julia stops by mid-morning with a latté for me and some new thing that she's taste testing for Angie and I take a little break with her, and we talk about the pastries, the sunshine, the D&D boys - anything but what's going to happen next.

I'M LESS of a big deal at school. Apparently none of my students have read my press clippings and don't particularly care that *The Chronicle* called my work "*evocative and sweetly melancholy.*" They just want to know, when are they going to get to ride a horse? Davis's equestrian

Anything Can Happen wish is starting to take on a momentum that none of the other activities did, although to be fair, we're comparing riding a real live *horse* to watching stripy little fish swim back and forth, so I get it. Every day I assure them that my friend Penny Clarke is on the case and is trying to track down a suitable equine candidate for a visit but just to be on the safe side they ask me about it every time they see me.

Tobey is the only one who doesn't seem caught up in the horse ride hysteria but that's probably because we're working on his Anything Can Happen request at the moment, which is going to provide him with a horse of his own. His wish, of course, was to fashion something having to do with Greek history and I think it was Max who came up with the idea of building a Trojan horse after leafing through a book with Tobey. It seemed like a good idea at the time - for one thing, there was the cool factor, but for another, as Max said, there wasn't anything made of wood that his grandfather couldn't fabricate. There was some initial disappointment when it had to be explained to Tobey that we would be completing a *scaled model* of the Trojan horse and not a full size replica with actual Athenian troops, but once he got over that little speed bump, he was all in.

Consequently, Alf has been randomly dropping by my classroom, usually with armloads of balsa wood sticks and bits of scrap wood that he and Max and Tobey are slowly piecing together out in the hallway. On one visit, Alf managed to let himself get roped into sitting in the class rocking chair and reading *Where the Wild Things Are* to everybody, so now every time he comes, he has to read a book to the bunch of them before he and his two assistants can go work on their horse. None of us have seen it yet, as they are careful to always cover their masterpiece with a canvas tarp and to hide it in the darkness under the stairs when they're not working on it, because they are planning a big reveal for it on Tobey's Anything Can Happen day.

Besides Alf, the most enthusiastic supporter of Tobey's project is Nana, who has taken it upon herself to outfit the whole class in Greek costumes for the big day. She read an article about autism recently that highlighted the importance of meeting the child wherever they are - in Ancient Greece, if necessary - and she seems to really be throwing herself into the project. Penny Clarke, who is a talented seamstress has jumped on the bandwagon as well and the two of them are busy almost every afternoon now, haunting the fabric store and rooting through the remnants pile for pieces of cloth that they can turn into something the kids can wear. They've already produced a surprising number of things out of old blankets and are testing out a plan to make laurel wreaths for everyone which is going to involve rather a lot of plastic leaves and hot glue gunning, but they seem to be very invested in it and it occurs to me that Nana might be trying hard not to think about my job offers, too.

AND SO IT IS, on a Friday afternoon in late April, that our little subterranean classroom is transformed into a tiny pocket of Ancient Greece. Everyone present is wearing some variation of traditional Ancient Greek clothing, which, I am told in brusque terms by Penny Clarke are not togas, but are in fact *chitons* and *himations,* since togas were from the Ancient Roman period, as every well educated person knows.

Penny Clarke, it must be said, looks particularly regal wearing her *chiton* and *himation* over her tweed skirt and silk blouse, but the costume of the day is surely Tobey's. Using old bits of clothes and rather a lot of cardboard, Max and Miss Holly have put together a very impressive Greek hoplite costume for him, complete with a paper maché helmet and a very long cardboard spear, which I repeatedly have to take back from Wally and Davis before they put out someone's eye. They are both deeply regretting not having picked an Anything Can Happen day that included a weapon, although Wally is quick to remind me that his Anything Can Happen wish specifically required something that explodes. I choose to be selectively deaf to this and redirect him to the laurel wreaths station where Angie is working the hot glue gun like she was born to it.

Alf surprises everyone with small wooden horses that he has carved and he sets up a little workspace just outside the fire exit where he and Max take each of the kids and walk them through the process of carefully applying stain and varnish to their tiny take-home horses. Then, once everyone has had a go at that and we have a neat line of shiny figurines left to dry, we all head back inside to where Nana and Penny Clarke have set up the snack table and they dole out goblets of grape juice and little squares of baklava and and we all sit in a circle for Tobey's presentation.

There is a genuine gasp from all present when Max and Alf roll in Tobey's Trojan horse - it's nearly as tall as Tobey and it is spectacular. The bits of balsa wood look like real planks and somehow they've perfectly captured the delicate curve of the horse's neck. It looks elegant and fierce and exactly like tiny Athenians might come pouring out at any moment. Everyone has a lot to say, and they pelt Tobey with so many questions about this intriguing artifact, that he looks a little spooked for a minute and Miss Holly has to go stand beside him and institute a "Hands Up to Talk" policy.

And then there he is, centre stage, in front of everyone, with his paper maché helmet occasionally falling down over his eyes, making deliberate and well-practiced eye contact with one person after another, answering their questions and lapsing into occasional editorializing about the gods and Socrates. I don't actually hear much of it because all I can think is that he's standing on the same spot as he was the day the fire alarm went off last September, and how he howled like a wounded animal, and how far we've all come since then.

When he finishes, he looks over at Max, who gives him a high five, and everyone claps and cheers.

And then a goblin walks into the classroom with a tray of take out coffees from the Second Chance Café and Isabelle screams like a banshee and everything goes a bit sideways for a while.

IN HINDSIGHT, it was pretty funny - Julia had thought that we might all appreciate some caffeine and Drew had heard we were all wearing costumes and just wanted to inject his own bit of nerd humour into things, so there he was, in his standard uniform of jeans and t-shirt but with a very realistic head-covering mask with creepy, dagger-like teeth and yellow eyes and a pair of really disturbing holes where the nose should be. Long after he's taken it off and we've all spoken to Isabelle in comforting tones for a while, she's still loathe to even go near him. But eventually she rallies and even tries the mask on and chases Drew around making monster sounds of her own, so it looks like we'll all survive.

Finally, we settle in to watch a few episodes of *Professor Milo G. Hound's Race Through History* and Nana and Alf and Penny Clarke take their leave, while we watch a cartoon greyhound wearing a mortarboard and academic robe explain the finer details of the Peloponnesian War.

Overall, it's a fine day, even with the mini-tantrum that Tobey falls prey to when we have to stop the video so that they can all catch their buses home - transitions are tricky for him, especially when he's not ready to be done with something - but a few encouraging words from Max, and Miss Holly's steady hand help set him back on course and eventually we get everybody packed off for home. It takes a little longer than usual to clean up and return the room to something that we can inhabit on Monday, so I'm well behind schedule and wondering what in the world we're going to do for supper when I finally climb into the Jeep to head home. Before I can turn the key in the ignition, though, my phone rings. It's Penny Clarke.

"Now, there's no need to panic," she says.

"Too late," I say, because my heart has just leaped into my mouth. "What's wrong?"

"I'm just here at the hospital with your grandmother, but everything is fine."

"What happened?"

"Well, as we were driving home, Violet mentioned that she'd been feeling a bit faint and had been having some dizziness - "

"This afternoon? She felt faint this afternoon? Why didn't she say something?"

"You know your grandmother, Olivia. When she sets her mind on something, there's no dissuading her."

"Oh my God, it's not another stroke, is it? Is her speech garbled? What are the doctors saying?" There's a conspicuous silence on the other end - possibly because I'm not letting Penny Clarke get a word in - and so I try to reel myself back in and wait for her to answer my many questions.

"She's *fine*," Penny Clarke says. "We just came to the hospital as a precaution. It's not a stroke. I think it's just some transient arrhythmia and they might have to adjust her beta-blockers but they're doing an ECG to be sure. If her QT intervals are fine, they'll probably just send her home."

"Okay, tell me all of that again in English," I say.

"Her heart was beating out of rhythm every once in a while so she felt dizzy. They'll adjust one of her medications. The doctors are just being thorough."

"Are they going to admit her?"

"We're just waiting on some tests but the doctor says she'd probably get a better rest at home."

"All right," I say. "So, everything is basically okay then?"

"It is. Which is why I told you that you didn't need to panic," she says. I can hear the smile in her voice and it's so deeply comforting that I have to blink back tears. "Olivia?" she says after a few seconds. "Are you there, dear? Are you all right?"

"I'm here, I'm fine," I say when I can find my voice again and I'm laughing a little now because I feel a bit embarrassed and at the same time like we've just dodged a bullet somehow. "I'm just leaving school now. Tell her I'll be there in a few minutes."

We hang up but I have to sit there for a while in the parking lot of the school and wait for my own heartbeat to slow a little before I can start the car.

I SPEED WALK my way across the hospital parking lot and through the halls, drawing odd looks from a few quarters which makes me think, for heaven's sake, have they never seen anybody in a rush to get to the emergency ward? But then I stand in line to see the check-in nurse, hoping to find out where they've put Nana and people are still shooting me funny looks and even the check-in nurse smirks at me when it's my turn but it's not until I spot Penny Clarke in the waiting room and she smothers a smile that I realize that although I had the foresight to change out of my *chiton* and my *himation* before I left the school, I did forget to take off my wreath of laurel leaves.

So I do that now, and jam it into my bag.

"It was, uh…dress up day, today," I say, to the check-in nurse. "At my school."

"Of course," she says, in a tone that suggests that's it's not really her business what sorts of things I like to wear. "Your grandmother just got back from the cardio lab. You can go in and see her."

I grab Penny Clarke and we are admitted to the inner sanctum and follow some lines on the floor until we find Nana, propped up on a gurney in a glassed-in room, a dozen menacing-looking computers looming around her but she's chatting up the nurse and they're both smiling and chuckling as if this was a strawberry social, so it's business as usual for Nana and somehow that helps a little.

I give her a kiss on the cheek and a long, tight hug. "Why didn't you tell someone that you thought you were going to faint?" I say.

"I didn't think I was actually *going* to faint, pet. I *felt* faint. There's a difference. And anyway, I feel perfectly fine now. Right as rain. I can't believe they're going to all this fuss."

And quite a fuss it is. The number of nurses and technicians and assorted personnel who drop by is a little intimidating, and every one of them wants to listen to her heart or peer intently at the computer screen that's displaying all her cardiac statistics. Naturally, Penny Clarke grills each of them but Nana is mainly concerned about the poor dogs who haven't had their post-supper walk, or come to think of it, their supper, so Penny Clarke offers to zip over to Nana's and take care of the pups. A few minutes after she leaves, Julia breezes in with coffee and sandwiches, which is especially lovely because I hadn't had a chance yet to sneak out of the emergency ward to phone her.

"Oh, Penny Clarke called me," she says, when I tell her I'm sorry I hadn't let her know where we were. "But I'd already heard from Angie and then from two different people who stopped by the café, including the ER charge nurse who was going off shift when you arrived and who assured me that Nana was doing fine." She gives Nana a quick peck and squeezes her hand. "If I'd thought you weren't doing well, I'd have been here two hours ago."

It occurs to me that the Stafford Falls grapevine is the most efficient means of communication on the planet and that Julia has probably even heard that I was wearing a laurel wreath when I arrived, but is just being too tactful to mention it.

She unwraps a sandwich for Nana and lays it out on the little rolling tray for her and sends me off in search of a cup of water, since Nana probably shouldn't have a cappuccino while they're trying to get her heart to beat in a more conservative and regular way, and when I come back, Julia meets me in the hallway outside of Nana's room, hugs me and says, "It's you I was worried about. Are you okay?"

"I'm a little scared, actually."

"Penny Clarke seems to think she's okay," Julia says. "Which counts for a lot in my book. Listen, Samantha is covering for me, so I have to get back to the café, but call me if you need anything at all or if anything changes."

"I will, but hopefully they'll just let her go home soon."

We go back into Nana's room to find her chatting with a new nurse and nibbling on her sandwich. Julia gives Nana a quick hug and Nana calls her a lamb for bringing us supplies and then she's gone.

It's a while before we're finally allowed to go and Nana seems completely knackered, but is trying not to let on. She needs more help than usual dressing herself and she leans heavily on me and on her cane as we make our way to the Jeep.

The dogs are so excited to see us, it's as if we've returned from the dead and after everyone has been thoroughly petted and told what a good dog they are, I offer to pour Nana a bath, but she's far too tired for all the climbing in and out. She's even too tired for a cup of tea she says, so I help her into her nightgown and tuck her in with all three dogs standing guard and I go run a hot bath for myself. It goes cold while I field calls from Penny Clarke, Angie, Julia, Mrs. Cameron next door, the Reverend Archie Lewis, Mrs. Skinner and Charlotte Ramsay, who I'm not sure if we think is sneaky anymore. I slip into Nana's room twice to check that she's all right, but she's so soundly asleep, she doesn't even hear me. Each time I open the door, Ophelia, who is lying on the mat beside Nana's bed, is illuminated by the light that spills in from the hall, and she lifts her glossy, black head from her paws and gives me a look as if to say, it's okay, we've got this.

IT'S SHORTLY after breakfast the next morning that Nana drops the bomb.

I'm just starting the dishes and waiting on calls back from Angie and Penny Clarke to arrange for one of them to come and stay with Nana this afternoon while I'm away at school, when Nana says, "Pet, come and sit down with me for a minute."

I've set Nana up in the Flowery Room with a cup of tea - the doors to the garden are open and the breeze that drifts in is heavy with the smell of water - the lake, or maybe there's rain coming. I come to the doorway with sudsy hands, intending to put her off until I've finished the washing up but something in her face makes me pause and instead, I grab a tea towel, dry my hands and go take my place on the couch by her rocking chair.

"Are you feeling all right? You're not dizzy are you?" I ask.

"I am perfectly fine," she says. "Just a little tired."

She does look tired, but there's something more. There is a shadow in the expression on her face, as if she's bracing herself against something and I have a sudden flash of sitting in this very spot many years ago, when Nana held my hand and told me in the gentlest way she could that Poppa wasn't coming home from the hospital.

"Nana, what is it?" I say.

"You know how much I love you, don't you, pet?" she says and she squeezes my hand.

"Yes," I say, "but at this exact moment, that's not making me feel any better."

Nana smiles at me and there is such affection in her look, then she says, "I've made a decision that affects you, but promise me you'll let me finish before you try to talk me out of it."

None of this sounds good but I just nod so that we can just get whatever it is out there and talk about it because every second that passes, the look on her face makes me more scared.

Lucy Boxer chooses this moment to come over to Nana and plop her head in Nana's lap to get some petting, so of course, Nana pauses long enough to stroke the velvety fur between her ears, and this big, brutish dog gives a series of contented snorts.

"Well, the long and short of it is this," Nana says. "I've decided to sell the house and move into Birch Haven."

I am so stunned, she may as well have announced that she's selling the house and moving to Tibet. "The nursing home in Winchester?" I say.

"I think these days they call it a retirement home," she says.

"I don't care if they call it Club Med," I say, "it's a nursing home and it's for sick, old people and you are neither of those things."

Lucy turns her very intense and slightly dyspeptic gaze in my direction and gives me one of her patented disapproving looks and I realize that my tone of voice has become a bit snippy.

"I'm sorry," I say. "I agreed to let you finish."

"There's not much to say, really," she says. "I just wanted to let you know that I'm going to have the house valued this week and that I'll probably put it on the market in a month or two."

"Nana, I know having that arrhythmia yesterday must have been scary, but the doctors seemed to think that it was just a little blip. You've been doing too much - you just need to rest for a little bit and I'm sure you'll bounce back."

"I know, but the fact is, I've been thinking about this for over a year and now more than ever, I think I have to be practical. I'd rather make these decisions now while I can, instead of after I've broken my hip or lost my memory or whatever other geriatric catastrophes await."

"Do you really think that's what's going to happen to you?"

She shrugs and smiles sadly. "The afternoon knows what the morning never suspected, pet." Lucy lays her head in Nana's lap and stares up at Nana with a devotion she usually reserves for the Sunday roast. "It will take some getting used to, but I think it's the right thing to do."

"Have you discussed this with Penny Clarke and Angie?"

"In broad terms, yes."

"And what do they think?"

"Angie is of the opinion that we're all going to live forever, and Penny Clarke says that Birch Haven has excellent nursing care."

"But you don't need nursing care."

"Eventually I will."

"Is that where you'd rather be? At Birch Haven?"

"Oh pet, I don't think anyone moves to a retirement home because that's where they'd *rather* be. What they'd rather is to be thirty five again and masters of their bladders. But we all get old and broken down and sometimes it's the most sensible thing to do. Beside, I'm told they have fitness classes and a movie night and bingo three times a week."

"You hate bingo."

"Maybe I'll give it another go," she says. "But what you need to focus on now is what job you're going to take. That needs to be your priority."

"Is that what this is really about then?"

"It's about what's best for each of us, but since you bring it up, Stafford Falls has many advantages and fine qualities, but it is not the centre of the art world. I may not agree with the way your mother expresses it, but she is right - it's criminal that you're not painting and living in that world. You have such a gift Olivia, and even more importantly, it makes you happy. That's what you need to be doing, not hanging around hospital waiting rooms all day long."

"I haven't just been hanging around hospital waiting rooms all day,

Nana," I say. "I've been having a life. A nice life. And now there's Julia to consider, too."

"I know, pet. And sometimes those long distance relationships can work out, but that's not for me to say. That's between the two of you. What I'm saying is that I don't want to be the thing that stands in the way of you moving forward."

"But what is it that *you* want, Nana?"

She strokes Lucy's head some more and smiles an odd little smile. "What I want is for you to be six years old again so I can make you peanut butter sandwiches for lunch and walk you to school. I want to work at the library and sit with your Poppa in the garden and watch the sun set and hear all about his day at work. But we can't always have what we want, pet."

She looks so wistful now that I wished I hadn't asked.

"There's no rush. I won't put the house on the market for another month or so," she says, but she can't quite look at me, it's as if she's already far away. And then she says, "Are you all right to walk the dogs on your own this morning? Only I'm so tired, I think I might just have a little lie down."

She hauls herself to her feet with the aid of her cane and makes her way out of the Flowery Room, the dogs following listlessly behind.

Outside in the garden, the rain begins to fall, softly, like a whisper.

CHAPTER 19

<u>No Good Deed</u>

Cynthia Osgoode has a complicated set of rules regarding weather and the cancellation of recess that can mostly be boiled down to this: unless the driving rain is accompanied by hurricane force winds and an impending tornado, the children *will* go outside for fresh air and exercise. Which is why I currently find myself standing by the play structure in a downpour, trying to keep the really small people from drowning themselves in the puddles and fervently wishing I'd listened to Nana when she told me to bring my raincoat.

I'm also wishing I owned a raincoat.

In addition to all of this, I'm trying really hard not to freak out because after two weeks of harbouring the (apparently fantastic) notion that Nana was somehow bluffing about selling the house and moving to a nursing home, it has all become very, very real. Not just because she went on another tour of Birch Haven, (although she has) and not just because Tyler Cooke with an e has been to our house three times to go over paperwork (and I like him less every time,) but because last night, after supper I came upon Nana, sitting in the Flowery Room, writing notes in the little leather portfolio that she takes to all her library board meetings. When I brought her a cup of tea, I noticed that it was not Official Library Business she was making notes on but that it was in fact care and feeding instructions for Lucy, Ophelia and Mortimer.

"What are your writing there?" I'd asked.

"Oh, just some things I want to remember when I talk to Penny Clarke and Angie tomorrow," she'd said.

"About the dogs?"

She'd nodded.

"Why do you need to talk to them about the dogs?"

She'd actually paused for a second before she answered, as if she'd been looking for the gentlest possible words. "They don't allow you to have dogs at Birch Haven, pet," she'd said. "But Penny Clarke has said she'd be happy to take Lucy, and Alf is just sick to have Ophelia. It's Angie who is going to need some convincing."

And just like that, I feel like I'm starring in the final scenes of *Old Yeller*.

"What about Mort?" I'd said. "What will happen to him?"

"I was thinking of talking to Julia about Mortimer," she'd said. "He just seems to adore her, but I don't want to impose, you know? It's quite a big responsibility. What do you think?"

I think someone has just punched me in the stomach, but I mumble something about Julia and Mort being meant for each other and quickly retreat to my room because my allergies have suddenly gotten very bad and my eyes appear to be leaking.

And now, I'm standing in the rain, with sodden children running back and forth and I'm thinking, maybe I could take the dogs with me, but as soon as I think this I know that it's a ridiculous idea because I can barely manage them in a big house with a yard and plenty of people to help me. And then I realize that at least if the dogs were still in Stafford Falls, Nana would be able to visit them, which unfortunately brings to mind an image of Ophelia being dragged away after a visit, her paws clawing fruitlessly at the linoleum floor, desperate to get back to Nana —

Mercifully, the bell rings to end this whole unfortunate exercise and I begin to shepherd my charges back through the quagmire of mud that used to be a playground, towards the school.

Eddie Spaghetti is waiting for me at the door with a steaming cup of tea.

"So it's still raining?" he asks.

I look down at the puddles forming at my feet. "Yeah, a little bit," I say.

He hands me the tea with a big smile and I'm not sure what makes me more suspicious, the hot drink or the grin.

"Do you have a minute?" he asks.

"Sure, I'm just going to go wring myself out," I say and we head for the stairs that lead to my little Greek hideaway.

"Remember that day in September," Eddie says, as we walk, "when you said, wow, I could really use a hand painting my classroom and I came and risked ten kinds of shit from Cynthia and I also brought beer and you said how grateful you were?"

"Do you need a favour, Eddie?"

"It's a small one, really, but I need you to be discreet."

"Well, now you've got my attention," I say.

He waits until we're in my room with the door closed to continue. "The regional basketball tournament is in two days in Winchester and I wondered if you would come as an extra supervisor. There's supply teacher coverage available and I could arrange it for you, if you want. So you don't have to ask Cynthia."

"Okay, but you realize that I know less than nothing about basketball, right?"

"Yeah, I don't need help coaching. I just need you to supervise the bus ride there and back, because I have an appointment in Winchester after the tournament and so I need to bring my car."

"Sure. I can do that. What's the discreet part?"

"The appointment is a job interview for a full-time vice principal position at a school in Winchester."

"Mr. Spaghetti," I say, "are you jumping ship?"

"No," he says, "not this minute, anyway. I'm just trying to get my name out there."

"And you don't want Cynthia to know?"

"I want to tell Cynthia when it's the right time," he says.

"And how will you know it's the right time?"

He ponders this for a moment. "One of us will probably be drunk," he says.

We laugh together and then we hear the small stampede that is my grade five math group coming down the stairs.

"So you'll do it?" he says.

"Only because it's you," I say and I toast him with my mug of tea.

"Thanks a million, Liv," he says, as he starts for the door. "And don't worry. Hardly any of them ever throw up on the bus anymore."

And then he's gone.

It's the next day when we first notice that something is wrong with Mortimer. When Nana goes to pick up their bowls after breakfast, she sees that Mort didn't eat his kibble, which is highly unusual since nothing can put that dog off his feed. What's worse is that it's possible that this wasn't the first time this happened but this might just be the first morning that we'd noticed it before Lucy could swoop in and hoover up everyone's leftovers.

But then, the morning of Eddie Spaghetti's basketball tournament, the left side of Mortimer's face balloons out as if he's been attacked in the night by a swarm of particularly vindictive bees and it dawns on us that perhaps Mort is having some dental issues. Nana phones the vet as soon as they open at seven, but the regular vet, whom we love, is on holidays and the fill-in vet is in surgery most of the day and can't possibly see Mortimer until six o'clock.

"It'll be okay," I say. "I'll be home from the tournament by five thirty and we'll take him straight to the vet then."

But honestly, Mort looks miserable and the side of his face is so swollen that his sparkling coal black eye is reduced to a winky little slit. Nana has set up a bed for him on the sofa with a fleece and a heating pad and he's laying there so quietly, not at all his usual peri-patetic little self. Ophelia and Lucy even seem subdued, as if they know something bad is going down, but I'm going to miss the bus if I don't get going, so I kiss Nana on the cheek, make her promise to call me if anything happens and I head off to school.

IT'S NOT SO MUCH the noise on the bus that gets to me but rather what sets the drums in my head to pounding is the *smell*: a subtle combina-tion of bus exhaust, farting pubescent boys, and whatever body spray one of them has doused himself in before boarding. The scent is so thick, you can almost see it, like some sort of hazy fug that hangs there in the aisle. Most of the trip, all I want to do is stick my head out the window so I can suck in lungfuls of non-toxic air.

At long last, we roll up to Winchester's newest high school, a cathedral of glass, brick and steel. Eddie Spaghetti is waiting outside on the sidewalk for us and he leads us through the throngs of kids and busses to the classroom where we can stash our stuff. It's funny to see our boys and the expressions on their faces as we make our way past clusters of cool, older kids and since Eddie has insisted that they all wear a proper shirt and tie for today's trip, they all look at once adorable and just a little odd, a bit like dogs who are made to wear glasses.

The rest of the morning is spent in one or another of the school's gyms, either playing a game or scouting out another team. The noise is remarkable: shouts and shrieks that echo around the cinderblock walls, punctuated by the incessant sneaker-on-wood squeak that is the signature sound of all basketball games. I try to follow the action and insert cheers at the appropriate places and I last as long as I can, but by half half past twelve, the headache is really starting to gain steam so I empty my bag in an attempt to find anything that might help the dull thudding in my temples. At the very bottom, I discover what I sincerely hope are two aspirin tablets and then I wander around looking for a water fountain so that I can chug the pills down.

I've just returned to my seat in the bleachers and am considering

leaving it again in order to find a quiet place to call Nana to see how
Mortimer is doing, when there is a nasty collision at mid-court - knee
vs forehead, with one of our boys on the shitty end of that stick. Eddie
flies out to check on his player and after a consultation with one of
the nice St. John's Ambulance volunteers, the poor rubber-legged boy
is dispatched to come sit with me, while he holds an ice pack to his
forehead. Upon interrogation, he tells me his name is Eamonn, that
his stomach feels "a little funny," but that he is otherwise all right. He's
so tight lipped, it's almost as if he's under orders not to divulge
anything to me, so I decide to leave him alone to enjoy his blossoming
concussion. I am trying to keep an eye out for when Max is in the
game, so that I can report back to Angie and Alf, but I quickly
remember how terrifically boring I find watching other people play
games, on top of which, the noise is making my head pound even
worse. I pull out my little sketchbook and a pen to hopefully distract
myself for a while by drawing. I'm several pages in when Eamonn
leans over and says, "You're really good at drawing people, Ms.
Sutton."

"Thanks," I say.

"Could you draw me?" he says.

"Sure. Do you want it with the goose egg on your forehead, or
without?"

Almost a smile. "Without, please."

I take a really good look at him as I draw - he's a gorgeous boy, big
pale blue eyes with cinnamon freckles on his nose and cheeks, and
curly hair in a shade of blonde that many women pay a lot of money
to have. He has fine bones and a patrician nose and if I was going to
do a proper portrait of him, I'd use watercolours because there is
something wispy and evanescent about him, despite his ice pack
bravado. When I finish it, I rip the page out of the book and give it to
him. He studies it with a hint of a smile, then says, "Thanks. My mom
will really like this."

There's a deafening buzzer just then, to mark the end of something
(The period? The quarter? The match? I am so out of my depth here,)
and Eddie signals for us to come along with the team for lunch. As a

special treat, Eddie has arranged for us to have lunch in the cafeteria, with real live high school students, most of whom tower over our guys, but who seem to find them amusing. We stake out a couple of tables in the corner and Eddie reminds the boys not to be morons in the lunch line. The looks of rapt attention on their faces as he talks to them is endearing - they would all follow him over a cliff if he suggested it, including, I am a little surprised to see, Adam, whom I've really only ever experienced in his capacity as part time evil genius and bully.

They all pile onto a table that's a safe distance from us. Max still gives Adam a wide berth, I notice, but the older, eighth grade boys seem to hold a lot of sway and they seem to approve of Max, so he sticks to their protective little huddle. Everybody tucks into their lunch, including Eddie who pulls a massive meatloaf sandwich out of his paper lunch bag and makes short work of it. I'm still unwrapping my salad and searching for the cutlery that I was sure I'd packed when he's on his feet again.

"I'm going to go track down some coffee for us," he says. He wads up his lunch bag and makes a fancy throw that lands right in the big garbage can by the door and all his players clap and cheer. A few minutes later, he's back with two mugs.

"You should see the fancy coffee machine they've got in their staffroom," he says. "I had to pay top dollar for these."

"You have my undying gratitude," I say.

There is a burst of laughter from our boys' table— Max has said something that has cracked up the eighth grade boys and they're all yucking it up together. Even Adam, who is sitting near them, is laughing.

"You know, I was skeptical that basketball was the answer to all the world's ills, but I see now that I was wrong," I say. "Being on this team has really helped Max. And Adam."

"Well, I think stopping the abuse played a pretty big role in helping Max," he says, "but as for Adam, I do think team sports are an excellent opportunity to teach someone how not to be such a dick."

I laugh. "Is that one of the pillars in your philosophy of education? 'Teach them not to be dicks?'"

"Yes," he says. "That and good penmanship. Good penmanship is very important."

Eamonn and another boy get up and come over to our table just then. "Ms. Sutton?" the boy who is not Eamonn says, "did you really draw this picture of Eamonn?"

"I did," I say.

"Could you show me how to draw a person's face like that?" Charlie asks me.

"Sure, sometime I could -" I start to say, but before I can finish, Charlie and Eamonn have both disappeared back to their table, only to reappear half a minute later with pencils, pages torn from their notebooks and expectant faces.

"Oh, you mean right now," I say.

"Guys, let Ms. Sutton finish her lunch," Eddie says.

"No, no, it's all right," I say. "Have a seat." I pull out my sketchbook and pen and pretty soon we're deep in a conversation about the proportions of the human face and Not Eamonn, whose name turns out to be Charlie, is telling me about how he wants to be an animator for video games and Eamonn is telling me he likes to build things and often finds it helpful to draw the thing he's building first and did I know what sort of job that could turn into? And then my phone buzzes with a text from Julia.

I'm at the vet with Nana and Mort. Call when you can.

Shit, shit, shit.

I excuse myself from the table and speed dial Julia.

"What's going on?" I say, when she answers.

"Mort gave your Nana a bit of a fright. His breathing had become quite laboured and she was pretty worried so she called me to see if I could take them to the vet right away."

"Is Mortimer all right?"

"He seems a little better," Julia says. "The vet thinks that he's got a little bit of fluid around his heart so they've given him some drugs for that and his breathing is better. The bigger problem at the moment is his tooth. Apparently, he's got a pretty bad abscess."

"Oh, poor guy."

"The thing is - he probably needs an extraction but that would require an anesthetic and the vet doesn't think a dog of Mort's age with a heart condition has a very good chance of surviving that. He basically told Nana, 'You might as well just put him down.'"

"Oh my God, he did not *say* that to her!"

"I may be paraphrasing a bit, but basically. To be fair though, we sort of got off on the wrong foot," Julia says.

"How so?"

"Well, I don't think he appreciated being dragged out of surgery - I guess it's marathon spay-the-kitty-cats-day here, but it seemed to me that it was an emergency, so when we showed up at the clinic and he wouldn't come and take a look at Mort, I made a little bit of a scene."

"You made a scene?"

"Just a little scene."

"On a scale of one to Shirley MacLaine in *Terms of Endearment*, exactly how little was this scene?"

"Oh, about a six. But I was prepared to go as high as an eight if I didn't get what I wanted."

"So what are they going to do?"

"They're going to give him some painkillers and a bunch of antibiotics to see if that can attack the infection at the heart of the abscess. Basically, it's a wait and cross our fingers strategy."

"How's Nana?"

"She looks a bit tired and she's worried, of course, but she's relieved that his breathing is better."

"Thank you so much for doing this," I say. "I'm sorry I wasn't there to take care of things."

"I'm glad she called me," she says. "I haven't had the opportunity to pitch a fit in quite a while. It was quite cathartic."

"I appreciate you using your fit-pitching skills to help out Mort and Nana," I say. "Tell Nana that I'll be home as soon as I can."

We hang up and I relay the information regarding Mort's medical drama to Eddie, who immediately starts digging around in his back-pack for his car keys.

"You should go," he says, "take my car, I'll take the bus back with the boys. You should be there in case things go south."

"No, no, no. You've got your interview after the tournament," I say. "You can't miss that."

He shrugs. "I'll reschedule."

"No, really, it's all right. It'll just be a few hours, and Julia's keeping tabs on things. It's fine. I don't want you to miss your interview."

Further debate on the question is interrupted by Charlie who is holding up a sketch for us to look at - it's Eddie as a superhero, complete with cape made out of what looks like noodles and the logo "Spaghettiman." It's a pretty good sketch - he's captured something of the line of Eddie's nose and brow and given him a chiseled haircut and a hell of a six pack.

Eddie gives a great belly laugh and asks Charlie to sign it, then he fastens it to the top of the pile of papers on his clipboard and admires it some more.

"Spaghettiman," he says. "I like that."

We play a lot more basketball. Or rather the boys do - all of them except Eamonn, whose mother comes to claim him early in the after-noon to take him to have his head examined. I mostly sit in the bleachers and cheer and draw, until my phone trills. My heart jumps because at first I think it's Julia and something's happened to Mortimer, but it's actually the guy from the fashion design school and I let it go to voice mail because I really don't want to talk about jobs and contracts and deadlines right now and in the end, it turns out it was just as well that I didn't pick up because he leaves a message saying that he really needs a answer from me about the job and I don't have one to give him.

They're all starting to breathe down my neck now, everybody wanting me to commit, but every time I think I've decided what I should do, I get this empty, queasy feeling in my stomach and I start to second guess myself. I'm fairly certain that I don't want to go back to the high school. Basically, I've had to admit that teaching art full-time in the public school system is a huge job that takes up all your time and energy in the pursuit of helping other people to create art, which is a noble endeavour, but ultimately results in you not creating any art of your own. (In a marathon session on the phone the other night, Pam told me that if I took the high school teaching job, she was going to call me "Mr. Holland," for the rest of our time on earth, and constantly ask me how my "Opus" was coming along. You can't buy friends like that.)

Thankfully, I'm distracted from all these existential and career thoughts by the excitement unfolding on the basketball court. Against the odds, our boys make it to the finals so I end up cheering myself hoarse - there's a brilliant moment when Max makes a basket and judging by the look of shock on his face, he's as surprised as anyone, and his teammates slap him on the back so hard that it nearly knocks him to his knees. Eddie seems to get everybody into the game for at least a few minutes and it comes right down to the final buzzer, but in the end, Stafford Falls Public School comes up short by 10 points. There is heartbreak on all the sweaty faces of our boys, but Eddie leads them in a cheer for the other team and then sends them to shake hands. A half hour later, they're all back in their shirts and ties and they're wearily trooping out to the bus for the trip home. Eddie has also changed into a clean shirt and is wearing a fancier tie and a suit jacket, so I barely recognize him as he leads them over to our bus.

"Wow, you look nice," I say.

"Look good, play good," he says. "Listen, thanks again, Liv, for filling in for me."

"Anytime. Good luck with the interview."

"I won't need luck," he says, as he slings his backpack over his shoulder and heads off. "For I am Spaghettiman and I am awesome."

SEVERAL PARENTS ARE late to come and pick up their offspring, and so it's the far side of six o'clock by the time I get home. Nana looks tired and worried and when I see Mortimer, I can see why. The swelling seems even worse tonight - the eye on the swollen side is completely shut now and he is exactly where I left him this morning, curled into a pathetic little ball on the sheep's fleece that Nana has arranged for him on the couch in the Flowery Room. Lucy Boxer has installed herself on the couch beside him with a stern expression on her face, acting as some sort of nurse/guard hybrid, so I retreat to the kitchen where I find Nana searching through the cupboards, looking for something that will make Mort's antibiotic and pain pills irresistible to him. We settle on a little cheddar to conceal the pill, with peanut butter smeared around it to disguise any lingering pharmaceutical smells he might pick up. It becomes quite clear just how shitty Mort is feeling when I offer him this delectable little tidbit and he sniffs it indifferently, then puts his chin back down on his paws. I try to reason with him and explain why it's vitally important that he take his pill and that it will make him feel better, but he is not swayed in the least by my arguments.

In the end, I have to strong arm the poor little guy, prying his tiny jaws open and shoving the pills into his mouth as far back as I can. When I've massaged his throat to make him swallow and even checked under his tongue to make sure the drugs are down the hatch, he's too tired to even shoot me death glares with his good eye, and he just whimpers and trembles and lies back down, and I feel terrible for being such a bully. The only thing that's worse is the look on Nana's face.

Nana and I try to eat a little dinner but neither of us is hungry and what's worse, we don't have much to say to each other. I don't know how to handle the uneasiness that has developed between us the past few weeks because we've never not been able to talk to each other. Even at the worst of times when I was a teenager and prone to moods and hormones and was generally behaving like a caricature of myself, at least we could talk. We didn't always agree - after all, I was being raised by my *grand*mother, she had to be behind the times, right? We were, however, always honest with each other and no matter how difficult, we talked about everything.

But these days, we're hardly speaking - partly because I don't want to talk about my impending job choices and partly because she won't discuss her decision to move into Heaven's Waiting Room, which pretty much leaves us with the topic of whether or not Lucy's new kibble has made her flatulence any better. So, yes, we talk about dog farts for half an hour.

Mercifully, the doorbell rings around eight thirty. It's Julia, bearing a bowl of fragrant chicken broth that she got from Mr. Wong at the Chinese restaurant that she's hoping might tempt Mort. He rallies a bit when he sees her, lifting his head and wagging his stubby tail, and when she sits beside him and offers him the bowl of broth, he gives a couple of licks out of politeness, but even this meagre effort seems to exhaust him and then he lies back down, his grotesquely swollen face snuggled against Julia's leg.

It is an excruciating evening - small talk so small that it's positively microscopic, punctuated by long silences. Julia does her best to distract us all by telling us about the goings-on at Six Perfections - the construction is well underway and progressing at quite a pace, which makes me wonder if they're employing the "Maximum Caffeination Strategy" that she used to get the café ready in time. Tenzin is apparently run off his feet, alternately wearing a bright yellow hardhat or a bee keeper's bonnet, both of which I think sound at once hilarious and yet oddly fitting, as if that's what he should have been wearing with his monk's robes all along.

By eleven o'clock, Nana looks so tired and pale that I'm worried she's going to have a recurrence of her arrhythmia so I suggest that maybe she should go to bed. Of course, she will hear nothing of the sort and I can tell that she's terrified that something bad will happen to Mort in the night while she's sleeping, so I tell her I will stay up with Mort and wake her if he takes a turn for the worse. Julia announces that she has to pop by the café to help Drew close up, but she offers to come back and keep me company on my Mortimer vigil and I'm so grateful that I don't even pretend to object.

Once I have Nana tucked in, I take Ophelia and Lucy out for a quick tour around the block, then I come back and coax Mort off his cushion and out to the garden for a pee. It's a beautiful night - balmy and clear, and I stand looking up at the stars for a long time while Mort decides exactly which of Nana's rose bushes he should water. We go back in and I help Mortimer up onto the couch and then lie down on the couch myself. He abandons the fleece in favour of curling up against my belly and I stroke his head and study his misshapen profile.

"You know, " I say to him, after a while, "I really thought that you were tougher than this, dude. I thought that when it was your time to go - which, by the way, I don't think it is - but when it *was* your time, I thought you would go out in a blaze of glory, foiling a bank robbery or fighting off a pack of rabid wolves or something big and bold, you know? Because, honestly, this is embarrassing. You simply cannot let your badass self be taken down by something as mundane as tooth decay."

I don't know whether or not Mort agrees with me, because he just snuggles closer to my tummy, sighs wearily and shuts his good eye.

Julia, because she is a perfect angel, comes back bearing coffees. She quietly lets herself in and for once the dogs don't go off like grenades because there's someone coming through the door. She asks if we have something that might "brighten up" the coffee and then she takes my place on the couch with Mort while I go fetch some of Nana's good Irish whiskey. We sit together, sipping our comforting spiked drinks and petting Mort.

After a while, Julia says, "Is everything okay with you and your Nana? It seemed a bit tense tonight."

"That would be because she's making a terrible decision about her future simply in order to push me out the door," I say, and even I'm a little surprised at how angry I sound.

"Well," Julia says. "Do you need one?"

"Do I need one what?"

"A push," she says and she's smiling, but her eyes are very serious. "Have you considered that maybe she's right?"

"Are you saying you think she should move to that nursing home?"

"Olivia," she says, and that's all she says, just those four syllables that comprise my name. She never calls me Liv or Livy which almost everyone does at some time, she always calls me 'Olivia,' but somehow when she says it, it doesn't sound formal or officious, it sounds joyful and sweet, like she just loves so much to say my name. But somewhere between the time she says my name and when she next starts to speak, I know in my heart that this time, it's not good.

"What?" I say.

"It's ironic because part of what I love about you is the fact that you are the kind of person who would give up everything to take care of her grandmother," she says, and it's as if she's talking to herself or maybe Mort, but then she looks at me and she's so sad. "You have to stop being angry at your Nana because she is just trying to give you the freedom to make a decision. And so should I."

"What are you talking about?"

She sighs, and it's a reluctant, weary sigh. "I've been thinking a lot about it and I'm worried that if you pass on these job offers and stay in Stafford Falls on my account, you're going to start to resent me."

"Julia, don't be -"

"No, hear me out. I'm not saying it would be next week or next month, but someday. Because if there are things out there in the bigger world that you want to be having and doing and you're only here because this is where I am, then you might begin to resent that and then eventually, you will begin to resent me. And being the thing that makes you unhappy…well, that would kill me." She tries to smile, but her eyes are filling up. "So, I think I need to let you go."

I have to sit up and carefully put down my cup because suddenly, I'm feeling really shaky. "Are you breaking up with with me?" I say.

"No, I'm not breaking up with you, I'm releasing you. It's not the same thing at all."

"Oh, I see. So we're still going to move in together sometime? Support each other, talk every day, having toe-curling sex?"

"Well, no," Julia says and she looks away. "I suppose not."

"Then it's exactly the same thing as breaking up. And it's not what I want."

"Olivia -"

"No, you don't get to decide that for both of us. Just like Nana doesn't get to decide -"

"But she does! Sweetheart, it's her life. If she wants to sell the house and move to Birch Haven, then she gets to do that. You shouldn't try to stop her."

"But she's only doing it for me. So I have to move back to the city and take a job there."

"Olivia, don't you see? She's doing it to *allow* you to move back to the city and take an *amazing* job there. She's doing it because she loves you. And so do I."

We go on in this vein for quite some time and I become increasingly angry because it's really hard to argue with someone who is so intent on telling you that they care about you and want the best for you, but I try anyway. Eventually, we fall into a somewhat loaded silence, punctuated only by Mortimer's wheezy little snores. A lot more of Nana's good whiskey is consumed. And that's all I remember.

IT's ONLY the moment that my eyes fly open that I even realize that I've fallen asleep. I'm sitting in Nana's rocking chair and at first I think it must still be the middle of the night because the sky outside the French doors is inky black, but then muted morning sounds come to me from the kitchen - the gurgle of the coffee maker, the clink of teaspoons - and then one thought finally works its way through the fog of my sleep hangover.

Mortimer.

His fleecy bed is empty.

Shit, shit, shit, I think as I haul myself to my feet and stagger out of the room, but I stop abruptly when I get to the kitchen, because Nana is up, and is sitting at the table with Mortimer on her lap. His face is still swollen, although not as much as yesterday - it's noticeably deflated, as if someone had let the air out of a balloon and in fact, now that I look at him, I can see that the swelling is down enough that he can open both eyes again, and although this strikes me as a little bit miraculous, at the moment, I'm more distracted by the fact that he is devouring a plate of scrambled eggs that Nana is holding for him.

"Oh, pet! I'm sorry we woke you," Nana says.

"There's coffee if you want some," Julia says. She's over at the stove, taking strips of bacon from Nana's big cast iron skillet and putting them on plates.

"He's eating," I say and I motion numbly towards Mort, who looks like he might be trying to lick the Blue Willow pattern right off the little plate.

"I know, isn't it wonderful?" Nana says. "Julia, I think he might want a bit more. Could you scramble him another egg?"

"Sure," Julia says and she pulls open the fridge door and peers inside. "Do you think he might like a little ham with this one? There's some leftovers here I could mince."

"He can have foie gras on toast points today if he wants them!" Nana says and we all laugh because it's all so improbable and marvellous, and also because it's funny to think of Mortimer, sporting a little black bow tie and top hat, eating fancy canapés.

And then the doorbell rings and everything stops.

The clock on the stove says it's 4:46 a.m., and I am frozen because nobody ever rings your doorbell at that hour with good news, and for just a second I think, if we don't answer it, nothing bad can happen.

But I do open the door and it's Miss Holly and Mike the Cop. The lights from the police cruiser in the driveway flash blue-white-red, blue-white-red, and Miss Holly's cheeks are stained with tears.

CHAPTER 20

Paddling in Eden

The details are at once mundane and surreal. Something as ordinary as stopping to help a woman with a flat tire - because that's the kind of guy Eddie Spaghetti was, that's how he'd been raised, you stopped and helped people - especially a woman with two little girls, and while they unloaded the tons of kid paraphernalia from the back so that Eddie could get at the spare tire, he'd told the woman about Bolognese and Carbonara and how they were the most perfect babies in the world, except for the fact that they never slept. And when they'd discovered that there was no jack, Eddie had said, no problem, I'll grab mine and he had stepped out from behind the van and been hit by a car before he'd taken three steps.

The police report left out a lot of details. Like the fact that the woman was on her way to a birthday party for one of her daughter's school friends and so they were all wearing their fancy party dresses; how the driver who hit Eddie was arguing with his wife by text message and was taking the corners a little too fast, and how Eddie's job interview had started late and gone long, so he'd phoned Connie before he'd left Winchester to say, I'm on my way and yes, I'll pick up milk and bread, and ten thousand other tiny details that all came together in such a way as to put Eddie Spaghetti, the first friend I made in Stafford Falls, into the path of a late model Mazda with a distracted, pissed off driver.

The paramedics say Eddie never regained consciousness and that's a blessing I suppose, but what I worry is that, as he stepped out from behind the van, he saw the car and and for that one split-second, he was afraid.

I don't let myself think about that very often.

He was Spaghettiman and he was awesome.

GRIEF IS A STRANGE THING. You think it's going to feel so much more like sadness, but it's not sadness at all, it's not nearly that simple - it's regret and despair and fear and rage and guilt and a hundred other things that ambush you from one moment to the next, that knock you to the ground and beat the very breath right out of you. Nana says that you get through it by degrees, that you learn to live with it, like walking forever with a pebble in your shoe. People try to say supportive things to me, encouraging things, hopeful things, but none of it helps and sometimes it makes everything worse and I want to scream at them. But then the night of Eddie's wake, just when I think I can't stand it anymore, Tenzin comes to the funeral home, resplendent as a sunrise in his orange robes, and he touches his forehead to mine for a long time, and then he sits beside me for hours and says nothing at all and somehow, that's what helps the most.

It's work that saves me - the kids, not the painting, because my canvas and brushes just sit there, untouched and useless, but the kids seem to need me like they need their next breath. There are grief counsellors at our school for the first few days and they mean well but they don't know any Mr. Spaghetti stories and that's all we want to do that first while, just sit together and tell Mr. Spaghetti stories as if we might somehow bring him back by invoking his memory so often.

The older kids take it hardest, at least outwardly, but there's a wave of tantrums and acting out in the younger ones, and they seem both angry at the world and more than anything, frightened, because if Mr. Spaghetti could just vanish from their lives in such a horrible and sudden way, then the world really is a dangerous, unpredictable place and who knows what the hell might happen next?

Which is exactly how I feel right now, but I don't tell them that.

Instead, we talk about how Mr. Spaghetti loved his tropical fish and what a good basketball player he was and how he always told such terrible jokes and we draw pictures of him playing with Bolognese and Carbonara, and now every day when our time together is over, Isabelle hugs me before she leaves.

Grief messes with your memory, too. There are a few moments that are chiseled into my brain and even when I don't want to think about them, they come back to me with startling clarity.

One of them is a moment near the very end of Eddie's funeral mass. St. Mary's, the big fortress-like Catholic church, was packed to the rafters, and people were filing by in an endless line to receive communion. The old pipe organ and the choir had chugged through a selection of hymns to pass the time, but the heat of the spring day and the sorrow were both oppressive and it was all I could do not to get to my feet and push my way through the crowd and out into the sunlight and air.

And then, a woman began to sing.

I've probably heard more renditions of *Ave Maria* than most people do in their lifetime, because my Poppa believed that Schubert's *Ave Maria* was perhaps the most perfect piece of music ever written and he had me listen to a hundred different recordings by the time I was six. But in all that time, I'd never heard anything like this.

This woman's voice was so pure and sweet that it made me think of Tenzin's singing bowl, and the whole church just stopped - I don't think anyone moved or breathed the entire time she sang. With every note, her voice reached down into our misery and cradled us and reminded us that, even though we couldn't feel it right now, there was still beauty in the world, somewhere. I sat there with my eyes closed and I let her lift me up and soothe me and when the last divine echo of her voice had faded and I could breathe again, I turned around and looked up into the choir loft to see who it was who could possibly have made such a sublime sound.

And there, standing beside the organ, tears streaming down her face, was Cynthia Osgoode.

It was like I'd never seen her before in my life.

SLOWLY, sadly, inevitably, life moves on. The awful stillness of suspended animation and emptiness gives way simply because there are things that must be done - walking the dogs, folding the laundry. Nana hires Alf to help get the house squared away for its inspection and so he's around a lot, touching up the paint, fiddling with the faucets, pruning some wayward bush or another. The house feels crowded and foreign and I want to escape it but I have nowhere to go - my "studio" feels equally claustrophobic because Penny Clarke is always hanging about and constantly seems to be on the verge of saying something but then thinking better of it, and I can't go to the café because even though Julia has been nothing but supportive in the wake of Eddie's death, I feel her slipping away. It's like she's slowly erasing herself from my life, as if we're playing some backwards game of 'Red Light, Green Light,' and one of these turns I'm going to look back and she'll be gone.

I phone the guy from the Northrop School of Design and tell him I'll take the job.

He's delighted.

THE FIRST SIGN that the kids are truly recovering is in early June, when they start to nag me about the horse again, but to be honest, I don't really mind, because I need something to distract me. Luckily, Penny Clarke has been on the case for weeks, and her friend Meredith who runs a riding stable outside of Stafford Falls has the perfect horse for us. Penny Clarke tells me all about 'Snapdragon' who is a Palomino gelding, a gentle chestnut fellow with flaxen mane and tail -

which doesn't mean a lot to me, but which seems to make Penny Clarke very excited. Best of all though, Meredith is willing to have all of us to her farm to take rides on the aforementioned Snapdragon for free - she has a nephew with autism and once she hears about Tobey, she insists that we be her guests. It feels too good to be true, so naturally that's when it all goes off the rails.

The volume of paperwork that Mrs. Demanksi hands me when I ask her about hiring a bus for our little field trip is the first indication that this might not be as straightforward as I'd hoped, but that little bureaucratic hurdle is nothing compared to the astronomical fee on the last page.

"I don't want to buy the bus," I say to Mrs. Demanski, "I just want to borrow it for a few hours."

"It's ridiculous what they charge," she says. "But there's just the one company around here, so they can set their price."

"But there's only a few of us going," I say. "Do they have smaller buses?"

She shakes her head. "Same price."

"Do we have a school fund that could cover this? Is there a budget for field trips?" I ask.

I can't tell if there's pity or admiration in her expression, but then she flicks her eyes in the direction of Miss Osgoode's closed door. "You can certainly ask," she says.

I sigh, walk to the door and prepare to knock.

"Wait," Mrs. Demanski says and she hands me a cellophane wrapped candy.

I thank her and knock.

Miss Osgoode bids me to enter but as always, she is busy scrutinizing something on her computer screen and as always, she makes me stand there waiting until she is finished perusing this crucial document. Then, she carefully removes her reading glasses and says, "What can I do for you, Ms Sutton?"

"It's about a field trip," I say and I tell her about Davis's Anything Can Happen wish to ride a horse and I tell her all about Snapdragon (although I'm sure I misuse a number of important equine vocabulary terms since I'm not one hundred percent certain what 'gelding' means) and I highlight how all of this is *free* and at *no cost* to us, and I even throw in the bit about how Meredith the Horse Lady has a nephew with autism, but that we can't do any of it unless we can get to Meredith's farm, and buses, I've just discovered, cost the earth, so…

I don't even get to the asking for money part before she starts shaking her head.

"It's quite impossible," she says. "We just don't have the funds."

"But it's just one bus," I say. "The sports teams get buses all the time."

"Yes, and that's planned into the budget in September. You can't come to me a few weeks before the end of the school year and expect me to magically make money appear."

"What if we were able to get some donations?" I say, and I am casting about now, frantically trying to think of some way to make this work because I don't want to have to be the one to tell Davis that he's the only kid in our class who's not going to get his wish, even though he's written a seven page report on horses and probably knows what gelding means. "Or what if Meredith could bring the horse here, to the school? She could give them rides around the schoolyard."

"Absolutely not," Miss Osgoode says. "It's patently unsafe and would be a huge disruption to the rest of the school."

"They're not going to be show jumping," I say. "A nice lady is just going to walk them around in a circle, that's all."

"Ms. Sutton, the liability that you would be exposing the school to is -"

I stop listening for a little while then, partly because she's starting to sound like my mother when she tries to explain economic theories to me, but also because I'm trying to organize my next argument, which is going to be based on how what I'm doing in the CRC class is actually working, how the kids are reading and writing, how Tobey is occasionally having actual conversations with people, how I'm doing such a good job but somehow it all just starts to sound whiny and immature in my head, like I'm a child who is begging her mother for a ride on a pony because she has been a Very Good Girl.

And then, just as Miss Osgoode is enlightening me on the role of the Risk Management Office at the school board and how my request would set all their risk-averse heads to spinning on their very cautious shoulders, for some reason I suddenly recall that moment at Eddie's funeral when this infuriating little woman started to sing *Ave Maria,* and then I am forced to remember again that Eddie is dead and I find I can't argue with her for one more minute.

I hold up my hand to stop her words. "I understand," I say. "Thank you for your time, Miss Osgoode."

She's so shocked by my capitulation that she sputters on a little while longer about deductibles and contributory negligence, but I've already started to move towards the door and I let her words wash over me. I have one hand on the door knob when something occurs to me. I pause and I give it a second and then a third thought and finally decide, no, it won't actually kill me to say something nice, so I turn back to face her.

"I've been meaning to tell you that I thought you sang brilliantly at Eddie's funeral," I say.

It's as if my words disarm her - at first she's stunned, but then her shoulders slump like I've knocked the wind out of her. "Thank you," she manages to say. "I was very fond of Mr. Spinella. I wanted to do something to honour him."

"You have a beautiful voice," I say.

"There was a time - " she starts to say and then it's as if she remembers who she's talking to and she shakes her head at her own folly.

"There was a time, what?" I say.

She sits back in her high-backed administrator's chair. "There was a time when it was all I wanted to do. For a while, in high school, it was my dream to perhaps someday sing professionally. But, that wasn't in the cards."

"Why not?"

"Oh, a hundred little reasons," she says. "Mainly, my parents felt...

well, they didn't see the point of studying music. I was the first person in my family to go to university and it didn't seem practical to them."

Then your parents were idiots and criminals I think, but I don't say this.

"But that's ancient history, now," she says. "I'm very proud of what I've accomplished. I wouldn't change a thing."

"Well," I say. "I hope I have the chance to hear you sing again sometime."

She smiles but can't quite meet my eyes. "Maybe on a happier occasion," she says and she's already putting her reading glasses back on and turning back to her computer screen.

I seize my chance to slip out the door.

Miss Holly is loitering by Mrs. Demanski's desk and they are both straining to appear casual and not at all like they've been trying to overhear my conversation with Miss Osgoode. They don't look surprised when I shake my head.

"All right," Miss Holly says, as we head back to our subterranean hangout, "then we'll just have to go to Plan B."

"I wasn't aware that we had a Plan B," I say.

"Thanks to Mrs. Demanski, we do," she says.

"Mrs. Demanski came up with a Plan B?"

"She did. She reminded me that Miss Osgoode is only in charge of events that take place on school property."

"So?"

"So," Miss Holly says, with a wide, satisfied grin, "Miss Osgoode is not the boss of Saturdays."

Clever old Mrs. Demanski.

To say that things began to snowball when Miss Holly and I convened with Penny Clarke and Nana at the Second Chance Café would be an injustice to the whole metaphor of giant cartoon snow-balls. I mean, this thing got out of hand *fast*. One minute we were organizing an intimate little meet and greet with Snapdragon at the park, and the next I was somehow hosting "The CRC Class Family

Medieval Barbecue Pot Luck and Science Show Extravaganza," with a guest list as long as my arm.

I blame Drew.

Ever since his cameo as a goblin at Tobey's Anything Can Happen day, Drew had sort of taken a shine to our little group of castoffs, and had begun dropping by the class once a week or so to read to the kids and more importantly, to be read to by them, a role of great honour which had previously only ever been filled by Mortimer. Of course, the girls thought Drew was dreamy and the boys thought he was the best thing since sliced bread because he could talk knowledgeably about such crucial topics as video games, Pokemon cards and which Avenger was, in actual fact, the coolest. He and Wally appeared to hit it off particularly well and they spent a lot of time deep in conversation about rocketry and things that could cause really loud explosions, and so it was Drew who reminded me that it wasn't just Davis's Anything Can Happen wish that hadn't yet been granted - I still owed Wally a Great Big Bang.

"So I was thinking," he says, as he sits himself down with Miss Holly, Penny Clarke, Nana and I at our window table at the Second Chance Café, "since we're having this party and all, we should make bottle rockets."

I let his generous use of 'we' go, because, frankly, I'll take whatever help I can get. "Aren't those kinds of fireworks illegal?" I ask.

"No, not that kind of bottle rocket," he says, "although you know what? You're right, we should totally have fireworks! Let me call the guys and see who knows where we could get some." And then he's off again, phone in hand, to pull somebody an espresso at the counter.

"All right," Penny Clarke says as she puts her phone down, "I've booked Meredith and Snapdragon for Saturday, the 21st."

"I've got Mike on the line," Miss Holly says, "and he thinks he can get us an eight burner propane gas grill for that day, but we need to pick it up. Do we know anyone with a truck?"

"I think Kylie's father has a truck for work," I say, and Penny Clarke grabs my parent contact list and picks up her phone again.

"What about tables, pet?" Nana says. "Are there enough picnic tables at the park?"

"We might need some extra tables to put out the food that people bring," I say.

"I'll call the New Vicar and see if we can borrow some folding tables from the church," she says, and she grabs her phone.

I'm just on hold with someone at the town hall, waiting to hear about what sort of permits we might need for public gatherings, barbecues, horse rides and bottle rocket launches when there is a lull at the counter and Drew reappears.

"Drew, these bottle rockets," I say, "are they safe?"

"It's just an empty plastic pop bottle that you partly fill with water and then pump air into. I mean, you probably shouldn't stick your head right over it when you set it off, that could kind of hurt, but they're harmless."

"So, no flames, no explosion, no flying debris?"

"Just water and air from a bicycle pump."

"Okay. If you'll be in charge of that, I guess we could do bottle rockets, then."

"Great!" he says. "And by the way, I was just asking Dave about fireworks and he reminded me that he and Pete used to do this science and magic show for birthday parties and stuff, and there's this one bit they do where they show you what chemicals you need to combine to make different colours of fireworks and they wonder if they could do their show for the kids that day. Because it would be, you know, educational."

"It sounds very educational," I say. "But what are the chances that something would explode?"

"Very small. Minute, really."

"Tell them not to make me regret saying yes," I say.

"Awesome! One last thing - they wonder if it's okay if they come in costume."

"What sort of costume?"

"Medieval knights."

"Sure," I say, because I'd really like this conversation to end. "Tell them to wear whatever they want."

Drew scurries away, happy as the proverbial clam, muttering something about finding enough lithium carbonate, and I add fireworks and jousting to the list of permits I need to inquire about.

WE HAVE A WEEK OF HOT, sticky weather and Nana's peonies start to bloom like crazy - overnight, the garden is transformed into a wild palette of pinks: salmon pink, cotton candy pink, coral pink and my favourite, a peony that I think should be called Hot Disco Pink, but which Nana informs me is in fact named for Princess Margaret, which then seems oddly fitting.

At the same moment that Nana's garden bursts into peony splendour, Penny Clarke's brother comes back from a vacation in Provence and so Penny Clarke comes into possession of several bottles of really good rosé. To most people, this might just sound like a typical week in June, but to my Nana and her friends, blooming peonies plus good booze in hand equals drinks party in the garden, the night before the Big CRC Event.

Unfortunately, and despite the multitude of cheerful pink flowers and the prospect of nice wine, I am in a dark mood, which started this morning about five minutes after Nana announced that tonight, after the drinks party, the dogs would all be going on a trial sleepover at their new homes. I don't know why this is bugging me so much, but all morning, as she packs their little overnight bags with food and treats and their favourite toys, I have to bite my tongue and stifle my impulse to sneak into the kitchen and unpack everything when she's not looking. At one point, I catch Ophelia staring at me, with a pleading, yet slightly reproachful look, as if she's saying, why are you not doing something about this?

Why, indeed.

I am pissy all afternoon at school, and I stew and fester and fume but somehow despite the heat, the squirrelly kids and Miss Holly reassuring me repeatedly that the Pot Luck and Horse Ride Fiasco will be a huge success, I survive the day and I drag myself home to grudgingly take part in Nana's little backyard social.

Penny Clarke is the first to arrive with the much ballyhooed rosé and she and Nana start to put together some charcuterie trays, much to the dogs' delight, because there are few things that dogs enjoy more than a nice selection of sliced meats and pâtés, spread out across all the counters. Penny Clarke is deep into a lecture on how it's actually the accompanying elements - the mustards, the gherkins, the olives - that can make or break a good charcuterie, when the doorbell rings again.

It's Angie and Alf, and Angie is in a lather because she was slated to bring the bread, and apparently the selection of baguette at the grocery store was disgraceful and she's loudly rueing the fact that she didn't take the time to bake the loaves herself, when the bell rings again.

It's Julia with Bea Wiseman, who is here for a few days to check on the construction at Six Perfections. Bea gives me a long hug and tells me how sorry she was to hear about Eddie Spaghetti, but there's an awkward moment with Julia - everything feels stiff and stilted and we can't seem to meet each other's eyes and I have a hollow feeling in my chest that I think might be loneliness, which is weird because I haven't even left yet. Everything is diffused by Mortimer though, because he's literally climbing over Lucy and Ophelia to get to Julia and while they have a happy reunion, I take Bea to the kitchen, where we unload the selection of specialty bits that Bea has brought from her favourite deli in the city. It's crowded and loud and hot and as soon as I can, I slip out to finish hauling lawn chairs and various extra pieces of patio furniture out of the garage and around to Nana's back yard.

Just as I'm finishing, Bea arrives with a glass of delicately pink wine for me. "Your grandmother asked me to tell you to see if you could find the fairy lights," she says. "She seemed to think you'd know what that meant."

"Already done," I say, and I point to the strings of white lights I've dug out of storage bins in the garage. "I just have to put them up."

"Let me give you a hand," she says, and we set about artfully arranging the little lights in the hedges that Alf has carefully trimmed. It's a beautiful evening, lush and warm, and Bea tells me all the news from Six Perfections as we work, how they're already booking retreats and conferences for the fall and how every time she starts to worry about whether or not they'll be ready in time, Tenzin laughs and says that one of two things will happen: either they will be ready or they will not, and either way, it will be an adventure.

Once we get all the lights hung, I plug them in and then we sit down to admire our handiwork and sip our wine. In the house, Angie is telling a story at quite a volume and everyone is laughing.

"Julia told me about your new job at the design school," she says, after a while. "When do you start?"

"September," I say, "but they've offered me the chance to redesign the syllabus for my course so I'd have to get going on that soon."

"It sounds like quite an opportunity," she says.

"It is."

She looks at me with a funny little smile. "Yet, you don't sound excited."

I think of all the things I should be excited about - the studio and office space that the school has arranged for me; the phone call from Bianca asking what new work I have for her to look at and if I'd like to give a talk in Berlin this fall - and I don't care about any of it.

"I don't want to go," I say suddenly, and it's such a relief to finally say it out loud, that I can feel my heart hammering at my ribcage, like I'd been holding my breath for a very long time.

"Change is hard," Bea says. "It can make you feel conflicted."

"No, I don't mean I feel conflicted," I say. "I mean, I *don't* want to go. I want to stay here. With Julia. And Nana."

Bea studies me carefully in the light of the sunset. "Have you told them that?"

"I keep trying to, but they're so busy making plans to shove me out the door for my own damn good, that I don't think they've even heard it." I take a healthy swig of my fancy Provencal rosé. "And now I feel like I have to go or they'll be disappointed in me."

"Oh, dear God, is that what you think?" Bea says, and she shakes her head and chuckles. "Olivia, trust me on this - if you decided to stay, they wouldn't feel disappointed. They would feel like they just won the lottery."

"No, they'll just go on and on about I shouldn't give up this job and these opportunities for them, because opportunities like this don't come along every day."

"Yes, but opportunities don't always equal happiness, do they?" Bea says. "We never know for certain how something will turn out."

Eddie Spaghetti pops into my mind, as he does a hundred times a day still, and I remember that I dreamed about him again last night, that we were playing Red Rover in his backyard and how utterly normal that felt. And of course, I start to cry.

Bea lets me weep for a minute and she just sits there, a little pillar of equanimity, and then after a while, she rummages in her handbag for a tissue for me. I blow my nose and try to pull myself together a bit.

"He had just stopped to help a woman with a flat tire," I say. "He was just being a good guy. If it can all turn on a dime like that - where is the sense in that, Bea? I mean, what is the point of any of this?"

Bea's smile is cryptic. "None of us has long, Olivia," she says. "What we have is now."

Her words hit me like a slap and I remember months ago, driving to Six Perfections through a dark winter night, hearing the story of Bea and Julia in the women's bathroom.

"Ask me the question," I say.

"The question?" she says.

"The question you asked Julia the day you talked her off the ceiling in the bathroom at the hospital," I say. "About the life that I want to be living. Ask me the question."

"My darling girl," she says, and she chuckles. "I don't think you need me to ask it."

She's right.

I put my glass down on the little wicker table between us, get to my feet and march into the house.

Everyone is in the kitchen, chatting and laughing, but I'm pushing such an emotional storm cloud ahead of me that all voices stop when I appear in the doorway. Even the dogs pause, frozen in the act of begging for cold cuts, and look at me.

"Pet, do you feel all right?" Nana says. "You look flushed."

"I'm fine, Nana," I say, "in fact, I'm better than fine, I'm *fantastic*, because I've just made a decision and it affects all of you, so I thought I should tell you about it."

And now they're all regarding me with slightly worried looks, as if they're not quite sure what's going to happen next. Everyone that is, except for Penny Clarke. She looks like she can't wait to hear it.

"I know I'm supposed to be very excited about this new job and all these new opportunities on the horizon, but the fact is that I'm not. And for too long now, things have just been happening to me and I've been going along with all of it. They weren't all bad things, but the point is that almost none of them were my decisions - they were either by accident or by default or by coincidence, but they weren't *my* decisions. Well, now I'm deciding.

"Nana, you can't sell the house and move into Birch Haven because I'm staying in Stafford Falls and I need someplace to live. Yes, I know I only came back here because you had a stroke but that doesn't mean this isn't where I'm supposed to be. I'm staying and you're staying and the dogs are staying, so I'm sorry to everybody who thought they were leaving with a dog tonight, but we're all staying right here, in this house."

Julia starts to open her mouth, but I beat her to the punch.

"And you! You can release me or let me go or whatever you want to call it but I'm telling you right now, I'm not going away. The job in the city is just a job. All I really want to do is paint and I can paint right here. I'll figure out the rest as I go - maybe I'll start a life drawing class at Birch Haven or maybe I'll open my own art school. And I'm not going to wake up in six months and resent you because I'm not doing this for you - I'm doing this for *me*. I'm being selfish because I want you, and I want this, so I'm staying."

It is really, really quiet when I finally stop talking, and Alf is very busy staring at his shoes, but everyone else seems some mixture of surprised and delighted.

"Pet, are you absolutely sure?" Nana says. "Are you sure this is what you want?"

"I'm sure, Nana," I say.

She shuffles over to me and kisses my cheek. "Well then, that's settled," she says. "All right everyone, let's give these two some privacy. Alf, be a lamb and bring the trays, would you?" And she shepherds everybody but Julia out to the garden, but not before Penny Clarke pats my arm and gives me an approving nod.

Julia just stands there, leaned against the counter, arms crossed, studying me.

"Sorry, I just realized that maybe I should've waited to talk to you about this when we were alone," I say.

"I don't mind," she says, but she doesn't move.

"Are we going to argue about this?" I say.

She shakes her head. "No, but if you're going to stay, we have to get you a proper studio space. You have to be able to paint and you can't paint forever on Penny Clarke's sunporch."

I shrug. "The light is really good."

"You know where else there is really good light? The rooms above the café," she says.

"You're right," I say. "But that's your apartment -I need more space, really."

"There'd be plenty of space if I moved all my furniture out," she says.

"But where would you..." I start to say and she smiles and then the light dawns. "Would you consider that? Moving in here with me? Well, with, you know, all of us?"

"I thought you'd never ask," she says, and she smiles the smile that I remember from the day we met, on the beach.

She holds out her arms to me and I fall into them and hang on tight.

"It is exactly like winning the lottery," I say.

"What?"

"You'll have to ask Bea."

It's quite a while before we join the party in the garden.

LATER, after all the rosé is gone and the last of the food has been finished and everyone has taken their leave, Nana puts Frank Sinatra on the stereo and goes to sit under the stars in her garden, with the fairy lights and her dogs, and Frank regales us with tales of how someday he will feel a glow, just thinking of the way we look tonight. Julia and I do the washing up, side by side at the kitchen sink, talking about the summer and the days after the summer, and washing each of Nana's wine glasses as if they were the newborn baby Buddha himself.

THE BIG ANYTHING Can Happen Event goes off brilliantly. Everybody assembles around four o'clock and there is an on-going soccer game (Tenzin turns out to be a selectively terrible goalie - he can't seem to stop a single kick delivered by anyone under the age of ten) and Pete and Dave do come dressed as knights which adds an aura of absurdity and elegance to the whole thing. There's enough food for a hundred people, which is good because by the time everybody and their parents (and a few grandparents) and all their siblings and all the special friends of CRC have shown up, we are a good chunk of the way to that number. Things really take off when Snapdragon and Meredith arrive and everyone takes turns going for little rides – Isabelle looks so tiny on such a huge beast, but proves herself to be quite the equestrian, and Davis, who has waited months for this day, just beams and beams. He's brought a cowboy hat for the occasion and pitches a bit of a fit when he has to trade it for a riding helmet but once he's astride the huge animal, all is forgotten and suddenly he's exuding a sort of cool that the Butch Cassidy would envy. Meredith leads him on a couple extra laps of the park and has him help remove Snapdragon's saddle and give him a quick brush, and Kylie nearly dies of jealousy.

The centrepiece of the day turns out to be the bottle rockets, though. Drew and his knightly team are all over it - they've set up a huge table with all the materials and tools the kids need to turn an empty soda bottle into a marginally dangerous projectile and then they take turns walking them down the lakefront, away from everybody to launch them. They really are like rockets - there is a great whooshing sound when they are let go and they shoot into the sky, spewing a water trail behind them. Wally is beside himself, running up and down the beach, clapping his hands. His rocket goes the furthest and the whole time it's in flight, he stands, riveted to the spot, his tiny hands on his cheeks, watching it soar into the heavens.

AND SUDDENLY, it's the end of June. It is weirdly quiet in my subterranean classroom, as I collect the last of my things and stuff them into a couple of cardboard boxes. Yesterday was the last day with the kids and so we've already said our goodbyes - my desk is piled with boxes of chocolates, an "I Heart My Teacher" mug and best of all, a letter from Isabelle that she wrote herself and that made me cry a little bit, and so now all that's left to do is pack my stuff and go. I've even brought Mrs. Demanski a bouquet from Nana's garden and said see you later to Miss Holly, who is spending today at the school board offices attending some training seminar about kids with autism that she should probably be running. We've promised to get together once a week for coffee at the Second Chance Café with our sketchbooks, because she has decided that she would like to learn to draw and possibly even paint and so I have the first student in my new art school.

I carry the first box up the fire exit stairs and out to my cheerful little Jeep, and by the time I return, there are two men in painter's overalls depositing ladders and cans of paint in the centre of the room.

"Hi," the older of them says. "Is this the CRC room? There's no number on the door."

"Yeah, this is the CRC room," I say. "You're here to paint?"

"Yup, work order from the school board," he says, but he's turning in a slow circle, taking in the colours, the chalkboard, the stencilled clouds. "Seems a shame though. This looks fresh."

I can't even think of what to say, so I pick up the last of my boxes, wish them a good day and leave my little Grecian sanctuary forever.

I sit for a while behind the wheel of the Jeep, enjoying the breeze and the feeling of summer stretching out in front of me. I feel giddy with possibility - there's going to be gardening with Nana, and paddling with Julia - she's going to teach me to kayak, which oddly, for someone who grew up on a vast, gorgeous body of water, I've never done. I'm going to drink lots of Julia's iced coffees and I'm going to paint a portrait of Eddie Spaghetti - two portraits actually, one as a boy, when I met him, and one as a father so Bolognese and Carbonara can know him.

I pull out my phone and send Julia a text:

I'm feeling kind of blue. Tell me something happy.

A few seconds later, she replies.

The Buddha is here!

I dial her number and she answers on the first ring.

"The actual Buddha?" I say.

"No, the Buddha statue for the meditation hall," she says and I can hear the smile in her voice. "Let's get Nana and go see it!"

Twenty minutes later we're all packed into the Second Chance Café van, Julia driving, Nana riding shotgun, me in the back with the dogs. We keep the windows down so the dogs can sniff the breeze and Lucy is wagging her stub of a tail so hard as she takes in all the summer smells that she nearly falls over. The sun is glinting off the lake every time we come around a curve and Nana is telling Julia that she wants to buy a barbecue so we can have cookouts in the garden - she actually calls them 'cookouts' - and Julia says we could go to Suckchester this weekend and take a look at some grills, if she'd like.

We pull in as the guys are yanking the quilted blankets off the giant Buddha. He is huge - easily six feet at the shoulder - and gorgeous: golden and majestic and inscrutable and so lovingly crafted that he takes my breath away.

Tenzin appears, smiling and clapping with glee, as if our arrival was the only thing that could possibly make his day better, and the dogs run to him to give him sloppy, wet greetings. I help Nana out of the van and she slips her arm through mine and we all set out along the path towards the meditation hall. The dogs race down the sloping lawns towards the lake.

This.

This, right now.

It's enough.

ACKNOWLEDGMENTS

This is a work of fiction - all of the people are made up and most of them are much nicer than anyone I know in real life. The dogs, however, are based on real dogs; two even retain their actual names. In addition, no less than four human characters are named for dogs I've known and loved.

I don't think the dogs would mind.

Sadly, Stafford Falls is a small town Arcadia that exists only in my imagination, although there are many days I wish with my whole heart that it was real.

Writing a book consists mainly of sitting alone in a room for long periods of time, but no book is ever written by yourself. I am endlessly grateful to the following people:

- My writing teachers: Anne, Liz, Julia, Stephen and Natalie

- All the early readers who offered encouragement, especially Teena, Kathy, Barb, Doris, Betty and Sonia. You'll never know how much it meant.

- Shauna, who reminded me that I was a writer who teaches.

- Milo, who was there for every single word.
- My mom, who made sure that it had a really good cover.
- Mariann, who so often said, I'll make dinner, you go write.
- And especially, my maternal grandmother, Olive Marguerite Boyer Martin, who probably wouldn't approve of some of the language, but who would totally love the story.

～

ABOUT THE AUTHOR

Patti Murphy loves to make up stories. In fact, only about half of what she ever says is actually true. She enjoys cool weather, warm sweaters and the way it smells right before it snows. When she is not writing, she can be found daydreaming or trying to brew the perfect cup of coffee. She lives in Ottawa with her partner and their very fierce little dog, Gavin.

I'd love to hear from you! Find me on the Interwebs at

www.PattiWritesBooks.com
patti@pattiwritesbook.com

 twitter.com/Patti_Writes

ALSO BY PATTI MURPHY

Book 2 in The Sutra Series:
"The Date Square Dharma"
Coming Fall 2018

Made in the USA
Middletown, DE
28 June 2018